WALLS OF BABYLON

A MEDIEVAL ROMANCE

BY KATHRYN LE VEQUE

Kathryn Le Veque Novels

Medieval Romance:

The de Russe Legacy:
The White Lord of Wellesbourne
The Dark One: Dark Knight
Beast
Lord of War: Black Angel
The Falls of Erith

The de Lohr Dynasty:
While Angels Slept (Lords of East Anglia)
Rise of the Defender
Spectre of the Sword
Unending Love
Archangel
Steelheart

Great Lords of le Bec:
Great Protector
To the Lady Born (House of de Royans)

Lords of Eire:
The Darkland (Master Knights of Connaught)
Black Sword
Echoes of Ancient Dreams (time travel)

De Wolfe Pack Series:
The Wolfe
Serpent
Scorpion (Saxon Lords of Hage – Also related to The Questing)
Walls of Babylon
The Lion of the North
Dark Destroyer

Ancient Kings of Anglecynn:
The Whispering Night
Netherworld

Battle Lords of de Velt:
The Dark Lord

Devil's Dominion

Reign of the House of de Winter:
Lespada
Swords and Shields (also related to The Questing, While Angels Slept)

De Reyne Domination:
Guardian of Darkness
The Fallen One (part of Dragonblade Series)

Unrelated characters or family groups:
The Gorgon (Also related to Lords of Thunder)
The Warrior Poet (St. John and de Gare)
Tender is the Knight (House of d'Vant)
Lord of Light
The Questing (related to The Dark Lord, Scorpion)
The Legend (House of Summerlin)

The Dragonblade Series: (Great Marcher Lords of de Lara)
Dragonblade
Island of Glass (House of St. Hever)
The Savage Curtain (Lords of Pembury)
The Fallen One (De Reyne Domination)
Fragments of Grace (House of St. Hever)
Lord of the Shadows
Queen of Lost Stars (House of St. Hever)

Lords of Thunder: The de Shera Brotherhood Trilogy
The Thunder Lord
The Thunder Warrior
The Thunder Knight

Time Travel Romance: (Saxon Lords of Hage)
The Crusader
Kingdom Come

Contemporary Romance:

Kathlyn Trent/Marcus Burton Series:
Valley of the Shadow
The Eden Factor
Canyon of the Sphinx

The American Heroes Series:
Resurrection
Fires of Autumn
Evenshade

Sea of Dreams
Purgatory

Other Contemporary Romance:
Lady of Heaven
Darkling, I Listen

Multi-author Collections/Anthologies:
With Dreams Only of You (USA Today bestseller)
Sirens of the Northern Seas (Viking romance)

Note: All Kathryn's novels are designed to be read as stand-alones, although many have cross-over characters or cross-over family groups. Novels that are grouped together have related characters or family groups.

Series are clearly marked. All series contain the same characters or family groups except the American Heroes Series, which is an anthology with unrelated characters.

There is NO particular chronological order for any of the novels because they can all be read as stand-alones, even the series.

For more information, find it in **A Reader's Guide to the Medieval World of Le Veque.**

TABLE OF CONTENTS

AUTHOR'S NOTE

Welcome to Kenton's story.

Ten years after THE LION OF THE NORTH, where Kenton le Bec was a secondary character, Kenton finds himself sworn to Richard Neville, Earl of Warwick. They are in the last days of the War of the Roses at this point and, as you'll see in the story, Kenton has played a big role in those final days. He has become Warwick's attack dog.

Atticus de Wolfe isn't in Kenton's story at all except by way of mention because Atticus, ten years down the road, has remained at Wolfe's Lair and is charged with holding the borders while Kenton runs off and plays the big, bad soldier with Warwick. Kenton is tough, intelligent, and no-nonsense, but we discover that he has one hell of an Achilles' heel in Lady Nicola Aubrey-Thorne.

Unlike some, or most, of my other books, there aren't any big connections in this novel. Conor de Birmingham, one of Kenton's knights, is a descendant of Devlin de Birmingham (*Black Sword*), and there are recognizable surnames in this novel, but no one who is of particularly note as far as relationships. Kenton, however, is the grandson of Richmond le Bec (*Great Protector*) and Kenton's uncle is a major secondary character in *BEAST* and his aunt is the heroine of that novel as well.

And as with THE LION OF THE NORTH, Kenton's story also involves a major battle. His tale sees the peripheral build up to probably the most definitive battle in the War of the Roses – the Battle of Barnet where Warwick was killed. It was after this battle that Edward finally seized the throne and ruled for several years unopposed, but this story isn't really about Barnet – it's a pure battle-and-politics-and-passion driven novel that has some serious highs and lows.

I hope you'll enjoy!

Hugs,
Kathryn

THE LEGEND BEGINS

Present time
Yorkshire, UK, East of Huddersfield
Babylon Castle

"ANOTHER OLD PILE of rocks," he said as he pulled into the tree-shrouded car park and they could see the castle ruins across the road. "Seriously, *another* old pile of rocks?"

The wife ignored his comment for the most part. "Yes, another old pile of rocks," she said as she opened the door and climbed out. "This is the last one for the day so you'll be spared any further misery after this."

The husband sighed heavily as he turned the car off and took the keys, climbing out of the car with far less enthusiasm than his wife. Already, she was standing at the end of the car park, looking at the ruins across the small road. The day had been misty and foggy for the most part but at this time in the afternoon, the gloom had lifted slightly. Still, it was rather cold and eerie, and exploring derelict old castles on a day like this was particularly spooky. The husband shut the car door and locked the car, making a face of utter and complete displeasure as he walked up behind his wife.

"Okay, so what's so great about this one that we haven't seen with the four other piles of rocks we've visited today?" he asked as they crossed the road to the ruins. "I'll be completely honest when I say they all look alike to me."

The wife didn't look at him as she spoke. "And I'll be completely honest when I say that any more honesty from you and I'm going to find some dark, dank dungeon and leave you there."

The husband eyed the wife; he was a little taller than she was, and stronger, but she could fight dirty in certain situations. More than that, he believed her. After all, he *had* been complaining quite a lot about the old castles she wanted to visit, but as a seventh-grade history teacher from California, things like old castles and old buildings and museums fascinated her. She wanted to take her experiences back to her students.

While she wanted to do the educational stuff, he wanted to check out the cities and the pubs, and maybe sit and watch a few football games. But he knew she wouldn't go for that. Therefore, he was tagging along much like a kid being forced to do something he didn't want to do. He really *didn't* want to do this and he was complaining every step of the way.

"Whatever," he said in a disgruntled tone, moving away from her so she couldn't grab hold of him, just in case she really meant to throw him in a dungeon. "So tell me about this old pile of rocks. What's so important about it?"

The wife came to a halt when they came off the road, looking up at the soaring gatehouse overhead. It was a massive structure, at least four stories in height, and the enormous curtain walls that were twenty feet high in places were still standing for the most part. The stone, a sort of light beige color, had darkened and stained over the centuries, but the age of the place didn't dampen the impact she felt while gazing upon it.

"Nobody is really sure," she said as they began to move through the gatehouse, once a grand thing with massive gates, now just a shell of what used to be. "It was built in the fourteenth century so it never saw any early action in the history of England, but it was documented to have been strategically important during the last part of the War of the Roses when Edward and Henry were going at it."

The husband was listening but he was already bored nearly out of his skull. All he could hear was *blah, blah, blah.* He had to make a conscious effort to prevent his eyes from rolling back in his head.

"Any famous knights or kings who lived here?" he asked.

They emerged from the gatehouse into a fairly significant inner ward, an uneven and muddy place. They could see the remains of an inner set of walls, now half of their original height because the local villages had plundered the stone to build their homes with a few hundred years before. The wife seemed fascinated by the massive outer walls and the seemingly ruined inner walls.

"Look at these walls," she said, pointing. "An inner set and an outer set. They call these concentric walls, you know. What seems odd is the fact that the inner walls are ruinous but the outer walls remain intact."

The husband was looking at what she was indicating. "Why is that odd?"

The wife shrugged. "Because, normally, the outer walls would be destroyed first," she said. "When Cromwell came through during the English Civil War, he bombarded a lot of these castles with canons so they couldn't be used by the enemy. He tore down walls and ripped apart the keeps and such. But these walls were evidently spared."

Now she was talking about a war and battles, which interested him somewhat. "Maybe he didn't come this far north."

The wife shook her head. "He did," she said. "But he left Babylon alone."

"Babylon?"

"That's the name of this castle."

The wife turned her attention to the massive four-storied keep to her left. It was mostly intact except for the roof and the floors. It was essentially just one enormous shell. She went over to the steps leading to the keep entry, which was a beautiful herringbone arch. She could peek inside but a permanent railing prevented her from going inside. It was a gigantic space.

"Wow," she said. "Look at how big this place was. You could put a hundred people on one floor alone."

The husband came up behind her, peering into the big, empty cavity of a building. "Big," he agreed. Then he turned to look out over the ward. "It doesn't look like there's much else to see here."

The wife ignored him; she was still looking into the keep, imagining the people who used to live here and love here. That was what she always imagined when she saw these great ruins. Her husband didn't understand that something drew her to these places and Babylon, in particular, held a fascination for her. It had since she'd first read about it years ago and when she and her husband were finally able to take their dream trip to England, Babylon was one of her non-negotiable destinations. Now, she was here, and it was totally worth the visit in her opinion. She could just feel the spirits of centuries past around her.

"Babylon Castle was built by the Thorne family," she said. "It guarded one of the major roads between Yorkshire and Manchester. There's supposed to be a great love story connected with it."

The husband was standing back in the muddy ward now, listening to his wife as she came away from the keep. He turned to look at the soaring structure behind him.

"What love story?" he asked. Then, he pointed upward. "Maybe Rapunzel lived up there and threw her hair out of the window for a soldier to climb up it."

The wife shook her head reproachfully. "No, Rapunzel didn't live here," she said with some disgust. "If you're not going to be serious about it, I won't tell you."

She started to walk away, rounding the side of the keep, and he followed. "Okay, I'm sorry," he said, although he didn't sound like he meant it. "What's the story?"

The wife glanced at him. "It's a local story," she said. "I found it while doing research online for all of the castles I wanted to see. Legend says that a lady knight held off a siege by another knight, but when he conquered the castle, she fell in love with him. They married and had something like ten kids. Lots of kids. Anyway, the legend also says that their ghosts are still here because, rather than go to heaven and separate after death, they chose to remain here on earth so they could always be together. Some say that when it gets really foggy, you can hear them calling to each other through the mists."

The husband made a face, looking around because there was a fairly heavy cloud cover this day. It was growing heavier as the sun began to set. "Beautiful," he snorted. "So there are ghosts here. Helloooooo!"

He called out, his voice reverberating off the ancient stone walls. The wife shushed him harshly.

"Be quiet," she hissed, slapping him on the arm. It didn't hurt because she really only slapped the jacket, but the message was obvious. "Why do you have to be so obnoxious?"

He was grinning at his sense of humor, sobering when he realized she didn't think it was all that funny. "Sorry," he said, although he didn't mean it. "I thought maybe they might call back."

The wife rolled her eyes at him; he was essentially ruining this visit for her and she was growing frustrated. "Will you please go wait for me in the car?" she said, unhappy. "I... I just want to be alone in here. Just go away for a few minutes, okay?"

Seeing he hurt her feelings, the husband tried to sound contrite. "I really am sorry," he said. "I'll behave."

The wife shook her head and pointed to the car. "Just go sit in the car," she said. "I'll be there in a minute."

With a shrug, the husband trudged off across the inner ward. The wife watched him until he went through the gatehouse and disappeared, heading to the car park across the street. Breathing a sigh of relief, she began to walk the inner ward, touching the stones that had obviously fallen from the inner walls, seeing the outlines of foundations against the walls that had been the outbuildings at one time.

She circled around the ward and ended up behind the keep where a well had been covered over with heavy wire, bolted down to prevent anyone from lifting it. The inner walls were particularly derelict back here, almost down to the ground, and she noticed what looked to be a bricked-up passage in the outer wall. She went over to it, running her hand along the bricked-up archway, wondering why it had been sealed up. Someone had evidently done it, long ago.

She felt such incredible fascination with the old ruins, fascination that was difficult to describe. Being a history major, ancient ruins very much intrigued her because she wondered more about the people who had lived there more than she wondered about their struggle of daily life or even the structure itself. She wondered what the people hoped for and wished on and dreamed about. Therefore, the legend about the lady knight and her lover was of particular interest to her, although she didn't know why. It was only a legend, of course, but she wondered if it was based on fact. She wondered if there really *had* been a lady knight and her enemy lover, now forever wandering the grounds of Babylon because they never wanted to be separated. As she stood there and touched the old stone, she could only think of one thing.

If these walls could talk....

She grinned, wondering if she should ask them. Her husband wasn't around so he wouldn't think she was insane. Putting both hands on the ancient rock that had stood for centuries, she spoke softly.

"If these great walls of Babylon could talk, what would they tell me?" she whispered.

She didn't really expect to receive an answer.

But she did.

~ YEAR OF OUR LORD 1471 ~
THE CONQUEST OF BABYLON

PROLOGUE

Early February
Lancashire/Yorkshire Border near the village of Moselden

S MOKE FROM THE campfires filled the night sky like misty gray ribbons. The smell was strong in the damp air, blanketing the landscape and infiltrating the nostrils of the living with the sharp, offensive odor. An encampment perched at the edge of a small forest, what tents there were arranged carefully towards the middle while a perimeter of soldiers made sure nothing came in or out without their knowledge. It was a dark time, a time of war and unrest, and these men fought for one of two powerful factions. In this case, there could be no definitive winner, though both sides were determined that there would be.

A larger tent sat towards the center of camp, the light from a massive bonfire dancing shadows across the canvas side. Several men squeezed inside the tent, all of them focused on a table that bore several sheets of well used, and sometimes torn, vellum. Familiar maps were drawn in lines of black and red with big rocks as anchors on the corners.

All of the tent's occupants wore chain mail and weapons to some degree, and some of them in full suits of armor. The smell of the night's smoke mingled with the body odors of men who had seen weeks of fighting, little food, and even less sleep. Their weariness was tempered by a sharp determination.

"We should be hearing something by now," a man with dirty, graying hair leaned over the maps, tapping a particular area with a stick. He wasn't terribly old but war and stress caused him to look much older than his age. "This siege has been days in the making. I cannot believe le Bec has not breached her by now. I sent him to accomplish a task and yet do I see the positive results."

"With all due respect, my lord," another man, younger but more expensively dressed, addressed him, "I am confident that Kenton le Bec will breach Babylon Castle by the end of the week. My lord Warwick must remember that Babylon is one of the more powerful strongholds in Yorkshire, and any competent army would have a difficult time breaching her. I believe patience…."

The man with the gray hair thumped the table sharply. "Patience is a virtue, indeed, but I was never a man to proclaim my virtues. It would be a lie, to be sure. And time is something we do not have in this case. Henry needs Gaylord Thorne's castle if we are to secure the region."

He pounded on the table again with his stick, shoving splinters into the vellum. The area in question was designated by a few thin red lines of ocher, sectioning off the most westerly region of the Yorkshire territory.

Every man in that tent knew they had to secure Babylon Castle, the gateway to the province, if they were to make any sort of advancement into the widely populated district of Yorkshire and, consequently, gain a serious foothold in their enemy's realm. They had been here before, many times, only to be turned away. But they had never come this close. The gray-haired man stared at the map again, his expression slackening as the ugly deeds of war passed through his exhausted mind.

"If we take Babylon, it is only a matter of time before we are able to launch against Leeds and Bradford." He repeated what every man already knew. "From Leeds, we sweep northeast until we reach York herself. With that entire region secured for Henry, we split Yorkshire and most assuredly hold the victory. But we must have Babylon."

He was back to thumping on the table, beating it like a drum. The younger man glanced at the others, seasoned war advisors to the legitimate king to England's throne, a claim that was disputed by the son of the late Richard, Duke of York. But Richard's son, Edward, had picked up the torch admirably and even now, years after his father's death, fought more viciously than his father ever had, which was why gaining a foothold in Yorkshire was so very imperative.

"Need we be reminded that le Bec has over a thousand men under his command," Warwick assured the others. "If anyone can take Babylon, it will be he."

The men in the tent grunted with agreement. "Not even Edward has a knight as powerful as le Bec," another man said solemnly. "We are fortunate, indeed."

A servant brought them more wine, fuel for the damp night. The men drank, mulled over the map, and pondered what the morning might bring. The gray-haired man finally sat at the table, staring pensively at the surface, his mind several miles away at the mighty fortress known as Babylon.

He could see it, sitting on a rise above the River Black in a dominating position above the village of Moselden, its concentric construction making it virtually impossible to breach. Two hundred years after Edward the First built his masterpiece castles throughout Wales, Babylon was raised in the tradition of that shining legacy when built by Gaylord Thorne's grandfather under permission from Richard the Second. Strategically, it was a force to be reckoned with because it guarded a major road from Lancashire into Yorkshire.

Somehow, the night passed into the chilly, cold dampness of early morning. The bonfire was burning low, spitting layers upon layers of smoke up into the air. The man with the gray hair had fallen asleep on his maps, while the advisors continued to mill around him. Though he could sleep, they would not. The night seemed to drag on endlessly until someone heard the shout of a sentry, which roused about half of the camp. The advisors tensed, waiting for the explanation for the alarm. Someone thought to rouse the gray-haired man, who stirred incoherently until a worn soldier suddenly appeared before him.

The man bowed unsteadily. He was dirty and disheveled, but his eyes held the glow of a man used to such hardship. The gray-haired man stared at him, suddenly tongue-tied.

"My Lord Warwick," the soldier said. "I bring news from Babylon."

The gray-haired man found his voice. "Give me something of joy, man."

"Babylon is ours, my lord," the soldier said with as much satisfaction as his weary manner could muster. "Le Bec secured her before nightfall and sends word to you of a decisive victory."

The advisors silently gloated. It was as they had hoped and predicted. The man with the gray hair closed his eyes, suddenly very quiet and very reverent. His eyes then opened again and he turned to his advisors. "It appears the saints and gods favor us," he said hoarsely. "Now, we will end it… or it will surely end me."

There was a prophetic ring to his words, more than any of them could ever imagine. Richard Neville, Earl of Warwick, had divined his own future.

CHAPTER ONE

G REAT OUTER WALLS soared to the sky with four corner towers, peppered with murder holes from which to shoot arrows at enemy soldiers. A narrow corridor separated the outer from the even taller inner walls, with a great gatehouse and a five-story keep lodged deep inside. Built from sandstone that had been quarried from the very earth around the castle, a big quarry that also created the moat, Babylon Castle was truly a sight to behold. Kenton le Bec thought so as he stood in the center of the inner bailey, eyeing his prize with the utmost satisfaction. Overhead, the day was dawning clear and surprisingly bright for winter weather and his mood was, for all of his exhaustion, amazingly light.

But his expression belied nothing of his inner emotions. The man could be as joyful as a child or as angry as a hornet and no one would know by looking at him. The only thing vassals and soldiers alike knew was that they feared him, and rightfully so. It wasn't so much that he was thought of as evil; it was more the fact that he was a master at the art of intimidation, so much so that the mere mention of his name within military circles brought chills and whispers of fear.

Peasants and nobles refused to discuss him at all for fear of incurring some distant curse from the know-all, see-all knight of the realm. Anyone who had served with Kenton le Bec knew that the man was unpredictable, unafraid, and as deadly as a snake. Even those closest to him knew to tread carefully, in any situation.

A knight emerged from the massive keep, taking the steps from the second floor entrance down to the muddy bailey. Most of the bodies from the battle had been cleaned up, but there were still a few in a pile near the entrance that were waiting to be burned. Whatever remained of Lord Thorne's fighting force was now outside the fortress, being held in a pen like a herd of animals while le Bec's men swarmed over Babylon like a horde of locusts.

There was a smell in the air, of the ugliness after a battle and the rotting dead. But the knights of le Bec's corps were used to the stench; they lived with it daily. The knight didn't even flinch as he stepped over someone's rotting hand, coming to a halt next to his towering liege.

"We've found them, Ken."

Only in private did the knight known as Conor de Birmingham address his superior informally. Having known Kenton since they were newly knighted, he was the only man who could get away with it. Kenton looked away from the walls of his latest acquisition and focused on the big, red-haired warrior.

"Where?"

"Hiding in the cellar beneath the kitchens."

"How many?"

"Lady Thorne, her three sons, and four servants."

"No sign of Gaylord?"

"None."

"Did you ask Lady Thorne?"

"She will not say a word."

Kenton's gaze moved in the direction of the keep; it was impossible to read his thoughts, but they were easy to guess. Conor followed his focus.

"Gerik and Ack are with her," Conor said. "Their manner is, shall we say, easier than yours or mine. Mayhap they will wrest something from her."

Kenton pondered that advice and promptly ignored it. He started towards the keep. "Gaylord Thorne's whereabouts continue to be unknown and he, along with this castle, are my objectives. Henry wants them both."

"So you intend to interrogate his wife yourself?"

"I intend to do what is necessary."

Conor thought of admonishing him to go easy on the woman, considering she was a delicate lady and knights of the realm were sworn to uphold the code of gentle treatment towards any female, even an enemy. But he bit his tongue; if the wench was foolish enough to resist Kenton, then she deserved whatever she received.

Kenton entered the cool, musty keep and found his way down into the kitchens. Located in the sub-level, it was a low-ceilinged room smelling of smoke and dung, and it was moderately warm. Off to the right, almost hidden behind a table, was an open trap door, and seated against the wall next to the door were several women and three small boys. Soldiers were tying the last of the bindings on the servants. Ducking under the low ceiling, as Kenton was several inches over six feet, he went over to the group.

Two of his knights stood hunched over, their heads brushing against the ceiling. The first man was bear-like with a head of thinning brown hair, while the other man was tall, able, with dark blond hair. Sir Gerik le Mon and Sir Ackerley Forbes, respectively, greeted Kenton with formality. They always greeted him with such manners, though they had served at the top of his command hierarchy for several years. It was the degree of respect that le Bec demanded.

"My lord," Gerik indicated the frightened, huddled people against the wall. "The elusive Lady Thorne and her household."

Kenton's piercing eyes gazed at Gerik a moment; if the man had anything to tell him, he was silently suggesting that now was a good time before he took matters into his own hands. He was weary from battle and in no mood to play games. But Gerik had nothing more to say and Kenton turned his attention to the terrified mass. The diplomacy of their captivity, brief though it were, was about to end.

The first thing he noticed was three little boys gazing back at him; the eldest was perhaps around five years of age, while the other two were identical twins and perhaps around three or four. They were all sandy-headed, well-formed, and regarded him with such challenge that Kenton nearly laughed. He might have, if he had remembered how to do it. To their left sat four cowering women, servants by their clothing, and to their left, it occurred to Kenton, sat the most beautiful woman he had ever seen.

He regarded her a moment, studying her porcelain features and the long, honey-colored hair that clung to her slender neck and spilled over her pale shoulders. She wasn't particularly young, nor was she old, but caught in that timeless limbo of a woman who is truly ageless. Were he to guess, he would suspect she was somewhere around her twenty-fifth year. But he had never seen a woman with her maturity look so positively perfect.

The woman gazed back at him with the emotionless expression of someone who had seen much in a lifetime. He knew she was terrified, but he admired the fact that she didn't show it. Wisdom had taught her that. Her magnificent eyes were the palest shade of green and her lips and cheeks were kissed a rosy hue. He had no idea how long he had been staring at her and suddenly felt very foolish that he had been doing so.

"You're le Bec?"

Kenton blinked, realizing the woman had brashly spoken first. But her voice was soft, soothing, like the pelt of a gentle rain on a warm summer night. He deliberately didn't answer her, slowly removing his gauntlets and tucking them into the elbow of the armor on his left arm.

"Your name, Madam?"

She was intentionally slow in replying. "Lady Nicola Aubrey-Thorne."

"Where is your husband, Lady Thorne?"

Her gaze lingered on him a moment before lowering. Kenton watched her long, thick lashes sweep her cheek defiantly. If nothing else, she was brave. Stupid, but brave. He would waste no more time with her. Kenton glanced at Conor and, with an imperceptible nod of his head, had the knight yank Lady Thorne to her feet.

The little boys went wild. Their hands were tied but their feet weren't, and the twins jumped up and began kicking the nearest knight, who happened to be Gerik. The serving women screamed and cried out to the boys, but the little men refused to listen. When Gerik put a large palm on each child's head and pushed them back to the floor, the eldest boy popped up, fully prepared to defend his mother to the death.

"Let her go!" he commanded. "You let my mother go or I'll get you, do you hear? *I'll get you!*"

Conor ignored the boys soundly. They may as well have been mice for all of the regard he gave them. He handed the struggling lady off to Kenton, who took her by the arm and pulled her across the kitchen. On the opposite side of the room, she was torn between defying the enormous knight and watching her little boys pick a fight. Welfare for her children won out.

"Tab!" Nicola hissed. "Stop it this instant. Teague, Tiernan, be quiet. Do you hear me? Be quiet!"

Her attention wasn't on Kenton. He braced one arm on either side of her head, forcing her to look at him without so much as laying a finger on her. The woman gazed up at him with those clear green eyes and Kenton stared back; he wanted to make sure she understood what he was about to say, plainly.

"Lady Thorne," he rumbled. "I will say this one time only, so listen carefully. I have come a long way and have lost many men in acquisition of this castle. It is now mine. You and your family are my prisoners. I will ask you where your husband is and you will tell me, truthfully, or I will remove those three boys from this place and you will never see them again. Is this in any way unclear, my lady?"

Nicola paled. "Since when do knights murder children?"

"My patience is at an end, Madam. You will give me the answer I seek."

Tears suddenly glimmered in her eyes. "I… please, you do not understand."

"I understand all too well that you are protecting an enemy of the rightful king of England."

"I am not protecting him at all. I am protecting my children."

"You speak in riddles. I told you I would not ask again."

"And I am trying to answer you. But you are not allowing me to do so."

Kenton didn't say anything. He just stared at her. Nicola knew he was not soft, nor sympathetic in any way. This was the great Kenton le Bec, a man feared and hated throughout the realm. Why he had to attack Babylon was a stroke of bitter luck. They had held out as long as they could. Now she could see it was all at an end.

She lowered her gaze and looked away. "I will… show you."

"You will tell me."

"*Please.*" Her tone was almost desperate. "I must show you."

"Madam, I am trying to be as tolerant as possible. Your stalling attempts are not well met."

"I am not stalling, my lord. But I would ask…. please, that if you must know, you must allow me to show you."

Kenton pondered that a moment. He didn't like to compromise a demand. It showed weakness. But he removed his arms and stood back, indicating for the moment that he would trust her word as a lady and allow her to show him where her husband was. He motioned to Conor.

"Stay here with the prisoners," he said. "I will take Gerik and Ack with me."

"Where are you going?"

"To find Lord Thorne."

Conor cocked an eyebrow but said nothing. He motioned to Gerik and Ackerley, who immediately went to their liege. The three knights followed Nicola from the kitchens, listening to the sobs of her youngest children undoubtedly thinking they would never see their mother again. From the great hall above the kitchens, she led them out into the bailey, hardly flinching at the death and destruction she saw there. Across the muck was a rather large, half-moon shaped structure built into the inner wall. There were long, thin windows on the curve of the structure, allowing weak light to penetrate into the gloom.

The interior was cool and dark, and Kenton immediately recognized the chapel. The majority of the room was set deep into the protective inner wall. Three pews were situated towards the front of the chamber and there were at least four sepulchers that he could see, two with large stone effigies affixed to the tomb.

Kenton paused by the door, thinking Gaylord to be a wise man to seek sanctuary within his own chapel. Public or private, the Holy Church had jurisdiction over all sacred meeting places and removing the man from here would prove controversial at best. He watched Nicola make her way over to one of the low-built, stone crypts.

"I am waiting, Madam."

She looked at him and he could see a tremendous sadness in the pale green eyes. Then she reluctantly patted the stone. "He's here."

Kenton cast her a long look. "Where?"

"In here."

"He's dead?"

"Aye."

"How long?"

"Four months now."

He made his way over to her, slowly, his gaze sweeping across the plain, gray tomb. There was nothing of decoration on it at all. Without remorse or emotion, he turned to his knights. "Open it."

Nicola was horrified. "No! You mustn't!"

"I must confirm your story, Madam. Surely you know that."

"But... you cannot violate his tomb!"

He cocked an eyebrow at her. "There is no name on this tomb. It could be empty for all I know and your husband could be halfway to Scotland by now. If he is not in here, your children will receive the punishment for your lies. You do realize that, of course."

"Of course I do, I'm no fool," she struggled not to become hysterical. "He is in there, I tell you. I would not lie with my children's lives at stake."

Gerik returned to the chapel bearing a heavy hammer. He marched straight to the sepulcher and raised the hammer above his head.

"Wait!" Nicola cried. "Please, hear me first before you smash it to bits and release this horrible secret!"

Gerik ignored her. He was in the process of bringing the hammer down when Kenton stopped him. His incredible strength halted what surely would have been a crushing blow. Kenton looked at the woman, his blue eyes hard.

"This is the second mention of such a secret. You will tell me now."

"I will. But please... do not smash the tomb."

Kenton sent Gerik aside, waiting with the hammer as a threat to her should she not do as she was told. The lady stood there a moment, distress etched on her lovely features.

"I am waiting, Madam."

She knew that. Lord, she knew that. "The children do not know that he is dead."

"Why not?"

She sighed heavily, claiming a seat on the nearest pew for support. There was lethargy in her manner, a resignation of someone who had been witness to far too much pain and suffering.

"I told them that he is away, fighting Edward's war."

"Why would you do that?"

The tears that had been on the surface since their introduction came forth and spilled down her creamy cheeks. Kenton felt a strange tugging in his chest, something he didn't recognize. Until he felt it again later in his life, he did not realize that it was compassion. He watched her wipe at her cheeks and summon bravery.

"My husband was not a kind man, my lord," she said quietly. "He... he would drink quite often and find delight in using me to alleviate his fury. My boys knew this, of course. One night, nearly six months ago, my husband was releasing his fury by taking his fists to me. Tab heard this and...."

"Tab?"

"My eldest son."

"Continue."

Nicola swallowed, her mouth dry with embarrassment and fear. "Tab heard what his father was doing to me. He raced into our chamber and drove a sword into his father's back. No one knows where he got the sword; he never would tell me. More than likely he stole it from a soldier. In any case, it wasn't a deep puncture, but it did wound him. But it wasn't the injury that killed Gaylord; it was the infection. My husband succumbed to the fever as a result of Tab's sword."

The tugging in Kenton's chest grew worse but he ignored it. "I still do not understand what the secret is."

Nicola looked at him, then, deep sorrow in her eyes. "Tab killed his father, my lord. He didn't mean to, but he was protecting me. Tab doesn't know; we never told him. He knew his father was sick, but to explain Gaylord's sudden absence, we told the boys that he recovered and went back to war. Tab cannot know that his father is dead, much less that he was the cause of it. If you smash this tomb to confirm that Gaylord is there, I do not know how I can keep it from him."

Kenton understood then. And from what he had seen of her eldest son in the kitchens, he had no doubt that the little lad was extremely protective of his mother and apparently for good reason. But he was a warrior, and he knew, perhaps more than anyone, that trust was misplaced in warfare. He took her by the arm and pulled her to her feet.

"I understand your dilemma, Madam," he tried not to sound harsh. "But you must also understand that I have certain obligations. I must locate Gaylord Thorne, and if I must destroy this tomb in order to do so, then so be it."

He handed her off to Gerik, trading the lady for the hammer. Nicola didn't fly into a panic as she had nearly done before; she was beyond that. She simply stood there, staring at him with those great green eyes.

"Do you not trust my word, my lord?" she asked softly.

Kenton couldn't believe it; a chill actually raced up his spine. Whether it be from her tone or her words, he wasn't certain. All he knew was that this woman was somehow trying to bewitch him and he was tremendously annoyed by it. He wouldn't look at her, nor would he answer.

"Please, Sir Kenton," she begged quietly. "Please do not do this terrible thing."

Kenton raised the tool. As Gerik pulled Nicola from the chapel, the last thing she heard was the hammer being slammed against the cold stone of Gaylord Thorne's tomb.

THEY HADN'T TOUCHED the keep yet, but she knew that was only a matter of time. Nicola sat in the solar she loved so well, gazing about at her furnishings, wondering what she was going to lose and how soon she was going to lose it. More than likely the soldiers would take everything, considering them spoils of war. She tried not to let her depression show, but it was difficult.

Tab sat at her feet, pretending to busy himself with the wheel of a toy cart. One of the twins had broken it and even at five years of age, Tab was mature beyond his years and was able to make the simple repair. He had learned at an early age to depend on himself or his mother, because his father was a cruel, vicious man who was only to be feared. Teague and Tiernan lay on the floor over by the hearth, playing with small wooden soldiers as they usually did. There were some old rushes between them, making a prime battle ground for their typical game of war. Nicola watched them distractedly, befuddled by the events of the past several days and concerned for her future and for her sons' future.

So Kenton le Bec had them. She'd heard the name before, many times in the past, for the man was said to be King Henry's, and Warwick's, most powerful knight. He wasn't a baron or an earl, but a mere knight, leading a thousand men into the most battle-weary regions of the country all in the name of the king. Everyone in York-shire, or England for that matter, was terrified of him, herself included.

He was the biggest man she had ever seen, with enormous arms the size of small trees. What she remembered of her observations, other than his colossal size, was the fact that he had blue eyes, and they were strikingly emphasized by a face that was as tanned as leather. And the face itself was tremendously intimidating, as she recollected; his jaw was square, and his cheekbones were sharp and angled. Other than that, she hadn't any other observations because he had worn his armor and helm the entire time. Not that she cared about the rest of him in any manner, but she was willing to wager he had horns underneath his helm. Anyone who would smash a dead man's tomb had to be purely evil, though it was merely the act of the desecration she found offensive. The fact that the knight had transgressed against Gaylord had no effect on her whatsoever.

A tray suddenly appeared beside her, distracting her from her thoughts. Nicola glanced up into the face of a young serving woman. She was petite and pretty in a pale sort of way. The girl smiled and offered her a cup on the outstretched tray.

"Mead, my lady," she said.

Nicola took a cup. "So they are letting you move freely within the keep, Janet?"

The girl shrugged, handing a cup of goat's milk with cinnamon to Tad. "There are soldiers about, watching our every move. But for the most part, we have been allowed to go back to our work."

Nicola sipped the mead. It was sweet and tangy. "What of the knights?"

Janet knew what had happened to Gaylord's crypt. All of the adults knew. She eyed the boys before continuing. "There are several around the castle, my lady. But I was talking to Hermenia and she seems to think that there are a select few in actual command."

Hermenia was the old cook who also did the sewing and other

household chores. She also gossiped like a magpie. "I see," Nicola said. "Will you impart to me her wisdom, then?"

Janet smiled at the sarcasm. "Le Bec is unquestionably in command, but he has been seen relaying orders to three or four other knights, who then go about and make sure the deeds are carried out. But there are lesser knights all over the walls and out in the countryside where they hold our soldiers. I believe Hermenia has counted more knights than she has fingers and toes."

Nicola didn't like the sound of that. But she knew as much, considering it had only taken three days for Babylon to fall. Fortifications or not, her husband had only two hundred men and simply by le Bec's sheer numbers and siege tower had they fallen.

"You and Hermenia will keep inside," she instructed. "Liesl and Raven, too. I'll not have the lot of you being abused by enemy soldiers."

Janet nodded. "I've already told them as much, my lady."

Nicola took another drink of her mead, this time deeply. "Especially Liesl and Raven. God's Bones, but those two are silly and pliable."

"They're young, my lady," Janet said. "Why do you think my mother sent them here, to serve with me? She hoped they would grow up."

Nicola realized she sounded harsh and smiled at the woman who had served her faithfully for many years. She set the cup back on the tray just as the objects of her reproach, two very young girls of fifteen and sixteen years, entered the solar. Liesl, plain and pale like her older sister, and Raven, with dark hair and dark eyes, carried food for the boys. They had been as much companions and older sisters to the brood and Nicola was, in truth, thankful for their help. When Gaylord had beaten her ill for days on end, the sisters took care of her boys, and the little ones loved them.

"The knights are gathering in the great hall, my lady," Raven said. "I fear they are up to no good."

Nicola's stomach lurched, but outwardly she remained calm. A gaggle of knights could never be a good thing.

"They are in control of Babylon now and we will do as they command. But," she held up a finger, "I would have the two of you and your sister stay up here in the family apartments. I will not have you catching their attention in any way."

Raven was all butterflies and innocence, pretending she was not capable of such things, while Liesl simply looked frightened. "We have no intention of catching their attention, my lady," Raven said. "We plan to stay far, far away from them."

Nicola didn't think that would last, at least not by the knight's standpoint. The reality was that someone had to serve the meals, which Liesl and Raven usually did. So did Janet. Keeping her girls from the knights and fighting men might prove difficult, but she would do her best to protect them. She sighed and stood up, stretching her legs as she walked across the room to the narrow lancet window.

The countryside beyond was green and moderately cool in the fall air. The breeze was chilly but she stood there a moment, letting it caress her, forgetting for a moment that she was captive in her own castle. But then again, she had been Gaylord's captive for many years, so it was something she was accustomed to. She had resigned herself to the state of her life so many years ago that it was difficult to think of it any other way.

She heard one of the girls gasp behind her and she turned around. Standing in the doorway was a big blond knight. He eyed her appraisingly.

"Lord le Bec will have a word with you, Madam," he said.

Nicola had no intention of arguing, though her heart was pounding in her chest. Before she could make it to the door, the twins were up and ready to do battle.

"You leave my mother alone!" Teague spoke with his terrible lisp.

Tiernan didn't even speak; he simply ran at the knight and began punching his leg. The knight just stood there as Nicola calmly pulled her son aside and whispered something in his ear. Then she murmured something to the other twin and both boys turned back, pouting, to their toys. With a deep breath, she winked at Tab to reassure him and left with the knight. She could hear Tiernan crying as she walked towards the stairs and it nearly broke her heart. For the second time that day, their mother was being taken away.

Raven had been right; there were several knights gathered in the great hall. It was a long room with a huge hearth at one end and the colors of the House of Thorne flying from the open beams. The blond knight silently indicated a man standing next to the hearth and it took Nicola a moment to realize she was looking at le Bec without his helm.

She hadn't recognized him. He sported a head of short, spikey dark hair, standing up from dirt and sweat. He had pieces of his plate armor off and as she approached him, she was terrified anew by the size of the man. He had a neck like a tree trunk.

Le Bec was studying the stone carvings of the hearth. Nicola stood a respectful distance away, silently, waiting for him to acknowledge her. After what seemed a small eternity, he looked at her with deep blue eyes. The mere expression on his face made her feel as if a bucket of cold water had just been thrown on her. She could almost taste her fear, but she would never let him know it.

"Lady Thorne," he moved from the hearth towards the long table that sat in the middle of the room. He perched his bulk on a corner and looked at her. "I am pleased that you did not lie to me."

"My lord?"

"Your husband. His body was in the crypt."

"You know my husband on sight, my lord?"

"I know all my enemies on sight."

"I was not aware you had ever met my husband, my lord."

Kenton nodded faintly. "On two occasions, once at a tourney and once in London."

Nicola didn't know what else to say. She simply stood there, feeling dumb and scrutinized. "If that is all, then I shall return to my children, my lord."

"That is *not* all."

He let her stand there for several more long, drawn out moments.

Eyes lowered, she could hear the sounds around her. For the number of men in the room, it was eerily quiet. She knew they were all staring at her and she resisted the urge to snap at them.

"Babylon is mine," Kenton said after an eternal and uncomfortable pause. "And with that reasoning, you and your household are also mine. Now that Gaylord is accounted for, it is time for you to be dealt with."

Her head snapped up. "What does that mean – *dealt* with?"

His face was like stone. "Exactly that," he said. "I've no use for a pampered lady about the place. Babylon will be a military installation from this day forward."

He had succeeded in stirring her indignation. "Allow me to put your mind at ease, Sir Kenton," she said sternly. "I am not, as you put it, a pampered lady. I am a functional part of this house and hold and run it quite efficiently."

Kenton didn't doubt for one second that she was not as capable as she said she was. He sensed a strength in her that set her apart from other noble women he had known and it was oddly intriguing. But he had a decision to make, strength or no.

"I'll harbor no nursery here with miniature ruffians running about," he said. "Your children have no place here."

"They were born here. They have more right to be here than you do."

Over her left shoulder, Kenton could see Conor fighting off a smile. Gerik and Ackerley stood well off to the side, shocked that the lady prisoner should speak to their liege so. Kenton sighed softly and crooked a finger at her, beckoning her towards him. Wary but unwilling to disobey, Nicola moved forward, stopped, then kept walking when he motioned her closer. She brushed up against his massive thigh when he finally stopped beckoning. Inches from him, she could feel his hot breath in her face and it was wildly intimidating and strangely curious all at the same time.

"Madam," Kenton's voice was low and quiet, "I have battled the most powerful armies this world has to offer and I have no intention of fighting with the likes of you. I will tell you this one time only; you will cease this insolence or I will toss you and your children in the vault and throw away the key. Is that, in any way, unclear?"

She struggled between fear and indignation. "Forgive me if I have been insolent, my lord," she said. "But I would like to know when the truth has been considered insolent."

"You're doing it right now."

"Am I? I was not aware."

He gazed into her pale green eyes, again feeling that strange tingle in his chest, only this time it was a warm, tightening sensation. It was not unpleasant but he thought perhaps he was becoming ill. The sensation unnerved him.

"You are, indeed, aware," he growled. "And this type of behavior will cease."

His tone was enough to make her back down. "As you say, my lord."

He stared at her, trying to discern if she was lying. He read nothing but fortitude and truth in her eyes. He almost read a challenge. Unbalanced, his jaw began to flex in an uncharacteristic display of emotion.

"You and your brood will keep to the apartments until I decide what's to be done with you. Under no circumstances will I see your children in the great hall or anywhere outside of the keep. If I catch one of them, he shall be mine."

"For what purpose?"

He couldn't believe she was being combative after what he had just told her. "How's that?"

She was quite serious. "I asked you for what purpose, my lord," she repeated. "If you catch one of my boys, what will you do with him? Surely you don't intend to make use of him in the midst of your mighty military installation."

He just stared at her in amazement. He swore he could see a twinkle of sarcasm in her eye and it nearly drove him mad. The woman was *toying* with him. He knew he had to tend to her attitude here and now, or all would be lost.

"Throw her in the vault," he commanded.

The twinkle fled from Nicola's eye. Conor came up and grasped her by the arm, tugging her back towards the door to the kitchens.

Kenton couldn't even watch the expression on her face as she was taken away; he was far too angry, but he realized he was very close to immediately countering the order. He had done it purely from spite.

He heard the door to the kitchens slam and that strange tug in his chest started again.

CHAPTER TWO

Babylon's keep

H E COULDN'T SLEEP.

It wasn't surprising given the events of the day. Much had happened and there was still much to do but, try as he might, thoughts of the stubborn and willful Lady Nicola kept filling his mind.

His knights had split up the night watch, leaving him to conduct his own business, which was good considering how much trouble he was having concentrating on anything other than that blond slip of a woman he had tossed into the vault. It was odd, truly, because Kenton was a professional soldier, meaning he had no family or wife or even a home of his own. He was Warwick's attack dog and he'd been doing it for over ten years, taking his crack squad of nearly one thousand men and doing Warwick's dirty work. He'd had more than his share of victories and perhaps one or two failures in all that time. His record as an aggressive warrior was excellent and Warwick had rewarded him well for his skills. He was quite wealthy. But when it came to women, he was relatively untried. He simply tried to steer clear of them. He'd seen too many good men fall to their seductive ways.

Therefore, a beautiful, fiery widow was something of a mystery and an object of intimidation to him; there, he'd admitted it. Lady Nicola was intimidating. Whenever the woman entered his orbit, he felt strange, as if she were weaving some magic upon him. He didn't like it.

Or perhaps he did. He hadn't decided yet because he was so unaccustomed to such things.

But as he walked the dark, smaller hall of the entry level of the keep, there was something bothering him even more than Lady Thorne and the web of spells she cast over him, something that had been on his mind since they'd breached the great walls of Babylon. All thoughts of the lovely temptress aside, it was clear from the condition of Gaylord's body that the man had been dead for months, which brought about a very valid question – if Gaylord Thorne had been dead for months, then *who* had led the defenses against him?

Aye, it was thoughts of Babylon's defenses that weighed heavily upon him at the moment. When they'd swept the castle earlier in the day, they had come across old soldiers mostly and two old knights. Kenton assumed that one of the knights had been in charge but one of them seemed to be unable to speak intelligibly and the other one seemed apathetic to the entire situation. It had been very odd. In fact, this entire place, the massive structure of enormous walls and soaring keep, was odd. There was something unsettling about the place, like it had secrets yet untold. Kenton wondered if he would ever discover them.

So he pondered his thoughts as he walked the dark level of the keep. The servants had vanished for the night and all he could hear was an occasional shout outside from one of his soldiers, men who had Babylon bottled up tightly for the night. The darkened hall had long, slender lancet windows for ventilation and sounds from the night outside drifted inside. The hall, located on the second-floor entry level, took up about half of the floor. It was two-stories tall and cut up into the third floor above, with a minstrel gallery that was accessed from the third floor.

He hadn't yet made it up to the third and fourth floors, the family sleeping rooms, mostly because he had been busy taking inventory of the wealth of what appeared to be Gaylord's solar but also two smaller rooms that were evidently for Lady Thorne's use because there were all manner of sewing and weaving looms in both of them. There was plate on the hearth of all three chambers, a box of coins in the larger solar, and a variety of possessions that included fine quills, elaborate ink wells, parchment for writing, various cups and chalices made from fine metals, and there were even several exquisite books that Kenton had come across.

There were also a variety of smaller closets, small windowless rooms where the servants stored things, but he hadn't paid much attention to those smaller closets yet. He was rather surprised to see them, for most keeps didn't possess such built-in storage, but Babylon evidently did. He was rather curious to get a look at what was inside the cubbies he had located.

Thinking on heading back to the large solar to get a closer look at the wealth he had acquired, Kenton passed into the entry hall with the stairs that led to the upper floors. The staircase was a big, supported structure that hugged one wall, following the line of the wall down until it came to a ninety-degree corner and then following the line of that wall until it reached the bottom. It was supported by big stone pillars that continued all the way up to the ceiling, as if caging in the staircase, and was quite an impressive architectural feat. Kenton had never seen another flight of stairs like it. As he moved out into the entry room to take another look at the big, sweeping staircase, he thought he caught a glimpse of movement near the top of the stairs.

It was dark in the entry save the silver moonbeams that poured in through two lancet windows above the arched entry door. It wasn't enough light to see clearly but was enough to illuminate movement. Hand to the hilt of the dirk that was sheathed at his belt, he slipped underneath he staircase and silently made his way to the bottom of the steps, unseen by whoever was at the top of the flight. If it was a Thorne assassin, he planned to make short work out of him.

He was prepared.

He'd quickly gone into stalking mode. His natural resting state was one of defense, anyway, but an unknown entity in his proximity was cause for alarm. In silence, he made his way to the base of the stairs, peering up into the darkened staircase to see if he could make anything out – friend or foe. He took the first two steps, not making a sound, and it was another eight steps before the landing where the staircase took a sharp right turn and continued up to the third floor above.

Kenton had learned long ago to remain calm in situations such as this. His heart rate had barely increased and his breathing was still quite steady, all signs of a man who had faced death before and knew how to survive it. Chances are, he thought, the assassin was a servant who had no idea that he was the one now being stalked. The tables were turned.

Kenton's grip tightened on his dirk, preparing to withdraw it and plant it squarely in whoever was lurking about in the darkness. Body tightly coiled, ready to spring, he reached the landing of the stairs only to be confronted with something crouching against the stone stair railing just as he turned the corner.

"Argggh!"

It was a very small person with some kind of coverlet over its head, now jumping up and clawing the air in his direction. Genuinely startled, Kenton actually took a step back as the small figure, covered with a linen sheet, jumped up and down and continued clawing at the air.

"*Ooooooooo!*"

More noise from the figure as it suddenly turned tail and ran back up the stairs as fast as its little legs would carry it. Kenton stood on the landing, frowning, as the figure went to hide behind one of the support pillars. The problem was that there was already a second small person hiding behind that same pillar and the little ghost who had tried to scare him got pushed out. But the little figure scrambled to its feet and chose another pillar to hide behind.

Kenton stood on the landing below and watched all of the hissing and pushing going on. His initial surprise was now tempered with realization and perhaps impatience. With a heavy sigh, he let go of the hilt of his dirk and began to take the stairs, going in hunt of the figures that were lying in wait for him. He was about halfway to the top when another figure, with what looked like a woman's linen shift over its head, jumped out at him from a pillar on the right.

"Ooooooo!" the figure said threateningly in a very heavy lisp. "I am going to curse you!"

Kenton came to a pause, hands on his hips as he faced his nemesis. "Is that so?" he said rather casually.

"It is!"

"Do as you must."

That seemed to stump the little figure for a moment; it paused as if confused but quickly took up clawing the air again.

"You are afraid!" it told him in a terrible lisp. "Go away and do not come back or you will be cursed!"

In spite of himself, Kenton found himself fighting off a grin. "I see," he said, wiping his hand over his mouth to hide the smirk. "Then you may as well curse me for I am not leaving."

That thoroughly stumped the figure and it came to a halt, turning to look up the staircase and into the shadows as if seeking silent support. It didn't take long for the walls to come alive with two more small figures, with coverlets over their heads, as they rushed down the steps. One of them even tripped, rolling down a stair or two, before picking itself up and recovering. It rubbed an elbow painfully.

"Go away!" the biggest of the trio pointed imperiously at Kenton. "You are not wanted here! Go away or you will be sorry!"

Kenton recognized the voice as that of Lady Thorne's eldest son. It was the same commanding tone the lad had used when he had ordered Kenton to leave his mother alone earlier in the day. With no more patience for their foolery, Kenton reached out and yanked the pale covering off of the lad's head.

Hair mussed, Tab glared up at Kenton with as much courage as a five-year-old boy could muster. In truth, the lad was beyond courageous, showing no fear in the face of his conquerors. Kenton had to admit that the boy's bravery impressed him. He was foolish, but brave nonetheless. Kenton held up the dusty, white coverlet.

"What are you doing with this?" he asked drolly.

Tab was scowling fiercely. "We were scaring you away!"

Kenton cocked an eyebrow. "Scaring me?"

Standing next to him, Teague pulled the woman's shift off his head and reached out, tugging on the hem of Kenton's tunic until Kenton looked down at him.

"We are ghosts," he said with his pronounced lisp. "Were you not afraid?"

He was quite serious and Kenton gazed down at the child, feeling an odd tugging in his chest, something between compassion and humor. For as much as these children were out and about when they should not be, he had to admit that he found it somewhat funny simply because they were dead serious about it.

"Nay," Kenton told the child flatly. "I do not believe in ghosts. And you were told to stay to your apartments."

Teague was thoroughly confused. "But everyone is afraid of ghosts."

"I am not."

Teague wasn't sure what to say to that. He looked at Tab, the eldest, for help. Tab was quick to intervene.

"It is our duty to chase you away," he said. "You are the enemy and we must protect Babylon. Mother does not allow us to fight with real swords so we are going to scare you away instead."

Kenton realized that, for the second time in as many minutes, he was struggling not to grin. The lad was determined to rid his keep of the enemy; Kenton could see that. But it was also clear that the boy did not understand the concept of a captor/captive relationship and it was up to Kenton to educate him. He'd already thrown their defiant mother in the vault and he wasn't beyond tossing her children in after her. He sighed faintly.

"Your tactics did not work," he said. "You will return to your apartments now or I will take my hand to your backside. I suspect your mother has not disciplined you nearly enough, therefore, that lesson will fall to me."

Teague, standing the closest, tugged on his tunic again until the man looked down at him. "Mam says that it is not very nice to hit," Teague said.

Kenton's smile nearly broke through at the innocent comment and he realized that, quite possibly, he would have difficulty carrying out his threat against these lads. They were quite naïve in their view of the world, it seemed, and that was something he didn't recognize. The world was a hard and dangerous place to him but somehow, within these walls of Babylon, the world was not such a terrible place to these children. Enemies could be chased away by the threat of ghosts and hitting was not a nice thing to do. Was it truly possible there was such innocence left in this world?

"It is also not very nice to disobey my order," he said, pointing back up the steps. "Return to your rooms. I will not tell you again."

Teague opened his mouth again, no doubt to tell Kenton that his demands were not very nice, but they were distracted by a rattling sound in the entry down below. Kenton turned towards the sound, back on the defensive, as the three little boys gasped with fear. Tiernan, the silent child, actually latched on to Kenton's leg and would not let go. Startled, Kenton looked down to see the utter terror on the child's face.

"Hurry!" Tab suddenly ran at him, grabbing hold of his hand and trying to pull him down. "Get down! We must hide!"

Kenton was preparing to outright refuse when Teague grabbed hold of him, too, and between the three boys, Kenton somehow found himself seated on the cold stone steps. They had managed to drag him down although he couldn't have shown much resistance if they were so easily able to do it. His reaction puzzled him, allowing children to tug him to the floor. There were gaps in the railing that he could see through to the entry level below and more rattling could be heard, echoing off the old walls of the keep. Before Kenton realized what had happened, he had both twins on his lap and Tab hanging over his shoulder, pointing to the darkness below.

"Look!" he said. "Now the ghost will come. You will see!"

Kenton frowned at Tab, exasperation coming from the usually emotionless knight. "There are no such things as ghosts," he repeated what he'd said earlier.

Tab, the serious young man, suddenly looked less than his usual brave self. He was jabbing a finger in the direction of the darkness down below.

"Look, now," he hissed. "Make no sound or else the ghost will come and get us!"

Kenton truly had no idea what the child was referring to but before he could ask, he heard a door open in the entry below. Curious, he turned to see where the sound was coming from. There were at least three smaller closet-like storage rooms he had come across down there as well as the large solar and the two rooms used by Lady Thorne. He thought he'd swept the keep quite thoroughly for any unknown inhabitants but he evidently hadn't. As he watched, a small half-door that was built into the wall near the base of the stairs suddenly lurched open.

Kenton could see feet emerge; small, dirty stocking feet. It was clear that a person was emerging from the door but they were doing it lying down, on their belly, as if they were crawling out backwards. It was all very strange. As Kenton and the boys watched, a woman dressed in tatters of a fine pale gown emerged from the small closet and stood up. Her gray hair was wild and long, like ribbons of smoke floating about her. Suddenly, she began whirling around, like a dancer, leaping into the air and twirling about. Her movements were surprisingly graceful and fluid and, at one point, it seemed as if she picked up a partner because then she began to dance as if she were intertwined with a lover.

It was all quite odd but strangely fascinating. The woman's long, graceful arms swung about as she danced on her toes and then holding her arms to her as if relishing her imaginary partner's embrace. She had no idea of her audience on the stairs above, watching her every movement. Her dance was a private one, imagining a world that no longer existed except in her mind. At one point, she touched her face, her mouth, and then her hands trailed to her breasts where she fondled herself rather sensually.

On the stairs above, Kenton instinctively put his big hands over Teague and Tiernan's eyes so they would not see the woman suggestively caress herself. It was a provocative and unseemly show for young boys to witness, at least in Kenton's view. Tiernan sat there with a hand over his eyes and tried to remove it by shaking his head around, but Teague lifted his hands and pulled Kenton's fingers away. Teague was torn between great curiosity and terror, just as Tab was, but Tiernan continued to sit there with Kenton's hand over his eyes, trying to remove it by simply shaking his head. He ended up rubbing snot from his running nose all over Kenton's palm and, when Kenton realized it, he yanked his hand away in disgust and wiped the mucus off on Tiernan's tunic and hair.

Meanwhile, the show continued down below. The woman was back to dancing with her invisible lover, leaping over the floor and disappearing into the smaller hall with its two-storied reach. Kenton stood up enough so that he could see what the woman was doing. She was simply skipping and whirling over the floor, avoiding the dogs that were sleeping by the hearth, and climbing up on one of the tables as she continued her bizarre dance. She was in a world of her own, dancing to an unseen orchestra and enjoying the company of unseen partners.

Abruptly, the woman ended her dance on the table and fled the room, rushing into the darkened entry hall and heading for the staircase. Kenton, with two little boys on his lap and one child hanging over his shoulder, watched as the woman ran halfway up the stairs, all wild gray hair and tattered clothing. When her gaze fell upon the four men seated on the stairs, men who had been watching her every move, she let out a hideous hiss and bared her rotted black teeth at them.

Kenton didn't move; he remained still as stone, preparing to unsheathe his dirk if she took another step towards him. On his lap,

Tiernan covered his eyes in horror as Teague shoved his fingers into his mouth, biting his fingers in terror. Kenton couldn't even see what Tab was doing, but he was fairly certain the lad was taking refuge behind his broad back. In any case, the old woman hissed again, a terrible sound, and rushed back down the stairs. As Kenton peered through the railing, she dove back into her closet and slammed the door.

All was suddenly still and quiet in the darkened entry. Kenton kept his gaze on the closet to see if the old woman would emerge again, but all remained silent. After several moments, he glanced at the boys on his lap to see that they were frozen in the same terrified positions as they had been when the woman had hissed at them. Behind him, he could feel Tab shifting around.

"Who *was* that?" Kenton asked any boy who could answer him.

Tab spoke. "The ghost," he insisted. "She lives here."

Kenton craned his head around to look at the boy, only to see that he was absolutely serious. It occurred to him that perhaps Tab didn't really know who the woman was, but Kenton suspected who did.

In fact, he was sure of it.

IT TOOK NICOLA a moment to realize that someone was opening the vault door. Down in the dank darkness on the sub-level below the gatehouse, the rattling of metal was deafening against the moss-slick stone walls. Rubbing her eyes of sleep, Nicola blinked her eyes in the darkness, struggling to focus, only to realize that Kenton was entering her cell. And he was not alone.

Tab and Teague were walking beside him and Tiernan was in the man's arms. Shocked and fearful to see her children, Nicola rolled to her knees and held out her arms to her sons. Tab and Teague rushed to her.

"What is wrong?" she asked, terrified for her boys. "Why are you here? What have you done?"

Tab hugged his mother fiercely. "We tried to scare him away but he would not leave," he told her. "The ghost could not scare him away, either!"

Kenton stood before her, gazing down at the woman as she hugged her children. There was something very sweet and gentle about it, something quite loving. Kenton had forgotten that there could be such tenderness in the world, for he couldn't remember a time in his life when he had known any.

He tried to put Tiernan down but the frightened boy clung to him. He couldn't just force the child to his feet so he stood there, awkwardly holding him. Still, there was something strangely comforting in holding a child. Very strange, indeed. Fighting off unfamiliar feelings of tenderness, Kenton focused on the reason for his visit.

"We saw the woman in the closet, Madam," he said, his voice low. "Who is she?"

Nicola was somewhat confused by the question. "The woman in the closet?" she repeated.

"The one at the base of the stairs, near the entry."

The light of recognition went on in Nicola's eyes. "Ah," she said. "That is my husband's mother."

Kenton was rather surprised by the answer. "His *mother*?" he confirmed. "What on earth is the woman doing in that closet?"

Nicola snuggled with two out of her three boys, almost too much for her petite lap. "She has been in that cubby as long as I can recall," she said, kissing Teague's head gently. "She is quite mad but quite harmless so long as she is left alone."

Kenton mulled over the information. "She hissed menacingly at us."

"She will do that if confronted."

"Your sons believe she is a ghost."

Nicola shrugged. "She comes out at night and dances through the lower floors in her tattered clothing and wild hair," she said. "If you were a child, what would that look like to you?"

Kenton conceded the point. "A ghost," he admitted. "She will be removed, however. I cannot have the woman disrupting my keep."

Nicola gazed up at him, her brow furrowed with concern. "But I told you she is harmless so long as she is left alone," she said. "If you try to remove her, she could become quite violent."

Kenton's face was like stone. "That is not my concern," he said. "I will do what is necessary in order to remove her. There will be no mad relatives loose in my keep."

Nicola regarded him a moment. Then she looked away, shaking her head. "*Your* keep," she muttered. "You have been here less than a day and already it is your keep."

"I told you it was my keep the moment I entered the gates of Babylon. What part of that statement did you not understand?"

Nicola sighed softly. It was evident she was very weary and somewhat defeated, but the fire of resistance was still in those beautiful eyes. Kenton could see it. He suspected a woman as strong and fiery as Lady Thorne would never be completely subdued, ever.

"It took you days to breach Babylon," she muttered. "It did not come so easy. It was not as if I easily gave it up to you."

Kenton's jaw ticked. Now, she was touching on a subject he had been wondering about since nearly the moment he'd breached the gatehouse – *who* was in charge of Babylon's defenses?

"And so it did not," he said, forcing Tiernan down to his feet. As the boy ran to his mother, Kenton crouched down a few feet away, watching the four of them very carefully. Mostly, he was watching Nicola. "As impenetrable as Babylon is, the fact remains that there are only a handful of soldiers and knights seeing to her defenses. You held off a substantial army for days with very few resources which is to be commended, but in the end, you still fell to me. That is a fact."

Nicola's head jerked to him, her eyes flaring with rebellion. "You mounted our walls with ladders," she said. "We stemmed your tide for almost five days before the end came."

"But the end did come and Babylon is mine."

He said it with such finality, such arrogance. Nicola, who had thus far remained somewhat calm and submissive throughout the conversation, began to feel the fire of resistance surge in her veins. She didn't like le Bec's attitude or his possessiveness when it came to something that did not belong to him. This was the home that her boys would inherit and for no other reason than that, she had to fight for it. She held no grand memories of Babylon. In truth, she equated the fortress to her marriage to Gaylord. It was a cold, sometimes painful, and always an intimidating thing. But it was her children's legacy and she would fight for it, no matter what.

"It is yours and Henry's for now," she said, hazard in her tone. "But soon enough, Edward shall regain it. I hope I am here to see that day."

Kenton heard the hatred in her words. Hatred of him, of Henry, and perhaps of war in general. It was difficult to know. But he could see such strength in the woman as she spoke. That fire he'd seen since the beginning of their acquaintance was still there, smoldering, waiting to flare once more. She could still be a viable threat to him and he knew it. The logical thing would be to get rid of her for his own protection but he couldn't seem to make a decision about it, which confused him.

Threats must be eliminated!

"It is quite possible that you will be," he said evenly. "But until that time, your fortress, and everything within it, belongs to me."

Nicola held his gaze a moment longer before turning away. She simply couldn't stomach the triumph in his eyes. "It would not be yours if I had more men," she murmured, "and if I was better at commanding. If I'd had those two factors, you would still be outside the walls and I would be laughing at your futility."

A twinkle came to Kenton's eye, suspecting he now had his answer about the leader of Babylon's defenses. In hindsight, he knew it all along. He wasn't surprised in the least and he found himself impressed with a woman that should be strong enough to hold off an army.

"Where are all of Gaylord's men?" he asked in an oddly conversational manner, as if there was no force or demand behind it. "Babylon has been known to carry thousands."

Nicola was still looking away from him, her gaze averted to the darkened shadows of the vault. There wasn't any reason not to tell him everything. It wasn't as if she had any secrets left to keep.

"Gaylord sent them on to the Duke of York to reinforce the lines for Edward," she said quietly. "He saw no reason to leave more than a few dozen men to man Babylon, knowing she was unbreachable. Imagine what his surprise would be to know that was not the case."

"Why did you not recall them from York?"

She shrugged. "I did not see the need until your army came upon us. By then, it was too late."

Kenton digested the information, thinking that a good deal now made sense. With Thorne's men away reinforcing Edward, Babylon was truly his. His men were currently still housed outside of the castle walls in an encampment that had been set up before the siege but he now thought it a good idea to fold up camp and bring everyone inside. Word would spread that Babylon was now in Lancastrian hands and he fully expected retaliation at some point, but before that could happen, he wanted Babylon sealed up.

His gaze moved to Lady Thorne and his thoughts followed. Having a woman at a military installation was a distraction and having her entire family there was unacceptable, and that thought alone swayed his decision towards sending Lady Thorne away. He'd been uncertain only a few second before but now, knowing what Babylon was to become for Henry's cause, he knew he had no choice. The woman, and her children, had to go.

"Babylon is now held for the rightful king," he said, telling her what she had already heard before. "You should know that I have sent word to Warwick. He will soon be moving his men here to assume command and we will be using Babylon as a base for further action in the north. With that said, there will be no room for you and your children and servants. Do you have somewhere else to go?"

Nicola looked at him again, her eyes wide with distress and surprise. "This is our home," she said, rather hotly. "Of course we have nowhere else to go."

"You cannot remain."

Nicola was stricken. "Why not?" she demanded. "I will keep the boys out of the way. We will not interfere with your operations. Moreover, you need me. I told you that before you threw me into the vault. I run this house and hold quite efficiently and with a large army arriving, I should think my function would be very valuable to you. You want your men fed and housed, do you not? I know how to do that. I serve a purpose."

I serve a purpose. He was coming to think that she was correct; he would have thousands of men here, including commanders, and if they did not have someone to run the household and provide meals and other functions, one of the men would have to do it and they more than likely would not do it nearly so well. Besides, he didn't exactly want to send her away. There; he admitted it. It was the entire reason behind his indecision and he found himself wavering once again on his inclination to send her away. She was beautiful and intelligent. She intrigued him. At least, she was starting to.

"We shall see," he said vaguely. "Since you do not have anywhere else to go, for now, I will allow you to remain, but only until other arrangements can be made. Furthermore, I will make it clear that Babylon can only have one master and that is me. Is that in any way unclear?"

"It is clear."

"You are not in charge."

"I understand."

He eyed her, knowing she was saying it simply to agree with him. He knew she didn't mean it. With a grunt, perhaps of resignation, he turned for the cell door.

"You are released from this place," he told her. "Take your children and return to your apartments. You will remain there until further instructions. Do you comprehend?"

Stiffly, Nicola began to rise. Tab was trying to help her to her feet.

"Aye," she said, brushing off the dirt and straw from her knees. "What will happen now?"

Kenton stood at the cell door, indicating for her to walk through it. "Go back to your rooms," he told her again. "The business of Babylon is no longer your affair. From this point on, you will obey implicitly or you will find yourself back in this vault permanently."

Nicola didn't reply, mostly because she knew he meant it. She had pushed the man repeatedly and he had shown her his capabilities. He had no problem throwing a woman in the vault. The next time, he might put her in here and truly keep her here forever. Her pride was a difficult thing to swallow and so was her rebellion, but for her children's sake, she had to. At least for the moment.

Silently, she grasped the twins by the hand and, with Tab in tow, slipped from the vault and back to the keep where Liesl and Raven and Janet were very glad to see them. They tried to return to a sense of normalcy quickly, unbalanced by the events of the day and uncertain of their future.

With the boys settled in for the night, Nicola remained awake, struggling to accept the new state of her world and wondering what the morrow would bring.

Never could she have imagined the scope of the invasion that was about to happen.

Babylon's very fabric was about to change.

CHAPTER THREE

A s Kenton had predicted, Warwick and his advisors arrived the next day.

Having never seen Babylon Castle from the interior, Neville was more than impressed with the structure. From its imposing gray-stoned walls to its towering keep, Warwick could see how the fortress gained its reputation based purely on what he was seeing. All of it was quite impressive.

The colors of Henry flew from the battlements, the sounds of the banners flapping in the breeze drawing Warwick's attention. Dismounting his steed, he gazed up, thinking it was a rather fine sight to see Henry's standards dominating the castle. It was a sight he wasn't sure if he would ever see.

"You have arrived safely, my lord," came a voice behind him. "Welcome to Babylon."

Warwick turned, grinning, to see Kenton walking towards him. "And so I have," he said. He swept his arm out to indicate his surroundings. "I am pleased, Kenton. You and the Trouble Trio have done well."

Kenton cracked a half-grin; Warwick meant Conor, Gerik, and Ackerley. Years ago, when they had served the Earl of Thetford, they had earned the nicknames Trouble, More Trouble, and Lucifer's Brother. In fact, Atticus de Wolfe, The Lion of the North, and the current Baron Killham, had given them that name. They wore it like a badge of honor and had for almost ten years. Now, however, they were simply called the Trouble Trio. Anyone in Henry's service knew what that name meant – three of the most powerful knights on the border. Serving under Kenton le Bec, however, the four of them were nearly invincible.

"Thank you, my lord," Kenton said. "It was something of a task, but we managed."

Warwick nodded, his gaze lingering on the walls. "This is more than I had hoped for," he said. "From the looks of those walls, it is no wonder it took as long as it did to secure it."

Kenton glanced up at the walls, wriggling his dark eyebrows as he remembered the effort it took to mount them. "It was no simple feat, I assure you," he said. "Mayhap you noted the slope of the ground as you approached the castle. It makes it very difficult to get a foothold for the ladders or siege engines on such an angle. That is what took us so long."

Warwick grunted in understanding. "Indeed," he said. His gaze upon the surrounding fortress turned wistful. "We have wanted Babylon for quite some time. With her capture, it will make many things possible for Henry. He will be very pleased. Now, show me this place so that I may gloat in your victory."

With a half-grin, Kenton took the lead as Warwick and his advisors, eight decorated and powerful men, followed. "As you can see, the bailey is large enough to house thousands. There is a troop house on the south side, built into the curtain wall, that can house at least a thousand men. There is also knight housing and various other shelters we can lodge men in and those we cannot fit into individual structures can be housed in the great hall and the keep. The entire fortress is self-sufficient and self-contained."

Warwick listened with interest. "And Gaylord Thorne?" he asked. "We have been friends and allies in the past you, you know. He is a pragmatic and somewhat brutal man. I cannot imagine he turned this all over to you so easily."

Kenton looked at him as they walked. "He is dead," he replied. "He died four months ago. I confirmed his body in the family crypt, buried in the chapel."

Warwick was surprised. "Dead, you say?" he repeated. "How?"

"A festering wound from what I was told."

Warwick found it all very interesting and, in truth, very satisfying. It was one less thing to worry about. Although he and Gaylord had been friends in years past when both of them had served Edward, he didn't particularly care for the man. "This is unexpected," he said. "I had thought to have the man as a prisoner. At least, I had hoped."

Kenton's mind moved to the family Thorne had left behind. "We have his wife and sons as hostages," he told Warwick. "Lady Thorne has thus far proven to be as formidable as her husband, more so in some respects. You will find your conversations with her interesting should you decide to interrogate her."

"Have you interrogated her yet?"

Kenton nodded. "Somewhat," he said. "It is my sense that she doesn't know anything critical to our cause but she does bear watching. I would not put it past her to try and slip a dagger into the ribs of the enemy."

Warwick paused in their walk, eyeing him. "Is she dangerous, then?"

Kenton shook his head. "I do not believe so, in truth," he said. "But she is a staunch supporter of Edward. She had made that clear. I have consigned her and her children to the fourth floor of the keep where there are three small rooms. She will be more easily watched from there."

Warwick thought on the situation. "She should be removed," he said. "I can send her to Warwick Castle as a hostage. She might prove valuable."

"With Thorne dead? I am not sure what value she would have."

Warwick shrugged. "That is true," he said. "Still, I am not entirely sure I am comfortable with her on the loose."

Kenton cleared his throat softly. He couldn't believe he was about to defend a woman who had been a combative shrew from the start.

"This is a rather large fortress," he said, eyeing Warwick for the man's reaction as he spoke. "It is in need of a chatelaine who knows the fortress intimately. It is my intention to keep Lady Thorne here to oversee the keep and the daily functions of the castle. If I send her away, I will have to assign one of my men to do woman's work and that will not make the lucky candidate very happy."

Warwick laughed softly. "There is truth in what you say," he said. "Very well; Lady Thorne will remain. But mind she does not poison our food."

Kenton nodded. "She will have a guard with her constantly."

Satisfied with the utilization of Lady Thorne, the two men continued with their tour of Babylon and Warwick was increasingly impressed with the acquisition of the fortress. But the truth was that he was weary and, eventually, Kenton took him into the keep and put him in the large, comfortable master's chamber that overlooked the bailey and the gatehouse.

Kenton wondered if he should send for Nicola to help settle Warwick but thought better of it. He didn't think she would be too receptive to help settle a man who had essentially taken over her fortress and her very world for that matter. So he ordered his men to assist Warwick and, soon enough, the man was settled down in the lavish master's chamber. The last Kenton saw of him, he was sprawled out wearily on Gaylord Thorne's comfortable bed.

Leaving Warwick to rest in the chamber of his conquered enemy, Kenton resisted the urge to take the small flight upstairs up to the fourth floor to check on Lady Thorne. He was perfectly within his right to check up on the woman, but she would only end up provoking him in some manner and he would leave angry and frustrated. Interesting how hordes of men couldn't invite his temper but a small, lovely slip of a woman could.

Fighting off a smile at the thought of their verbal battles, which he evidently wasn't as frustrated with as he tried to convince himself, he headed down to the bailey with the intention of overseeing the settling of the rest of Warwick's men.

But thoughts of Lady Thorne lingered.

THEY'D SPENT MOST of the morning moving their possessions up from the third floor family chambers and into the fourth floor small rooms, which were meant for servants to sleep in. Now, the three small rooms had become her living quarters and Nicola was determined to make the best of it. There wasn't much she could do about it, anyway. She had to make the best of it, thankful that she was at least out of the vault. It could have been much worse.

Between her, Liesl, Raven, Janet, and the three boys, they had made short work out of moving their possessions. The beds, however, were another matter; one of Kenton's men, the man she had been introduced to as Conor de Birmingham, helped bring the boys' little beds up to one of the rooms. There were already two beds in one of the chambers, beds that weren't entirely uncomfortable, and Conor wouldn't allow her to bring the big master's bed upstairs. That bed, he said, had to remain.

Nicola didn't fight him on it, assuming as he did that Kenton would more than likely be sleeping on it. But she did want her coverlets and bed linens. Fearful that Conor wouldn't let her bring linens and other items upstairs, she waited until the red-haired knight left before going back to her former chamber and removing what she could. When she was finished, the chamber was nearly stripped.

Pleased in a sadistic way that she had left virtually nothing for le Bec to use in the master's chamber, she threw herself into organizing her current apartments. They were cluttered and small, but she would make do. As she supervised her servants as the women put clothing away and organized personal care and other items, the boys were playing in their small chamber. As usual, Teague had his little wooden knights on the floor, with their spears, while Tab was bossing Tiernan around and telling the boy to push the little beds into a certain configuration.

Tab was very good at giving orders and Nicola paused in her duties to smile at her eldest son who had a natural air of command about him. He was much like his father in that respect; Gaylord had a very commanding persona. He was decisive and unbending, something Tab tended to be as well.

Nicola watched Tab as he helped Tiernan push a little bed around, realizing that her eldest son had more of his father in him than she cared to admit. He had proved that the night he had rammed a sword into Gaylord's back as the man beat his mother. Nicola's smile turned to something of a grimace. She would have to make sure Gaylord's tendency for physical violence didn't also manifest itself in Tab. She could never do much about her husband to that regard but she could certainly do something about her son. He would not repeat the mistakes of his father. And he would never, ever know that his actions had led to Gaylord's demise. She could only pray that le Bec and his knights would help keep her secret.

"My lady," Janet said, catching her attention.

Jolted from her train of thought, Nicola turned to her little maid. "Aye?"

Janet had been rummaging around in one of the baskets of clothing that had been brought up from the master's chamber. She scooted over to Nicola, keeping her voice low.

"I think something was left behind, my lady," she said, wringing her hands nervously. "I cannot find the items you use for your woman's time. No bindings, no moss… I believe it was all left behind."

Nicola lifted her eyebrows, unconcerned. "No need to worry," she said. "I will go down and retrieve it."

Janet was still nervous. "It seems that Henry's men do not want us out of our rooms, my lady," she said. "I do not want you to get into trouble. I will go."

Nicola shook her head. "I will go," she insisted. "You remain here and tend the boys. Soon they will be hungry and we shall have to go to the kitchens."

Janet's worried appearance increased. "But we are to remain here, my lady."

Nicola moved to the chamber door, turning to glance at her servant. "Le Bec will have to release us, eventually," she told her. "His men will need to be fed at some point. He needs someone to manage the house and hold. I am confident we shall not spend the remainder of our days in this stone prison."

Janet wasn't entirely convinced but didn't say any more. Nicola quit the chamber and shut the door softly behind her, making her way to the small flight of stairs built into the wall of the keep that led down to the floor below. It was dark in the stairwell and she paused, listening for sounds of le Bec or his men. In truth, she didn't want to run into the man and risk being punished again for being caught out of her rooms, so she very carefully made her way down to the third floor.

The familiar smells of her former chambers greeted her. She was edgy standing on the landing, fearful that le Bec was about to make an appearance and throw her in the vault again for disobeying him. Even though she wished nothing but ill on the man, she was still afraid of what he might do when provoked. He'd proven that he wasn't reluctant to punish her and even though taunting had become something of a game, she didn't want to push him over the edge.

Therefore, not wanting to be caught, she immediately headed to the master's chambers, seeking the small basket of products she used for her personal needs. Usually, it was under the bed but the moment she opened the door, she noticed that since the time she had moved most of her possessions upstairs, le Bec had entered the master's chambers and fell asleep on the bed. He was covered up with the only coverlet she had left, including his head, but his feet were sticking out. He still had his boots on.

Frowning at dirty boots on her mattress, which wasn't so much her mattress any longer, she tiptoed inside the chamber and headed for the bed. The old wooden floors creaked now and again and she froze every time one let out a squealing noise, watching the bed to see if the sound had awakened le Bec. He must have been a very sound sleeper because, so far, nothing seemed to have disturbed him. Encouraged, Nicola closed the gap between her and the bed and went to her knees, peering underneath it in search of her items.

There was still some clutter underneath the bed but she saw the basket she was looking for on the other side. Her arm wasn't long enough to reach it. Still on her knees, she crawled around the bed to the other side, hoping to grab her basket and flee before le Bec realized she was in the room and tried to kill her because he thought she was an intruder. The floor was still creaking a bit but she ignored it. It was impossible for the floor not to creak so she simply tried to be careful about it. Just as she neared the basket, as it was within her grasp, a hand from the bed shot out and grabbed her.

"You are a lovely wench," the voice said. It was *not* le Bec. "Did Kenton send you to me? Good man. Come here and warm me."

Startled, not to mention terrified, Nicola smacked the man's hand as he grabbed her rather brutally. He yanked at her, pulling her halfway onto the bed, but she threw out a fist and shoved it into the man's face, still half-covered by the coverlet. The man grunted and loosened his hold, enough so that she was able to pull away, but it wasn't enough to run completely. He grabbed her again, more forcefully, and Nicola was rightly panicked.

The old, iron fire poker was next to the bed where Tab had left it. He had been playing with it earlier when they had all been in the chamber, removing items, and she had forced him to set it aside. She didn't allow her boys to play with sharp things even though Tab had an affinity for them. He'd proven that many times, most recently with the sword that had impaled his father. With the iron poker in arm's length, she swiped at it even as the man pulled at her, getting a grip on the pointed end of it. As the man pulled her onto the bed again, she took hold of the poker and brought it down on the body still buried within the blanket.

The man grunted again as she brought the poker down, twice, before he finally let her go. Seized with panic, Nicola beat the man soundly as he lay wrapped up in the coverlet, racing all around the bed from every angle, whacking at him with all her strength. The man protested vehemently and at one point, tossed the cover off his head so he could try to get hold of the poker, but Nicola whacked him on the knees and he howled, trying to protect his legs.

"You... you beast!" she cried angrily. "You *fiend*! How dare you grab for me! I am not a whore!"

The man roared. "Woman, cease your battle!"

Nicola was furious as well as frightened. She hit him one last time, on the thigh near his buttocks, and backed away from the bed with the poker wielded in front of her defensively. She backed up towards the door.

"Touch me again and this is only a foretaste of what is to come," she hissed, grabbing at the door latch and throwing it open. "You have been warned!"

With that, Nicola fled the room, having no idea who she had just thrashed. When Kenton came up later to discuss a few items with Warwick, he was astonished to hear the man describe his violent encounter with a woman who beat him soundly with a fire poker.

Warwick was laughing as he told the story, but Kenton was not laughing; based on Warwick's description of the beautiful, volatile woman, Kenton knew it could only be one person. He only knew of one woman at Babylon with enough bravery and foolishness to do such a thing. He was embarrassed as well as furious, convinced that Lady Thorne had purposely sought Warwick to issue her own particular brand of rebellion against him.

When Warwick finished his tale, snorting and giggling, Kenton had all he could take. He was going to put that woman over his knee and spank her into submission as he should have done the first time they met. Obviously, the vault did little good to quell her rebellion. He would see if his hand to her backside would.

Politely excusing himself, he made his way up to the fourth floor.

NICOLA WAS DOZING in a big chair with Teague lying across her lap and Tiernan sleeping upon her shoulder. After fleeing her former chamber and the wicked man who now slept there, it had taken her a while to calm her fright. She kept thinking of that terrible man, and of how he had grabbed her, trying not to think of what would have happened had she not broken away. Perhaps le Bec had a very valid reason for telling her to stay to her apartments and it hadn't merely been because he was a cruel captor. Perhaps it had been for her own safety. That hadn't really occurred to her until now.

Feeling rather sheepish, she had finally settled down in the nearest chair, taking a cup of stale wine from Janet to help calm her nerves, but the twins were upset and restless, so she had turned her focus to them in the hopes of settling them down. She eventually calmed, they calmed, and the boys finally fell asleep. Exhausted from a night of very little sleep herself, Nicola closed her eyes and dozed off right along with them.

Until the door to her chamber flew open and le Bec was standing there in all of his hulking glory. Startled by the servants' cry when the door slammed back, Nicola sat up so fast that she nearly dumped Teague onto the floor. She grabbed both boys to make sure they didn't fall as she looked up at le Bec, wide-eyed with surprise.

"My lord!" she gasped. "What is the….?"

He didn't let her finish. He took three massive steps over to her and picked up Tiernan from her shoulder, extending the now-squealing child to the nearest frightened servant.

"A word, Madam," he said as he then reached down to pick up Teague, who was taken quickly by Janet. "You will come with me."

With both children off of her, Kenton grasped Nicola by the arm and pulled her up from the chair, practically dragging her across the chamber and slamming the door. Nicola, now being pulled down the steep stairs behind him, tried to catch herself from falling but it was difficult when he was tugging so forcefully.

"What on earth is the matter?" she demanded. "Stop pulling me!"

Kenton ignored her as he dragged her down to the third level. Nearing the bottom of the steps, she slipped in her struggles and plowed right into the back of him. Kenton had hold of her enough so that she didn't fall, but when they reached the landing, she began to fight ferociously.

"Let go!" she demanded, smacking at his hand. "By what right do you treat me like this? You will release me immediately!"

Kenton didn't say a word. He utterly ignored her demands and the hand that was hitting his wrist as he pulled her into the chamber that used to belong to her children. Once inside the smaller chamber that was oddly vacant and quite dusty, he shut the chamber door and released her. Nicola stumbled away from him, furious, and ended up on the opposite side of the chamber. Torn between fear and outrage, she glared at him.

"Why did you do that?" she hissed.

Kenton faced Nicola with more patience than he felt. He wasn't entirely used to losing his temper, at least not with a woman, so he struggled to calm the rage that was burning in his chest. He would tell her why he had dragged her down to this chamber before he blistered her undoubtedly lovely backside. But first, he had to try to explain his position without yelling at her. It was a difficult struggle.

"You," he said, pointing a finger at her, "are very close to being put into the vault permanently. Did you think I would not be told of your actions?"

Nicola was now confused as well as furious. "What actions?" she asked. "What are you babbling about, le Bec?"

Kenton's eyebrows lifted. "Babbling, am I?" he said, his jaw ticking as he came one step closer to losing his temper. He might even wring her lovely little neck if he was angry enough. "Did you truly believe your actions against Warwick would go untold?"

Her sense of confusion grew. "Warwick?" she repeated. "What do you mean?"

"You know exactly what I mean. Did you think I would not find out what you did to him?"

"But I have never met the man!"

"You will not lie to me."

Nicola threw up her hands, bewildered. "I am not lying," she said. "I swear that I have not met the man!"

His eyes narrowed and he jabbed a big finger at her again. "You beat him with a fire poker," he said hotly. "He has shown me his bruises and even though he could not tell me the name of the woman who did it, the physical description was enough. It was *you*."

Suddenly, Nicola realized what he was talking about. *The evil man in her chamber!* The entire incident came flooding back and, now, things made a good deal of sense. Exasperated, she shook her head.

"I did not know that was Warwick," she insisted. "I have never met the man. How could I know it was him?"

There was some logic to that statement but Kenton didn't acknowledge it. He rested his big fists on his hips in a gesture that just preceded him running across the room, grabbing her, and spanking her until he had satisfaction. He was already figuring out how he could cut off her escape route.

"Then if you did not know it was him, why did you beat him?" he wanted to know. "You deliberately set out to thrash the man."

"I did not!"

It was Kenton's turn to throw his hands up in the air. "Your actions speak otherwise, Madam," he said. "Know that I intend to punish you so it would be wise for you to tell me the truth."

Nicola didn't want to go to the vault again. She moved away from him, preparing for the mad dash that would undoubtedly follow when he began to chase her around the room.

"I swear to you that I did not know it was Warwick," she insisted, now less angry and more frightened. "I was in the chamber for a very good reason – after moving all of my possessions up to the fourth level, I realized I had left something very important behind. Upon entering the chamber, I saw that someone was asleep on the bed and assumed it was you, so I was very quiet as I made my way to the bed so I could look underneath it for the basket I had left behind. As I looked underneath, the man in the bed grabbed me and called me a whore. He wanted me to warm his bed. So… so I hit him. I will not be taken for a whore, le Bec, not by anyone. I am within my right to defend myself."

Kenton was listening with some astonishment to the entire explanation. It was nearly exactly what Warwick had told him and, as much as he hated to admit it, he believed her. He was quite sure she would not know Warwick on sight and quite sure that the woman, although cunning and intelligent, would not lie to him. She'd proven that when she had shown him Gaylord's tomb. He didn't want to believe her; for all of the frustration and embarrassment she had caused him, he truly wanted to punish her. There was great satisfaction in that thought. But the fact remained that he did, indeed, believe her. An exasperated sigh escaped his lips and he hung his head, shaking it sorrowfully.

"God's Blood," he hissed. "Is it true? Did you truly go in there without the intent to beat him?"

Nicola nodded her head. "Why would I do such a thing?" she asked, hoping he believed her. "Why would I risk being put back in the vault again?"

Kenton shook his head. "I would not know this," he said flatly. "You have challenged me from the moment I set foot in Babylon, so I cannot pretend to anticipate anything you do. You seem to take delight in pushing me."

Nicola's expression was guarded. "And you seem to take delight in pushing me."

He looked at her, then. "I do not push, Madam," he said. "I mean everything I say. My words are not meant as suggestions or hints. They are meant to be obeyed without question."

Nicola didn't know what to say to that. The fury of the situation had thankfully blown over but she was still very uncertain as to his motives or what he planned to do. When she didn't reply, he lifted his eyebrows expectantly at her.

"Have you nothing to say to me?" he asked.

Nicola shook her head but she was feeling increasingly incensed by the way he was treating her. The man was big and powerful, and he used that size and power against her. She did, in fact, have something to say.

"You had no reason to drag me down here as you did before you knew all of the facts," she said, sounding hurt and angry. "I was, in fact, Warwick's victim, yet you treated me as if I had been the attacker. Your sense of justice is twisted, le Bec. Is this your idea of fairness?"

He cocked his head. "Who said anything about being fair?" he wanted to know. "Warwick supersedes you and me and everyone else at Babylon, so when the man tells me that a beautiful woman thrashed him, I believed him."

Nicola's eyes flashed. "I *did* thrash him," she said. "God knows what would have happened had I not. I will not be taken into any man's bed, le Bec, so you may as well know that now. If anyone tries, I will do to them what I did to Warwick."

She was angrily marching towards the chamber door now, where he was standing. The more furious she became, the more he cooled and regained his composure. He supposed she had every right to be angry but he would not acknowledge the fact. The woman had to know she could not soften him or change his mind. She had to know she had no effect on him.

… or did she?

Startled to realize that, perhaps, her moods did have an effect on him, he grabbed her wrist as she reached out to unlatch the door.

"I will not tell you this again," he said, gazing down into that lovely, angry face. "You will remain to your rooms for now. You will not come out for any reason until I personally release you."

Her jaw ticked as she looked at his massive hand holding her wrist. His hand was so big that it covered half her forearm. Still, she couldn't help but notice the heat of his flesh against hers. There was something in that heat that made her heart leap strangely.

"Take your hand from me," she growled.

He very nearly smiled; the woman was, if nothing else, courageous. Perhaps it was foolish in the face of a man more than twice her size, but she was courageous nonetheless. He admired that in a strange way.

"Not until we are clear," he said, matching her tone. "Do you understand you are not to leave your rooms?"

"Aye."

"Swear this to me."

She wouldn't look at him. "I swear it, you bas... that is, I swear it, my lord."

He ignored the slander that had nearly slipped from her lips. "You will obey me without hesitation from now on," he said, watching the disgust ripple across her face. "Is that clear?"

"It is."

"Swear it to me."

"I swear."

He didn't believe her but he kept his opinion to himself; perhaps she truly believed her vow. Knowing what he did of the woman, however, he did not. He released her arm.

"I will summon you in time to prepare the nooning meal," he told her as she yanked the door open. "I will expect a feast."

Nicola didn't say anything. She simply marched from the room and stomped up the stairs that led to the fourth floor. Kenton stood in the doorway, watching her shapely backside until she disappeared from view. He could only imagine what the woman was thinking of him and the situation in general. She was proud and she was brave. As much as those qualities in a woman frustrated him, they were also admirable. Therefore, he could fairly read her mind at the moment, the mind of a woman who wasn't afraid to swing a fire poker to defend herself. He was fairly certain she wanted to swing the fire poker at him.

The thought made him grin.

CHAPTER FOUR

T HEY STARTED ARRIVING just before the nooning meal. Hordes of
men, weary from a march across rugged territory, trudged into the
bailey like beaten animals. The day was cold and cloudy in contrast to
the sun the day before, and rain threatened, adding to the gloomy
ambiance.

Kenton stood on top of the inner wall, watching Henry's troops
filter in through the gatehouse and into the inner bailey. Conor, Gerik,
and Ackerley were down in the courtyard, segregating men and making
sure to send the wagons on to the stables while keeping the men
gathered in the ward. Great houses were arriving, men in support of
Henry who had been in skirmishes all over Yorkshire in the past few
months. Now, they had a base from which to launch the rest of their
conquest of the north. The plan was to march on Harrogate before the
end of the week and preparations had to be immediate.

Kenton was pleased with the progress, though one would never
know it by looking at him. The men filtering in through the gates would
look up and see him atop the wall like a mighty sentinel and they would
raise their weapons in salute. Le Bec gazed back at them, his eyes hard
enough to cut steel and calculating enough to anticipate the ultimate
victory.

By early afternoon he was ready to leave his post and go down and
mingle with the men. But a speck on the green horizon caught his

attention, a small flick that grew in size until it sprouted arms and legs and became a man on horseback. The rider was alone but Kenton didn't give it much thought; there were still hundreds of men arriving at Babylon and the rider was more than likely a member of a detachment.

Therefore, he descended to the inner bailey without concern, visually inspecting the troops that were gathering there. Conor and Ackerley were in conversation with one of the commanders of a small army that had most recently arrived while Gerik had moved out of the fortress altogether and was now beyond the walls to estimate how many more men were coming. Already, with the volume of men coming, logistics were going to be difficult.

Kenton was engaged in a conversation with one of the Earl of Oxford's commanders when he heard someone call his name. He turned towards the sound to see Gerik making his way towards him quickly with a man in Warwick colors trotting along beside him. Already, there was concern in Gerik's eyes.

"My lord," Gerik said. "One of Warwick's scouts has returned. He brings news."

Kenton looked immediately to the weary soldier. "What news?"

The soldier was near the point of collapse. "Edward's troops, sire," he gasped. "About three hours south. They're moving on Babylon."

Kenton didn't change expressions, but Conor, having just joined him, hissed a curse. "How many?"

"Not as large as our force," the soldier said. "But we still have troops coming in from the southwest. We'll have to close the gates before they can reach us, leaving them vulnerable to Edward's army."

Already, Kenton's mind was working. "I am well aware of that," he said. "Can you give me a number on Edward's troops?"

The soldier nodded. "I would say one thousand, sire," the man replied. "'Tis a large force moving north from the village of Barnsley."

Kenton looked around the fortress, mentally calculating what he would be up against. "Barnsley," he repeated with disgust. "We had no reports of troops there. Why in the hell didn't our spies tell us of this?"

"Most of the army was reported to be towards York," Conor could see his liege's irritation. "If they're moving north from Barnsley, more than likely they were much further south. From Chester, even. Edward knew we were laying siege to Babylon and, I would wager to say, mobilized these troops to help defend the fortress."

"Then they have had days to move northward."

"Precisely."

Kenton pondered that. "What is our current count inside the castle, Conor?"

"One thousand, four hundred and fourteen men, my lord."

Kenton paused to think on that number. "With approximately eight hundred more still on approach and Edward's army due in three hours," he pondered. After a few more moments of deliberation, he turned to Conor. "Send several riders to the southwest with news of this. Have them intercept the rest of Henry's supporters and have them hold station for six hours, giving Edward's army time to reach us. Then, have them move quickly and attack the rear of Edward's force as they lay siege to Babylon. We shall mash Edward between our two armies and quash him."

It was a simple, yet effective, countermeasure and Conor was swiftly gone to carry out the command. Kenton wasn't worried in the least about the approaching siege, but he did want to seal up Babylon and prepare for the onslaught. One more hour and he would raise the drawbridge. Any troops that were unfortunate enough to be caught outside at that time would have to find cover.

Message delivered, Kenton dismissed Warwick's soldier. As the man went in search of food, Kenton spoke to Gerik.

"Find Lady Thorne and tell her that we will be in for a siege and to prepare to assist our surgeon with the wounded. She will do everything necessary to see that the man's life is made easier, considering we should have a fair amount of wounded once the battle is in full scale with the rear assault." Gerik turned to leave but Kenton stopped him with another directive. "And tell Warwick what is transpiring. I shall meet with him and the knights in the great hall in a half hour."

The knight acknowledged the order and departed, and Kenton moved forward with other things requiring his attention. There was much to do now and little time to do it. Huddling with Conor and Ackerley for a few minutes to finalize preparations, the three knights then went about seeking shelter for the soldiers that were in the bailey. Siege engines were a very real fear, hurling projectiles over the walls, and the men in the bailey would be caught in the open without protection if such things happened.

While Conor and Ackerley began moving men inside as much as they were able, or directing them around to the enclosed kitchen yards and stables with sod roofs, Kenton went to gather the commanders of the armies within the bailey to tell them what was transpiring. With a battle approaching, they would need to know.

The preparations moved smoothly enough, a given factor whenever Kenton was in charge. He was orderly and methodical, and the results were evident. He was busying himself with a group of soldiers who had just arrived from the smaller city of Huddersfield when Gerik suddenly appeared at his side, looking rather frustrated.

"A word, my lord?" Gerik said quietly.

Kenton was in the process of directing the soldiers in the construction of some make-shift shelters. He had a huge plank of wood in his hands, one that would have normally required two men to carry it. But Kenton handled the bulk easily. He turned to Gerik impatiently.

"What is it?" he asked.

Gerik was hoping for privacy but saw he would receive none. To ask for a confidential word would have been to irritate his already strained liege and this conversation, as it was, would not be an easy one. Therefore, he took a deep breath and proceeded.

"Lady Thorne wishes for me to tell you that she cannot help the surgeon," he said.

Kenton planted the beam vertically as a few soldiers moved in to secure it. "What do you mean?"

Gerik was hesitant to tell him the rest but he had no choice. "She says you have not personally given her permission to leave her chamber," he said. "Therefore, she cannot help the surgeon. She suggests...."

Kenton cast him a baleful eye. He was almost afraid of what he was about to hear. "Pray, what does she suggest?"

Gerik winced. "That if you want it done, then do it yourself."

Kenton stared at him. Then, his gaze trailed to the keep and he wiped his hands off on his tunic. "Is that what she said?"

"Word for word, my lord."

That confirmation was all it took to send Kenton back across the bailey, heading for the keep. Gerik watched his liege cross the muddy ward and up the articulated wooden stairs that led into the keep. He shook his head, sorry for the foolish Lady Thorne. The woman was in as fine a mood as Kenton was and, very shortly, there would be a great battle going on in the keep. Personally, he did not envy Kenton.

Kenton, however, did not envy Lady Thorne. The woman was as difficult as any he had ever encountered and, once again, he tried to keep his irritation in check as he entered the great hall, mounting the steps to the third floor. He could hear Warwick in the master chamber, talking to his advisors. By the time he hit the alcove on the fourth level, his irritation had been given time to build into a righteous fury. It seemed as if all the woman ever did was provoke fury in him. Fury and interest. As he approached the open chamber door that led to the Thorne rooms beyond, the first thing he saw was Teague, jumping out at him.

"Knight!" he said happily. "I have weaponsth, lots of weaponsth. See them?"

Kenton stopped so quickly that he nearly lost his balance. Only quick reflexes had saved Teague from being run over. The little boy was thrusting something up at him and Kenton saw that he had a handful of small wooden knights in one palm and several sharp sticks in the other.

"Where is your mother?" Kenton asked.

Teague pointed a full hand in the direction of the adjoining chamber. "In there," he said. "But how do you like my weaponsth? I made them mythelf."

He was referring to the sharp sticks, spears for his toy soldiers. Kenton had no time for such nonsense but that strange tugging in his chest again told him not to brush the boy off so easily. He was so innocent, something Kenton could barely remember. Innocence was for the very young, and sometimes, not even for them.

"Your weapons are fine." He didn't know what else to say. Moving past the child, he nearly bowled over the mother who had just appeared in the adjoining doorway.

Nicola patted her chest to restart her heart. "My lord, you gave me a start," she said. "I heard your voice and was just coming to see you."

He lifted an eyebrow at her. "A word, Madam."

"Of course."

"Alone."

She laughed ironically. "These are small rooms, my lord. With eight people about, this is as private as it gets."

He drew in a long, irritated sigh. Taking her by the arm, more gently than he had earlier in the day, he once again led her to the stairs and down to the third floor. They again headed into the children's former chamber, which now had evidently become their personal meeting room. Kenton quietly closed the door and turned to Nicola.

"Now," he growled. "I have had just about enough of this."

She knew what he was talking about but she was not about to back down. She was still furious from his treatment of her that morning and had every intention of letting him know it.

"Enough of what, my lord?" she asked innocently.

"Do not toy with me," he jabbed a huge finger at her. "You know exactly what I mean. I send Gerik up here to issue a simple command and even after your promises of obedience, you cannot abide by my wishes. It has been a battle with you since the moment I first lay eyes on you and I will have no more of it."

She was unaffected by his irritation. "There has been no battle, my lord. I have done everything you have asked."

"Christ," he slapped a hand to his forehead in an uncharacteristic display of emotion. "You have done what I have asked, aye, but not without struggle, insolence, and pure petulance. I threw you in the vault once before for your behavior and I have no qualms about doing it again."

"You have said that, repeatedly."

"I mean it."

She believed him. Nicola didn't want to go in the vault again but she was not as in control of her emotions as she needed to be. Outspokenness was a sin and she sinned regularly where that was concerned.

"Sir Kenton," she said deliberately. "Did you truly think you could conquer Babylon and expect that I, the Lady of Babylon, would simply fall at your feet and carry out your every whim without resistance just because you demand it?"

"Tread carefully, Madam."

"I *am* treading carefully," she was gaining steam. "But you show me none of the respect you are so haughty to demand, my lord. Have you once granted a request of mine? Have you once shown me any measure of regard? All you have done is go out of your way to show me how much disrespect you have for me and my household, yet you find it surprising when I show you the same measure of what you've given me."

His eyes were like shards of glass; hard and cutting. "You are my prisoner and an enemy of the true king," he said. "You personally directed the battle against my forces and any consideration you are given is more than you deserve."

Nicola wasn't surprised that he realized that, she'd all but told him as much. "If I had been any smarter in military ways, you would not have conquered us."

"But I did."

"Then you have what you want. You have Babylon. If you want any more than that, you'll have to take it by force because I shall not easily surrender anything more to you."

One moment he was standing across the room glaring at her. In the next, he was nearly on top of her, grabbing both arms and pulling them behind her back. It wasn't painful, but the message was obvious. Nicola found herself pressed up against his massive chest, her neck craned back sharply as his face loomed over her. His eyes, so piercing, bore straight through her.

"That, Madam," he said slowly, "can be arranged if that is your wish."

Nicola would not admit that provoking him had probably not been the best decision. Submission was foreign to her nature, something her husband had tried to beat into her on many occasions. She was a fighter and always had been, which had cost her much when Gaylord turned his fists against her.

"You may as well do as you will," she could hardly breathe for as tightly as he was holding her. "From someone who would use my children against me, one more vulgar offense would not surprise me."

Kenton had only meant to scare her. But he should have suspected a woman like Nicola would not have been so easily frightened. Now, as he gazed down at her, he felt a bolt of fire race through him like nothing he had ever experienced and he knew, instantly, that his bold move had backlashed on him. All he could do was stare at her beautiful face, her pink lips, and imagine what it would be like to taste her.

When his mouth descended on hers, roughly, one of her hands wriggled loose and he felt the sharp sting of her slap against his cheek. He felt another slap, and still another, but it only caused him to hold her closer and kiss her harder. He never realized when she stopped fighting him and started to respond; all he knew was that she was sweeter than he could have possibly imagined.

Kenton didn't know how long he kissed her, his tongue invading her honeyed mouth and his lips devouring hers. But he had to taste the rest of her and his mouth moved over her chin, her cheeks, and her slender neck.

"You'll do as I say, you cheeky wench," he whispered hoarsely. "Or I swear you'll regret it. Do you understand?"

Nicola didn't understand anything at the moment. His kiss had terrified her at first, then it had warmed her from a spark of passion into a roaring blaze of lust. She had no idea she was capable of such emotions and she couldn't breathe, much less think straight. Was he asking her to make a decision?

"I... I...," she gasped.

"Tell me," he growled, his mouth against hers. "No more of your disobedience. Do as I say."

She could only whimper and he kissed her so hard that he drove his teeth into her lip, drawing blood. He tasted her blood and sucked on her lip, tasting more of it and loving it.

"Tell me."

He shook her slightly, his mouth still on her lips. Nicola nodded weakly, the only gesture she could manage.

"No more insolence?"

She shook her head.

"No more tantrums?"

She shook her head again and Kenton paused long enough to look at her flushed face before kissing her again. How it was possible to smile and kiss at the same time, he didn't know. But he knew he was doing it.

Kenton didn't know how he got away from her. He was walking across the inner bailey before he realized she was out of his arms. He remembered leaving her standing in that small chamber with a dazed look on her face, but not much more than that. With an approaching battle, he was fully aware of how muddled his mind was, distracted by thoughts he had forgotten were possible. It was essential that he come to his senses. He had to push thoughts of Lady Thorne from his mind.

It was easier said than done.

TRUE TO THE word of the messenger, Edward's troops began arriving exactly three hours later. Babylon was ready. But rather than begin the siege immediately, they set up an encampment a quarter of a mile away and hunkered down for the approaching night.

Babylon was stuffed to the rafters with soldiers. For as big as the keep was, it was still close to bursting with all of the men that were now sheltered inside it. Nicola knew this because Janet and Liesl had been down in the small feasting hall that was part of the keep, trying to help the cook and several male servants feed the multitude of men. Most of the armies had brought their own provisions but some had not, especially those who had been traveling for weeks on end. The second cook of Babylon, a man who had been cooking at Babylon since the days of Gaylord's father, had been forced to butcher a fat pig and, even now, the scent of cooking pork filled the air of the castle.

The aroma of roast pig wafted into the windows of their fourth floor prison, making the little boys very hungry. Janet and Liesl had brought the children bread and cheese and small apples, but they wanted the meat that they could smell cooking. As the servant women fed the boys with what they could bring from the kitchen, Nicola stood at one of the lancet windows that faced east to the gates of Babylon, oddly inactive with all of the things that needed to be attended to. When she should have been seeing to her duties as chatelaine, all she could seem to do was think on Kenton le Bec.

Distracting thoughts that had only grown worse over the progression of the day. This man who had so brutally confiscated her home, smashed her husband's tomb, and thrown her in the vault was now occupying a good deal of her mental energy.

And then there was the kiss… she had finally determined that it was the kiss that had her so terribly distracted. A kiss such as she had never known in her life, one of passion and power and lust that made her heart race and her knees weak. There was something incredibly virile and masculine about Kenton le Bec and it wasn't merely his size and strength. He had eyes the color of the deep blue ocean and there was something mysterious within those murky depths. It was both unnerving and intriguing.

I am a fool, she thought to herself as she pondered le Bec and his heated kiss. The man terrified her, yet he also brought out curiosity and interest she didn't know she had towards the opposite sex. Having been married to Gaylord since sixteen years of age, all she knew of men was the rough brutality of a husband who used his wife as an object of his lust.

Coupling with Gaylord had been something she dreaded, a daily occurrence because he felt it was his right to have relations with his wife wherever and whenever he pleased. There had been times he had cornered her in the kitchen, in their children's chamber, or even in the hall. Humiliated, she'd been forced to allow him to do as he pleased. Tab had been conceived as he'd bent her over the butcher's block in the kitchen right after they had been married and the twins had been conceived in a darkened corner of the hall as drunk soldiers had played gambling games nearby. It had been a humiliating, degrading experience for her more times than she could count. Therefore, le Bec's kiss had her extraordinarily fearful. But it also had her intrigued.

He had her intrigued.

Deeply confused, and deeply torn, Nicola remained lost to her thoughts as the world went on around her. As much as she had enjoyed Kenton's kiss, and the truth was that she had, she refused to allow the man to turn her into his whore. Perhaps it was that thought that terrified her the most – submitting to yet another man even though she found this one very attractive. Still, there was something in her that refused to be toyed with. If she could not have the man's respect, then he could not have her. At least, that was her stance in theory although practice would be somewhat different. Men ruled the world. Women were merely possessions.

She was Kenton's possession.

Therefore, her only choice was to leave, to escape the situation. He had wanted to send her away once before but she had begged to stay, telling him that she had nowhere else to go. The truth was that she had a widowed aunt in Gloucester that she could go to. The woman was her father's sister and, as of three years ago, Aunt Eve was still alive. Nicola had told le Bec she had nowhere to go mostly because Babylon was her home and it was Tab's legacy. As of his father's death, Tab had not only inherited the castle but also his father's title, Baron Marsden. Nicola wasn't entirely sure le Bec was aware of that and she certainly didn't want to tell him. A very young baron with a great castle would make an excellent hostage. Therefore, more for Tab's sake than for her own, she knew she had to leave.

Bearing that in mind, Nicola turned away from the lancet window. She had to find le Bec and ask permission to go to her aunt in Glouces-ter. She had to get out of Babylon, and quickly. As she made her way to the door, Teague tried to follow her, his hands full of little wooden soldiers, but she gently distracted the boy. When he was focused on an errant toy soldier that had fallen on the floor, she quickly fled the room.

Taking the narrow stairs down to the next floor, she was wary about Warwick in the master's chamber but the door was shut and she quickly scurried past it. The great staircase was up ahead and she took it down to the hall level of Babylon where enemy soldiers and servants were about. Unfamiliar soldiers were crowded around the feasting table that usually held her family and it was not a happy sight for her to see Henry's men touching things that belonged to her. Henry's filth was infecting the hall.

In fact, it was not a happy sight to see how many men had arrived over the past day. It seemed like thousands. Now, they were truly overrun by Henry. She'd known it all along but seeing the reality of it, with hundreds of greedy soldiers all over her keep, hit her in the gut. It was sickening. With determination, she sought out le Bec.

She had every intention to go outside and send one of his soldiers running for him but as she passed by Gaylord's solar, she caught a glimpse of men inside. Pausing by the door, she tried to remain out of sight whilst searching for le Bec but the angle of the open door made it impossible. As soon as she stepped towards the doorway, nearly everyone in the room saw her, including le Bec. He was standing by Gaylord's big, heavy desk, looking at a map as the man she'd come to understand as Warwick pointed to something on the vellum. As soon as Kenton saw her, he moved away from the desk and stepped in her direction.

"Lady Thorne," he said, his deep tone neutral. "Do you require something?"

Nicola stepped back, out of the doorway, as he approached. In fact, for every step he took towards her, she took two back. Kenton finally came to realize this and came to a halt just outside of the doorway as Nicola stood a few feet away, eyeing him warily.

"I... I have an urgent need to speak with you, my lord," she said, addressing him formally. The gesture of respect, given their history, sounded odd coming from her lips. "I did not realize you were in conference."

Kenton glanced over his shoulder into the solar where Warwick continued discussing the coming battle in tones he couldn't quite hear. "It is of no consequence," he said, returning his attention to her and trying not to look at her mouth, that sweet and luscious mouth he had kissed so eagerly. "What is your wish, Lady Thorne?"

Nicola glanced around nervously, as if she didn't want anyone to hear what she had to say. Or perhaps she was nervous with all of the men sworn to Henry in her home. In any case, she seemed more nervous and unsure than Kenton had ever seen her.

"I have come to understand that Edward has brought an army to our door," she finally said.

Kenton nodded. "He has."

Nicola thought he seemed rather unconcerned with an army about to attack. "I could see them from my chamber."

"Is that what you came to speak with me about?"

Nicola shook her head. "I came to ask for your permission to leave

Babylon," she said. "You ordered me to leave once before but when I told you we had nowhere to go, you permitted me to stay. I have reconsidered that offer and I would like to take my family and go."

Kenton regarded her carefully. "Madam, we have an army outside of our gates," he said, taking a few steps towards her to close the gap between them. "You are not going anywhere."

She tried not to let his denial frighten her. "We will be no trouble," she said. "I will take my servants with me, the female servants, and leave the rest. Mayhap we will need a small escort, only a couple of men, but with all of the men under your command, surely that will not be a hardship."

He was close enough to reach out and grasp her elbow. It wasn't a tight grasp, but the message was clear. "We will not discuss this now," he said. "I have more important things on my mind and shuttling you through an enemy army is not one of them."

Nicola didn't like to be pushed around. Moreover, the last time he grabbed her, she'd let him do wicked things to her. She tried to pull away but make it seem as if she wasn't. "But the enemy army you speak of is not an enemy to me," she insisted. "They are loyal to Edward, as was my husband. Surely they will allow me to leave unmolested."

"Mayhap," he said, "but I am not going to take that chance. Return to your chamber now. I will send for you if and when I need you."

He still had his hand on her arm. Nicola, now flustered, indiscreetly pulled herself from his grip. "Will we be allowed to leave when this action is over, then?" she demanded. "Or do you intend to keep us permanently?"

His eyes were intense. "I have no time to argue this," he put his hand on her again and turned her back for the stairs. "Do as I ask. Return to your children until I send for you."

Nicola didn't like being manhandled and resisted him. "You will do me the courtesy of answering my question," she said. "Do you intend to keep us permanently?"

He could see that she wasn't going to leave without some kind of clarification. The woman was as stubborn as he'd ever seen but, still, he found the quality oddly admirable. It also made her rather attractive. He was coming to realize that he liked her when she was flustered or angry. That spark, that fire, inflamed him in a good way. He supposed that if he didn't answer her question, they might be here all night, so he thought he'd better tell her something. Certainly not what he was thinking; *because I do not want you to go*. He would have to think of something.

"Only yesterday you were telling me what a valuable asset you were to Babylon," he pointed out. "Now you wish to leave?"

"Aye."

"Why?"

"It does not matter the reasons. Suffice it to say that I wish to leave."

"And go where? You said you had nowhere to go."

"I have a widowed aunt near London. We will live with her."

He just looked at her. In fact, he hadn't taken his eyes off of her from the moment he grabbed her. Nicola had seen that look in his eyes once before, just before he kissed her. She was frightened and warmed at the same time. Finally, he simply nodded his head.

"Nay," he said quietly. "I do not plan to keep you permanently. It would be better if you left. Therefore, I will grant your request but only after this military situation has settled. Will that suffice?"

He gave in far too easily. She thought she would have had a much more difficult struggle on her hands. She began to think that perhaps she hadn't been very nice about her request, more demanding than asking. Perhaps she shouldn't have taken that tone with him. He wasn't acting like a man who wanted to keep her as his concubine.

Now she was wholly confused. Unable to meet his gaze, she turned back towards the stairs.

"It will," she said softly. "You have my thanks."

Kenton didn't reply. He watched her climb a couple of steps and then she paused, looking at him over her shoulder. "Do you think Edward's army will triumph?"

It was a surprising question. He blinked slowly, pondering his answer. "That would please you?"

She didn't reply in the affirmative right away. Instead, she seemed to mull over her answer, unable to look directly at him as she did so. After a moment, she nodded her head.

"He is the rightful king, you know," she said softly.

Kenton almost smiled at her boldness. She was loyal to young Edward to the end. "A matter of opinion, Madam."

"What will happen to you and your army if he wins?"

Kenton crossed his enormous arms thoughtfully. "The men-at-arms will be captives, at least for a while," he said. "Then they will be pressed into service for Edward. I, on the other hand, will probably stand trial for treason and be executed."

Nicola didn't like the sound of that at all. She shouldn't care in the least, but deep down, she didn't want to see Kenton executed. She turned on the staircase and came down a couple of steps, looking at him with distress in her expression.

"But you are not a nobleman," she pointed out. "You are only a knight. Why should they execute you?"

He was rather touched by her concern. "Because I lead Henry's armies," he said quietly. "I am Warwick's attack dog and I have caused a good deal of damage to Edward's cause for many years. With me eliminated, Edward's war machine will have the advantage. It would be a great victory for them to see me out of action."

Nicola wasn't aware of how distressed she sounded. *Distress for him.* "But surely they would give you the opportunity to swear fealty to Edward," she said. "Everyone knows of your military brilliance and I imagine it would be a great waste to do away with you."

She had paid him a compliment without realizing it but she became quite aware when he smiled at her, dipping his head gallantly.

"I am honored by your confidence in my abilities, Madam," he said. "Coming from you, that is quite flattering."

Nicola's cheeks turned red. She had said too much and, struggling to recover her composure, she quickly turned away and resumed ascending the steps. Kenton's gaze lingered on her until she disappeared from view, and even then he had a visual image in his mind far longer than he should have. His men were demanding his attention, for a battle lay on the horizon, and it was all he could do to concentrate on what needed to be done to keep them all alive.

Thoughts of the delicious Lady Thorne overwhelmed his mind.

CHAPTER FIVE

E DWARD'S ARMY MOBILIZED at first light.

Nicola had been in a deep sleep next to Tab when the shouts of men gradually roused her. Rubbing the sleep from her eyes, she went to the lancet window only to be met by a furious tide of soldiers upon the walls of Babylon. Projectiles and smoke were everywhere. The sun was barely breaking in the east and, already, a full scale assault was at hand.

Nicola sighed heavily; battles were always such an ugly business. Babylon had seen more than its share over the past several days. Her walls were strong, but they weren't invincible. When Kenton had laid siege, he had taken great catapults and pummeled the outer walls with great stone projectiles, creating cracks and divots everywhere. The drawbridge had been partially destroyed and was now, in the midst of this battle, the weakest point. Nicola had no way of knowing that Kenton had put a concentration of men on the bridge to try and stem the tide of Edward's men, and the skirmish was growing uglier by the moment.

She became aware of Tab standing next to her, his green eyes watching the smoke and fighting below. He was such a stoic creature, unafraid, and she put her arm around his small shoulders and together they watched the battle unfold.

By mid-morning, there was a heavy haze of smoke in the air. Edward's army had been shooting flaming projectiles and other long arrows over the walls, and the number of wounded was growing. One of Kenton's knights had come up to request that Nicola help with the injured and she agreed without a fight. Leaving her crying twins with Tab and Raven, she took Janet, Liesl and Hermenia with her. The bloodied men were being collected in the great hall, running red rivers over her wooden floors, but Nicola saw their pain more than the mussed flooring and immediately went to work. These were Edward's men and they needed her help.

Kenton's barber surgeon was an old man that barely spoke a word, but he moved like lightning among the wounded, stitching holes and removing arrows. He didn't give Nicola and her servants any instructions other than to start where they were most needed, which is exactly what they did. Hair pulled back to the nape of her neck and a heavy broadcloth apron over a durable blue surcoat, Nicola went to work on a boy with two big arrows in him. He died before she could remove the second arrow and from that moment on, her mood was full of sorrow and disgust.

Yet it was only the beginning of what was to come.

By noon the hall was half-full of weak, dying men. The smell of coagulating blood was thick. Nicola and Janet were working on a man who had fallen on his own sword, jamming mail and dirt deep into his stomach. While Janet would wash away debris with watered whisky, Nicola would pick the mail out piece by piece, causing the man agonizing pain. He wasn't the silent sort and it was nerve-wracking work.

Finally, the man was clean enough for Janet to stitch him up and Nicola went on to the next injured man. Every time they would bring in a fallen soldier, she would look up to see if it was Kenton and was relieved when it wasn't. She thought herself rather silly for being so concerned for the man but, secretly, she couldn't help it. Her attention was naturally on him, being in the heat of battle as he was.

Still, she had spent several hours in the great hall and had yet to see him. To her, that was a good sign even as she kept trying to tell herself that she didn't care what happened to him. It was a lie. Kenton's luck soon ran out, however. By early afternoon, Gerik came racing into the great hall, shouting for the surgeon. Those terrible words Nicola had been dreading had finally come to pass.

"Le Bec has been hit!" Gerik bellowed. "Come now, man, and assist!"

Nicola was bent over a man with a cut over his eye, stitching carefully. But she passed the duty off to Liesl and leapt over the wounded prostrate on the floor in order to quickly reach the door where they were bringing Kenton in.

Instead of being carried, however, he was walking under his own power. The hilt of an arrow stuck out from the joints in his armor, between the shoulder and the breast plate. He was bleeding profusely. But instead of pain on his face, Nicola only saw annoyance. Their eyes met and Nicola felt what was surely a physical blow; she knew of no other way to describe it. Good or bad, she couldn't tell. All she knew was that she was feeling far more about this enemy knight than she should have.

She had to help him.

Nicola practically shoved the old surgeon out of the way so she could take a better look at the wound. A cursory examination told her that it was embedded deep.

"Take him up to the master's chamber," she ordered the knights that had accompanied him. "Careful going up the stairs. And do not jostle the arrow!"

Kenton, in moderate pain in spite of his appearance, watched Nicola take charge, giving orders as well as any battle commander. When their eyes had met, he had felt the physical impact, too. He also felt a good deal of comfort, which he couldn't adequately describe. All he knew was that the sight of her had taken away any anxiety or unease he may have felt.

Therefore, he didn't say a word as she helped him up the narrow steps, unnecessary since he was quite capable of doing it by himself, but she was determined to aid him so he let her. She raced into the master chamber ahead of him, throwing Warwick's personal effects aside in order to make room for him. Kenton thought it was all quite comical and he was touched by it.

He was touched by *her*.

Arrow jutting into the air, he sat gingerly on the bed as Nicola went to work removing his armor. He glanced at her face occasionally, seeing intense concentration. He also noticed that she refused to meet his eye. Ackerley and Gerik also helped with the armor removal, helping her unhinge plates, and soon they had all of his protection removed from his arms and torso. Then Nicola asked for a dagger, which Ackerley produced, and she used it to cut off Kenton's damp padded tunic underneath. Finally naked from the waist up, Kenton lay back on the pillows, carefully, feeling more pain when he lay down than when he was standing. Nicola and the surgeon took a closer look at the projectile.

"It could be lodged beneath his collar bone," the surgeon said. "We must take great care removing it."

Nicola knew she wasn't strong enough to pull the arrow free, so she wisely backed off and let the men take charge of the operation. Going to the chamber door, she sent Janet running for bandages, whisky, and hot water, waiting impatiently while the girl carried out her request. She stood there nervously while the old surgeon broke off the hilt of the arrow, turning away when Gerik and Ackerley held Kenton fast and the surgeon ripped the head free. Things like that had never bothered her before and she had no idea why they should bother her now, but she suddenly had a very queasy feeling at the thought of Kenton's injury. Though he never uttered a sound, she could only imagine the pain. Once the arrowhead was free, however, she took charge.

Nicola chased the knights from the room. The surgeon had worse-off men to attend to downstairs and determined that Kenton's wound wasn't life-threatening. Nicola bent over Kenton as Janet held the bowl of watered whisky, gently cleansing the wound and trying to determine the best course of action for sealing it up. She sent Janet to collect the finest silk thread she could find.

"'Tis not that bad," Kenton's voice was low.

She glanced up at him. "'Tis bad enough. It will require several stitches."

"A scratch," he argued.

"A wound," she countered in a tone that suggested he not argue with her.

She kept her gaze averted, picking bits of mail from the outside of the wound that the whisky bath had missed. Even though she was focused on the wound, she found it very hard to concentrate now that she was faced with a half-naked man on a bed, no less. All of that warm, muscular flesh had her quite distracted in spite of the circumstances. She could feel the searing heat from his skin against her hands as if the man were intentionally burning her. She wondered what it would feel like if he....

"Is that for me to drink to ease the pain when you stab me with your needle?"

Startled from her lustful thoughts, Nicola looked up from the wound, seeing that he was indicating the half-full bottle of whisky Janet had left sitting next to the bed. She shook her head and went back to work.

"It is to cleanse it before I stitch it so you will not come down with a fever," she replied.

His eyes never left her face. "If you just left it the way it was, you'd be finishing what Edward started out to accomplish."

She met his gaze that time, noting the twinkle in his eye. The normally deadly-serious man was actually toying with her. But she was in no mood to tease or be teased.

"I can just as easily go back to the great hall and tend those men who are truly injured," she said irritably. "If you sincerely wish for me to let Edward's murder attempt take its course, then I can abide by your wish."

"Do what you feel is right, of course."

He wouldn't rise to her mood. He maintained an even, steady tone with her. Nicola didn't know why she was irritated with his attempt at lightheartedness; perhaps it was because she had been so worried and he wasn't. He wasn't concerned for his injury in the least. She wasn't sure how to deal with his nonchalance. Sighing, Nicola picked up the bottle and held it out to him.

"You may as well drink," she said. "Mayhap it will indeed ease your pain."

He reached out, slowly, to take it from her. His fingers moved across hers, briefly, but he might as well have pinched her from the way she jumped. He took a long, deep drink, smacking his lips with satisfaction.

"Irish whisky," he commented.

"You know it?"

"Aye," he set the bottle to rest on the bed beside him. "Another drink and I can tell you what city it was aged in and, more than likely, by a professional or an amateur."

He took another drink. "Well?" she said.

He licked his lips as he looked at her. "Dublin. Professional. Aged in a beechwood cask as opposed to oak to temper the flavor."

Nicola's eyes twinkled with some mirth at a man who could so easily identify an alcoholic drink. "There was a time when ale and wine were sufficient enough," she said. "Now whisky fills the flask of every soldier from Kent to Northumbria."

"It takes less to get a man drunk."

There was a knowing gleam in her eye. "Including you?"

"I do not get drunk," he replied, almost stiffly. "It dulls a man's senses. And I must have all of mine."

"You are different from the rest, then?"

"What do you mean?"

"I mean that most men look forward to getting uproariously drunk and care not about their wits. But you do?"

"I do. In my line of work, it is imperative."

Janet entered the chamber bearing silk thread that was nearly transparent and a bone-sharp needle. Nicola took the items and sent the girl back down to the great hall where there were many men in great need. She could handle le Bec on her own.

Kenton watched her carefully as she prepared for the coming task. She seemed quite unwilling to look at him as she laid out precise measures of thread. But she did look him in the eye, apologetically, right before she doused his open wound with the straight, pure whisky. Kenton didn't react to the excruciating pain other than to close his eyes a moment. Nicola bent over him and went to work.

Her stitches were tiny and swift. She was temptingly close, biting her tongue as she worked quickly and surely. Kenton watched her face, feeling her breath on his shoulder and her hair against his flesh. It was one of the most arousing moments he could ever recall, having her so close yet knowing it was inappropriate to touch her, at least at the moment. He wouldn't give in to his lustful impulses as he had before. She was being standoffish and he was sure their kiss earlier had everything to do with it. He started to get that strange tightness in his chest again and he turned away.

"Is this paining you?" Nicola asked.

He shook his head. "No."

"I'm almost finished."

"Good. I need to return to the progress of the siege."

She stopped in mid-stitch. "You are going back to the battle?"

"Of course."

She looked at him, completely baffled. "But this is a serious wound," she said firmly. "You must rest. You lost a goodly amount of blood and…."

He reached up and put a hand on her arm before she could gain a head of steam. "I have cut myself shaving worse than this," he insisted quietly. "Though your concern is appreciated, it is unnecessary. Finish your stitching and that will be the end of it."

She stared at him, unsure how to react. Frustration was the first thing that came to mind as she bent back over him and finished the last few stitches. "I can see that I am wasting my time," she punctuated her words by stabbing him perhaps a little harder than necessary. "Therefore, your wound is now sealed and you are free to go out and make yourself another hole, bigger than this one. And don't think I'll lift a finger to help you."

She gathered her things in a huff. Kenton lay there, watching her vent, smirking at her animation. When she passed too close to the bed, he reached out and grabbed her. One good yank and she was practically laying across his outstretched body, twisted so that her face was in his. Kenton's eyes devoured her.

"Madam," he said slowly, "not only will I not break your careful stitches, I will most certainly not create a bigger hole, as you so bluntly put it. This I vow."

He was too close, too hot, too intense. Nicola could feel her face growing warm. "I… I believe you," she stammered.

"Do you truly?"

"Aye."

"Then no more temper tantrums. I interpret them as a lack of faith in my abilities, which contradicts what you were saying earlier. Are you always so fickle?"

"I am not fickle at all. But I do not want to see…."

She trailed off and he was seized with her potential train of thought. Kenton, sensing what she was about to say, encouraged her.

"What do you not want to see?" he asked softly.

She was having difficulty answering him, difficulty meeting his gaze. Everything about him was overwhelming her. "We have enough wounded without you going back to the battle and making yourself a target. The biggest target of all, I might add."

"You did not answer my question. What do you not want to see?"

He wasn't going to let her go peaceably. She scowled at his persistence. "I do not want to see you end up with another wound," she snapped before she could stop herself. "Will you let me up, please?"

He couldn't think of a good reason not to let go of her, so he did. She stood up, dropping the needle on his leg and reaching down to pick it up. Her fingers came into contact with his massive thigh and even though it was covered by armor and mail, she could still feel the heat. It was terrifying in a giddy sort of way. She was halfway across the floor when his voice stopped her.

"My thanks, Lady Thorne," he said, his voice low. "I am in your debt."

She turned around to see that he was standing up, gingerly trying to rotate the shoulder to see just how much movement he had out of it. He was determined to return to the battle and she stood there a moment, more worried than she cared to admit.

"Take care that you do not injure yourself further," she said quietly.

She started to quit the room but he called after her. "Wait."

She paused at the door. "Aye?"

He stood there a moment, staring at her. Then, slowly, he walked over to her, all the time rotating his shoulder and testing his injury. Nicola thought he might have concern with it somehow, that perhaps her stitches were too tight and he was concerned with them tearing. But he didn't say a word. Leaning over, he grasped her with his good arm and pulled her against him, slanting his mouth hungrily over hers. It was a sweet kiss, one full of promise and passion, and Nicola immediately folded. Not a flicker of resistance did she give as Kenton suckled her lips, his tongue licking at her, his teeth nibbling on the tender flesh of her lower lip. It was a kiss among kisses, a taunt of the pleasures of the flesh that the man was capable of, and Nicola collapsed against him and let him do whatever he pleased.

But the kiss went no further even though she surely would have let him. When he finally stopped kissing her, he didn't release her. He simply gazed into her flushed face, his eyes glimmering warmly at her. A flicker of a knowing smile crossed his lips and he let her go, turning to head out of the chamber, still rotating the arm, walking away as if he hadn't just sucked the breath right out of her.

But he had. Nicola stood, rooted to the spot, long after he was gone. Her heart was pounding and she couldn't quite catch her breath. She realized she was quivering. Her hands were shaking so that she was about to lose the needle she was still holding.

Carefully, she sat down on the bed behind her simply to regain her wits. Was it truly possible for a man's kiss to overwhelm one so much that they could barely think? Evidently, it was, but she had never experienced such a thing. She had no idea that a man's touch could be so thrilling. In a sense, as much as Kenton le Bec's presence was an unwelcome thing, it was also coming to be something that excited her. The man was taking liberties and she was letting him.

Did she truly want to leave Babylon when the potential for something so thrilling was here? When *Kenton* was here?

... she wondered.

CHAPTER SIX

T HE BATTLE FOR Babylon waged for six additional days, only brought to an end when a furious storm rolled in and very nearly drowned Edward's army out. The moat of Babylon filled up and overflowed, creating great torrents of water and mud and debris that rolled downhill and into Edward's encampment at the base of the hill that held the castle. At first, the storm was very cold rain but as the day passed, the temperature dropped and it turned into miserable, slushy snow. It turned into torrents of a mess.

At that point, it was misery for everyone. The men inside of Babylon had to deal with a bailey full of mud and puddles of half-frozen water, and because of the siege by Kenton and his men the previous week, supplies were running low. Babylon had, in essence, been at war for weeks upon end without any reprieve or chance to replenish supplies. Because of this, Nicola and the old cook, Hermenia, were forced to become very creative with what remaining supplies they had left.

The big pig that had been slaughtered and roasted at the commencement of the battle was now only skin and bones, and Hermenia had the cook fry the skin in hot fat to make big crunchy slabs, giving the men something more to fill their bellies. There were a few more pigs in the stables, not as fully grown as Nicola would have liked, but she had little choice in slaughtering them if she was going to feed a castle full of men, including her sons. Therefore, she had Hermenia slaughter three young pigs and the meat was roasted and put into great pots to be made into stew that would feed the army for days.

Dried winter vegetables went into the pots – dried beans, peas, turnips, carrots, old celery leaves, and slabs of raw pig fat to season up the broth. There was salt, fortunately, and sacks of peppercorns, so the stew was well-seasoned as it bubbled away in three big pots out in the kitchen yard. Hermenia and a few soldiers rigged canvas covers over the pots so that the falling snow wouldn't ruin it and they stood back, bellies rumbling, as the delicious smells of cooking pork filled the air.

Unfortunately, hunger eventually won over and men began eating it before it was completely cooked. As they entered the seventh day of siege and the black clouds overhead showed no sign of stopping, the men of Babylon sucked down the bubbling stew, hot and salty. Liesl and Raven, helping old Hermenia, manage to fill two big bowls of it for Nicola and the boys and, along with some cheese Hermenia had stashed away and stale bread, took it up to the family's chambers on the fourth floor. There, the three little boys devoured the meal whilst Nicola and her serving women took the leavings.

During the past seven days, Nicola hadn't seen much of Kenton. He'd spent all of his time upon the walls of Babylon, fighting off Edward's forces or launching offensives against them. She had seen him from her window on several occasions, a massive man in frozen armor upon those mighty walls, a fixture there as if he'd been defending Babylon his entire life.

Nicola came to wish that he had been defending Babylon all this time instead of Gaylord, a secret fantasy that Kenton was her husband and not Gaylord, the man who had beat her, the man who had ultimately been killed by his own son in an ironic twist of fate. What if Kenton was her husband and he was here, defending Babylon against an enemy, protecting their children and their home. To even think on such a silly fantasy gave her a warm, giddy feeling, something to dream about and secretly entertain whilst warfare and death went on around her. Truly, there were plenty of both.

Nicola had spent every day of the siege down in the great hall, helping Kenton's surgeon with the wounded. Some men were hardly injured whilst others had sustained mortal injuries. One young man had been hit by an arrow through the belly, severing his spine, and the remainder of his life was measured in hours. Nicola sat with him, telling him stories she often told her sons, stories of valor and great deeds, while the young man quietly died. That death had particularly affected her, seeing a young life cut so needlessly short. After that, she'd retreated to her room for the rest of the night and into the day. She was finished with death for a while.

She was fairly certain that Kenton knew of her presence in the great hall, among the wounded, because she saw his knights several times – the big red-haired knight, the one that looked like a bear, and then the blond knight with the thick neck. They had come in, usually bearing wounded, and they would notice her. She knew that because she always turned to see if it was Kenton coming into the hall, so her gaze would lock with that of whatever knight happened to be there, but so far Kenton had yet to set foot back into the hall of the wounded. She was certain his knights had gone back to Kenton and told him that the Lady of Babylon was doing her duty.

She hoped, in some way, her dedication to his men would earn his respect as a woman who was capable of performing under pressure. As the days passed and the battle raged, she realized that she wanted it. From a man she was terrified of in his first days at Babylon to a man she was increasingly enamored with, her opinion and thoughts of Kenton le Bec were rapidly changing.

All thoughts of Kenton aside, Nicola also saw Warwick on occasion, which usually caused her to flush red and run in the opposite direction. Like Kenton, the man had remained in the heat of the action, upon the walls, fighting off men who had once been allied with him. Nicola knew that Warwick had once been allied with Edward because Gaylord had fought with the man in years past, so Warwick was something of a distasteful enigma to her – she didn't understand a man who could switch sides so easily from one king to another. Gaylord had once told her Warwick tended to side with the man he knew could provide him with the most power. To her, Warwick was a sword that could be bought.

Towards the end of the seventh day of the siege, the snow began to fall in earnest and it was a white-out condition that saw both armies retreat into shelter. Those in Babylon were much better protected than Edward's army and by the time dawn began to color the eastern horizon on the next day, the snow eased enough for Edward's army to leave.

Conditions were too terrible to continue the siege and the commander in charge of Edward's forces was willing to concede defeat. His men were exhausted, freezing, and hungry, so without any fanfare or fuss, Edward's army skulked off at first light, leaving the walls of Babylon, and her inhabitants, relatively intact.

Upon the great walls that embraced Babylon's keep and occupants, Warwick, Kenton, and his knights were watching the retreat of Edward's forces. The snow was still falling, sticking to the skin and eyelashes, although it wasn't falling nearly as hard as it had been earlier. Kenton stood next to Warwick as they watched the figures through the mist disbanding below, fading off into the falling snow and leaving the land stripped and devastated behind them.

"They are heading southeast," Warwick said. "They will cross the Black River, pass Huddersfield, and it is my guess they might head to Conisbrough Castle to regroup. It would be wise to take a contingent of men after them to harass them while they are weak. They could potentially splinter. That would further weaken Edward's strength in this area."

Kenton, with snowflakes hanging off of his dark eyelashes, looked at the man. "Do you want me to take some men and go after them?"

Warwick shook his head. "I was referring to me," he said, turning away from the wall and wiping the melted snowflakes off of his face.

"There is a larger contingent of Henry's men in Wakefield at the moment and I will join them. Now that Babylon has held, I have every confidence it will continue to hold. Your duty, Kenton, will be in subduing the surrounding countryside and claiming it for Henry. You will also keep this road and exact tolls from anyone who travels upon it. This is a very important road between Lancashire and Yorkshire. It is imperative that Henry control it."

Kenton nodded sharply. "Aye, my lord."

Warwick began to take the stairs down through the gatehouse, narrow spiral stairs that were difficult to navigate for men of Kenton's size. He ended up taking the steps sideways, following Warwick down.

"Rochdale is to the west, Kenton," Warwick said, bumping his shoulder armor against the frozen stone walls. "It is imperative that the town be brought under Henry's control. That will be your next task – to subdue and control Rochdale before moving on to Manchester."

Kenton nodded. "I thought as much," he said. "Rochdale and Manchester are big towns. I will need at least a thousand men or more to cover them."

Warwick reached the bottom of the steps, into the cold, muddy gatehouse. "You shall keep fourteen hundred men," he said. "I want Babylon well supplied with soldiers. I will take the rest with me, on to Wakefield. You will send word to me when Rochdale is under your control and we will celebrate once you contain Manchester. You are the Lord of Babylon now, Kenton. Command your realm with fairness and swift action."

"I will, my lord."

They were heading out of the gatehouse now as a group, out into the inner ward that was full of men camping on the frozen ground. A thick haze of smoke from the fires blanketed the area, made worse by the snow that was falling. It kept the smoke low and heavy, stinging their eyes as they walked through it.

"One last thing, Kenton," Warwick said as they made their way to the keep. "Be wary of Conisbrough Castle to the south of you. Edward owns it. It is stocked with his men. I've not yet heard of the castle taking any punitive action in this area, but it is a foregone conclusion that they know Babylon now belongs to Henry. As I said, it is my belief that the retreating army will head there to gather more forces. That will bring the garrison to your doorstep."

Kenton was well aware of Conisbrough, a very big castle that belonged to Edward. "Indeed, my lord," he said. "I shall watch them closely."

Warwick's gaze was moving up, through the smoke, to focus on the monstrous keep ahead. "Edward is undoubtedly unhappy that we now have Babylon," he said, an ominous hint of warning to his tone. "The siege we experienced over the past few days might only be the beginning. I have a feeling there will be many such sieges to come. That being the case, I will reinforce your knight ranks with two additional knights who have been in my service for a couple of years. Sir Matthew Wellesbourne and Sir Gaston de Russe are two of the finest men I have ever seen in action. They may be young but they are seasoned. They fight like men who have been doing it their entire lives. I believe they will make an excellent addition to your ranks. You will rely on them heavily. I trust their judgment and so will you."

Kenton thought on Wellesbourne and de Russe; he knew them both and his opinion was the same as Warwick's – he'd never seen finer knights. In fact, he was quite pleased with Warwick's suggestion.

"I know Matt and Gaston," he said. "I have fought with them in the past on occasion, although they have mostly been with you and not out with me and my strike force. I am honored that you would leave them in my command, my lord."

Warwick paused by the steps that led up into the keep. "Wellesbourne is very much loved by the men and will make an excellent commander by your right hand," he said. "No offense intended for de Birmingham or Forbes or le Mon, but Wellesbourne has a wisdom that nearly exceeds mine. And de Russe... God's Blood, you know his reputation. He rips men apart with his bare hands."

Kenton cracked a grin. "I have seen evidence of that," he said. "I have heard rumor that the men have started calling him The Dark One."

"It is no rumor."

Kenton chuckled. "Then I will try to stay on his good side."

Warwick's gaze lingered on Kenton. "I would suspect he had better stay on *yours*," he said. Then, he turned for the keep. "I will meet with my advisors now and we will plan our advance on Wakefield. Where will you be so that I can send Wellesbourne and de Russe to you?"

Kenton gestured inside the keep. "Into the hall," he said. "I've not eaten since yesterday. They can find me in there."

Warwick simply nodded and took the stairs into the keep with Kenton on his heels. But they separated as soon as they entered the tall, two-storied entry. Warwick went into Gaylord's solar to the right of the entry whilst Kenton continued on into the hall in front of him. His thoughts were lingering on Wellesbourne and de Russe but he was quickly distracted at the sight of all of the wounded in the hall and the great hearth that was breathing smoke and sparks into the room in a vain attempt to ward off the cold. Stepping further into the hall with the hope of obtaining something to eat, he spied Nicola almost immediately.

The chatelaine of Babylon was kneeling down next to a wounded man, feeding him something out of a bowl. Kenton took a moment to simply look at her; her lovely blond hair was braided, tucked back into a kerchief, and her beautiful face held a warm and comforting expression. God, he'd never seen anything so lovely or reassuring in his entire life.

It was a weak moment, one weak with emotion and fatigue. All he wanted to do at that moment was go to Nicola and take her in his arms, taking solace in her warm and soft body, feeling her flesh in his hands and her scent in his nostrils to remind him that there were still things of beauty left in the world. War seemed to erase all memories of peace and joy from him. At the moment, he was feeling fairly exhausted and desolate. He realized, at that moment, that he needed her.

Needed her!

It was a shocking thought. He'd never needed anyone or anything in his life.

Until now.

As if she could sense his presence and perhaps even his thoughts, Nicola suddenly looked up and saw Kenton standing several feet away. He was pale and sporting a growth of dark beard. Their eyes locked and, quickly, she passed the bowl she was holding off to one of her serving women, hovering behind her. She wiped her hands on her apron as she approached Kenton.

"So you are alive," she commented. She meant it to be a wry quip but it ended up coming out as a concerned statement. "I had wondered. I have not seen you in days. How is your shoulder?"

The sound of her sweet, gentle voice was like music to his ears. He had missed it. "It has healed completely thanks to your tending."

"I must take the stitches out."

"No need. I removed them myself."

Nicola winced at the sound of that particularly unsavory action, removing stitches from oneself. But she wasn't surprised that Kenton would do such a thing. The man seemed impervious to pain or fear or anything else that men considered a weakness.

"I could have just as easily done it for you," she said quietly, not knowing what else to say on the matter. She changed subjects. "How goes the battle? Does it show any signs of ending?"

He nodded. "It has already ended," he said. "Edward's army is retreating and Babylon has emerged triumphant."

Nicola was relieved to know that the battles, for the moment, were over. "But for how long?" she asked. "I cannot imagine that Edward will leave Babylon to Henry without much more than a single attempt to regain it."

Kenton shook his head. "More than likely not," he said quietly. "But for now, Babylon will know a measure of peace."

Nicola thought on that. She wasn't eager to face more battles, at least not any time soon. She looked around the room to the wounded men crowding the hall and she sighed heavily.

"Hopefully these men will be much better by the time we face another attack," she said. Then, she looked at Kenton again and realized that the man looked as if he were on the verge of collapse. His pale face was paler and his eyes were dark-circled. She hadn't really noticed his fatigue until this moment. "Come and sit, Kenton. You must be famished. I will bring you some food."

Kenton. It was the first time he'd heard his name from her lips and he instantly, deeply loved the sound of it. He never knew his name could sound so good. She'd only called him "my lord" once or twice and most of the time she ignored any semblance of title at all. She was very clear in that she had no respect for him and his position at Babylon. But he didn't care about any of that at the moment. He wanted to hear her call him Kenton for always. It was the most natural of things coming out of her delicious mouth.

Without replying, he sat down at the end of the feasting table, one with wounded men lying on top of it. He simply sat because she told him to and he watched as she scurried away, off to a section of the hall he couldn't see but he knew that area had a servant's alcove and a door that had stairs leading down to the kitchen yard. When she was gone, it was as if a light had gone out of the hall. It seemed like a darker and more dismal place. Feeling more exhausted by the second, Kenton raked his fingers through his dark hair, thinking on washing and shaving his face before trying to catch a few hours of sleep. Or maybe he wouldn't. Truth be told, he was much too tired to plan anything beyond the next few moments.

Nicola reappeared a short time later with a tray of food. She was followed by one of her serving women, the dark-haired girl named Raven, the one that his knights had been eyeing, as the girl carried a pitcher and some other items. Nicola practically ran up to the table and set the tray down in front of him.

"I have some lovely, hot stew for you," she said, putting a big, wooden bowl full of something steaming in front of him. She also began to put various other things in front of him. "I found a spoon, too. Oh, and here is some cheese and bread, and Raven has brought warmed wine for you. I hope this will be enough. Our provisions are quite low so I cannot offer you more than this."

Kenton simply nodded as he picked up the spoon and plowed into the stew. It was hot and salty and delicious. The bread wasn't very fresh but it didn't matter; he tore apart the chunk and dipped it in the stew, slurping it up. He was so hungry that he hadn't noticed Nicola now moving away from the table to leave him to eat in peace, but when he realized she was leaving, he called her back.

"My lady," he said, motioning for her to sit when she turned to look at him. "Please sit. Tell me about our lack of provisions. I fear that we shall have to remedy the situation quickly with the number of men we have within the walls of Babylon. Are we truly so low on stores?"

Nicola sat down on the opposite side of the table, watching the man wolf down his food. "Unfortunately, due to the fact that Babylon has suffered through two sieges in close succession, our provisions are quite low," she said, hoping it didn't sound like a reprimand because he, in fact, had been the aggressor in one of those sieges. "We are nearly out of flour and we could use meat – any kind of meat. I do not want to kill all of my pigs this winter because we need offspring to breed more food for next year."

Kenton, still eating, listened to her seriously. "You are chatelaine," he said. "What would you suggest?"

Nicola didn't stop to think that this was nearly the first rational and serious conversation they'd ever had that didn't involve stolen kisses or anger or harsh words. He was showing respect for her opinion and she was showing him respect in kind. It was a calm exchange of information, the first between them.

"Rochdale and Manchester are about ten miles to the west," she said. "Manchester has a big market every Sunday where we can purchase a good deal of stores, but I fear with all of these men we are sheltering, we will need an entire herd of pigs or sheep to feed them. We will also need grain for the animals if we can get it. This winter has been difficult so it will come at a premium if we can even find it."

Kenton was nearly at the end of his meal but it was clear that he was carefully considering the problem. "Tomorrow is Sunday," he said. "I am not entirely certain, however, it would be wise to leave Babylon so soon after a siege. Even though Edward's army has departed, they could still be lurking nearby."

Nicola shook her head. "Lurking or not, we must go," she said firmly. "We cannot wait another week. We will be boiling hides for soup if that happens."

"The situation is desperate, then?"

"It is."

He lifted his dark eyebrows at her. "Then tomorrow we travel."

Nicola nodded, satisfied, but then she began to look around the hall. Her movements were almost nervous. "There was a chest in Gaylord's solar that contained coin," she said, lowering her voice. "I do not know what has become of it, but I would assume you have it. That is what we must use to pay for the provisions."

Kenton wiped at his mouth and downed what was left in his cup. "I have it in a secure place," he said. "I will bring enough coinage to secure what we need."

Nicola tried not to think about the fact that he essentially stole Gaylord's money which, at his death, became her money. She understood the rules of the spoils of war. Therefore, she simply sighed and tried not to sound as if she resented the fact that he took most of the coinage belonging to her family. Not all, but most. She still had some tucked away with her possessions. Seemingly at the end of their conversation, she moved to leave.

"Very well," she said. "We should leave well before first light tomorrow to make it to Manchester when the farmers are arriving. I want first pick of their wares."

Kenton eyed her as she stood up. "It is generous of you to worry over our provisions enough so that you should delay your leaving Babylon," he said. It was a leading statement. He wanted to see if she had, indeed, been serious about leaving in the first place because it had been on his mind since she'd first spoken of it. "When did you plan on going to your widowed aunt?"

Nicola came to a halt, looking at him with an expression between surprise and hesitation. She cleared her throat softly. "I... I had not thought on it," she said. "I suppose I will leave when it is convenient for you to send a few men with me as escort."

"That could take a very long time. I need my men here at Babylon."

Her brow furrowed. "How long?"

"I have no way of knowing."

"Surely we are talking about weeks here, not months or even years."

He wiped at his mouth and wondering if he was sounding as if he didn't want her to leave at all. Part of him hoped she understood that, but most of him was embarrassed that he could even think such a thing. Since when did he want to keep a woman around? The answer to that question was very simple but in order to save his male pride, he thought of another excuse.

"I have no one else to be chatelaine," he said, "at least no one with your experience. At the moment, you are quite valuable to me. I would consider it a favor if you would delay your departure until such time as I no longer have a need for you. Right now, I need you."

There was a hint of something more in that last statement, something that suggested he needed her for more than to simply run a household. Nicola caught of whiff of it, like a ribbon of smoke that tantalized and then was quickly gone. *I need you.* Was it possible that he did in more ways than she realized?

Madness! She quickly scolded herself. *You are mad to believe this knight, the enemy, has interest in you! You should clearly have no interest in him!*

Aye, she knew that. God help her, she did. But the giddy beating of her heart and the pull of his deep blue eyes told her otherwise.

"Then… then I shall remain for a time if I truly serve a purpose," she stammered, wondering why her mouth was so dry. "I would not wish to leave you in a quandary."

"That is very gracious of you, Madam."

"But you *will* provide me with an escort at the appropriate time?"

"If time and situation permits, I will take you myself."

She felt both better and worse by that statement. Perhaps she was reading too much into his "I need you" statement if he was willing to personally escort her to her aunt's. Fearful to become the man's whore but not too fearful to become one if she actually meant something to him, her mind was wracked with turmoil and confusion.

Therefore, she simply nodded her head and moved away from the table, passing within close proximity as she did. Before she could get away completely, Kenton reached out and grasped her hand as she passed by and she immediately stopped, heart beating in her ears and her breathing coming in little gasps. His touch had that effect on her. As she watched, he lifted her hand to his lips and kissed it tenderly.

"I hope you will not leave," he confided. "I hope you will choose to remain of your own free will."

With that, he dropped her hand, stood up, and moved away from the table in the opposite direction. Nicola simply stood there, her hand still nearly in the position he had left it, out in front of her as if he were still holding it. She watched the enormous knight leave the hall and out into the entry beyond before disappearing from her sight altogether. All the while, Nicola simply stood there, her focus still on the last place she saw Kenton, her heart still beating wildly from the kiss to her hand.

Dear God…, she thought, *is it really possible that he should want me to remain? And is it equally possible that I will?*

Of course she would. She knew she would. She didn't want to leave him, either. Nicola fought off a grin, realizing that, for the first time in her life, she was actually attracted to someone and entrenched in the throes of a giddy infatuation. She'd never experienced anything like it but, as she was coming to realize, thoughts of Kenton were making her feel rather as if she were walking on clouds. It was the most wonderful feeling in the world.

"My lady?"

A soft female voice floated up behind her, distracting her from foolish, silly, warm thoughts of Kenton le Bec. She turned to see Raven standing behind her. When Nicola looked at the girl, the young lass smiled.

"The little lads will be hungry, my lady," she said. "It is the evening now. We should take them what food we can carry."

Nicola nodded swiftly; *too* swiftly, embarrassed she had been caught in reflections of Kenton le Bec.

"Of course," she said, shooing Raven in the direction of the kitchen yard. "Let us take all we can. Le Bec is going to take me into Manchester tomorrow so that we may purchase more supplies, thankfully."

Raven scooted well ahead of her mistress, heading for the kitchens. She heard Lady Thorne's statement about purchasing more supplies and she had seen the entire exchange between the lady and the big knight known as Kenton le Bec. Raven and her sisters were coming to suspect that there might be something of an attraction between the pair and le Bec, in spite of his fierce reputation, seemed a far better character than Gaylord Thorne. Raven, Janet, and Liesl genuinely loved their lady and they had hated Gaylord Thorne for the way the man treated her. Certainly it was not an ideal situation to find solace with the enemy, but Raven and her sisters found themselves hoping just that.

As Raven and Nicola gathered more food for the boys from the steaming pots of stew, which was by now boiled-down and very thick since it was a few days old, Raven couldn't help but notice that her lady seemed distracted. She kept glancing to the walls overhead or looking behind her at the kitchen yard gate as if expecting someone to appear. Raven knew, just as her lady did, who the woman was expecting to appear.

The powerful form of Kenton le Bec.

~ A NEW DAY DAWNS ~

CHAPTER SEVEN

The next day

NICOLA WAS FAIRLY certain that she had never been so cold in her entire life.

It was an hour before dawn as the party from Babylon set out for Manchester's market. Wrapped in the warmest clothes she had, which included a woolen shift, woolen hose, a heavy traveling dress, and a cloak lined with rabbit fur, she was still feeling the bite of the weather. Her face felt as if it was half-frozen already and they had barely left the gatehouse.

But she kept quiet about the cold because she knew that all of them were feeling it. The clouds had cleared up overnight and a brilliant blue sky await them for their travels to Manchester. At least that part of the trip would be pleasant.

Beside her, Tab rode astride his fat roan pony because Nicola had pleaded with Kenton to allow the boy to come. Tab was mature for his age, a good traveler, and the lad had begged to go. Nicola could not deny him and Kenton had given his permission without much resistance, so Nicola and Tab rode happily, side by side, right in front of the big wagon that they brought to carry their provisions home in.

In spite of the cold, it was already turning out to be a fine day and a good ride. The road was in unusually good condition given the weather as of late, with dirty snow drifts piled up along the side of the road. In spite of the cold, it felt good to be free of Babylon's confines but Nicola very quickly saw the damage to the land left by two successive sieges. Trees were stripped bare and the land was generally beaten and desolate. Remnants of cooking fires littered the ground. There were also big pits spaced around, dug so the men could relieve themselves. The smell of human sewage was heavy.

But the smell cleared up as soon as they got away from Babylon and down the road a mile or two. The frozen landscape appeared a bit more attractive as they headed east towards Rochdale and Manchester. The horses were rather frisky, having been corralled for so long, and twice Tab's pony bucked and tried to throw the boy, but he remained steady in the saddle. Kenton, who was riding in front of them, finally told Tab to run the pony up the road and back again so the beast would settle down, and Tab happily complied. Nicola watched with concern as Tab's fat-butt pony raced up the muddy road.

"'Tis a fine animal, Lady Thorne," Kenton said when he noticed her look of distress at her son riding at such breakneck speed. "Your son rides him quite well."

Nicola's gaze was on her son in the distance, riding hard as the mud flew. "He has been riding since before he could walk," she said. "His father insisted."

Kenton watched the boy nimbly turn the animal around at the crest of the road and head back in their direction. "That was wise," he said. "Where did he plan for your son to foster? He is coming of age, you know. If arrangements have already been made, then I would know of them since I now oversee your family."

There was haughtiness in that statement but Nicola ignored it. In fact, she began to reflect on her fantasy of Kenton being her husband and the master of Babylon as if Gaylord Thorne had never existed. It was still a lovely, secret fantasy, but one she just as quickly chased away. She didn't want to be caught dreaming of the man. *Dreaming of the enemy.* She struggled to focus on his question.

"He is only five years of age," she said. "He is too young to foster."

"I was sent to foster at four years of age."

Nicola frowned. "Ridiculous," she said. "That is far too young."

Kenton's lips twitched with a smile. "My mother tells the tale that I was four years of age whilst my father says that I was more like eight years of age," he said. "They cannot agree. Mother insists I was four."

Nicola could see that he was struggling not to smile at what was undoubtedly a heated topic between his parents. She couldn't help but grin. "I am sure to your mother, you were still her baby whether or not you were four or eight," she said, her gaze moving back to Tab who was thundering towards them. "I know how she feels."

Kenton opened his mouth to reply but Tab's pony suddenly slipped in the mud and went down, pitching Tab over its head. Tab went sailing into a snow drift, face-first, as his mother shrieked. She spurred her horse towards her son but Kenton was already there well before she was, reaching out to help the boy from the dirty snow. Odd how Kenton beat her to her own son, as if the boy meant something to him. As he pulled the lad free, someone went to see to the pony.

"Tab!" Nicola gasped, pulling her son into her arms. "Are you well? Did you injure yourself?"

Tab, frowning, was wiping snow and dirt off his face. "Nay," he said, grumpy and embarrassed. "I am not hurt. Is my pony well?"

Tab pulled from his mother's embrace, more concerned for the pony than for himself. He went to the beast as one of the knights who had accompanied them was checking the animal over. As Tab petted the pony, looking it over with great concern, the knight was running his hands all over the animal's limbs.

"He seems sound," the knight told Tab. "I believe he is well. He merely slipped."

Tab nodded silently although he still looked the pony over, just for his own comfort. He took the reins from the big knight as Kenton helped the boy to mount again.

"That was quite a tumble, young Thorne," the knight who had tended the pony said. "You fall as well as any knight."

Kenton snorted. "Knights do not fall, Matt."

Sir Matthew Wellesbourne laughed, a very easy smile on his handsome face. "If you have been told they do not, then someone is telling you lies," he said. "And if you think *you* have not, then there are men who will say differently."

Kenton cocked a dark eyebrow. "Nay, there are not. All witnesses have been eliminated."

"I believe you."

Matthew grinned at Kenton, and then at Nicola, before turning away to collect his big white mount. Kenton pointed to Matthew as the man mounted his steed.

"That is Matthew Wellesbourne," he told Nicola. "A finer knight has never walked this earth, Lady Thorne. He is under my command now and shall be at your service."

Nicola turned to look at the big knight who had helped her son and saw that he was still smiling at her, now dipping his head politely in her direction.

"Lady Thorne," he said. "'Tis an honor to make your acquaintance."

Nicola simply smiled politely and returned her attention back to Tab, who was now wrestling with his frisky pony.

"Tab," she said hesitantly. "Mayhap... mayhap you should ride on the wagon. Your pony is quite wild this morn."

Tab frowned at his mother. "I can ride him," he insisted. "I must show him I am the master!"

With that, he spurred the pony back down the road. Kenton watched the boy go, turning to flick a hand at Wellesbourne, who spurred his big rouncey after the boy. Nicola, frowning, watched them ride down the road after each other.

"You must let your boy become a man, Mother," Kenton said softly. "Tab is capable. You must let him make his own mistakes and take his own falls."

Nicola turned to look at the man, realizing he was fairly close to her. He had obviously been watching her tense expression, concern for

her son and his lively pony. She was torn between agreeing with him
and her motherly instincts.

"Why must he become a man at such a young age?" she wanted to
know. "Why can he not simply enjoy being a child for now?"

Kenton's lips twitched with a smile, his gaze warm upon her. "Because he wants very badly to grow up," he said softly. "He wants to be a
man and take care of his mother and brothers. You must let him do this
and not undermine his confidence by reminding him that he is still a
child. Children have ruled kingdoms, my lady, and they have done it
quite well. Tab is a fine young lad and he will make a fine man thanks
to you, so you must let him grow up."

It was a very kind thing to say, one that touched Nicola deeply. It
also softened her up to Kenton's suggestion that Tab must be allowed to
grow up. Reluctantly, she turned her attention to Tab and Wellesbourne, far down the road.

"I suppose you are correct," she said. "When Gaylord passed away,
Tab inherited everything from his father. He is already a baron. I
suppose I should…."

Horrified, Nicola realized she had divulged information she had
sworn never to reveal to Kenton. *A young baron would make a fine
hostage,* she had once told herself. Now, she could kick herself for
revealing what should not have been revealed. She prayed that Kenton
didn't catch on to what she had said, but there was no way around it.
She had been clear and Kenton caught on right away.

"I was not aware that Thorne was titled," he said. "What title did
Tab inherit?"

Nicola sighed heavily. "Baron Marsden," she said. "His lands run all
the way to Rochdale to the west."

Kenton didn't seem to be overly impressed or concerned over a
titled five-year-old boy. "I also inherited a title when I was young," he
said. "My mother's father died when I was six years of age and I
inherited the Dunscar barony from him."

Nicola turned to look at him, mildly impressed. "You are titled also?"

"I am," he replied. "I have a castle in Yorkshire that belongs to me also, through my mother, called Steelmoor Castle. Unfortunately, Edward likes it a great deal and I have been forced many times over the years to return to defend it. Henry keeps a big contingent of men there."

Nicola simply nodded. She wanted off the subject of young barons should Kenton come up with the idea to use Tab somehow because of it. Silently, she turned back to her palfrey and Kenton came up behind her, helping her to mount the horse. Quite literally, he lifted her up and put her on it and she smiled politely to the man to thank him. Stone-faced Kenton smiled back.

The rest of their ride into Manchester was uneventful but before they entered the city proper, Kenton had his ten-man escort, including two knights, remove their tunics bearing Warwick's colors. He didn't want to charge into town announcing who he was even though Manchester was mostly held for Henry. Still, it was his directive and duty to secure the entire town for Henry's cause but until he could do that, they had to tread carefully. He didn't want to get into a fight with Nicola and Tab in their midst.

By the time the party entered the city walls, the sun was starting to rise and people were leaving the big church at the conclusion of matins. The church of St. Mary was very old, having been built on the site of an even older church, and it had been packed with worshippers on this frozen morning.

As their group progressed into the heart of the city, they followed the flock of worshippers towards the street of the great market, as most people in Manchester, and in other great cities, usually did their shopping on Sundays after worship. Soon enough, the big street with its many vendors opened up wide before them and the patterned protocol of market shopping was in full swing.

With the street in sight, Kenton called a halt to the party. There was palatable excitement in the air, the bustle and hustle of a busy city around them, and Kenton moved their group off of the main road and up against a building that was both a residence and a seamstress according to the painted sign above the door. Leaving two men-at-arms guarding the horses and the wagon, Kenton took Nicola, Tab, Wellesbourne, and the remaining eight soldiers to the street where farmers and merchants were doing their business for the day.

The very first vendor they went to was a sheep farmer. The man had his sheep in a makeshift corral, great wooly beasts with spindly black legs. Several of the ewes were pregnant, the farmer told Kenton, and Kenton had the man point them out. Meanwhile, Tab wanted to pet the fuzzy animals, including three tiny lambs, and ducked under the corral railing, pursuing the sheep as they walked in a nervous bunch away from the boy. Nicola alternately negotiated with the farmer and told Tab to get away from the sheep. The boy was chasing them in circles around the corral, so much so that it looked like someone was stirring a great pot of sheep. Still, he managed to catch one of the lambs and he hugged the beast happily.

Nicola was very good at bartering and Kenton stood out of her way as she deftly handled the farmer; as Babylon's chatelaine, she was much better at negotiating good prices than he was. Kenton wasn't one to negotiate at all, which Nicola was to discover with the next merchant. After they purchased six pregnant ewes, three ewes with lambs, and a ram from the sheep farmer, they moved on next to a man who had dozens of sacks of grain – oats, rye, barley, and wheat – and his stall was the most crowded.

It was somewhat of a frenzy with a dozen customers demanding service. Unwilling to wait his turn amongst the throng of people, Kenton had Wellesbourne and the soldiers chase all of the customers away by flashing swords and balled fists, and then Kenton went to the merchant and put the tip of a dagger to the man's throat and demanded the best deal for all of his sacks. Exasperated, Nicola was forced to step in, remove the dagger from the man's throat, and negotiate for the price for every single sack of grain the man had. They needed it badly and were willing to pay.

Fortunately, the farmer wasn't one to hold a grudge against a man who held a blade to him and soon enough, the men-at-arms were loading the bags of grain onto the wagon. The farmer, who had a great deal of land to the north of Manchester, had been very smart about storing his grain so it would not become wet or moist and grow mold during the winter months. He'd kept it very dry, off the ground on pallets of wood and stone, and therefore he'd made it a valuable and quality crop. It was a good haul.

All told, Nicola had purchased twenty sacks of oats, eighteen sacks of barley, eleven sacks of rye, and twenty-three sacks of wheat. She explained to Kenton as the wagon was loaded that mixing the wheat with the rye or oats would stretch out the supply. She estimated that they could feed twelve hundred people for a couple of months on what they had, providing they were careful with rations. That would take them into late spring with good planning.

Kenton listened to her speak of measurements and stores with a great deal of interest. She was very knowledgeable on such things, which impressed him. She had been well-schooled in the duties of a chatelaine and he quickly learned to defer to her in all things. As the day began to dawn brighter and the market was in full swing, Kenton sent Wellesbourne and four additional soldiers back to guard the provisions wagon with all of that grain stored in it while he moved with Nicola and Tab through the market stalls.

Four men-at-arms trailed them, keeping an eye out for anything threatening, which was a good thing because Nicola seemed to have all of Kenton's focus. There could have been an entire army of Edward's men behind him and he wouldn't have noticed. Having spent the majority of his time with Nicola fighting with her or being in some kind of argument with her one way or another, to find themselves in a peaceful and pleasant situation was rather disorienting but wholly wonderful.

Nicola had an adorable little habit of wrinkling her nose when speaking of something serious or distasteful, and she had just the slightest bit of a lisp that Teague had inherited, although his was much more pronounced. Kenton found her lisp utterly charming. *She* was charming. That belligerent, aggressive woman he had first come to know had a sweet side to her that was quite overwhelming.

But along with his admiration and his increasing interest, he couldn't help the thoughts of Gaylord Thorne that filled his mind. He recalled the first time he'd met Nicola, how she'd spoken of Gaylord taking his fists to her. Then he looked at Tab, holding his mother's hand, and thought of the young boy who had stolen a sword in order to protect his mother from his father; on any normal day with any normal people, such thoughts would not have distressed him. Fathers being stabbed by their children weren't particularly strange things in his world, a world of warfare and death. But given that it had happened to Nicola, and to Tab, he felt some pity for them.

Odd, he wasn't one given to pity, but he did know one thing – if Gaylord Thorne wasn't dead by now, then knowing how the man treated his wife and sons, Kenton realized that he surely would have killed the man himself and would have felt absolutely no guilt about it. Nicola and Tab and those two silly twins deserved all of the protection he could provide and all of the protection he wanted to give.

He wanted very much to give it.

A cold breeze was picking up as they made their way to a man who was selling dried peas and beans, great bushels of them, but they were detoured when Tab caught a whiff of something wonderful. The lad let go of his mother's hand and fled in the direction of the smell, which ended up being a baker who was baking tarts with eggs and cheese and herbs in them.

The tart crusts were made from rye because of the expensive nature of wheat during the winter months, but it created a wonderful savory dish that Tab begged for. Kenton, the Keeper of the Purse, relented and bought two for the boy, who happily wolfed them down. Then Kenton looked to the men behind him, his men-at-arms, and he could see that they were hungry, too. Pursing his lips irritably, he ended up purchasing all of the tarts and the seven of them, including Nicola, stuffed themselves on the delicious pies.

Bellies full for the first time in days, they returned to the farmer with the bushels of dried peas and beans but they had to pass a smithy in order to get there. Nicola, Kenton, and the men-at-arms saw nothing unusual or spectacular with the smithy but Tab did. He saw small swords that the man had made, suspended from the roof of his stall. He stopped to admire the swords as the others continued on but it didn't take Nicola long to notice she was missing her child. Quickly, she dashed back to take him by the hand and pull him along, but he dug his heels in.

"Mam!" he cried, pointing to the smaller blades hanging from the ceiling. "Look at the swords!"

Nicola didn't even look. She was tugging at her son. "Come along, Tab," she said firmly. "You must not delay our business. Sir Kenton will not be pleased."

"Pleased about what?" Kenton asked, coming up behind them. "What is so interesting here?"

Tab didn't hesitate; he pointed to the swords. "Those," he said. "They... they are small for boys. Like me."

Kenton's lips twitched with a smile. He knew what the lad meant. He wanted a sword. Kenton pointed to the blades. "Those are called batons," he told him. "They are not real swords. They are meant for training."

Tab's face fell. "Oh," he said, dejected, his longing gaze still lingering on the swords. "Am... am I old enough to train?"

Nicola scowled. "You are *not* old...."

Kenton cut her off, gently done, but putting a hand out to stop her from finishing her sentence. "How old are you, young Tab?"

Tab didn't hesitate. "I have seen five summers," he said. "I will see six summers soon!"

Kenton's eyebrows lifted as if impressed. "Then you are old enough to train," he said firmly. "You should go into training immediately."

Nicola's mouth popped open in concern and outrage. "But... but....!"

Kenton wasn't looking at her at all. He put his hand on Tab's shoulder and turned the boy around so he was looking into the smithy shack. Kenton caught the attention of the fat, red-faced smithy as the man worked over the hot coals.

"You, there," he said to the smithy. "My young friend wishes to see some of those batons you have hanging from the ceiling. Bring them over here so we might inspect them."

As Kenton and Tab hovered over the small swords that the smithy put before them, Nicola went to stand on the other side of her son, frowning greatly at what was going on. "Sir Kenton," she said, struggling not to become irate at the fact that she was being ignored. "My son is much too young to learn how to use a sword."

Kenton was still focused on the four or five smaller swords that the smithy was laying in front of him. "He is the perfect age to be well-taught," he said evenly. "I am surprised your husband did not already start his education."

Nicola was growing increasingly angry. "The boys are *too* young," she said again. "Moreover, Gaylord was busy with Edward. He did not have time to train his sons."

Kenton lifted his head to look at her. "I have time for them," he said. "I will make sure they are properly instructed on the use of weapons."

Nicola's jaw ticked. "I forbid it."

Those were the Magic Mother Words as far as Kenton was concerned. He was willing to push the woman, even ignore her in his quest to have his wishes known, but when she started throwing around words like "forbid", it was time for him to reason with her. He didn't know why; she was his captive and a captor didn't usually have to reason with a prisoner, but if he was honest with himself that captor/prisoner relationship had dissolved days ago. Now, they simply coexisted side by side and he liked it that way. He didn't want to upset or anger her. Leaving Tab all but drooling over the small swords, he reached around the back of the boy, took Nicola by the elbow, and pulled her away from her son. They came to a halt a few feet away and Kenton faced her.

"What did I tell you earlier?" he said quietly. "Your son must be allowed to become a man. Learning how to fight with weapons is part of that growth."

Nicola's brow furrowed. "But why now?" she asked. "He is still a little boy. And why should you take such an interest in him and his education? He is not your son."

It was like throwing cold water on a fire. Kenton's warm expression faded and, as Nicola watched, his eyes, so recently glimmering with kindness, suddenly went cold. He let go of her elbow.

"You are correct, of course," he said, his voice without the gentleness it had held only moments earlier. "I apologize if I have overstepped my bounds. If you want your son to remain uneducated and useless for the rest of his life and fall prey to men who were properly trained as children, then that is your affair. I will not interfere in the manner in which you wish to raise your sons."

With that, he turned away from her and went to the men-at-arms, who were also looking at the small swords over Tab's shoulder. He snapped orders to the men and they began to follow him to the stall where the farmer had bushels of dried vegetables. His manner was businesslike and professional, and not once did he look at Tab as he took his men away. He simply moved on, leaving Tab and Nicola behind.

Nicola watched him go, thinking that perhaps she had been too harsh with him. She *had* been rather brusque, but in her opinion, he had forced her hand. He was not listening to her when it came to Tab and that had infuriated her. Perhaps the man was trying to do something kind for her son, but in any case, he should not have ignored her.

Fighting off an increasing sense of guilt, she went to take Tab by the hand and dragged the unhappy child away from the batons and on towards the vegetable farmer where Kenton and his men were gathering.

Kenton remained standoffish while Nicola went about the task of purchasing dried beans and peas and other items from the farmer. Tab went to stand next to the knight, his young face looking up at the man with great longing for the swords they had left behind, but Kenton wouldn't acknowledge him. Tab did all he could to get Kenton to look at him as Nicola bartered with the farmer but, in the end, Kenton wouldn't look at him at all. His expressionless face was like stone.

Frustrated, Tab finally slipped his hand into Kenton's big, gloved fingers and held on to the knight tightly even though Kenton wouldn't respond. Tab squeezed the man's hand but Kenton wouldn't squeeze back. Finally, Tab dropped his hand, and his head, and went off to stand by himself in dejected silence as Nicola negotiated with the farmer. It was a sad moment for the young boy because, for once in his life, he had a male figure who was interested in him, a man who had been kind to him. That had never really happened in his life. All he knew of men, and in particular his father, was cold ruthlessness. But Kenton was different. He thought that perhaps Kenton might even like him. But that was evidently not the case.

In truth, Kenton liked him a great deal and that was where the problem lay. Nicola's words had wounded him. Aye, she had. He could admit it. *He is not your son.* Up until that moment, Kenton hadn't really thought about Tab's relationship to him one way or another. He simply saw a young boy who desperately needed a man's guidance. In fact, Tab was the same age Kenton's son would have been had he lived.

The gloom of remembrance settled. God, he hadn't thought of his son in ages; he tried *not* to think about it. He tried not to think of the child who had been born to the young wife he'd taken those six years ago, a frail but pretty girl who wasn't able to tolerate the strain of childbirth. Delivering Kenton's enormous son had killed her and ultimately the child hadn't survived, either.

Nay, he didn't like to think on that event or on the guilt that had followed him since. He silently scolded himself for allowing his feelings to get the better of him and attach themselves to young Tab Thorne. He shouldn't have opened himself up to feel something for the boy. Even so, the fatherless boy and the boyless father were establishing a connection, both of them seeking something they lost or had possibly never had – affection. Kenton knew it wasn't healthy for him. With that thought, he tried to be thankful for Nicola's sharp and hurtful words bringing him to his senses.

"There," Nicola said, approaching him. "I believe we settled on a fair price. If you can have your men carry the sacks to the wagon, we can be on our way."

Kenton whistled between his teeth and motioned to his men, who began picking up the bushels of dried vegetables and shuttling them in the direction of the wagon. Nicola pretended to watch what they were doing, making sure they took everything she had agreed to pay for, but the truth was that she was distracted by Kenton and his brooding presence behind her. The man hadn't moved from his spot since they'd left the smithy and she couldn't help but notice Tab, standing off by himself in sad silence.

Both men wounded by her words, now separated, whereas before they had been very happy and companionable. Nicola sighed heavily, thinking that perhaps she had been too harsh with them both. She had always raised her children alone, with no help from Gaylord, who saw children as an inconvenience more than anything. It was difficult to accept advice on raising her boys, but from a man's perspective, perhaps Kenton only meant well. He had no hidden agenda or ulterior motive with Tab. At least, she didn't think so. He seemed to be truly interested in her son's welfare and she was starting to overcome her fear of Kenton using Tab as a hostage. She supposed only time would truly tell on that account, but she didn't sense any ill-will from Kenton. In fact, she only sensed kindness.

Nicola cast a sidelong glance at Kenton, who was standing with his enormous arms folded across his chest as he watched his men load up the wagon. Then, she looked at Tab, who was kicking at the ground dejectedly several feet away. Swallowing her pride, and her fear, she went over to her son and took his hand.

"Come with me," she said quietly.

Tab followed, unhappy, until he realized that his mother was returning to the smithy shack. The smithy had already put the small swords away but Nicola had the man present them again, much to Tab's delight. As the boy fawned over the weaponry, Nicola turned her head in Kenton's direction and spoke loudly.

"I do not know what would make a good sword for you, Tab," she said to Kenton's turned back. "I would hope that someone knowledgeable in such things would help us decide."

Kenton would have had to be deaf not to hear her but instead of turning in her direction, he headed the other way, back towards the wagon. It was clear that he did not wish to speak with her in any case. Undeterred, Nicola scurried after him.

"Sir Kenton," she called. When he kept walking, she came to a frustrated halt and raised her voice. "Sir Kenton, *please!*"

He slowed his pace before coming to an unsteady halt, turning in her direction. The expressionless face was hard. "How may I be of service, Madam?"

So he was going to be difficult about it. Nicola braced herself. "Will you please help Tab select a sword?" she asked politely.

To her surprise, he shook his head. "Nay, Madam," he said. "As you pointed out, he is not my son. It would be presumptuous to make any decisions for him."

Nicola tried not to become angry at his stubborn stance. She had caused it and she knew it, so she did the only thing she could. She apologized.

"It was wrong of me to say that," she said, lowering her voice. "Forgive me. But I... I have never had anyone take such an interest in my children. Not even their father. I simply... Sir Kenton, it is my job to protect them. I have tried to be both mother and father to them, as their father would not be bothered with his own children. To see you take interest in my son… mayhap you can understand or mayhap you cannot… he likes you a great deal and he must not become attached to the man who holds him and everything he owns captive. I cannot let you hurt or influence him, yet you have been very kind to him. I find it all very confusing and confusion makes me protective. I cannot explain it any better than that."

Her halting apology took some of the sting out of Kenton. The truth was that he hadn't thought of it from Nicola's point of view, only his own. With a pensive sigh, he made his way over to her, slowly, looking at the ground as he walked as if there were a good deal on his mind. He came to stand in front of her, still looking at his feet as if mulling over something great and troubling. When he finally spoke, it was quietly.

"It is not my intention to hurt or influence your sons," he finally said. "They are young men in need of male guidance and they have none. It was presumptuous of me to try to fit that role."

Nicola was feeling terribly guilty now. "You are our captor," she said, bewilderment evident in her soft voice. "How can I allow an enemy to guide my sons?"

He looked at her, then. "Do you look at me as your enemy?"

Nicola nodded. Then, she shrugged. She didn't seem to know how to respond. "That is what you are, isn't it?"

Kenton wasn't sure how to respond, either. God help him, he should have been decisive about it. He was indeed her captor. But he couldn't seem to bring himself to take a firm stance on it. His confusion gave way to frustration.

"I am," he said. "But it… Nicola, we have been through a great deal together, you and I. We have seen war and death and we have come out of it somehow oddly unified. When I look at you, I do not see an enemy. I see a beautiful, intelligent, and desirable woman and when I look at your sons, I see three young men desperately in need of someone to guide them. But mayhap there is more to it than that… my own son would have been Tab's age had he lived and when I see Tab, I see what I would hope my own son would have been like – intelligent and brave and strong. It has drawn me to Tab, and to you, and for that, I am sorry. I have confessed my weakness. But it will not happen again."

Ashamed by his confession, he started to turn away but Nicola reached out and grasped his arm before he could move away complete-ly. She held him fast even though he could have very easily pulled away from her. He didn't seem to want to. He kept his eyes on the ground, embarrassed to look at her, as Nicola moved close so only he could hear her.

"I did not know you were married," she said, feeling great disap-pointment and even anger towards him and hoping that it didn't show. What married man would kiss a woman the way he had kissed her? "You never made any indication that you had a wife. In fact...."

He cut her off, suspecting what she was about to say. "My wife died with my son," he confessed. "I hope you do not think I would have kissed you as I have with a wife at home."

Nicola was vastly relieved to hear that. "I do not know you very well," she admitted. "I had hoped you would not make advances towards me if you were married."

He shook his head, his jaw ticking. "Never," he said with finality. "Some men with wives think nothing of bedding another woman but I am not that sort. My loyalty, once given, cannot be revoked."

Nicola believed him without question. She was coming to see the character of the man, her captor, and he did not seem the disloyal type – not to his king and not to a wife. Therefore, she very much believed him.

"Then I am so very sorry for your loss," she murmured in that sweet, honeyed voice that sent chills up his spine. "I did not know of your loss but I completely understand. I, too, lost a child last fall. I still weep for my baby, the little girl who never even drew a breath. So I understand your loss very well. As for Tab, he has been forced to grow up quickly. You already know he is very protective of me, protective enough that he killed his father because of it. I suppose I am very protective over him, sometimes to the extreme. He is such a gentle and thoughtful creature and I do not want to see him hurt."

Kenton was looking at her by then, his gaze guarded. "He is a fine young man already," he said hoarsely. "Again, if I overstepped myself, I am sorry."

Nicola squeezed his arm. In fact, she moved closer to him and ended up holding his big hand. When she squeezed it, he squeezed back.

"If you tell me your intentions with him are honorable, then I shall believe you," she whispered. "Forgive me for being cruel to you when you were only trying to be kind to my son."

Kenton's heart was beating so hard that he felt as if it were about to burst from his chest. His limbs ached and his breathing was painful and labored as Nicola stirred emotions within him that he'd never known before. She had him thinking on his dead son yet again with her confession of a dead daughter. Was it possible that she truly understood the loss of a child? He was letting himself feel things that he had forbidden himself to even entertain; Nicola was bringing them out in him. He was connecting to her as he'd never connected to anyone in his life. Reaching out his free hand, he cupped her sweet face in his enormous palm.

"I will always be kind to your son, Nicola," he confirmed, "as I will always be kind to you. I hope you know that."

Nicola laid her cheek against his gloved hand, feeling such sweetness and warmth from the man. He stirred emotions within her breast that she'd never experienced, emotions of thrill and adoration and desire. This man, her enemy, stirred up her very soul but as she gazed up into his face, her eyes twinkled with a delightful hint of mischief.

"You were not kind at first."

"Neither were you."

She laughed, as did he. "I suppose we were both to blame," she said. He dropped his hand from her face and shook his head. "I will shoulder no blame whatsoever," he told her. "You were stubborn and belligerent. I was forced to react in kind."

She frowned at him, although there was jest in her actions. "You subdued my home," she pointed out. "How was I supposed to act?"

He shrugged, the blue eyes twinkling. "Just as you did, I suppose," he said. "But you should know that I still live in fear of that stubborn, belligerent woman."

He was teasing her and Nicola burst out laughing. "I do not believe that for one moment," she declared, but was interrupted by Tab, over at the smithy stall, calling for her. She waved to her son and faced Kenton once more. "Will you please help him select a weapon? I would be most honored if you would help guide my son in these matters for I know nothing of them."

Kenton's lips twitched with a smile. Of course he could not refuse her. As he opened his mouth to respond, Wellesbourne abruptly appeared at his side.

"Trouble, Kenton," he said, his young face grim. "There is an entire column of Edward's supporters heading in from the south. We spotted them at the southern edge of the market. We must depart quickly to avoid being seen."

Kenton's head snapped around, looking to the southern portion of the market as he strained to see what Wellesbourne was talking about.

"Only fools would wear standards into a town and risk running into men who might be your enemy," he grumbled. "Did you see colors?"

Wellesbourne was looking in the same direction that Kenton was. "Three stags against a field of blue," he said seriously.

Kenton looked at him. "Derby," he said with some disgust and confusion. "What on earth would the man be doing here this far north?"

Wellesbourne cocked an eyebrow. "He could be part of the contingent that left us yesterday," he said. "I would wager to say that the army that kept us bottled up for the past week is still in this area. They will need to recover and restore their supplies much as we have had to do."

Kenton knew that. He also knew that if those men realized another group of armed soldiers had purchased all of the supplies, there might be trouble. They would very well have to defend their food stores. He pointed in the direction of the wagon.

"Get the men moving, Matt," he said. "We will catch up."

Wellesbourne went on the run, back to the provisions wagon and the majority of the men-at-arms. They were still loading up the dried beans and peas and at Wellesbourne's prompting, began loading at a furious pace. In fact, the wagon began moving even as they were still loading, but they managed to get everything onto the wagon with little spillage. As the wagon took off down the road, heading north towards the road that would take them back to Babylon, Kenton rushed to Tab's side. When the boy realized that he was being taken away from the swords again, he balked.

"But can't I have one?" he pleaded as Kenton grabbed him by the shoulder. "Can I have this one?"

He made a grab for the nearest sword and held it up, nearly poking Kenton in the face with it. Kenton, swayed by the look of desperation in the young man's eyes, spoke quickly to the smithy.

"How much for this one?" he asked, looking over his shoulder to see if any of Derby's men were in sight. "But be warned that I will only give you two silver marks and nothing more, so take it or leave it."

The smithy extended his hand. "Sold, my lord," he said. "It will make a fine weapon for the boy."

Quickly, Kenton dug into his purse and pulled forth two silver marks, elaborately etched coins, and put them into the man's hand. And with that, Tab had his very first weapon. The child was so gleeful that he was practically walking on air.

But there was no time to waste with celebration or joy. Kenton pulled Nicola and Tab along with him, rushing back to the spot where the wagon used to be. Two men-at-arms were waiting for them, holding the horses, and Kenton quickly seated Tab followed by Nicola, who was fairly deft and mounting her own horse. Kenton leapt onto his own steed, a charcoal-gray brute from Belgium, and the five of them took off at a fairly clipped pace through the town.

Outside of Manchester, they caught up with the provisions wagon and the rest of the men, making their way in haste back to the welcoming walls of Babylon.

CHAPTER EIGHT

One week later

S HE HAD HAIR as black as a raven's wing, which was appropriate considering her name was Raven. Young, with a sweet and round body, and firm flesh, Wellesbourne knew he wasn't the first man who had bedded her. In fact, she knew far too much about the pleasures of the flesh to be as virginal as she pretended.

Matthew had kept her in his bed all night, physically feasting on all she had to offer. She knew too much about how to make a man squirm; when he was embedded in her body, she would tighten her slick walls around him and fondle his testicles, which only made him mad with lust. Then she would push him over on his back and ride him as one would ride a wild animal and Matthew would spend his time with his hands on her breasts as she plunged her body down on him over and over again. Her climaxes were loud and often, which only fueled his passion. He liked to feel her releases around him. It made him feel virile and masculine.

He woke up on this bright but cold morning to Raven's mouth on his manhood, her heated lips and wicked tongue working him up into a stiffness that would only be sated when he spilled himself into her mouth, but the odd thing was that it felt very much as if there were two mouths upon him and when he lifted the coverlet, he could see Raven and another woman, her pale sister he thought, working him into a frenzy.

Two women. Wellesbourne rather liked that and he lay back and permitted the women to pleasure him until he could stand it no more. He grabbed Raven by the hair because she was the closest to him, pushed her over onto her belly and mounted her from behind as the other woman latched onto his mouth and kissed him furiously as he thrust into Raven. He fondled the pale woman's breasts as he kissed her, repeatedly impaling Raven on his big, hard manhood, and he enjoyed every minute of it.

It had been a long time since he'd had double the pleasure like this, even if the pale girl wasn't the beauty her sister was. Still, she had some skill. He managed to pull out of Raven's tight body before releasing himself, sending ribbons of pearl-colored liquid onto Raven's smooth back. Then, and only then, did the other woman stop kissing him as she climbed off the bed and used the end of the coverlet to wipe off Raven's back. Then, she climbed back into bed with Raven and the two began giggling.

Exhausted from a night of sexual activity that had both drained and rejuvenated him, Matthew went to the basin in his chamber and splashed cold water on his face. He had duties to attend to even though he wanted to crawl back into bed with the two giggling women. Wellesbourne was the best of the best, a serious knight with great training and wisdom and skill, but he was also oversexed. It tended to be the butt of jokes from those who knew him well.

Matthew loved women, loved to bed them, and was sweet and kind to those he managed to deflower. But there was no sense of marriage or of having a lasting relationship in his mind or heart; he was too young for either. Therefore, he bedded every woman who caught his fancy and left a string of heartbroken hearts from Dover to Newcastle. Tales of Matthew Wellesbourne's sexual exploits were almost as legendary as his knightly reputation.

A knock on the door distracted him from flirting with the two women in his bed. Rolling his eyes with frustration at the interruption, he went to the door, completely nude, and put his hand on the latch.

"Who goes there?" he demanded.

A deeply frightening voice answered. "If you do not open the door, you will find out in the most painful way possible."

With a grin, Matthew opened the door to find Gaston de Russe standing there. Impossibly enormous, powerful, dark, and frightening, Gaston de Russe was as ominous and terrifying as Matthew was congenial and benevolent. The two were also the best of friends as well as cousins. Gaston shoved the door open and stepped into the room, immediately spying the women in Matthew's bed. He sighed heavily.

"Why am I not surprised?" he grumbled, pointing to the women and then flicking his hand in the direction of the door. "Out, both of you. I will not tell you again."

Orders from the knight they called The Dark One were not meant to be questioned or disobeyed. The women began to scurry, picking up their clothes from the floor, trying to dress and protect their modesty from the big, dark knight, which was a ridiculous thing to do. It wasn't as if he gave any care to either one of them. He did, however, turn his back on them to face Matthew as the women frantically dressed.

"Did you get any sleep?" he asked Matthew wryly.

Matthew was still grinning at his big cousin. "Of course I did," he said, turning away and going in search of his breeches. "At least, I think I did. A little, I suppose. Come to think of it, I do not know."

Gaston shook his head at the man, resigned to Matthew's behavior. "Your father said he was going to marry you off soon," he said. "Maybe that will curtail these primal urges you seem to have."

Matthew found his leather bottoms and pulled them on. "Not any time soon," he sniffed. "My father has been threatening to betroth me for a few years now but he has yet to do it."

"Doesn't he have someone in mind?"

Matthew shrugged. "He says he does," he replied. "The niece of an ally, I think. Howard Terrington. Do you remember him?"

Gaston nodded his head. "I do indeed," he said. "I do not like him.

He is shifty and I do not trust him. His niece, you say?"

Matthew made a face. "She is only five years of age," he said, unhappy. "I am sure I can talk my father out of it."

Gaston cracked a smile. "Why?" he asked. "You will have to marry, eventually. If your wife is five years of age then you will not have to marry her for quite some time, at least another ten years of so."

Matthew simply shook his head as he secured the ties on his breeches. He glanced up as Raven and the other woman ran past him, fully clothed, and disappeared into the darkened corridors beyond. He sighed.

"Is that what you came to talk to me about?" he asked Gaston, irritated. "You want to know when I am getting married?"

Gaston grunted and shook his head, moving over to the bed and sniffing the air. "Jesus Christ," he hissed. "It smells as if animals have been mating in here."

Matthew crossed his muscular arms over his broad chest. "Did you also come to criticize me?"

Gaston fought off a grin as he moved to the lancet window that overlooked the eastern portion of Babylon's walls. "Nay," he said, pleased that he had managed to annoy his usually easy-going cousin. "I came to talk to you about le Bec. Has he said anything more to you about the move on Manchester?"

Matthew shook his head. "Not since Warwick departed last week," he said. "Why do you ask?"

Gaston was looking out over the countryside. The snows had melted surprisingly fast because the past week had been clear weather with bright sun. Now, all he could see were fields of dead grass beneath the sunshine. Below him in the inner ward, the castle was going about its business and the sections of wall that had been damaged by two successive sieges were being repaired from a quarry nearby. Aye, everything was back to normal. But it shouldn't have been. He turned to Matthew.

"Warwick gave Kenton specific instructions to plan for the subjugation of Rochdale and Manchester," he said. "Kenton should have at least have come up with a plan during this past week but I have heard nothing. I thought he might have said something to you."

Matthew uncrossed his arms and looked away, heading to the chair where his heavy woolen tunic was slung over the back. He collected his tunic and pulled it over his curly blond hair.

"He has not said anything to me about it," he replied, somewhat subdued. "Have you asked de Birmingham or Forbes or le Mon?"

Gaston nodded. "They are as much in the dark as we are."

Matthew pondered that a moment. "Kenton has been too busy with Lady Thorne and her children to worry about a siege on Manchester."

Gaston nodded. "I know," he agreed. "I have seen it, too. So have his men. I suppose that was the point I was driving at. Le Bec is very distracted and if word gets back to Warwick, he will not be pleased."

Matthew knew that. "We have fought with Kenton le Bec since we were both knighted," he said. "He is the consummate knight, professional and perfect. He was at Towton, for Christ's Sake, and survived it, so that is some indication to the man's skill. But I also heard he lost a wife and child a few years ago. It is not wrong for a man to want to fill that void, Gaston."

Gaston glanced at him. "Nay, it is not wrong," he said, "but Warwick will not see it that way. Do not take my statements as condemnation against le Bec; I respect and admire him a great deal. But if Warwick finds out he has been distracted by Lady Thorne, it is quite possible that Warwick will send the lady away. You know this as well as I do. If he is forced to do that, it will not go well for le Bec."

Matthew sat down on the chair to pull his boots on. "Then mayhap we should bring that up to the man."

Gaston shrugged. "And if he does not respond? Do we send word to Warwick that le Bec is otherwise occupied and Manchester will have to wait?"

Matthew shook his head. "We do *not*," he said. "Gaston, I have no great love for Warwick. You know that. My loyalty would much rather be with le Bec for I know he is a true and loyal knight. I feel in this case that we must speak with le Bec and voice our concerns, for his sake. If le Bec does not move on Manchester, Warwick will come down on him. Even if he knows that, he must be reminded. Mayhap that is all he needs – a reminder that we are expecting something great from him. And so is Warwick."

Gaston nodded with some resignation. "I never thought I would see the day where Kenton le Bec would stray from his orders."

Matthew finished with his boots and stood up. "He has not strayed," he replied steadily. "He is simply off course a bit. A beautiful woman will do that to a man."

"Not me."

"You are not a man."

Matthew barely dodged the giant fist that came flying out at him. With a grin, he led the way from his chamber as the pair went in search of Kenton le Bec. The man had to be set on course again or bad tidings in the form of Warwick's wrath could befall him. Matthew and Gaston would try to prevent it if they could.

As the knights passed down the stairs that would take them to the entry level one floor below, they failed to see two little forms tucked back in the alcove that was just outside of Matthew's door.

Raven and Liesl were hovering there, having heard everything Matthew and Gaston had spoken of. They were young, and naturally curious, and the conversation about le Bec and Lady Thorne did not surprise either of them. Spending as much time as they did around Lady Thorne, they knew she spent a great deal of time with le Bec. And they knew she seemed to like it.

But hearing the knights speak of the attention between Kenton and Nicola, they wondered if they shouldn't say something to Lady Thorne about it. Perhaps she would want to know that Kenton's knights were suspicious of their lord's behavior and that it could cause problems with Warwick. They brought the information to the attention of Janet, who told them to keep their silly mouths closed. It was none of their business, anyway, and if rumors got started, Janet swore she would take a switch to them both.

Therefore, the girls kept their mouths closed, at least to rumors, but when it came to Matthew Wellesbourne, their mouths were anything but closed.

He rather liked it that way.

CHAPTER NINE

"PULL!" KENTON COMMANDED. "If you do not pull, he will get away!"

Teague was trying as hard as he could but the fish seemed stronger than he was. It was only a small pond, one inside the kitchen yard where they kept a supply of fish, but the trout had grown fat in the winter time feeding off of the algae in the pond and they were more than a match for three small boys.

It was cold in the shadow of the keep this day even though the sun was shining and the sky above was a bright blue. The boys were crowded around the pond with a fishing line and hook that Kenton had given them. It all started when Tab told the man one evening over mutton stew that he didn't know how to fish, nor had he ever been fishing, which prompted Kenton to remedy the situation. Gerik, who could make just about anything, helped Kenton make three fishing lines for the boys to use.

Even now, in the cold of the kitchen yard, Kenton and Gerik were teaching their young captives to fish using the lines. Gone were the days of keeping the boys confined to the fourth floor apartments; that had ended the day Kenton had returned from Manchester with Lady Thorne. The family was allowed free rein about the castle and Lady Thorne was freely permitted to return to her duties as Lady of Babylon as if she and her family were not prisoners. Much had changed after that day, in fact.

Kenton had changed.

But the knights hadn't said anything about the obvious change in the man and his attention towards Lady Thorne and her brood. A good example of his change in attitude was the fishing. The Kenton le Bec of old would have never done such a thing and he certainly would not have done it with captive children. But he was doing it now and he had Gerik roped into it. Not that Gerik minded because he could be a rather relaxed character at times. He wasn't thinking what the other knights were thinking: *what has happened to le Bec?* But, wisely, no one said a word. No one wanted to enrage le Bec.

As Kenton and Gerik lingered around the edge of the castle pond, supervising, the fishing was going well enough for Tab and Teague but Tiernan hadn't had a bite since they'd started. The three-year-old was quite frustrated to the point where his mother had to intervene. Bundled up against the cold, Nicola helped Tiernan toss the line and tug on it to lure the fish in. Kenton was helping Tab while the big, bear-like knight was being quite patient with Teague, who became very upset when a fish he thought he caught swam away. He'd tried to pull on it just like Kenton told him to but the fish still escaped. Frustrated, he kept tossing his line into the murky water, hoping to lure it back.

Tiernan, the silent child, was the first one to catch a fish, which utterly discouraged Tab and Teague. Tab was determined not to let his baby brother best him and continued trying very hard while Teague, eventually bored and dejected, left the pond and ran over to the corral where the lambs were huddled with their mothers. He was more interested in playing with a lamb, which he carried out of the corral and ran to show his mother. The little lamb's legs were dangling as Teague excitedly brought the little beast to display to his mother and brothers. When he put the little creature on the ground, the lamb took off running and, delighted, Teague and Tiernan followed. So did Nicola, trying to keep control of her frisky twins.

Now, there was only one child fishing in the murky castle pond but

Tab was determined to catch as many fish as he could. He confiscated his brothers' fishing lines and tried to work all three as Kenton and Gerik helped.

"Pull, lad," Kenton encouraged Tab again. "But not too hard; you do not want to tear the hook out of his mouth. He'll get away if you do."

Tab was biting his lip, concentrating on all three lines. "But he is pulling away from me."

"Then you must pull harder. Show him that you are in command."

Tab glanced at the knight even as he started to become entangled in the fishing lines. "He is just a fish," he said. "He will not know I am in command. He only understands fish things."

Kenton grinned. "That is true," he said. "But all creatures understand force. You must show him your force is stronger than his."

Tab pondered that idea for a moment. "That is what men do, isn't it?" he asked. "Try to prove their force is stronger than someone else's?"

Kenton's smile faded at the simple but true concept of war, and life in general, from the young lad. "That is quite true," he said. "You are very astute."

"What does that mean?"

"It means wise."

Tab liked that thought. He felt complimented, praised even. In fact, this entire afternoon had been filled with something he'd never experienced before – a man taking an interest in him with something as small as fishing. Not even his own father had ever done that. But this big knight, the man who had conquered his castle, was taking a great deal of interest in him and his brothers. That was utterly new in Tab's world.

With that in mind, he tried very hard to manage the three lines. In some way, he wanted to make Sir Kenton proud of him and what he was doing. He liked it very much when the man gave him his approval, filling a need in the boy that had never been met. It was a need Tab never even knew he had.

"I am going to show this fish that I am bigger and stronger than he is," he declared. "I will show *all* of the fish I am bigger and stronger. I will catch them all!"

Kenton stood next to the boy, his smile returning at the lad's boast. "You can try," he said. "But it may prove difficult. Fish are very fast."

"I am faster!"

"They may not wish to be caught, then."

Tab was resolute. "I will catch them, anyway," he said. "When I catch them, I will cut their heads off and eat them!"

Kenton snorted, putting a big hand on Tab's blond head. "I believe you."

Tab looked up, grinning openly at Kenton before returning his attention to the tangled fishing lines. When Gerik, standing a few feet away, tried to help untangle them, Kenton waved his knight off. This was Tab's fight, after all, and they would let him fight it alone. It seemed that all the boy needed was a bit of encouragement, which Kenton was happy to provide.

Kenton's gaze moved from Tab to the boy's mother several feet away as she trailed after the twins. The boys were playing with the little lamb and Nicola meandered after them, smiling at her little boys and their frolics. Kenton was starting to notice everything about her now, from the way her hair fell against her neck to the dimple in her chin when she would smile. If he'd merely been fascinated with her before, the past several days had seen him become completely enamored with her and everything about her. Every movement, every word enthralled him. His attention increasingly on her, he couldn't help but move in her direction. It seemed the most natural of things.

Nicola, meanwhile, had no idea she was being stalked. She had moved away from the pond and was following the twins as they played with the little lamb, which was becoming quite frisky and playful. It would jump in the air and try to head-butt the little boys, who were delighted at the antics. Nicola stood back, grinning, as Teague was butted by the little lamb and fell over, giggling.

"My lady," came a quiet, deep voice from behind. "I fear we may have an issue."

Nicola turned around to see Kenton standing behind her, a faint smile on his face. She smiled in return, instantly, as she had so many times over the past few days. Ever since the return from Manchester, Kenton was ready to smile at her and she was ready to smile in return. Gone was the serious, stone-faced knight she had first become acquainted with. Gone was the belligerence between them. These days, there were no arguments. Thankfully, there was peace.

"What issue is that?" she asked.

Kenton threw a thumb over his shoulder at Tab, who was standing by the pond's edge with Gerik behind him. "Young Tab has declared he will not stop fishing until he has caught every fish in the pond," he said. "I have tried to suggest that such a thing may not be possible but you may wish to speak with him as well."

Nicola looked at her eldest boy with two fishing lines in his hands. She laughed softly. "He is quite determined once his mind is set," she said. "But I will see what I can do."

Kenton nodded, his gaze lingering warmly on her as it had so often over the past few days. "I am sure that you can move mountains with him," he said softly. "At least, you could with me."

Nicola looked up into his handsome face, feeling quite warm and giddy by his statement. He had flirted with her quite heavily over the past few days but it hadn't gone beyond that. He hadn't even kissed her. It was as if he were trying to charm her into submission first, which she nearly liked better. She'd never had a man try to charm her in her life.

"How flattering, my lord," she said, lowering her lashes coyly. It was something she'd learned to do with him as of late, something he seemed to like a great deal. "You are too kind."

He snorted. "I tell the truth," he said, eyeing her. "I was wondering, in fact...."

He trailed off and she cocked her head, smiling at him. "What were you wondering?" she asked.

He cleared his throat softly. "I was wondering if tonight after sup, if you would join me in the solar for warmed wine and conversation," he said, somewhat awkwardly. He wasn't a man used to *asking* anything; all he ever gave were commands. "I would be pleased if you would be agreeable."

Nicola smiled broadly. "Conversation?" she repeated, toying with him. "Whatever could we speak of?"

"Many things."

"You must give me an example."

Kenton pursed his lips. He could see that she was jesting with him. "We will discuss how obstinate you are. And how beautiful."

She laughed softly. "May we also speak of how forceful and determined you are?"

"Those are my good qualities."

Her laughter grew. "Then I would be honored to converse with you about such things," she said. "I must put the boys to bed first but I would be happy to join you when I have finished."

"Then I shall look forward to it."

Nicola flushed sweetly, flattered by his invitation. So much had changed between them over the past week that it was as if they were two entirely different people who had only just met, and whose attraction to one another had been obvious and strong from the onset. She was so caught up in gazing at the man, who was looking at her rather bashfully, that she was genuinely startled when the lamb butted Tiernan, catching the boy off balance, and he fell down on a rock. He howled at his scraped knee.

Forgetting the sweet flirt with Kenton, Nicola picked her son off the ground and soothed his tears. He had a bit of blood, and his breeches were torn, so she begged leave from Kenton and took both twins into the keep with her.

Kenton watched her go, his gaze lingering on the seductive sway of her hips as she walked. In fact, he couldn't see anything else but her. He was consumed by the shapely vision, recalling snippets of her voice and flashes of her smile now that she was out of his sight. He had no idea how long Conor had been standing next to him when he finally noticed the man. He tried not to appear surprised or off-guard, but he couldn't quite manage it. He flinched.

"God's Bones," he muttered. "Why would you sneak up on me like that?"

Conor was looking at him with a glimmer in his eye. "You have always heard me approach before."

Kenton knew exactly what he meant. He'd been very distracted with Nicola, so distracted that those uncanny senses he usually had, like feeling a man sneak up on him, had been dulled. Rather than become angry about it, because it was the truth, Kenton simply shrugged and avoided acknowledging what Conor already knew. He tried not to appear embarrassed.

"What do you want?" he asked simply.

Conor threw a thumb over his shoulder, in the direction of the inner ward. "Wellesbourne and de Russe have need to speak with you," he said. "Are you available?"

Kenton nodded. "I am," he said as he began to move towards the ward. He was eager to move past the fact he'd flinched like a woman when Conor came upon him. "Where are they?"

Conor moved with him. "By the stables," he said. "They were looking for you. I told them I would send you to them."

Kenton's gaze was moving to the ward and the stables beyond as he approached the gate in the wall that separated the kitchen yard from the rest of the inner ward. "Did they tell you what they wished to speak of?"

Conor shook his head. "Nay," he replied. "Do you want me to accompany you?"

"You may as well."

They passed through the kitchen gate, an arched portal that was built into the thickness of the wall. A very heavy iron grate was built into it, separating the kitchen yard from the inner ward. Kenton and Conor moved into the inner ward, which was crowded with men camping in various circles. Since there were so many men stationed at

Babylon now, what men couldn't fit into the keep or hall had to stay outside in the elements, so the inner ward was peppered with small encampments that surrounded small fires.

Smoke from those fires lingered heavy in the cold air, so much so that Kenton's eyes were stinging because of it. As he and Conor approached the stables, they were met by Wellesbourne and de Russe emerging. Wellesbourne smiled, that easy smile that came so readily to him, at the sight of Kenton.

"Can I talk you into selling me your stud?" he asked. "I have a beautiful roan mare that would breed spectacular animals from him."

Kenton shook his head firmly. "That stallion is closer to me than a brother," he said. "I would sooner cut off my right hand than sell the beast."

Wellesbourne shrugged. "It was worth a try," he said. "Mayhap you will permit me to breed my mare to him, anyway. We shall breed them twice and each take a result."

Kenton cocked his head thoughtfully. "I would consider that," he said. "But I will get the first offspring."

Matthew chuckled. "Agreed," he said. "My mare is at Wellesbourne Castle so at some point, we will need to take your stud to Wellesbourne to accomplish this great task."

Kenton simply nodded, looking between Wellesbourne and de Russe, who had thus far remained silent. That wasn't unusual with Gaston, however. The man didn't speak much. Kenton's gaze lingered on the pair.

"I understand you two wish to speak with me," he said. "Shall we go inside the keep or do you wish to speak to me here?"

Wellesbourne immediately moved for the keep. "Inside," he said. "The smoke in the ward is burning my eyes to cinder. If I remain out here any longer, I shall go blind."

Kenton nodded silently but suspected that wasn't the only reason they wanted to move inside. It was much more private in there, away from the ears of the soldiers, and he sensed that Wellesbourne wanted that privacy. It made him very curious as to what, exactly, Welles-bourne and de Russe wished to speak with him about. His curiosity grew to epic proportions, so much so that by the time they reached the solar inside the keep of Babylon, they were barely inside the room when Kenton came to a halt and turned to them. He was out of patience.

"What is this about?" he nearly demanded. "What is so important that we had to come where it was private to discuss it?"

Matthew kept his gaze on Kenton even though Gaston cast Matthew a long look. As the knight known as The Dark One moved for the pitcher of wine that was over near the cluttered table, Matthew didn't keep Kenton waiting. It was clear that the man was impatient, which already put the conversation on edge before it even started.

"Matters of Warwick, my lord," Matthew said evenly. "The last we were told, you were to be planning the acquisition of Rochdale and Manchester for Henry. We have been at Babylon over a week and have not heard of these plans yet. We would like to offer to help you with the planning if you have not already done so."

It was a very polite way of asking Kenton if he'd moved forward with obeying Warwick's directives. Kenton knew that; he knew it very well. Wellesbourne was asking it in the kindest way possible – there were no accusations or condemnation that plans which should have been made, or at least discussed, days ago had not yet even been considered.

Even so, Kenton could already feel guilt creeping into his veins. He felt defensive. These seasoned knights knew he had orders and they further knew he hadn't done anything about them. They would have been fools not to have figured out why he hadn't acted on anything yet, and these men were no fools. It was then that Kenton began to realize that every knight under his command must have known his distraction with Lady Thorne. There was no way they could not have known. He'd been far too obvious about it, even careless about it.

Wellesbourne's question should have come along much sooner than it had. Kenton, struggling to know what to feel about the query and the reasons behind it, turned for the messy table that held maps and parchment and other implements that a warring commander needed to carry out orders. That *he* needed to carry out orders. Orders he had, for the past week, soundly ignored.

"The truth is that I have not considered any plans to march on Rochdale or Manchester yet," he said, sighing. It was the truth. "My priority has been to ensure the men inside the castle were fed and there was some semblance of a military installation formed. One cannot launch attacks if one's men are not well fed or even well rested. Most of the men within these walls have been fighting battles for the better part of six months, me included. A few days rest for them has been the priority. Has that not occurred to you?"

Matthew shook his head. "It has not," he admitted. "I suppose that is why you are the commander and we are not. You are correct in that they need food and rest. Forgive me for questioning your methods, le Bec. We were only offering to assist if you needed it."

Kenton couldn't get too angry about it although he knew that wasn't entirely the truth. "Is it?" he asked, cocking a doubtful eyebrow. "This would not have anything to do with the time I have spent with Lady Thorne, would it?"

Wellesbourne lifted his eyebrows, unwilling to answer, as he turned to glance at de Russe, who was already halfway in to a full cup of wine. De Russe noticed that Wellesbourne was looking at him, perhaps seeking some support for their actions. Even if Wellesbourne was unwilling to answer, perhaps trying to be tactful, de Russe had no such compunction. The man was candid to a fault.

"It does," de Russe said bluntly. "You have spent a great deal of time with a woman who is your captive. Le Bec, your motives are your own. We will not question what you do with the woman. But should Warwick catch wind of your attention towards her, and should he also catch wind of the fact that you have not yet moved against Rochdale or Manchester, he might make it difficult for you."

It was a very honest answer and Kenton was well aware. His jaw ticked, thinking on his reply, but it was Conor who made the first move. He put himself between Kenton and de Russe, glaring at de Russe as Kenton had not seen the man glare, ever. The big, red-haired knight's nostrils flared as he faced down de Russe.

"You are not in command, de Russe," he growled. "Kenton le Bec is in charge of Babylon and of the western road, and you will not question the man in any fashion."

Gaston was at least a head and a half taller than Conor. Compared to the men around him, and they were all big men, de Russe was a giant. His smoke-colored eyes narrowed at de Birmingham.

"Someone has to question him since you and your comrades have not had the courage to do so," he said, slandering Conor's bravery in the first strike of their verbal battle. "Everyone at Babylon knows that le Bec is interested in Lady Thorne. He makes it obvious every single day, but soon that interest and his lack of action in carrying out Warwick's orders is going to get back to Warwick and we are all going to be in trouble because of it. Did that not occur to you?"

Conor was balling a fist which almost always preceded him throwing a punch. Against de Russe, that would be suicide. Conor was an excellent knight but simply by sheer size and strength alone, de Russe could quite easily harm him. Kenton, knowing this, stepped around the table and quickly put himself between the pair.

"Conor, go and summon Gerik and Ackerley," he said quietly. "Go, now. Bring them here. We must all discuss this."

Conor's cheeks were flushed with rage. "But…."

"Carry out my order. I will not tell you again."

Conor was having great difficulty complying but, ultimately, he was an obedient knight. He had never refused an order from Kenton and he wasn't going to start now. Glaring daggers at de Russe, he quit the solar to carry out Kenton's order. When the knight was gone, Kenton turned to de Russe.

"He is as fast as lightning," he said in a low voice. "You may crush him in the end, but you would not come away undamaged. If I hear that you two have battled it out, I will send you away. Is that clear?"

De Russe nodded, unimpressed by Kenton's assessment of de Birmingham's skills. "It is," he said. "But if he strikes first, I will defend myself."

"Understood," Kenton replied, his gaze lingering on the big and mighty de Russe. "Did it ever occur to you and Wellesbourne that I have spent time with Lady Thorne for reasons other than bedding the woman, which I've not done in any case?"

De Russe shook his head faintly as Kenton looked to Wellesbourne. "Did it occur to you?"

Matthew shook his head. "I am not entirely sure what you mean."

Kenton lifted his eyebrows and moved away from the pair. "You two are very young," he said, heading back to the cluttered table. "Wellesbourne, how old are you?"

"I have seen twenty-two years in August," Matthew replied. He jabbed a thumb in Gaston's direction. "He saw twenty-two years in April."

Kenton's focus moved between them. "Twenty-two years," he muttered. "You both make me feel very old at nearly forty years. But the point is that I have seen much more than you have in my lifetime. There is more to winning a war than simply overpowering castles and laying siege to cities. Sometimes the mental aspect of war is far more critical."

Matthew crossed his big arms curiously. "What do you mean?"

Kenton pulled up a stool and sat next to the table. "You must win minds over more than bodies," he said. "Lady Thorne was married to Gaylord Thorne, an enemy of Henry, for many years. She knows his allies and mayhap she even knows what they have discussed. There could be treachery afoot that I do not know about. I cannot beat any information out of the woman. It is in my best interest to be gentle with her in order to discover what she knows. Hell, already I know that it is impossible to threaten the woman into submission. I have tried. Now, I am trying another tactic."

It made sense. Matthew looked to Gaston, who simply poured himself another cup of wine. Matthew was beginning to feel badly about their thoughts towards Kenton, thinking the man had been off-course because of a lovely woman, but he wasn't sure how Gaston felt about any of it because Gaston wouldn't look at him. Gaston had great difficulty in admitting that he was wrong, in any case. Although Matthew wasn't entirely sure that what Kenton was telling them was the entire truth, he didn't argue with the man. He gave him the benefit of the doubt.

"Then I greatly admire your wisdom," he said to Kenton. "Forgive us if we overstepped our bounds. It was out of concern, I assure you."

Kenton nodded, now feeling extremely guilty that he had lied to these knights. He hadn't been doing anything of the sort with Nicola, being kind to her to extract intelligence from her, but he wanted them to think he was. Kenton paid attention to Nicola because he wanted to, pure and simple. It had nothing to do with pressing her for information because he was quite sure she didn't know what her husband had been involved in. But for nosy young knights, he would put them in their place and lie to them. It sounded logical, logical enough that they believed him. At least, he hoped so.

"I am grateful for your concern," he said simply. "But now that you are here, let us finally speak of the move on Rochdale and Manchester. I agree that we must move as soon as possible to claim those cities, mayhap as early as next week. The men are supplied and rested so there is no longer any reason to delay."

Matthew nodded firmly, snapping his fingers at Gaston to join them as he moved closer to the table where Kenton was pulling forth a map of Lancashire. Gaston, downing his second cup of wine, obeyed the wordless command and moved towards the table as well. He, too, was eager to move past the uncomfortable conversation of the last few minutes. Now, they would move forward with Warwick's orders and le Bec was doing what he had been ordered to do – plan the advancement of Henry's cause. Matthew and Gaston were satisfied.

Conor, Gerik, and Ackerley joined them several minutes later and the six of them plunged into some serious war planning. Kenton wasn't oblivious to Conor and Gerik and Ackerley as they glared at de Russe over Kenton's head and, at one point, Kenton quite pointedly stepped on Conor's toe when the man began to grumble over a suggestion from de Russe. Conor took the hint, and his injured toe, and moved away from the table. Kenton didn't want any animosity between men who would face battle together so it was important to quell whatever hard feelings had arisen. Conor behaved himself for the rest of the day and the situation soon settled somewhat.

But the settled situation between the knights would be the only settled situation Kenton would face. He discovered that quite clearly when he entered the hall for the evening meal and quickly realized that Nicola was avoiding him. Concerned, as well as oddly hurt, he let her. He didn't know what was wrong but he intended to find out.

When the meal was finished, he went on a hunt for the Lady of Babylon.

CHAPTER TEN

TIERNAN'S KNEE WAS hardly worth the fuss the child put up over it. When Nicola brought the twins back to their fourth floor apartments and gently tended the child's scraped knee, she had to shake her head over the fit the child was putting up. Janet held the boy and soothed him while Mam eased the sting of the wound and promised to bring him some treats from the kitchen. That seemed to ease Tiernan's pain and she left him cuddling with the servant woman while she made her way down to the lower floors.

Headed down the narrow spiral stairs that led to the entry level, she passed by Raven and Liesl on their way up. It was mid-morning and the girls were carrying fresh linens and freshly baked rye bread and salty butter for the boys to eat. Nicola told them where she was going, to seek something tempting from the kitchens for Tiernan, and instructed the young women to bathe the boys while she was gone. The young women agreed and continued up the stairs, but not before Nicola saw a very big love bite on the top of Raven's left shoulder. It then occurred to her that Liesl appeared somewhat disheveled and weary as well.

Thoughts lingering on the two young women, Nicola continued down the steps. She was trying to recollect when last she saw them. As always, they slept in her apartments and she had seen them when they had all gone to bed the night before. But this was the first time she had seen them all morning. Janet had been in the room when she'd awoken

---

but the two younger girls had not. The love bite on Raven's shoulder told her where the women had spent their evening.

Knights. She had been concerned from the onset that dark and lovely Raven and impressionable Liesl would fall victim to le Bec's men. Truth be told, she believed the girls had been bedded by some of Gaylord's men, too, so it wasn't simply le Bec's knights who were using them for comfort. She'd said something to Gaylord about it, once, months ago before he died, and he had simply told her to keep her mouth shut, so she had. But with Gaylord gone and her relationship with Kenton much better than it had ever been with her husband, she intended to say something to him about it. She didn't want bastards running around Babylon. They had enough to deal with without the added burden of children to unwed girl-servants.

Indeed, it was something to discuss with Kenton, sooner rather than later. Although she intended to head to the kitchen to see if old Hermenia had something to tempt Tiernan and cheer him up, her thoughts were lingering on Kenton and his knights. She knew he was around, somewhere nearby as he always was, and she thought to seek him out before ending up at the kitchen.

There was business on her mind but the truth was that she simply wanted to see Kenton again. Her thoughts were never far from him these days, his sweetly awkward flirtation and his kindness towards her and her boys. She was quite smitten with the man, if she were to admit such a thing, neglecting the fact that he was her captor. That word, that situation, didn't seem to exist any longer. The days since their visit to Manchester had seen to that. Things were more wonderful at Babylon these days than they had ever been, at least as far as her happiness. For the first time in her life, she was actually happy.

With thoughts of handsome Kenton on her mind, Nicola was heading for the keep entry with the intention of looking outside for Kenton when voices from Gaylord's solar caught her attention. The door wasn't quite closed and there were multiple male voices coming forth. Nicola thought she heard Kenton's voice and moved closer, timidly, wondering if she could interrupt their conversation or if she should simply wait for another time. In order to do that, she listened to a few snips of the dialogue to see if they were seriously discussing something or if they were simply talking about something inconsequential.

She soon found out.

"… was married to Gaylord Thorne, an enemy of Henry, for many years. She knows his allies and mayhap she even knows what they have discussed. There could be treachery afoot that I do not know about. I cannot beat any information out of the woman. It is in my best interest to be gentle with her in order to discover what she knows. Hell, already I know that it is impossible to threaten the woman into submission. I have tried. Now, I am trying another tactic."

It was Kenton, discussing her with as much emotion or enthusiasm as one would discuss the enemy. *The enemy.* Stunned, Nicola moved back, away from the door, her mind reeling and her heart sinking. With Kenton's words rolling over and over in her head, she stumbled away from the solar door, moving blindly for the entry and rushing from the keep. As she ran, she could only think of one thing – *he spoke of me as if I am nothing to him but his enemy.*

I *am* the enemy!

In a humiliated daze, she found herself out in the inner ward, surrounded by enemy soldiers, who were all looking at the lady of the keep with some interest. They all knew who she was and they all knew that le Bec had been keeping company with her, which was why no one moved to speak with her in any fashion. To do so would incur the wrath of le Bec.

But Nicola wasn't aware of what the soldiers were thinking, nor did she care. She passed through the gate that separated the inner ward from the kitchen yard, immediately hit by the smell of roasting pig. Hermenia and a couple of the soldiers had killed one of the remaining young pigs and the scent was heavy in the yard.

The old cook was stirring one of the three big pots of stew that they seemed to have going at any given time. Since their return from

Manchester, the pots would hold different things – porridge to fill empty bellies, or beans and pork fat, or even mutton stew. There was always something going and the smells were often overwhelming in the cold, heavy air.

Nicola came to a halt just inside the gate, watching old Hermenia stir a pot full of provisions she and Kenton had brought back from Manchester. The mere remembrance of that day, that lovely day when he spoke so sweetly to her, now brought a knot to the pit of her stomach. Now, the shock of his words was wearing off and the realization was hitting. *It was true, all of it.* She stood there a moment, sinking further and further into despair.

The reality was staggering – she was smitten with a man who had only been using her. She couldn't even begin to describe the desolation she felt, the sheer anguish at her own idiocy. Why hadn't she realized that before that Kenton was only using her? How could she have been so foolish? He'd played upon her emotions and, like a silly woman, she had let him. She had agreed most readily to everything he said or did as of late, his tall and dark handsomeness blinding her to the truth of the man's character.

He was her enemy and she had all but given him the key to her heart.

Dear God, why hadn't she seen any of this before?

No one had touched her heart, ever, and for good reason. Now, she knew without a doubt that all men were liars and abusers. Gaylord abused her body but Kenton abused her soul. Never again would she allow a man to betray her. Never again would she be stupid to his true motives. At that moment, something inside of Nicola died just a little bit, something warm and soft and loving. It died because she killed it.

She would not make the same mistake ever again.

Turning away from the sight of the food, she wandered back over to the stables were the animals were crowded in, eating grain and dried fruits as given to them by the stable servants. Nicola wandered all the way to the back of the stable, into a stall where Tab's pony was happily

147

crunching oats, and sat heavily near the manger. The tears came then.

She wept all afternoon but when she finally emerged from the stables, it was with greater resolve than ever before. If Kenton thought he was going to use her, then he was sadly mistaken. It was she who now had a plan.

Kenton le Bec would not have the last laugh in all of this.

She would.

THE EVENING FEAST was a fragrant and sticky affair, with so many men crowding into the great hall of Babylon that the air itself was not only warm, it was moist. Men were sweating because of the roaring blaze in the malfunctioning hearth, coughing as they ate with all of the smoke in the room. But it was much better than the alternative, being out in the snowy February night.

Dark clouds had rolled in throughout the afternoon and as the sun set, a dusting of white powder began to fall. The inner and outer wards still had dirty snow in them from the last snowfall, so the new snow was simply piling onto the dirty black mounds that were already there. It made for wet and miserable conditions, so there were many men crowded inside the hall and inside the keep, trying to stay dry and warm.

Fortunately, there was enough food to feed them. Hermenia and her help had a pork and bean stew that included carrots and parsnips, great chunks of grainy bread, butter, cheese, big slabs of fried, salty pig skin, tart apple pies with cinnamon and cloves and honey, and ultimately a good deal of warmed wine.

In all, it made for pleasant feasting with the exception of Gaylord's mad mother having emerged from her closeted hovel in the entry to create an interruption. The woman's nightly dance had continued in spite of the strange army at Babylon and Kenton had deliberately forgotten about his intention to remove her, mostly because he was fairly certain such a move would upset Nicola and her sons, and he did not wish to upset them. Therefore, he tolerated the old woman who would emerge from her hole near the mural stairs in the entry, dance around a bit, and then hiss and run back into her closet when she saw all of the men gazing back at her. She was such a regular occurrence that men were starting to place bets as to the exact time she would appear. Betting on the crazy old woman was now a nightly happening.

And this night was no different, although the woman with the wild hair had made a very brief appearance before rushing back into her closet and slamming the door. Kenton and his knights were seated at the end of the big feasting table, enjoying the warmth and food and ignoring the mad woman in the entry. Kenton, in fact, had spent the evening watching Nicola, her three female servants, and several male servants provide food and drink to a room full of soldiers.

In evenings past, she had brought her boys to the table and she would sit with the knights, which made for good company because she was smart and witty and made excellent conversation, but tonight she seemed unable to take the time to sit. With the snow and bad weather, even those men camping in the inner ward had come inside to get out of the cold and the damp. The hall was standing room only.

But Kenton ignored the crowd of men as he continued to watch Nicola as she made sure the servants provided adequately to each table. When she finally came near the big table with a steaming pitcher of hot wine to fill the cups, Kenton reached out and gently grasped her arm.

"Lady Thorne," he said, relishing the close proximity of her as she leaned over the table to pour wine into Wellesbourne's cup. "Will you not sit and eat with us this night? Surely you must eat at some point."

Nicola had spent the entire evening avoiding looking at Kenton; she didn't want to look into that beautiful face and be reminded of what a fool she had been. She didn't want to be reminded of how badly her heart hurt. But she also didn't want him to think anything between them had changed so she forced herself to look at him, smiling weakly.

"I will try," she said. "There are many men in the hall tonight and the servants are quite busy. They need my guidance."

"But we need your company," Kenton said, his eyes glimmering at her. "Will you not sit, even for a moment?"

Nicola very much wanted to refuse him but she steeled herself. If she refused, he might think something was wrong, that she was upset with him, and she didn't want him to think that. She wanted him to think that everything was still right between them and that his attempts to probe her were still in full swing.

Nay, she wouldn't give in to the pain she was feeling. Instead, she gazed at the man steadily. She wanted him to believe all was still well and that her heart wasn't shattered in a million little pieces of pain. But it was difficult, oh so difficult. Everything in her body was screaming with anguish as she looked at the man, wishing he had truly been sincere in his attentions. But he hadn't been. He'd lied to her. Quietly, she set the pitcher down and sat on the bench next to Kenton.

"There," she said, forcing a smile. "I suppose I can sit for a moment or two. What great plans do you all have for this evening? Will there be another game of chance that I will be forced to keep my children from? They are very interested in the dice, you know."

The knights around the table all grinned to varying degrees. "Where are your sons?" Kenton asked. "They are usually here with us, demanding stories."

Nicola shook her head. "Tab seems to have a bit of the sniffles so I put the lot of them to bed early," she said, although it wasn't quite the truth. Tab had a stuffy nose, that was true, but she simply didn't want the boys to be around the enemy knights any longer. *She didn't want them to be around Kenton any longer.* "Once one child becomes ill, it runs through all of them, so I am trying to prevent that."

Kenton accepted her half-truthful explanation without question. "Tab was very proud of the six fish he caught," he told her. "Why are they not on the menu?"

Her smile turned real in spite of herself. "They were on *his* menu, not yours," she said. "He wanted to eat his fish so I had the cook prepare them just for him and his brothers. Surely you cannot object to that."

Kenton shook his head. "Not at all," he said. "I am glad he was able to eat the fruits of his labor."

Nicola nodded, still with the smile upon her face, as she thought on how to start the next part of the conversation. She'd spent the entire afternoon planning her vengeance against the man and the commencement of that vengeance had to start with knowing his future plans.

Now, she was the one in control because she was wise to his scheme. Now, she would treat Kenton as he had treated her; *as the enemy*. All she could think of was defeating him at his own game. He would not get the better of her.

It was time to put her plan into action.

"I do not intend to pry, my lord, but for the sake of the provisions at Babylon, may I ask what your immediately plans are?" she asked politely. "The provisions we have, at least the grain that we have, will last for another month, two at the most, so I must plan what I will need if you and your army plan to remain here for the next few months. Since there are so many mouths to feed, I must plan our needs as far in advance as I can. Would you be kind enough to give me any information to that regard?"

It was a perfectly logical and normal request and Kenton took it as such. Had he suspected what she really had in mind by asking the question, he would have thrown her in the vault and left her there. Truth be told, he also would have been extremely hurt by her actions. Instead, he was oblivious. He reached out for his wine cup and drank of the tart, warm liquid.

"We will be here at least through the summer," he said. "There is much I need to accomplish in that time."

Nicola was all innocence as she continued her probing questions. "You have not already accomplished it by gaining Babylon itself?"

He shook his head, casually moving closer to her as he leaned upon the tabletop, his arm against hers as he looked over his shoulder at her.

"Babylon was only the beginning," he told her, his voice lowered. "There is more to do."

Nicola pretended to look both thoughtful and somewhat distressed. "I see," she said, having trouble looking into his glittering eyes and not feeling her courage waver. She was still desperately attracted to him. "Will you... will you be leaving, then, to lay more sieges? Will you still return to Babylon after you do?"

By this time, the other knights had turned to their own conversation because Kenton was singularly focused on Lady Thorne and she on him. No one wanted to be part of a two-person conversation that surely didn't include them. Therefore, no one heard what Kenton was saying to Nicola.

"I will always return to Babylon," he said softly. "I will always return to you. I thought I made that clear."

It was like a dagger to her heart to her those words. *He is lying to you!* Her mind screamed. *Do not believe him! Be strong!*

"Where will you go?" she asked softly, trying so hard to resist his sweetness without trying to appear that she was. His gaze was trying to suck her in as she desperately resisted. "I only ask because... because if you do not come back, I want to know where to look for you."

He reached over and gently touched her hand, his flesh against hers, sending bolts of heat shooting through her tender body.

"You would look for me if I did not return?" he asked. "That is kind of you. I did not know you cared so much as to do that."

Nicola averted her gaze, looking at her lap as her cheeks flushed red. She simply couldn't look at him any longer. She was starting to feel sick, her heart palpitating. She wanted very much to leave and it was a struggle not to give in to that feeling. There was so much hurt inside of her at the moment that it was consuming her and his gentle words only made it worse.

Kenton, seeing her subdued manner, smiled faintly. He thought, or at least he hoped, it was because she was upset over the thought of his death. He touched her hand again.

"Not to worry," he whispered. "As I said, I will always return to you. But we will be departing in two days for Manchester and Rochdale. I am under orders to bring those towns into Henry's fold. Right now, they are still under contention between both sides, so even though I will be gone from Babylon, I will still be close by. I will be back as soon as I can."

Manchester and Rochdale. He told her his plans without hesitation, because he trusted her. That was clear. Nicola lifted her gaze to him, seeing such warmth and affection in his eyes. It was shattering, all of it. God, it was so difficult to resist!

"Rochdale is closer," she said softly. "Do you go there first?"

He nodded faintly. "More than likely."

She paused a moment, a strategic pause to make it sound as if she cared for him and about what he did. *But she did still care for him!* "Then you go to war again," she said softly.

"That is my vocation, Madam. Surely it does not surprise you."

She shook her head, looking to her lap again. "Do... do you think the wars will ever stop?"

He watched her lowered blond head, imagining that he could smell her hair from where he sat. He very much wanted to kiss that lowered head to give her comfort.

"They must," he said, reaching over to collect his cup again. "We have all been fighting each other far too long so, at some point, they must stop. One king will reign and we must all accept that."

She cast him a sidelong glance. "And if it is Edward?"

Kenton shrugged. "If he is the ultimate victor, then I shall have to accept it as well," he said. "But until that time, I will do all I can to ensure that he is not the ultimate victor."

She was looking at him more seriously now. "But why?" she asked a genuine question, one that wasn't designed to press him for information. "Why must you fight for a king who is mad? Why not serve a king who would be an excellent ruler with no bouts of madness?"

Kenton cocked an eyebrow, mostly in thought. "Because Henry is the rightful king," he said simply. "Mad or not, the throne is his. It does not belong to Edward."

It was plainly put and Nicola could not dispute it. In fact, as she gazed into his eyes, she could almost see his point. But not quite; she had to pull herself away from him. That magnetic pull between them was too much to bear. Collecting her pitcher of warm wine, she stood up.

"I have taken too much time away from my duties," she said, stepping away from the bench. "I must return."

Kenton reached out, his hand brushing her arm. "Will you return when you can?"

Nicola looked at him, her gaze guarded. "I will try."

"Will I see you after sup? You promised me that I could."

Nicola simply nodded. Kenton smiled at her and she smiled in return, although it was stiffly done. Head down, she took off across the room with her warmed wine, heading into the servants alcove and disappearing into the darkness.

Kenton watched her go, mostly because he liked to watch her hips as they swayed alluringly. She had a delicious figure and his eyes were always drawn to her hips and buttocks. Most often he would watch her and imagine how her tender backside would feel in his hands, imagining the silken texture of her skin. He knew for a fact that he was going to bed the woman before he left for Manchester but he could see that talk of his departure upset her.

He knew that his knights would not have agreed with him telling her their future plans, but he saw no harm in it. His heart swelled with joy knowing that she did not want him to leave. Surely that was her only trouble, the reason behind her quiet manner and lowered head. Aye, he would bed her and prove to her that he would return to her. Nothing, not even an assault on Manchester, could keep him from her. Not now, not ever.

With a smile, he returned to his wine, already reflecting over the joy of their reunion once he returned home from battle. He'd never had anything so thrilling or wonderful to look forward to. Now, he had Nicola to look forward to.

Little did he realize that the reality of such bright joy would soon take a definitive turn for the dark.

When Nicola left the hall, she went straight to the stables where she found a young groom who was healthy and energetic. He was also loyal to the House of Thorne and not to Henry's soldiers who had taken over Babylon. Nicola knew the young man, and knew he was trustworthy, and she sent him that night through the postern gate of Babylon, riding south to Conisbrough with a message for the garrison commander there. It was a vicious, snowy night so she knew it would take a couple of days at the very least to reach Conisbrough, a very large outpost of soldiers loyal to Edward, but she was confident the young man would make it. She struggled not to feel guilty for doing what she must.

For betraying the man who had tried to betray her first.

The tides of the battle for Babylon were about to change.

~THE BETRAYAL~

CHAPTER ELEVEN

Conisbrough Castle
Two and a half days later

"THAT IS WHAT the boy said," a man clad in heavy tunics and a cloak of fur against the freezing temperatures spoke. "Warwick's army is moving out of Babylon in an attempt to capture Rochdale and Manchester."

In the second floor main chamber set deep within Conisbrough's enormous keep, the man's words had an ominous echo. There were several men in the chamber, huddled near the enormous hearth with the elaborate mantel, blazing hot enough to cause them to sweat. But the chill of the day had been particularly bitter and under the guise of discussing their recent failure at Babylon Castle and what to do about it, the men who had sought refuge at Conisbrough had gathered with the garrison commander. What they really wanted to do was eat, drink, soak up a bit of warmth, and forget about the past week that had seen them defeated by the weather more than they had actually been defeated by the Henry loyalists who now held Babylon. Still, it had all been a bitter blow.

But this latest news has the men perking up, listening to what Brome St. John, the garrison commander of Conisbrough, was saying about a rider that had recently stumbled through the gates of the castle. Half-frozen, the young man had relayed some stunning information.

Truthfully, all men in the chamber sat straight when they heard this news but Lord Saxilby, the baron who had led the assault against Babylon to regain it, was listening more closely than any of them.

"They are *leaving* Babylon?" Lord Saxilby wanted to make sure he heard correctly. "How would this lad know? Where did he come from?"

Brome St. John was a very big man with long blond hair, bunched up around his shoulders with ice crystals sticking to it. He moved closer to the fire, pulling off his gloves. "He claims to be from Babylon," he replied, holding his cold hands up to the blaze. "He said that Lady Thorne sent him. I know Lady Thorne and I know her husband. Gaylord Thorne is loyal to the bone for Edward. It would make sense that Lady Thorne would send word to us of the enemy's movements."

Lord Saxilby, a short man with a strong constitution and a great acumen for battle, listened seriously. "We all know Gaylord Thorne," he pointed out. "But you say that Lady Thorne sent the information? Why not Gaylord?"

Brome shook his head. "This I would not know," he said. "The messenger specifically said Lady Thorne. He did not make mention of Gaylord."

Lord Saxilby mulled over that odd fact, which concerned him. "Strange that he did not mention Gaylord," he muttered. "Of course, Babylon has seen much war over the past few weeks so it is quite possible that Gaylord did not survive it."

"That is a possibility."

Lord Saxilby rubbed his chin. "If that is the case, then it would truly be unfortunate," he said. "There is no man more loyal to Edward than Gaylord Thorne and only a man desperate to relay information about the enemy would be foolish enough to send a messenger in such weather. Where is the rider now, Brome? You will bring him to us to interrogate."

Brome glanced at the group of fur-clad, cold, and weary men. "The lad is nearly dead with cold," he said. "My men are tending to him to try and warm him. Give him some time to recover before you are tearing into him with your questions. Meanwhile, I would say that we have some very vital information as to the movements of Henry's forces at Babylon. More than that, we have the name of the man who commands them."

"Who?" Lord Saxilby demanded.

Brome looked at him. "Kenton le Bec," he said, his voice low as if to emphasize the seriousness of that declaration. "Grandson of the great Richmond le Bec. He serves Warwick directly, my lord. He is known as Warwick's attack dog."

Lord Saxilby's expression didn't display the surprise nor the disappointment he felt but it came out in his tone, anyway. "Le Bec," he hissed, scratching his head. "Now I understand a great deal. No wonder we could not breach the walls. Not only was Warwick inside Babylon, but so was le Bec. I do not feel nearly as humiliated as I did only moments ago. A defeat by both Warwick and le Bec is nothing to be ashamed over because, combined, they are nearly invincible."

The group of men grumbled in both agreement and disagreement. "I knew le Bec years ago," another man spoke. Hugh Fitzalan was the son of a great war baron as well and had a long history of switching sides from Henry to Edward and back again. "He was at Towton and survived. He survived the second battle at St. Albans as well as the battle at Mortimer's Cross. The list goes on and on. The man cannot be defeated. Some swear he is the devil incarnate because of his ability to survive in battle."

Brome looked to Fitzalan. "He is *not* the devil," he said, "although his reputation would have us believing otherwise. It would be a great feat indeed to kill or capture le Bec."

"Edward will want him," Lord Saxilby said, moving closer to the fire where Brome was standing. "If we are able to capture the man and send him to Edward, Warwick's war machine would be severely damaged. It would be a triumph for Edward's cause."

Brome knew that. He nodded his head slowly, pondering the information the half-dead messenger had given them.

"Then let us discuss this information Lady Thorne's messenger brought," he said. "He said that Henry's forces were moving quickly to Rochdale and to Manchester. Reason would dictate that if she said they were moving quickly, then that would mean in the next few days or a week at the very least. Since the messenger took almost three days to arrive here, it would be logical to assume that le Bec and his men are moving as we speak, or at mayhap they already have. In any case, it is imperative that we mobilize the men and march north to Rochdale to see if we can intercept le Bec's army."

The group grumbled, mostly in agreement, although they were reluctant to jump out into the freezing weather so soon after having spent so much time in it as of late. Still, St. John's logic made sense.

"If we march north to Rochdale, we can cut off the road between Babylon and Rochdale and presumably put our army between le Bec and Babylon," Lord Saxilby pointed out. "Let us assume that le Bec takes most of his men out of Babylon because he will need a good deal of men to capture Rochdale and Manchester. That being the case, he would leave a skeleton army at Babylon. If we position ourselves between his army at Rochdale and Babylon, we could block him from returning whilst we lay siege to Babylon and reclaim her for Edward."

It was a reasonable and sound plan, one which the men in the room agreed with for the most part. Still, going back out to fight in this weather did not appeal to them, especially if victory was not assured.

"What of Warwick?" one of the men wanted to know. He was skinny and shaggy-haired. "He was at Babylon all during the siege and then when we retreated, he chased us for a day until turning away and heading northeast. Do we know where he is? Could he not easily return to help defend Babylon?"

Brome shook his head. "My spies tell me that Warwick has moved on to Wakefield," he said. "He is gathered there with a group of Henry's supporters. Even if he is told that Babylon, and le Bec, are compromised, he cannot move fast enough to assist. It is my belief that we can destroy le Bec's army and regain Babylon before Warwick can arrive."

Lord Saxilby shook his head. "That is a bold assumption," he said. "We laid siege for a week at Babylon and were unable to take her. What makes you think this second attempt will be successful? We will still be fighting le Bec."

Brome's gaze was intense. "Because neither I nor my men were with you the first time," he said. "You brought nine hundred and eighty-seven men to my doorstep, Saxilby. I carry eleven hundred men at this garrison. Even if I leave three hundred men here, that still gives us almost two thousand men to go after le Bec once he has separated himself from Babylon. We will split the army in half and send half after le Bec and half to Babylon to breach her. We cannot fail."

Saxilby wasn't convinced by the arrogant knight's assertion. "We have no way of knowing just how many men le Bec is commanding," he said. "There could be a couple of thousand men in Babylon we were not aware of. The walls are so tall that we could not see. If le Bec brings a sizable army out of the castle, we would be foolish to split our forces against him."

Brome would not be discouraged. "Mayhap," he agreed vaguely. "But we will not know until we see what le Bec has to offer. It is my suggestion that we mobilize the men and move out as quickly as we can. If le Bec is already marching to Rochdale and Manchester, then we must keep the element of surprise on our side. He will not know we are coming until it is too late."

Lord Saxilby couldn't disagree. In fact, it was a perfect opportunity to regain Babylon and defeat one of Warwick's best knights. They had failed in their first attempt to regain Babylon. God willing, they would not fail in their second.

Interrogation of the messenger an hour later revealed that Gaylord Thorne had not been at Babylon throughout the successive siege, which begged the question as to the man's whereabouts. Surely he knew his castle has been compromised. But neither Brome nor Lord Saxilby could give any consideration to the missing Gaylord Thorne. They had a task to accomplish and little time to do it for time, it would seem, was of the essence.

Lord Saxilby gave great thanks for the loyal Lady Thorne and her half-frozen messenger.

"MY LADY?"

Kenton's voice was soft, coming from behind. Bent over a bin of rye grain that seemed to have a bit of mold on it, Nicola gasped with the surprise of his unexpected appearance. He had cornered her down in the storeroom of Babylon, the vaults beneath the keep, and there was no one around. In the cold and dark dampness, she could only see Kenton's face in the torchlight.

"God's Bones," she muttered, patting her chest as she tried to catch her breath. "You gave me a start."

Kenton smiled faintly. "I asked the cook where you were and she told me," he said, trying to see what she had been looking at. "What are you doing down here?"

Nicola was nervous, extremely nervous. She'd spent the past three days avoiding him, pretending she was working, or with her sick children, who now all had sniffles and running noses, and she'd seen very little of Kenton even if thoughts of him had been heavy on her mind. Try as she might, she couldn't seem to shake him and the betrayal she felt from the man had eaten a nasty, rotted hole into her soul. But now, here he was, and they were alone. Her heart pounded loudly in her ears as she struggled not to look at him.

"The rye grain," she said, pointing to the basket at her feet. "There seems to be some rot on it. I was trying to see if we can salvage it."

He took a step closer, his gaze on the big basket of grain. "Oh?" he said, sounding concerned. "Is this isolated or is there mold on other grains as well?"

Nicola took a step away from him as he came closer. She didn't want to be within arm's length of him should he try to grab her. "Just the rye, I believe," she said. "If we can scrape it away, it may be salvageable."

Kenton wasn't a fool. He could see that she was moving away from him. He'd hardly seen her over the past three days and was coming to think that she was avoiding him, although he had no idea why. He had been wracking his brain with their conversations since returning from Manchester, trying to see if there was anything questionable or offensive he'd said to her that might make her avoid him. He honestly couldn't think of anything and the separation from the woman was starting to wear greatly on him. His army was prepared to depart Babylon and he at least wanted to bid the woman a private farewell. He wanted that memory to hold on to, to sustain him, to give him something to look forward to upon his return.

Already, he missed her.

"I am sure that under your expert guidance, it will be saved," he said, eyeing her and noticing that she would not look at him. It made his heart hurt in ways he never imagined it could. "My lady, may I ask a question?"

Nicola was still looking at the basket of grain. "Aye."

"Have I done or said something that would cause you to avoid me?"

Nicola was startled by the question but just as quickly, she felt cornered. Cornered and angry and guilty. Swiftly, she shook her head.

"Nay," she said, stammering and moving away from him even further. "I… I have been busy and my children are ill. There is much on my mind."

Kenton sighed. He didn't believe her for one minute and his heart sank. "Nicola, please," he begged softly. "I must have done or said something. It is clear you do not wish to be around me and not knowing what I have done is eating at me. Please tell me. Whatever it is, I apologize profusely. I would never do anything to knowingly hurt or offend you."

He had managed to push her a little too far with his gentle words. Her anger surfaced and she tried to move away from him further but ended up stumbling over a bushel of grain. When he reached out to prevent her from falling, she lashed out at him savagely and smacked his head away.

"Do not touch me," she hissed. "Leave me alone!"

Kenton stood there, looking at her with an expression of naked confusion and desperation. "What have I done?" he pleaded. "Won't you tell me?"

Nicola shook her head furiously and before she could stop them, the tears started to come. Embarrassed, and feeling pain she'd struggled to push aside, she tried to turn away from him.

"Please go," she whispered. "Go away and do what you must do in order to carry out your orders. Just... leave me alone."

Kenton could see the tears and each droplet was like an arrow to his heart. Pricks of agony that he couldn't help and he couldn't stop. But he didn't move. "What did I do to upset you so?" he asked again. "Nicola, won't you tell me?"

She sniffled, trying to discreetly wipe away tears. "There is nothing to tell, Sir Kenton," she said. "I asked you to go. I would be grateful if you would oblige me."

Kenton knew one thing: he wasn't leaving, not until he knew what he had done to upset her so. He'd never felt such desperation or angst in his entire life. He'd never felt such emotion over a woman and therefore truly had no idea how to gracefully handle what he was feeling. As she stood there and quietly wept, Kenton sat heavily on a barrel behind him. He wasn't leaving until he knew.

"I am not a man given to emotion, Nicola," he said softly. "I have seen much war and death in my lifetime, of those close to me, enough so that I have learned to dull my feelings when it comes to another human being. I thought I was doing quite well until I met you but now I see that I am a weak fool when it comes to you. Right now, I cannot breathe for all of the pain I am feeling, knowing that I have somehow hurt or offended you. Clearly, I have done something and you will not tell me what it is. I am not leaving until you do."

Rather than ease or comfort her, his words inflamed her and she whirled on him, infuriated. "You will cease with your sweet words," she hissed. "All that comes out of your mouth are lies and coercion. You have been doing it since you came to Babylon and I will no longer listen to you, so cease with your attempts to be kind. I am immune to them."

His brow furrowed in puzzlement. "Lies and coercion?" he repeated, rather taken aback at such strong words. "How could you think....?"

She cut him off, rudely. "Stop it!" she shouted, putting her hands over her ears. "You only lie to gain your wants but I am not listening to you any longer! I know the truth, Kenton le Bec, so you can stop pretending to be kind and attentive. Your actions are filled with lies just like the rest of you. If you want to know what I know about Edward's movements or my husband's allies, then I wish you would simply ask me. You did not have to pretend to be kind to me in order to gain your wants."

Kenton was stunned. "Is that what you think?" he asked, aghast. "That I have been pretending to be kind to you in order to extract information?"

Nicola burst into painful sobs. She was trying to keep her hands over her ears but she couldn't do that and point for the ladder that led from the vault, so she was forced to drop a hand and gesture most strongly towards the exit.

"Get *out*," she screamed at him. "Get out and leave me alone. I do not want to see you again, ever!"

Kenton was pale with sorrow and anguish. He could hardly believe what he was hearing. "Who told you this about me?" he demanded, his voice hoarse. "Who told you such lies that you would believe them?"

Nicola was beyond rational thought at that moment; all of the pain she had been feeling at the realization that Kenton had only been using her was flooding out all over the place, through her veins, bleeding out of her pores, and filling the very air around them with anguish. She started screaming at him.

"*Get out, get out!*" she roared. "God damn you to hell for what you've done to me, le Bec! God damn you for making me feel… for making me hope… get out of here before I kill you!"

She was far gone with rage and hysteria. Kenton sat there, watching her, realizing that he was close to tears himself. In those few stammered words, he could see that she had felt something for him as well. She felt something for him now. It was the only way to explain the utter agony she was exhibiting. She was feeling something for him just as he was feeling for her but somehow, someway, someone had poisoned her against him. Someone had lied to her. Someone had convinced her that his intentions were not honorable and she had believed them. He could see, simply by her reaction, that she was as heartbroken as he was.

He'd never felt so much pain in his life.

Quietly, he stood up and made his way over to the ladder, hearing Nicola's sobs all around him, echoing off of the cold walls of the vault. They were like blows to his body, causing him physical anguish. There was a lump in his throat as he put a hand on the ladder.

"I am leaving," he said, his voice tight, "but you will listen to me before I do. I do not know who has told you that my intentions towards you were dishonorable, but nothing could be further from the truth. I love you, Nicola Aubrey-Thorne, and when I return from Manchester, we will have this discussion again. If it takes the rest of my life to convince you that my feelings for you are true, then so be it. I am willing to give the rest of my life to you, and only you, because I have never loved anyone before. You are my first and, God willing, you will be my last. This is not over."

Nicola couldn't help but hear his words. They carved through her like knives, causing her entire body to weaken. *I love you.* No one, save her children, had ever told her that. Hearing those words from Kenton's lips was the most glorious and most tragic thing she could have ever experienced. She wanted to believe him, to tell him that she loved him also, but she couldn't bring herself to do it. He was lying… *wasn't he?*

Distraught, Nicola collapsed on the floor of the storage vault in a fit of deep sobs as Kenton mounted the stairs and left, just as she'd asked him to.

She never saw the tears on his face that he quickly wiped away before anyone else could see them.

CHAPTER TWELVE

K ENTON'S ARMY LEFT before dawn the next day when the weather had surprisingly cleared up. As the eastern sky turned shades of pink and purple, and dark clouds slashed across the heavens as a reminder of the terrible winter weather they'd so recently suffered, Kenton departed the great gates of Babylon with around twelve hundred men, leaving the remaining two hundred at Babylon to watch over the castle until he returned.

He took all of his knights with him except Conor, whom he left in charge of Babylon in his absence. Kenton didn't expect any trouble in the foreseeable future, as his spies had returned saying that the army that had attacked them the previous week had sought refuge at Conisbrough, and it was likely that an army that had suffered such a defeat wouldn't be ready to regroup any time soon. He gave them a month or two before they came out at him again, which was plenty of time to gain control of Manchester and then retreat back to Babylon. That was what he was counting on.

But even as he left Babylon, his heart was heavy after his encounter with Nicola the evening before. He'd tried to shake the sense of sorrow he felt, the sense of hurt, but he hadn't been able to do it. He was nearly desperate to know who had poisoned her against him but he would feel like a fool for asking any of his knights, so he didn't. He bottled everything up inside him. Consequently, his mood was darker than usual and the men sensed it. The preparations for the departure had run smoothly because his men, including the knights, were fearful of upsetting him.

Wellesbourne and de Russe had accomplished most of the preparation with the men whilst Gerik and Ackerley had been focused on the provisions, animals, and equipment. They were going to subdue a large city – and Rochdale was without perimeter walls – therefore, most of their weaponry was meant for hand-to-hand combat situations. Spears and shields were the main things they made sure the men were carrying with additional weaponry stationed in two big wagons they were bringing. The preparations ran all evening and most of the night.

While Kenton focused on his army, he assigned Conor to deal with Lady Thorne and the castle in general. The army needed to take supplies with them, as foraging in the dead of winter was difficult, so Conor and Gerik spent the most time with Nicola taking from her what she could spare the army. Kenton wasn't anywhere to be seen during this time, which seemed odd to both Conor and Gerik. Where Lady Thorne was, Kenton usually was, so it was then that they began to suspect a rift had arisen between the pair.

But they kept their thoughts to themselves because whatever was occurring between Kenton and Lady Thorne didn't matter in the great scheme of things. Nicola was polite and helpful with them but she wasn't particularly friendly and when they were finished stocking the army, she quickly vanished. Even as they left the gates of Babylon before dawn, she was nowhere to be seen. The lady had retreated to her apartments and there she apparently would stay.

Without the Lady of Babylon to see them off, Kenton and his army headed out into the dawn of a new day in the direction of Rochdale, which was about an hour's ride from Babylon. Since they were already close to their target, Kenton sent his scouts out almost immediately, along with Wellesbourne and de Russe, who rode ahead to get the lay of the land and decide what the best course of action would be. Battle was on the horizon and intelligence had to be gathered.

For Rochdale, a rather bustling burg to the northeast of Manchester, the course of action had been relatively easy. When de Russe and Wellesbourne rode into town to confront the lord mayor, who was also the town's surgeon and beer maker, and told the man to surrender his village or suffer the consequences to Warwick's forces, the beer-making surgeon-mayor had immediately folded. It would seem he was not willing to put up any manner of resistance and by noon that day, Rochdale was secured in the name of Henry.

Leaving about two hundred men in Rochdale to keep close tabs on the operations of the city including who came in or out, Kenton and his men camped on the north end of town that night as they planned to march on Manchester the following morning. Already, Kenton sent out scouts towards Manchester, including Wellesbourne and de Russe again, but Manchester turned out to be not so entirely welcoming to Henry's troops.

In fact, there were some of Edward's troops staying in the town, as Kenton had seen on the day they had done their shopping there, and those men were most resistant to le Bec's army or the suggestion that the town and its occupants were not loyal to Henry. It was an unfortunate stance, considering they were undermanned, and Wellesbourne and de Russe killed those who refused to surrender. But it was only a hint of what was to come.

On dawn of the following day, Manchester became a battleground.

CONOR SAT IN Gaylord Thorne's solar, reading a missive he'd just received from Kenton. Six days after leaving Babylon, Kenton and his army were in heavy fighting in Manchester; the city had not surrendered as easily as Rochdale had, and there was a definite Edwardian influence, so the pocket of fighting had been vicious indeed. Frustrated that he was not part of the fighting, Conor let the missive fall onto the table that had once been cluttered with cups and books and maps belonging to Gaylord.

Kenton hadn't paid any attention to the clutter but Conor, with time on his hands and boredom threatening, had organized the messy table. Now, everything was neat and orderly because that was the way he liked it. Even when the missive fell back to the tabletop, he simply couldn't leave it laying there so he put it neatly off to one side.

Sighing heavily, he struggled not to let his frustration show. Kenton was facing strong resistance at Manchester yet he was here, growing fat and lazy with his inactivity. He thought seriously on sending Kenton a missive and asking if he could trade places with Gerik or Ackerley, but he knew that Kenton would deny him. Neither Gerik nor Ackerley had the acumen to completely run a castle, but Conor was fairly certain his presence here was more than simply a nod to his command ability. He was fairly certain it was to keep him and de Russe separated.

With a grunt of displeasure, he sank back in the cushioned chair and put his muddy boots upon the tabletop, thinking heavily on Manchester and battles and Gaston de Russe. Since their harsh words those days ago, they had both managed to steer clear of one another or, at times when they could not avoid it, they had simply ignored each other. Conor thought he had been quite professional about his behavior towards de Russe and was therefore insulted that Kenton had chosen to take de Russe with him into battle and leave Conor behind. Conor was, in fact, grossly offended.

As he sat there and stewed about being left out of a battle, he caught sight of someone entering the solar. The boots came down off the table as one of his soldiers entered the chamber, edging close to the blazing hearth because it was quite warm in the room. The soldier had just come from the walls of Babylon where it was breezy and quite cold.

"My lord," the soldier said. "Two scouts have returned from their usual patrol to inform us that a large army is moving up from the south."

Conor stood up, concern on his pale features. "An army?" he repeated, confused. "Where on earth did they see this army?"

The soldier edged even closer to the warm blaze. "About three hours ago," he replied. "The scouts were on the edge of Huddersfield when they saw the army approaching from the south. They watched the army for as long as they could and they think that the army is traveling the road to the south of us, the road the parallels the road that runs from Huddersfield to Babylon and on into Rochdale. It seemed to the scouts that the army took a turn onto that road. They are now heading east, towards Manchester."

Manchester, where Kenton is. Conor didn't like that thought at all; he was thinking on the roads to the south of Babylon and of all of the big armies that were also to the south of them. *Conisbrough*, he thought ominously. Was it even possible? Of course it was. There could be no one else, at least no one that was any closer than the massive garrison of Conisbrough. Kenton suspected Conisbrough would move on Babylon at some point only he didn't think it would be so soon. He thought he had weeks, mayhap even months before that happened. Evidently, that was not to be the case. The more Conor thought on it, the more concerned he became.

"There are two roads south of us," he finally said. "One that is not very far at all; we can see it from the battlements. And there is a second road that is over the range of hills further to the south. Which road do they mean?"

The soldier wasn't entirely sure. "I believe the road that is over the hills," he said. "Shall you speak with the scouts, my lord? They are in the gatehouse."

Conor nodded firmly. "I will, indeed."

Conor charged from the solar followed by the soldier. He was in the entry, heading for the door to the keep, when he caught sight of Nicola as she emerged from the hall with her boys in tow. Tab was begging his mother for something while Teague seemed to be deliberately tripping Tiernan, who fell onto one knee with his brother's bullying and came up swinging. Nicola came to a stop and put out a hand, stilling the brotherly fight. Conor called out to her politely.

"My lady," he said. "If you require service of me, I will be upon the battlements."

Nicola had her hand on Teague's balled fists. "Very well," she said politely.

"I would assume the evening meal will be at its usual time?"

Nicola nodded. "It will."

With a forced smile, Conor quit the keep, heading towards the gatehouse beneath the cold and dark sky.

Nicola watched the man go, her thoughts lingering on him as she turned for the stairs that led to the upper levels. Conor had kept a polite distance from her and she from him, but even so, the distance wasn't enough. Every time she saw him she was reminded of Kenton, which wasn't particularly a surprise considering the man occupied nearly every waking thought.

Nicola thought that his departure would help her forget about him, to help her to hate him and all he represented, when, in fact, it did just the opposite. Time had tried to heal that ache. She wanted to go to him and tell him why she was so angry with him, so hurt, and hope that he had an explanation about his words that she could believe. She'd never even given him the chance to explain, but at the time, there had been no reason to. She had heard him speaking, unguarded, to his men. That was explanation enough.

... wasn't it?

Torn with grief and confusion and longing for a man who had only been using her, Nicola tried to shake off thoughts of Kenton le Bec as she directed the boys to the stairs. She trailed along behind them, stopping Teague from clobbering his brother again, as they made their way to the upper floor. They were nearly to the top of the flight of stairs when a soft call came from below.

"My lady?"

Nicola paused, looking down to see Janet standing in the darkened entry below. "What is it?" she asked.

Janet looked around nervously before silently motioning for Nicola to come to her. Nicola looked at her curiously and Janet did it again, this time pointing frantically in the direction of the kitchen. Curious, not to mention oddly concerned, Nicola instructed Tab to take his brothers up to their chambers. As Tab began dragging them up the remainder of the steps, Nicola went to Janet.

"What is the matter?" Nicola asked as she came off the stairs. "Why are you…?"

Janet shushed her softly. "Not here, my lady," she whispered. "Hurry, you must come with me."

She dashed off and Nicola quickly followed. Janet wasn't usually the jumpy type so the maid's manner had Nicola naturally intrigued. She soon found out why.

Seated just inside the kitchen door near the hearth, with a steaming cup of wine in his hand, sat the stable boy Nicola had sent to Conisbrough over a week ago. Hermenia was hovering over the lad, spooning great globs of hot stew into his frozen mouth, as Janet and Nicola entered the low-ceilinged kitchen. It was quite warm, and quite smoky, as Nicola quickly went to the shivering lad.

"Hux?" she gasped, reaching out to touch the boy and realizing that he was literally frozen solid; his clothes were hard with ice. "God's Bones, Hermenia. We must remove his clothing. It is like a block of ice!"

Hermenia set the bowl of stew down. "I know it, m'lady," she fretted. "But he couldn't move his face. I thought to warm it at the very first."

Nicola, Janet, and Hermenia began yanking pieces of clothing off the boy – the inadequate gloves, his shoes, a stiff wool coat, and a wrap around his head. It all came off, all frozen and wet, and Janet laid it on the hot floor in front of the hearth. Nicola shoved the lad upon his stool closer to the blaze and he, as well as his clothing, steamed as the warmth began to saturate through the wet and ice.

"Hux?" Nicola asked again, helping the lad drink the hot wine because he was having difficulty holding on to the cup. "What happened? How did you get back into the compound? Did the soldiers see you?"

The young man who had seen sixteen hard years shook his head. "They did not see me, m'lady," he assured her, teeth chattering. "I came up by way of the river and into the postern gate. Hermenia saw me first, through the gate, and chased the soldiers away so she could open it."

Nicola was glad the boy hadn't been caught entering by Kenton's eagle-eyed soldiers. "De Birmingham has men all over the walls," she muttered, thinking on the soldiers she had seen from her chamber window. "It is truly a miracle that you were not seen by them when you left the first time and now when you have returned. God must be on our side."

As the serving women nodded, Hux's pinched face grew very serious. "Where is le Bec, my lady?"

Nicola held the boys trembling hands, keeping them wrapped around the warm cup. "He left more than a week ago," she said. "He left for Rochdale and Manchester. I do not know what has happened, exactly, because I've not asked, but I heard that he took Rochdale with ease. He must be at Manchester by now."

"Then he is not here, my lady?"

"Nay."

The young man coughed and choked down another swallow of warm wine. "How many men and knights are here?"

Nicola was somewhat puzzled by the question. "Only one knight was left behind," she said. "Conor de Birmingham. There are mayhap two hundred men. Not very many at all. Le Bec took almost all of his men with him."

"And how many men do we have that are loyal to you and to Lord Gaylord?"

Nicola was increasingly puzzled by the questions. "As many as were here when le Bec took over the castle," she said. "Two of my husband's knights, the old pair, and thirty-seven men. That is all we had. Hux, why do you ask so many questions? What has happened?"

The young man took another long drink of wine, slurping it now that he was getting some feeling back into his lips. "Brome St. John of

Conisbrough Castle sent me back to you with a message," he said. "He says to tell you that he is taking men to engage Kenton le Bec but that he needs your help to regain Babylon for Edward. There are men from Conisbrough waiting in the woods to the south and they want to enter the castle. They want to take it back."

Nicola looked at him, both surprised and fearful by the information. "What do they want me to do?"

"Let them in, my lady."

Nicola rocked back on her heels, absorbing the request. She was being asked to open the gates to Conisbrough's garrison, to admit men that were loyal to Edward. They wanted to take the castle back, to restore it to its rightful self. Wasn't that what she wanted, too? To restore Babylon to Tab, as the rightful lord of Babylon? Kenton le Bec was a usurper, a common thief for stealing what did not belong to him. Now that he was away, it was a perfect time to gain it back. He would return to Babylon and find that it no longer belonged to him. She couldn't imagine that he would let it go so easily, but with seasoned soldiers inside her walls to stave him off, surely the walls would hold this time. Surely he would be the one leaving in defeat. That was what she wanted.

… wasn't it?

Perhaps it was, perhaps it wasn't. Nicola couldn't seem to summon her courage at the moment. She had sent word to Conisbrough to betray Kenton but somewhere over the past few days, she had wavered on that stance. That was never more obvious than at this moment. But she couldn't waver. Kenton wanted nothing more than to betray her. She had heard it from his own lips. But those same lips had told her that he loved her.

God, she was so confused!

"I cannot let them in through the gatehouse," she said. "The postern gate would be the only way and it will only allow one man in at a time. If someone were to see them…."

She trailed off, shaking her head, gazing back at the young man with some trepidation. But the young man seemed to have the courage and conviction she lacked.

"It can be done, m'lady," he assured her. "I must go back to them and show them the way. They can come in through the kitchen yard and into the keep through the kitchens. Those at the gatehouse cannot see the kitchens from where they are. It will be too late when they realize we will regain the castle."

The wheels were in motion and Nicola could not stop them. Men were here, ready to help her take back her castle, and she could not hesitate. She had to think on her sons and their future; they would not have a future if le Bec were to regain Babylon. Their legacy and wealth would belong to Kenton. *Think of your children!* She told herself. *Stop thinking with your heart and think with your head, you fool!*

"Very well," she finally said, but it was difficult to spit the words out. "Go back to Conisbrough's men and lead them to the postern gate. We shall try to get them into the kitchens unseen. How many men are there?"

"About forty, my lady," the young man replied. "Enough to make it to the gatehouse and open it."

"But there are at least two hundred men here."

"They will not be an issue if they are distracted."

Nicola's eyebrows lifted. "Are the Conisbrough men setting up a distraction for those on watch?"

The young man nodded. "I believe they are, but I do not know what it is, my lady," he said. Then, he set the cup aside and grabbed at his shoes and coat. "I must return. I must tell them our plans."

Nicola helped the young man dress in his wet, warm clothing, her manner now somewhat hesitant. Plans were in motion and she felt as if she were being swept along with evil by her own design. Of course, it was by her own design. She had sent word to Conisbrough and they had responded. Soon, Kenton le Bec and his men would be a memory at Babylon and nothing more. Soon, the nightmare would be over and her recollection of Kenton le Bec would be those of a man who had helped her to feel more, to understand more about herself, than anyone had ever done for her. If nothing else, she was grateful for what he had done for her. Betrayal or no, enemy or no, he had done this for her.

Think nothing else of the man, she told herself. *You are not allowed to think anything else of the man!*

Her heart, a fragile and protected thing, wasn't listening.

This night, to her, would forever be the night that she betrayed the man she loved.

A WEEK AFTER beginning the siege of Manchester, Kenton and his army was beginning to make ground.

Their attack had come from the northeast and was designed to allow the town's inhabitants to escape the carnage before the real show of force began. Kenton and his men gave the town exactly one day before they began to launch their attack in earnest, and on the dawn of the second day, they plowed into Manchester and began to sweep the city, subduing those who didn't flee and flushing out soldiers and other armed men who didn't belong there.

The Earl of Derby, who had been encamped to the south of the city, put up a serious fight on the third day when Kenton and his men were midway into the city. There was terrible fighting in the streets, alleyways, and even in houses. De Russe and Wellesbourne, always the advance team, got into a serious battle alongside the two hundred men they were commanding with a contingent of Derby's men just past Market Street, to the southwest on King Street. Derby had set up an ambush that ended up killing about ten of de Russe and Wellesbourne's soldiers, which spurred the knights into a bloody frenzy. No man was safe at that point, and de Russe in particular drew upon his bloody reputation and single-handedly put down eleven of Derby's men that he caught in a bathhouse. The bathhouse became a blood house.

The bloodshed continued to roll into a fourth and a fifth day after that. Fighting upon a field of battle versus fighting in close-quarters combat in a city was much different, and more exhausting, Kenton believed. As he had Gerik hold the northeast section of the city, he moved parallel to de Russe and Wellesbourne. While those two moved to subdue the southern part of the city, Kenton and Ackerley moved into the western section of the city and even secured the two main bridges over the River Irwell.

With the bridges secured, Kenton personally moved into the small portion of the city that was to the north of the river and struggled for two days to secure it. There were many people willing to fight back in this portion of the city and Kenton met with serious resistance. It was a brutal onslaught of attacks and counterattacks.

The sixth day of fighting saw most of the city under Kenton's control although there were pockets of fighting that seemed to move around throughout the city, making them difficult to quell. The biggest blow came when Ackerley took an arrow to the neck, a mortal blow that saw the man bleed to death as Kenton and a few other soldiers struggled to save him.

There was nothing anyone could do even though they tried, going through the motions of trying to save a man who was beyond help. Kenton, his hands covered in Ackerley's blood, held the man's hand as he had drown in his own blood, speaking quietly to him and assuring him that his wound wasn't mortal. He assured the man that he would be saved and that they would enjoy some time in London when the battle was over. Ackerley had died with a smile on his lips, thinking of alcohol and round women and the pleasures of London.

It had been a difficult death for Kenton to accept. Now, the trio of Trouble, More Trouble, and Lucifer's Brother was without Lucifer's Brother – the three friends of Conor, Gerik, and Ackerley were no more. Gerik had been informed of his friend's passing when the man's body had been sent back to Kenton's encampment on the north side of town. The wagon bearing Ackerley's body had passed by Gerik as the man held his post, and he had stopped the wagon a moment, touching his friend's still face one last time before waving the wagon onward.

After that, it was back to his duty bearing a broken heart. But war was war and he accepted that men died; it was just difficult to accept that one of those men had been Ackerley Forbes.

Ackerley's death greatly affected Kenton and Gerik even though they tried to pretend otherwise, but those who had fought alongside them for any length of time could tell. Even Wellesbourne and de Russe could tell. More than that, they understood and they stepped up their service. Wellesbourne took Ackerley's place next to Kenton, carrying out even the smallest order that Kenton may have had, while de Russe remained in control of the southern portion of the town.

Day seven dawned to see Kenton nearly in complete control of Manchester thanks to his skill as a commander and also thanks to his knights, who had worked very hard to ensure victory. The death of Ackerley seemed to spur something in them, something deep, and even though his men as a whole were exhausted and physically beaten, their spirits were good and the casualty rate had been surprisingly low. Of the nearly one thousand men he'd brought with him, having left two hundred in Rochdale, he'd only lost sixty, which he considered rather low for such a bloody battle. Finally, by the end of the seventh day, Kenton was confident that he could declare victory.

But there were details in that victory, both good and bad – Derby's men had been chased off and their encampment to the south end of town raided and burned, and Kenton now found himself with several very fine horses, tents, clothing, rugs, and even coinage from Derby's camp. He was quite pleased with the booty and allowed his men to divide most of the treasure trove among them, although Kenton kept the horses and the coinage. As evening finally fell on the seventh day and the fighting, for the most part, had ended, Kenton set up a perimeter around the majority of the town and declared Martial Law. People began coming back into the town, into their homes, to see what was salvageable. Kenton had not permitted his men to raid homes so what possessions that hadn't been inadvertently destroyed were still there, and the citizens were grateful for small mercies.

A peaceful night followed, a night that saw Kenton sleep heavily for a few hours with dreams of Nicola on his mind, until he was awoken before dawn by a panicked soldier. It would seem that a large army was already on the southern side of town and had managed to break through their perimeter. Kenton's soldiers were dying, now fighting for their lives against a fresh army, and de Russe and Wellesbourne were already riding to the south side of town to assess the situation.

Assessment or not, Kenton knew that the introduction of a fresh army against his exhausted one was a very bad thing indeed. He was dressed in a flash, with mail and plate armor, and he and Gerik began organizing their men to resist whatever army was now invading Manchester. Exhausted men, and wounded men, began forming lines against what was coming. There was a palpable sense of doom in the air, of coming death, but Kenton's men were ready for it. With le Bec leading the charge, their courage was limitless in the face of adversity.

Even so, Kenton wasn't fully prepared for the news that de Russe and Wellesbourne ultimately brought back to him; an army flying the standards of Edward and Fitzalan and Saxilby was now tearing through the southern end of town, with several mounted knights and men who hadn't been fighting for a week solid. Kenton's soldiers were dying left and right, and Wellesbourne had ordered the entire southern perimeter to retreat and fall back to Kenton's base camp. Based on that information, Kenton knew it was about as bad as it could get.

Mounting his heavy Belgian warmblood, a fat rouncey who was bred for battle, Kenton charged southward and straight into the mouth of hell.

CHAPTER THIRTEEN

Babylon

I T STARTED WITH a fire off to the northeast, a fire in the distance on the cold and snowy night that immediately created a brilliant spot of light across the barren landscape.

The gatehouse of Babylon faced northwest; therefore, the men at the gatehouse were turned away from the main gate by the sight of the fire in the distance. It was an extremely odd occurrence, one that had every man on the wall peering at the blaze in the distance, wondering what it could be. There were a few farms up in that area, farms that helped supply Babylon with cattle and other products, and there was also a small forest that they could see clustered up on the horizon. Other than those few landmarks, there was nothing else of note and certainly nothing that would create or otherwise warrant a fire the size of the one they were seeing.

Conor, wrapped heavily in wool and furs, watched the fire from the battlements. He had both of his scouts on the wall with him as well as the soldier who had originally come to give him the scouts' report. Word had spread through the men that a large army had been sighted well to the south, heading to Manchester, so the men knew that there was activity in the area.

The very air at Babylon was tense, knowing that danger was lurking about but uncertain as to what, exactly, that danger was. All they knew was that they could feel it in their veins and as the bright moon shone down upon them, a silver disc in the freezing night, there wasn't one man at Babylon that didn't sense the approach of something wicked and deadly.

Something terrible was coming.

Conor could feel it most of all. He had been charged with the safe-keeping of Babylon, after all, and he wasn't a man to fail at his post. He suspected that the fire in the distance was meant to draw them out, to see what was happening, and he had no intention of opening the gates to send out scouts. Therefore, he remained on the wall, watching the fire as it burned steadily. His curiosity was great, of course, but so was his sense of suspicion. Greater still was his sense of self-preservation. The fire in the distance wasn't a natural phenomenon; therefore, it would stand to reason that someone had created it.

So he stood there with his men, monitoring the fire in the distance as well as keeping watch over the gatehouse and the walls. The wall walk reached around the entire perimeter of the castle, including back near the slope of the hill where there were trees and a path from the river up to the kitchen's postern gate. The gate was heavily fortified, with an iron grate on the exterior of the wall as well as the interior of the wall, and it was very small, so much so that only one man could pass through it at a time and even that man had to be crouched down to go through it. It was purposely built to make movement difficult so any enemy trying to pass through would immediately be at a disadvantage.

When one passed through the postern gate, they were immediately in the outer ward, literally an area of space between the outer and inner walls that was no more than fifteen feet deep. Then there was a second opening cut into the interior wall that led to the kitchen yard beyond, which was the vast open space between the interior wall and the keep.

Conor kept men not only on the battlements, but also patrolling the space between the inner and outer walls. A soldier checked the postern gate with regularity, but this was where Conor made his grave mistake – he had the same man check the gate repeatedly, a solitary sentry who roamed alone because most of the men were on the wall. When that man was knocked unconscious by Nicola with a large fire poker so that she could unlock the postern gate and allow the Conisbrough men inside, no one knew anything about it until it was too late.

By then, the damage was done.

The first Conor realized there was trouble was when men in the inner ward bearing crossbows began firing at the sentries on the walls. Conor was barely missed by an arrow but the soldier standing next to him and one of the scouts who had seen the big army to the south weren't so lucky; they fell immediately, as did scores of other men hit by the barrage of arrows. As Conor and the others took cover on the walls and began to return fire, the men in the ward that had initially fired the arrows then charged the gatehouse, and the gate, and the battle for control of Babylon was on.

Conor could hear the fighting as he labored to stay low, away from the flying arrows, but even as he struggled to assess what had happened, deep down, he already knew. Somehow, someway, men had breached Babylon, and he made his way on his hands and knees towards the gatehouse to defend it. He was stunned to realize that men were able to enter Babylon in spite of the safeguards he had set up and it confirmed to him then that the fire in the distance had been a ruse. It had been meant to attract, and keep, their attention, which it had. While they had been watching the flames, the enemy had evidently mounted the walls.

Or perhaps they dug holes beneath them or even launched themselves over them. Whatever the case, Babylon was now compromised. Feeling very foolish, and very angry, Conor drew his broadsword and charged down the narrow spiral staircase of the gatehouse, only to be blocked by several of his soldiers who had already tried the same thing. They were dammed up by men at the entrance to the gatehouse down below, fighting to keep them from all coming down off the walls.

Conor began shoving men aside in his attempt to get down to where the fighting was. He was near the door and could see the battle going on beyond, near the portcullis. The great portcullis itself had already been partially lifted and men were pouring in through the breach. Conor had no idea where the enemy army had come from because he and his men had been keeping careful watch of the surrounding countryside. They even kept watch of the River Black, which ran to the south and west of Babylon, but there was vegetation on the banks of the river and Conor came to understand that the enemy army must have used the river itself to their advantage. While the fire burned, the army had moved in stealth upon Babylon and now, for their lack of awareness, Conor and his men were paying the price. God's Bones, he felt like such an idiot.

He had let Kenton down.

That was the worst dishonor he could possibly imagine, letting down le Bec, a man he so greatly admired and a man who had been kind to him. And man who had survived so much and had fought many great battles. The fury of Conor's failure breathed new life into his resolve and he shoved men aside, moving in between them, scratching and clawing to get free of the gatehouse stairs and to where the fighting was taking place. He was able to shoot through the doorway and into a tide of incoming hostiles. They seemed to be coming from everywhere. Conor had to find a way to stop them or die trying.

As the battle for Babylon was in full swing, a ragtag army headed towards Babylon from Rochdale, a group of beaten and fleeing men who had another group of men pursuing them. There were no standards flying, from anyone, and therefore no way to know that the ragtag army was what was left of Kenton's fighting force after the route at Manchester. There were three knights in the lead who, after seeing the siege of Babylon as it was illuminated by the big, silver moon, took their beaten and exhausted army to the south, to a minor road that ran towards the east.

There was no returning home for the fragments of Kenton le Bec's army so the remaining knights in command acted wisely and bypassed the besieged Babylon, choosing instead to take the remains of the army to safety elsewhere. Beaten and shattered, if they wanted to survive, they had little choice.

But neither Conor nor his men saw any of it. He was too busy try-ing to reclaim Babylon from the men that were quickly gaining the upper hand. With only two hundred men to defend Babylon, the battle was over almost the moment it started, but Conor never gave up. Not even when he was swarmed with enemy soldiers, who managed to disarm him and beat him fairly badly did he give up. He was still fighting until the last, until someone mercifully landed a heavy blow to his unprotected head which stilled the big, red-haired knight once and for all.

Then, and only then, did Conor stop resisting.

For him, it was over.

CHAPTER FOURTEEN

Manchester

Three days later

I T WAS DAWN on a particularly cold morning as Kenton sat in the icy grass beneath a barren oak tree on the south side of Manchester, shackled by the ankles and wrists. It was actually the first day he could remember being completely lucid since riding to battle against an army of Edward supporters who were trying to invade Manchester so soon after he had secured it.

Kenton had charged into the heat of the fighting and had performed magnificently until someone hit him on the head from behind, so hard that he had pitched over his horse and landed on his forehead. He'd been wearing a helm at the time, but the blow had knocked him cold. He'd awoken some time later to find himself tightly bound and quite obviously a prisoner, but he'd lost consciousness again for an unknown amount of time until regaining consciousness within the past hour or two.

He'd awoken, dazed, to a horrific headache and blurred vision on his left side. He was fairly certain he had a massive bruise or some kind of swelling on his forehead because his face was extremely tender and the blurriness in his left eye seemed to be because he couldn't open it completely. It had been dark when he'd awoken, and he'd been lying on his side, but he'd looked around enough to see that he was grouped with other prisoners, men under his command that he recognized.

"My lord?" came a hiss. "Sir Kenton, can you hear me?"

Kenton could see a pair of bound boots a foot or so away from his head. He must have groaned, or moved, or both, because the hiss came again.

"Sir Kenton?" the man said again. "Are you awake now? Can you speak?"

Kenton tried to move his head but it was very painful to do so. He ended up closing his eyes, trying to stave off the nausea. "Who is it?" he asked, his voice hoarse.

"'Tis Lewis, my lord," the man whispered loudly. "Camden Lewis. I have served you for...."

Kenton cut him off. "I know you," he said. "You are one of my senior soldiers. You have a brother who fell at Towton."

"Aye, my lord."

"Give me the situation, Lewis."

It was a formal request, from a commander to his soldier, because all things in Kenton's world were formal no matter what the circumstances. He could hear the soldier grunt, more than likely with irony.

"They got us good, my lord," the soldier muttered. "The garrison from Conisbrough, they are. From what we can gather, they were alerted that our army was in Manchester. We heard them speaking of it. They are looking for you in particular."

Kenton's eyes opened and he tried to look around. "How... how long?"

"Have you been unconscious?"

"Aye."

"Since the battle started two days ago," Lewis said. "I broke my foot at the beginning of the fight and they caught me easy. They brought you here right after I came, so it has been two days. You have been unconscious for that long."

Kenton was trying very hard to clear the cobwebs out of his mind. He remembered riding to the south end of Manchester, into a nasty skirmish, and fighting a big knight on a blond steed. But after that, he remembered very little. Flashes of sound and pain, mostly. His anxiety began to take root.

"What is happening now?" he asked.

Sitting up, and watching the St. John guards carefully as they monitored the gang of Warwick prisoners they had spread out in a field on the southeast side of town, Lewis spoke quietly.

"Nothing, my lord," the soldier mumbled. "The fighting is over. Conisbrough brought fresh men to a fight. They captured many of our men and more than likely killed as many."

"And my knights?"

Lewis shook his head. "Not here," he said. "Not with us. I heard some of the Conisbrough men speak of chasing a group of men back towards Babylon, including three knights, but I haven't heard any more of that."

Kenton blinked, struggling to think clearly. "Three knights," he mumbled. "With Forbes gone, it had to be le Mon and Wellesbourne and de Russe. That means they were not killed."

"I would say not, my lord."

Kenton felt a great deal of relief at that. "Then I am thankful."

Lewis stopped himself from replying when one of the St. John soldiers happened to hear conversation and glance back at the group of prisoners to see who was talking. Lewis kept his head down until the soldier lost interest and turned back around.

"Mayhap the knights will summon help from Babylon," he whispered.

Kenton drew in a deep breath, turning his head slightly and trying to loosen his neck up. It was so incredibly stiff. "What help?" he questioned. "I left a mere two hundred men back at Babylon. If we are to be helped, it will not come from them. Warwick is in Wakefield; hopefully, men have already ridden to tell him what has happened. If assistance comes, it will come from Warwick."

The same St. John soldier turned around because he heard conversation a second time. Lewis dropped his head, pretending to be dozing, until the soldier turned back around once more.

"We must keep quiet, m'lord," he said. "They know you are a knight and they hope you are one of Kenton le Bec's knights. I do not think they know they have le Bec himself but they keep asking the men if you are le Bec. No one will confirm it."

Kenton lay there, thinking of the loyalty of his men, feeling like such a complete and utter failure. He had been fighting since seventeen years of age. He'd seen several major battles in that time and had survived all of them. To allow himself to become captured in a mere skirmish was insulting at the very least. He could still hardly believe it. Still, it was dangerous for his men to deny who he was. Soon enough, whoever his captors were would start using strong-arm tactics to gain answers and his men would suffer. This Kenton could not allow. In order to save his men, and perhaps even himself, he had to announce his identity. At least his men would be spared if he told them who he was. At least, that was the hope.

"Lewis," he whispered, "are there Conisbrough soldiers around?"

Lewis eyed the gang of them several feet away. "Aye, my lord."

"Call them over."

Lewis looked at him, shocked. "But... why?" he asked. "You don't want to engage them, my lord."

Kenton tried to lift his head, to look at Lewis, but it was just too painful. "Call them now. I will not tell you again."

Lewis was quickly growing distraught. He had no idea what le Bec had in mind but he knew he didn't like it. "Please, my lord," he hissed. "They are looking for you. They want to use you, probably as an example to the others. They may even want to send you as a prize to Edward. Surely you cannot...!"

"If you do not call them, I will."

Lewis gazed at the man, feeling a good deal of sorrow. He couldn't stomach the thought of the great Kenton le Bec in Edward's hands but it occurred to him that le Bec might have something else in mind. He hoped that was the case. Eyeing Kenton as the man tried to lift his head, Lewis turned with great reluctance to the group of soldiers about twenty feet away.

"Oy!" he yelled. "You, there! Come over here!"

Several of the soldiers turned to look at him, frowning. "Quiet, you," one of them threatened, holding up a balled fist. "If I come over there, you are not going to like it."

Lewis pursed his lips ironically. "I already do not like it," he said. "'Tis not my idea to ask you over here. I have been told to do it."

Now, he had the attention of most of the soldiers who were standing in the group. "By whom?" one of the men demanded.

Before Lewis could reply, Kenton spoke in that deep, commanding boom that his men knew so well. It was a tone not meant to be disobeyed.

"By me," he said. "You want le Bec? I will turn him over to you."

Lewis' worst fears were confirmed. He began hissing at Kenton, shaking his head. "Nay, my lord," he said through clenched teeth. "You *mustn't!*"

Kenton ignored Lewis as four or five Conisbrough soldiers made their way over to him, wandering amongst the captured Warwick soldiers. By their expressions, it was clear they were wary, looking at Lewis and the enormous knight who was lying beside him. The soldier who seemed to be in charge scowled.

"Where is le Bec?" he demanded.

Kenton peered up at the soldier, a seasoned man, bearing a tunic of yellow, blue, and red, which were Edward's colors. He could see the shields and lions. Before he could open his mouth, however, Lewis spoke.

"Here," he said quickly. "I am le Bec."

The warrior bearing Edward's tunic looked at Lewis, his brow furrowing. "You?" he repeated in obvious disbelief. "You are an old and broken fool. You are not le Bec."

Lewis geared up to argue but Kenton spoke, more loudly, which positively killed his aching head. "He is not but I am," he said. "Tell your commander that Kenton le Bec wishes to speak with him."

The group of Conisbrough soldiers was much more inclined to believe that the massive knight with the head wound was Kenton le Bec. In fact, their expressions held varied degrees of surprise and pleasure with a fair amount of hatred mixed in. The soldier bearing Edward's tunic crouched down next to Kenton, looking him over thoroughly.

For a moment, no one spoke. The soldier on his knees next to Kenton seemed to be drawing it all in, the sheer size of the man, digesting the image before him and coming to realize that he believed him. The knight was older, which they knew le Bec to be, and the equipment they had stripped him of had been expensive and well-used. Aye, it was easy to believe this injured man was who he said he was. The more the soldier looked at him, the more pleased he became.

"So you are the great Kenton le Bec," he said rhetorically, though not impolitely. "You have a good deal of courage admitting it."

Kenton stopped trying to lift his head; there was too much pain and he was bound so tightly that he couldn't get his balance even if he could sit up. So he lay there, gazing up at a man who would just as easily kill him as speak with him. Kenton had never felt so vulnerable in his life.

"Not courage," Kenton sighed. "I am being practical. You are going to beat the information out of my men, anyway, so I am saving you the trouble. Tell your commander I wish to speak with him."

The soldier's gaze lingered on him. There was still a chance that the knight could be lying but there were those that knew Kenton le Bec on sight; Saxilby, who had been wounded in the battle, claimed to be one of them but the man was unable to move because of a bad gash to his back and hip. The soldier presumed he could discover if the big Warwick knight was being truthful easily enough.

"I've a better idea," he said, motioning to the soldiers who had accompanied him. "We will take you to him."

Four men reached down to lift Kenton up as one of them unshack-led his ankles. If they wanted him to walk, he couldn't do it with his feet bound. Kenton bit off a groan of agony as he was lifted up, fighting off the pain and dizziness that swamped him. He couldn't stand on his own so the Conisbrough soldiers nearly completely supported him as Kenton tried to gain his bearings. It was clear that he was in terrible shape.

It was a status that didn't go unnoticed by Kenton's men and they began to protest the treatment of their brave commander. Lewis in particular was very concerned.

"Be careful with the man," he demanded. "Can you not see how badly injured he is? Take care with him!"

Around him, other men began to shout, louder than before. Soon, an entire chorus arose, demanding that the Conisbrough soldiers be cautious with le Bec. Kenton, hearing their cries, labored through the swaying and nausea, trying to stand on his own feet. The voices in support of his condition infuriated him.

"Enough!" he roared at his men. "You all bellow and whine like old women! Shut your mouths allow me my dignity!"

The men instantly ceased their protests, which told the Conisbrough soldiers that, indeed, the big knight they were dragging away was a man of respect. More than that, he had given an order that was instantly obeyed. Only a man in command would require such obedience and it was clear that his men loved him. That was blatantly obvious. That being the case, the soldier in command slapped the colleague who was holding Kenton up by the right arm.

"Be careful with him," he said pointedly. "He has a bad wound to the head. Where is the surgeon?"

One of the four men supporting Kenton spoke. "Last I saw he was in Saxilby's tent," he said. "Are we taking him there?"

The soldier in command nodded firmly, eyeing the bruise on Kenton's forehead. Now he, too, was inclined to be careful with the man now that the realization of his identity was confirmed by dozens of prisoners, men who were clearly subservient to him. *Kenton le Bec in the flesh,* the soldier thought. If he were to admit it, he was a bit awed.

He never thought he'd meet such a legendary knight, a man among men in the annals of the battle for the throne. Aye, he was awed, indeed.

"We are," he finally said. "I think there are a few people who would like to meet him."

The last Kenton's men saw of him, he was being dragged off towards a cluster of tents set up on the south side of Manchester and there wasn't one man in witness who didn't have a sinking feeling in the pit of his stomach. They all knew why le Bec had revealed himself because le Bec knew, as they did, that sooner or later, the Conisbrough men would try to beat le Bec's identity out of them. They had all been resolved to resist but Kenton had other ideas; he wasn't about to let his men take a beating protecting him. That wasn't how Kenton le Bec operated.

Heroics often went beyond mere battlefield behavior. Heroics were in the character of men and in their sacrifices.

Kenton had sacrificed his safety for the sake of his men.

Now, all his men could do was pray.

CHAPTER FIFTEEN

Babylon Castle

"**M**AM, ARE THERE more battles to come?" Tab asked, looking up at his mother with his big green eyes. "Will we have more fighting?"

In their fourth floor chambers at the top of Babylon's keep, Nicola was watching the activity in the inner ward down below. Raven was over by one of the little beds with Tiernan, who was still sniffling and sick, whilst Janet and Liesl were looking out of the windows as well, watching the bustle down below just as Nicola was. None of them particularly liked what they saw.

It was the morning after the breach of Babylon and Edward's banners were once again flying high from the battlements. The day was clear and bright, but to Nicola, it was the most desolate and horrible day she could have ever witnessed. A night of fighting had seen Babylon fall back into the hands of Edward's supporters, but all she could think of was the fact that she had betrayed Kenton and his men. She didn't even know what had become of Conor, the man left in charge when Kenton had departed. All she knew was that it had been a nasty battle, all night, and she had watched it all from the safety of her room.

As morning dawned, she stood at the window, pale and gray, wrapped in a heavy cloak against the cold morning temperatures and wondering what her treachery had brought them all. It was her hurt and anger at Kenton that had compelled her to send the missive to Conisbrough before she thought the entire thing through. Hurt and anger and fear that she was about to be preyed upon by a man who had made it clear to his comrades that his only intent was to use her. Now, all she could feel was deep regret and sorrow that she hadn't confronted him before she acted. She should have asked Kenton about his hurtful words and, at the very least, allow him to explain himself.

But she didn't.

I love you....

Those were the last words he had spoken to her, not knowing that the wheels of betrayal were already in motion. Now, guilt threatened to consume her as she viewed the results of her treachery against Kenton and his men.

In the end, she was the one to win the battle for Babylon but there was no joy in that victory, only sorrow.

"I do not think there will be any more battles," she finally said, putting her hand on Tab's blond head. "I think the battles are over for now."

The serving women heard her, Janet and Liesl standing by the other window that faced east. They, too, were feeling uncertainty and guilt about the entire situation. They were well aware that their lady's missive to Conisbrough had started this trouble and they were further aware that it was Lady Thorne who had opened the postern gate to let the enemy in, but they said nothing about it. It was not their place to question their lady even though their hearts, like Nicola's, were heavy. So much death and destruction. Over on the bed with Tiernan, Raven was sniffling so much that Nicola finally looked over at her only to see tears in the woman's eyes.

"Raven?" Nicola asked with concern. "Why do you weep?"

Raven shook her head, wiping quickly at her eyes. "It... it is nothing, my lady," she said. "I... I suppose I am simply frightened by the battles. We have seen much."

Liesl and Janet were looking at their sister with varied degrees of concern and disapproval. Liesl, the younger and more foolish one, spoke.

"She weeps because she is in love with Matthew Wellesbourne," she said accusingly. "She is in love with an enemy knight and she is afraid for him! She thinks he is dead!"

Raven's head shot up and she hissed at her sister as Janet tried to calm the pair. "Quiet, both of you," Janet scolded. "Lady Thorne does not need to hear any of this foolishness."

"Shut your lips!" Raven snapped at Liesl. "You are jealous because he only looks at me and not you!"

Janet turned Liesl around and shoved her towards Nicola and Tab. "Silence!" Janet barked. "Go stand somewhere else. You will speak no more!"

Grumbling and mumbling, Liesl wandered away, towards one of the boys' little beds, and began fussing with the linens as if straightening out the bed when the truth was she wasn't doing much good of anything. She was only trying to keep her hands busy and her mind off of her sister's hateful words before she said something they would all regret.

Nicola eyed the young serving woman with some concern, suspecting there might be more to the story than she was being told. It seemed to her that Janet and Raven were both quite nervous about it. After a moment, she returned her attention to Raven.

"Is this true, Raven?" she asked quietly. "Do you love Wellesbourne?"

Raven shook her head, but her lower lip was trembling. "I... I tried to stay away from the knights just as you said, my lady."

Nicola shook her head. "Yet you did not," she replied. "Do not lie to me. I know you did not stay away from them. So it's Wellesbourne, is it? I do not suppose there will be any Wellesbourne bastards running around come winter, will there?"

Raven flushed a dull red, hanging her head in shame. Liesl, too, was fairly red-faced and she kept her head lowered where Nicola could not see her disgrace as well. Janet, feeling mortified on behalf of her foolish and loose sisters, cleared her throat softly.

"I am sure there will not be, my lady," she said, eyeing her sisters. "If there are, then be assured I will send the child and its mother back to my mother, where both will be tended. I would not permit them to remain here and shame the House of Thorne."

Raven, humiliated by her older sister's words, was unable to control her anger. "There may be other bastards, too," she snarled at Janet. "You cannot point all blame at me. I am not the only one who has been warming a knight's bed."

Janet was aghast. "How dare you say such things in front of Lady Thorne," she hissed. "Shut your silly mouth, girl, or I'll send you back to Mother this very day."

Raven would not be silence. "I heard Wellesbourne and de Russe speak of other women who give themselves over to the knights," she said. "You know I have. I told you about it and you told me not to tell!"

Janet lifted her hand to slap her sister but Nicola stopped her. "What is this she is speaking of?" she demanded, moving closer to Raven as she sat on Tiernan's bed. "Raven, what do you mean? Who were Wellesbourne and de Russe speaking of?"

Infuriated, ashamed, and with little tact, Raven turned her guarded gaze to Nicola, "You, my lady," she said, her voice quiet and trembling. "I heard them speak of you but Janet told me not to tell you."

Shocked, Nicola looked at Janet, who was very close to boxing her sister's silly ears. "It was foolish talk, my lady," Janet explained, trying to downplay the importance of such gossip. "Raven and Liesl overheard the knights speaking of you. It was simply gossip."

"It was *not* simply gossip!" Raven insisted. "They were speaking of Lady Thorne and Kenton le Bec, and they were concerned that le Bec was paying too much attention to Lady Thorne, so much so that they were fearful that Warwick would discover his interest in Lady Thorne and send her away!"

Nicola's mouth popped open in surprise as Liesl, behind her, spoke up. "It is true, my lady," she said. "We heard them say that Sir Kenton had orders from Warwick that he was not fulfilling because he was smitten by you. They said that they were going to speak to Kenton about you but I do not know if they did."

Nicola stared at Liesl in horror, digesting what she'd been told. "How would you know such a thing?" she asked, her voice oddly hollow. "How in the world would you hear these men speak of me?"

Raven lost some of her indignant stance. "We… we were near Matthew's chamber and heard them speaking," she said, refusing to admit that they had deliberately been listening in. "Both Matthew and Gaston speak rather loudly and we couldn't help but hear them. It seemed to me that they were going to tell Sir Kenton that he must follow Warwick's orders or he would be in trouble."

Nicola blinked, somewhat stumped by the information. "In trouble with Warwick?"

Raven nodded. "Because of you."

"How long ago did you hear this?"

"Just over a week ago, my lady. Not very long at all."

Just over a week ago. The words, all of them, were tumbling around in Nicola's head and she labored to make sense of everything, like pieces to a puzzle that did not yet fit together but somehow, someway, she began to suspect that all of it had something to do with that terrible day when she heard Kenton dismiss her as something to be used. The timeline seemed close enough; *just over a week ago.* Weren't Wellesbourne and de Russe in the solar with Kenton when she heard the man speak those terrible words? She thought she may have heard their voices and she knew that Kenton was speaking to his knights, but she hadn't known who, exactly, he had been speaking with.

What if it had, indeed, been Wellesbourne and de Russe confronting him about spending an abundance of attention on Lady Thorne and threatening to go to Warwick with the information? *What if…* what if Kenton had merely told them he was using her so they would not tell Warwick of his behavior? What if Kenton had lied about his true intentions towards her, lying to his knights so they would not betray him or his feelings to their liege?

What if he was simply defending his true intentions towards her to throw them off the scent?

Oh, God....

Heavily, Nicola sat on the bed behind her. The truth was that her knees gave out and she simply plopped down onto it. There had been no conscious choice to sit. Her knees would no longer hold her. She sat there a moment, gripping the edge of the bed, wondering if her act of betrayal had been based on Kenton trying to keep the two of them together. *Warwick would send you away.* Kenton didn't want her to be sent away.

He was trying to keep them together.

I love you....

Nicola could hardly breathe through the horror she was feeling. Dear God, was it possible? Had he truly only been trying to throw Wellesbourne and de Russe off his trail? Why, oh why, hadn't she confronted him about his words? Why hadn't she asked him to explain himself? Instead, she had believed the worst and her feelings of pain and betrayal had taken over her common sense. She had betrayed the man who loved her.

Whom *she* loved.

Aye, she loved him. She couldn't remember when she hadn't. Now, her treachery had cost her everything, including the man she loved.

Dear God... what have I done?

Forcing herself to breathe, to think, Nicola stood up from the bed unsteadily. She had to go downstairs, to see to the status of Babylon and to see what her act of betrayal had done to Kenton's men. She suddenly felt quite protective of them, as misplaced and late as those feelings were. Smoothing at her hair, her mind wandering to thoughts of Kenton and the degree of damage she had done to him, she moved for the chamber door.

"Thank you for telling me what Wellesbourne and de Russe had said about me," she said, her voice trembling with emotion. "But it truly doesn't matter what they think now, does it? Babylon is back in the hands of Edward, where it belongs, and it is time for me to assess the situation. I will also procure some food for the boys while I am gone, but you will remain here and bolt the door. Do not open it for anyone but me. Is that clear?"

Janet, Raven, and Liesl nodded fearfully but Tab came up next to his mother and clutched her hand.

"I will go with you," he said.

Nicola was momentarily forced away from her tumultuous thoughts, gazing down at her son and thinking his offer sounded very grown-up. "There is no need," she said. "I will return as soon as I can."

Tab was serious. "But you may need protection," he said. "I will protect you."

It was a sweet thing to say and Nicola couldn't help but smile at her brave boy. "Protection from what?" she asked. "These men are loyal to Edward. They will not harm me."

Tab remained quite serious. He went to the door and opened it for his mother. "Come along," he said. "I will escort you. We do not know these men and they could be cruel."

"If they are cruel, then I do not want you where they are. I want you here, safe."

"If they are cruel, then I will defend you."

There was no arguing with him, as his mind was made up. Fighting off a grin at Tab's chivalrous behavior, Nicola obediently went to the door just as her son had asked. When she quit the room, Tab followed her onto the dark landing beyond and shut the door behind his mother. He was the first one down the stairs as she followed.

The third floor of the keep was very quiet, as it had been since Kenton and his men had departed, and the smile faded from Nicola's face as she was once again reminded of his absence and of what she had done. Gazing into the two empty chambers on this level, the ones that the knights had once used, left her feeling sick and hollow. At some point, she simply couldn't look at the rooms anymore; the longer she stared at them, remembering who was once in them, the more sickened she became.

Nicola and Tab made their way down the great staircase to the entry level below, their senses heightened and their manner cautious. The hall to their left and the solar straight ahead seemed to be empty and they couldn't hear any voices, nor any sounds except those coming from outside. Quickly, Nicola hurried through the dark, smelly hall and to the alcove at the far end that led to the kitchen where she found Hermenia out in the yard bent over a steaming pot of grainy porridge. When the old cook saw her mistress, she crowed with delight.

"M'lady!" she gasped. "Ye survived the onslaught!"

Nicola nodded as the old woman reached out to grasp her hand, kissing it, and Tab went to the pot to see if there was anything interesting cooking inside. He stuck his finger into the bubbling gruel, hissing when he burned it. He sucked the gruel off his burned finger as Nicola pulled him away from the scalding pot.

"We were safe in our chambers all night," she told the cook. "And you? Where did you spend the night?"

The old woman pointed to the kitchen. "In there," she said. "I bolted all of the doors so no one could get in, but they found me this morning and told me to feed the men. I asked what men and they said I was to feed the army. My lady, these men are sworn to Edward. There is a new army here after last night."

Nicola looked around the yard, noting that it seemed untouched and unchanged from the last time she saw it. No looting, no destruction. The sheep that she and Kenton had purchased were still over in their corral, munching on their feed, and right next to the corral was the postern gate. She stared at the gate a moment, remembering her role in the recapture of Babylon. It had been pivotal, for without her, none of this would have happened. Depressed, she forced herself to turn away.

"I know," she muttered. "I must find the commander and discover what is to become of Babylon. We are back in Edward's hands now and I must know what their plans are."

Hermenia nodded, pointing to the gate that led from the kitchen yard out into the inner ward. "A knight was just here," she said. "He was the one who told me to feed the men. He can't have gone far."

She was urging Nicola towards the kitchen yard gate and Nicola took the suggestion. She hurried to the gate with Tab on her heels, both of them peering outside into the inner ward to see what it looked like beyond. It was muddy and they could see signs of damage. Here and there were men sitting against the inner wall either injured or simply resting, but she couldn't see much more than that.

Timidly, she opened the gate, yanking on it when the hinges stuck. The rusted iron hinges often gave her trouble and when the mud would shift after heavy rain, the gate would sometimes be wedged closed. Fortunately, she was able to squeeze through it, out into the inner ward, as Tab followed close behind.

Nicola was several steps into the inner ward when she realized that Babylon appeared much worse off at eye level than it did from her perch above. The walls weren't damaged but there were injured men everywhere and the gatehouse was in shambles. She gasped when she saw the great portcullis off-track, hanging at an angle, and there were men she did not recognize trying to fix it. The big gates themselves were wide open and one of them seemed to be unhinged. Men were milling about and there was a group of soldiers, Kenton's soldiers, who were being corralled.

Shocked at the sight of the devastation, Nicola called to the first soldier she came across.

"Where is your commander?" she demanded. "I am Lady Thorne and this is my home. Take me to your commander immediately."

The soldier, who had been assigned to collect fallen weapons, eyed Nicola strangely for a moment. She thought he might actually deny her simply by the expression on his face, but after a moment he leaned the used arrows he had been collecting against the wall of the keep and pointed towards the gatehouse.

"He is over there, my lady," he said.

"Take me to him."

The soldier turned for the gatehouse without another word. Nicola, grasping Tab's hand tightly, followed through the muck and mud. She passed by men who were badly wounded and being tended to by other soldiers, but she tried not to look at them. She tried not to look at any of them because every man reminded her of Kenton. Most of the wounded she saw were, in fact, Kenton's men, and she knew that if they saw her, they more than likely recognized her. Perhaps they even blamed her for what happened. Or perhaps they were hoping she would save them. In any case, she simply couldn't look at them. She was afraid that if she did, she would weep.

Weep with guilt.

The gatehouse seemed to be the busiest area in the inner ward and the soldier led her through the crowd of men trying to repair the unhinged gate, straight to a big man in armor and shoulder-length blond hair. The soldier muttered something to the armored man, who then looked at Nicola with both surprise and interest. He pushed the soldier aside as he went to her.

"Lady Thorne?" he asked politely.

Nicola eyed the large knight, who was not unhandsome. "Aye," she replied. "Who are you?"

The knight smiled politely. "I am Brome St. John, commander of Conisbrough Castle," he said. "We have answered your missive, my lady. I hope we have responded to your liking."

Nicola sighed, although she tried to cover it. It was simply a reaction to his statement; *I hope we have responded to your liking.* She couldn't say what she was thinking, that she wished she'd never sent the damnable message. But she was certainly thinking it.

"Thank you for your response," she said, hoping she didn't sound ungrateful for all of the effort. "Then it is safe to say Edward once again controls Babylon?"

Brome nodded. "He does, indeed," he said, looking to Tab. "And this is your son, my lady?"

Nicola nodded. "This is my eldest son, Tab," she said. "There are two more boys, younger. You will see them about, too."

Brome smiled faintly at Tab, who was looking up at him with a great deal of hostility. "You have a fine young man by your side, my lady," he said, wondering why the child looked as if he wanted to kill him. He tore his eyes off the boy, his expression somewhat hesitant as he fixed on Nicola. "I have not yet seen Lord Thorne. Do you know where I can find him?"

Nicola wasn't sure what to say, at least in front of Tab. She endured the same question from Kenton those weeks back and she'd physically had to show the man where Gaylord was and she didn't want to go through that again. The destruction of Gaylord's tomb had been traumatizing and she was still fearful that Tab would hear whispers of what Kenton's men had discovered. As she tried to come up with a generic answer, Tab suddenly spoke.

"My father is dead," the boy said without emotion.

Nicola gasped, her eyes wide with astonishment as she turned to her son. But Tab was looking seriously at Brome, who gazed back at the boy with curiosity as well as disbelief.

"Dead?" Brome repeated. Then, he looked to Nicola. "Is this true, my lady?"

Nicola heard the question but she was looking at Tab, having no idea what to say to him. Was the boy simply making excuses for his missing father? Or did he truly know the man was dead? There was only one way to find out.

"Why would you say such a thing, Tab?" she asked, great emotion in her voice. "Your father has not been at Babylon for several months, that is true, but why would you say he is dead?"

Tab looked to his mother and it seemed to Nicola that there was no innocence left in his face at all. Just as he was trying to be a man by escorting her and declaring to protect her from harm, it seemed as if

Tab had done a good deal of growing in a very short amount of time as of late.

If she thought about it, hard, it all seemed to start when Kenton began spending some time around him, helping him learn to fish or otherwise paying attention to the lad. Perhaps Kenton's influence not only spread over her, but over her boys as well. They knew him to be a man of his word, a man who did not beat their mother as their father had, and someone who had taken time with them. Through the eyes of a child, Kenton was someone to be admired and emulated. Young Tab was emulating perhaps the only hero he'd ever known as her little boy tried to become a man.

"Because he is," Tab said to his mother, without any hint of distress. "I know that Papa is buried in the chapel."

His words were like an arrow to Nicola's heart. She completely ignored Brome as she knelt beside her son, grasping the boy by the arms. Her touch was gentle but unmistakably supportive as she tried to determine just how much he knew and what, in fact, she should say to him. Gazing into his green eyes, she didn't see much point in continuing the lie.

He knew.

"How do you know?" she asked softly. "I never told you."

Tab wasn't clear what had his mother so upset. "Papa was very sick and suddenly he was gone," he said. "I heard some of Kenton's knights say they found him in the chapel but I did not say anything because I did not want Teague or Tiernan to know. They still think he is off fighting wars. I know you do not want them to be afraid that Papa is not coming home so we should not tell them until they are older."

Tears filled Nicola's eyes at her son being so noble and strong for the sake of his younger brothers, keeping a secret he did not have to keep. It was all so very brave of him. But beneath that bravery, it began to occur to her that Tab didn't seem to know *how* his father died, a result of the wound that Tab himself had inflicted. He had mentioned his father being ill so he knew that much, but it was evident he didn't know *why* his father had taken ill. Therefore, she didn't venture on to that subject. It was best not to. Even if Tab knew his father was dead, Nicola would take the reasons behind it to her grave.

"I am sorry I did not tell you myself," she said softly. "I did not want to upset you. I planned on telling you and your brothers when you were a bit older and could understand."

Tab pondered his mother's words. After a moment, he shrugged his slender shoulders. "It does not matter," he said. "Papa wasn't a nice man sometimes. He hurt you. I stopped him from hurting you the last time."

Nicola grunted softly, embarrassed that a strange knight was hearing her deepest family secrets. "Aye... you did, Tab," she insisted weakly. "But that is all over now. We do not have to worry over that any longer."

Tab watched his mother as she wiped the tears from her eyes. He didn't like to see her upset but when the subject was his father, she was always upset. He frowned.

"It was better when Sir Kenton was here," he said. "You didn't cry at all. When I get bigger, I am not going to fight for Edward like my father did. I am going to fight for Henry with Sir Kenton!"

Nicola gasped, standing up quickly and putting herself between her son and Brome. "Tab!" she gasped, trying to push her rebellious son behind her, out of the man's wrath. She gazed up at the knight, fear in her eyes. "He... is young and weary of war, my lord. We have seen much of it over the past few weeks. This is our third siege in such time and I am afraid it has worn on him, as it has worn on all of us. Forgive him."

Brome was fighting off a grin at the very bold Tab Thorne. He'd actually learned a great deal over the past few moments listening to Tab speak of his father and of Sir Kenton. It was clear that the boy had no real love for his father, but he clearly had some manner of feeling for Kenton le Bec. He found that rather odd that a child should speak fondly of an enemy soldier but, then again, he had no way of knowing what had gone on with le Bec's occupation of Babylon. There could be much more to the story than he was being told.

"He's an admirer of le Bec, is he?" Brome said after a moment. "I cannot blame him. There is much to be admired with le Bec from a military standpoint. But I must say that, knowing that your husband is dead, it must have been very difficult for you with knights like le Bec holding Babylon. Were you treated fairly, my lady?"

Nicola nodded without hesitation. "Very fairly," she replied. "Sir Kenton and his men were kind to us."

Brome bobbed his head as if relieved. "I am glad to hear that," he said. "You were very brave to send the missive to me at Conisbrough, my lady. You risked much."

I risked my very soul, Nicola thought gloomily. As she looked into Brome's features, she was suddenly very desperate for news of Kenton; she had to know the depths of horror she had brought down upon Kenton and his men. St. John would be the man to ask.

"Did you capture Sir Kenton, then?" she asked, trying not to sound too curious or eager or desperate. "I told you he was going to Manchester. Did you find him?"

Brome nodded. "I received word from Manchester this morning," he said. "I am told that le Bec's army has been routed. It is a complete victory for Edward and you are to thank, my lady. Without you, we could not have defeated le Bec. We owe you much."

Nicola felt as if she'd been hit in the stomach. "A... a complete victory?" she stammered. "Are... are you sure? Le Bec has been defeated?"

Brome continued to nod. "That is what I have been told," he said. "You see, my lady, when you sent your missive to Conisbrough, it was full of men who had just come from one of the recent sieges of Babylon. I had at least two thousand men at Conisbrough and when we received your missive, we were able to use the information to plan the defeat of Warwick, and le Bec, once and for all in this area. I sent the majority of the troops to Manchester to fight le Bec's army while a small contingent of men took Babylon back from within. You were instrumental in that, my lady. I was there when you opened the postern gate for us last night. As I said, we have much to thank you for. We could not have been victorious without you."

Nicola stared at the man, thinking she had never felt less heroic in her life. Her loyalties and emotions were all mashed up, twisted, only to be spit out in ways she couldn't clearly decipher. All she knew was that she had made a massive mistake. That was becoming abundantly clear.

She wondered if it was a mistake she could right.

"Did you capture le Bec?" she asked again because it seemed as if he had not answered that particular question.

Brome politely moved her and Tab aside as men bearing great planks of wood moved to repair the unhinged gate. "I have not received word of that," he said. "But we do have many prisoners. It is possible he is among that group."

Nicola didn't know if she felt better or worse by that statement. Was it possible that Kenton got away? "If you have him, what will you do with him?" she asked.

Brome shrugged. "Take him back to Conisbrough, I am sure," he said. "After that, I will send him to Edward. The king will be thrilled to have such a prize as Kenton le Bec."

Nicola was feeling increasingly sick at the prospect, the realization that Kenton, if a prisoner, would be sent to Edward as some great, triumphant prize. A seasoned knight, who was born and bred for battle, reduced to a trophy. A pawn in the game between Henry and Edward. God, she felt so ill at the mere thought.

But something more filled her thoughts. If Kenton was sent to Edward, it was quite possible she would never see him again. He would be taken away and locked up forever. She could not live with herself if she didn't see him one last time, to confess her sins and explain why she had committed them, and ask for an explanation of his terrible words, the ones that had driven her over the brink of sorrow and paranoia.

It was too late for apologies and she knew it. Perhaps it was too late for anything and perhaps Kenton wouldn't care about her feelings or her motives. But for her own peace of mind, she had to clear her conscience. She had to see the man one last time, the man who had made her feel things she never imagined she was capable of feeling. But he was the enemy and he had been intent on using her; those were the facts as she knew them. But perhaps they weren't facts at all.

Perhaps she had been the real enemy all along.

It was she, after all, who had done the betraying.

"I see," she murmured after a moment. "But you will take him to Conisbrough first?"

"I will."

"Then you will do me a favor," Nicola said. "There is much I wish to say to Kenton le Bec now that he will be a prisoner of Edward. The man spent two weeks at Babylon and in that time... well, it does not matter. I have a few things to say to him. It is my right, as his former captive."

Brome appeared doubtful. "My lady, I...."

"It is my right," Nicola insisted again, louder. She was growing agitated. "He smashed my husband's tomb and stole from us. It is my right to have a few final words with him before you take him away forever. I demand it."

Brome wouldn't argue with her. It was evident that seeing le Bec meant a good deal to her. Perhaps she wanted to spit in his face, which he really couldn't blame her for. She had spent days, weeks, with the man, under submission. He could understand her need to tell him exactly what she thought of him and the damage he'd done.

"Very well," Brome sighed. "If it is your wish, I will make it so."

Nicola struggled to calm her agitation, pleased that he had given in to her request. As if he'd had a choice. "My thanks," she said, putting her hand on Tab's shoulder with the intention of leading him away. But she paused. "What of the le Bec knight who was in charge of Babylon? Where is he?"

Brome tilted his head in the direction of the gatehouse structure that contained the vaults. "He is locked away," he said. "I am not entirely sure of his health because my men beat him soundly, but he is still alive."

Nicola struggled to keep the great concern off her features. "I would see that one, too," she said, trying to sound angry. "I have a few things to say to him as well."

Brome complied, mostly because he didn't want a scene with Lady Thorne. The woman was determined to speak with the knights who had held her and her family hostage and he would not stand in the way. There was certainly some sense of vengeance there against her former captors. Without another word, he motioned her to following him to the vaults, and that's exactly what Nicola did.

Down into the moldering, dank depths of Babylon's horrid vaults.

CHAPTER SIXTEEN

Outside of Wakefield, Yorkshire

"WE HAVE NO way of knowing how they knew we were in Manchester," Matthew said. "All we know is that we were overrun with troops bearing the standards of Saxilby and Fitzalan, the same bastards who had laid siege to Babylon the week before. This time, however, they were heavily reinforced with garrison troops. Someone said they were from Conisbrough. We could see Edward's colors everywhere."

WARWICK HAD ONE of the more comfortable encampments when traveling, with big tents and creature comforts to suit him. Even now, as Wellesbourne and de Russe stood exhausted and beaten before him, Warwick was quite comfortable with his blazing brazier and piles of furs. He sat at his portable desk, the one he always traveled with, listening to a harrowing and disheartening tale. His gaze upon Wellesbourne and de Russe was not one of pleasantness.

"So you ran," he said flatly. "You left le Bec behind."

De Russe, displeased at having his courage questioned, spoke. "It was not a matter of running, I assure you," he said, his voice low and rumbling. "We had been fighting for a week and our men were exhausted. Edward's supporters rolled into the south side of town and began taking back the town one street at a time. We moved to meet them and we met them strongly, but they were fresh and we were not. The last I saw of le Bec, he rode straight into a particularly bad skirmish and was unseated. We tried to get to him but we were driven back. We were very nearly captured ourselves. With le Bec down and the men scattering, we gathered what troops we could and headed back to Babylon to gain what reinforcements that we could, but Babylon was under attack as well. It would have been foolish to try and engage whoever was after Babylon with our meager numbers. That being the case, we came straight to you to inform you what has happened."

Warwick was glaring up at the big knight. He knew de Russe wasn't a coward and he knew the same about Wellesbourne. Still, he was upset with the loss of Babylon. He'd heard the story twice now, once from Wellesbourne and now from de Russe, but he was still disheartened and angry.

"Manchester was hit when le Bec had secured it and Babylon was hit simultaneously," he muttered, rolling the facts over in his mind as he tried to make some sense of them. Then, he began to shake his head, wagging it back and forth. "God's Bones, this stress is more than I can bear right now. I have enough on my mind. I've received word that Edward's armies are sailing up from Calais, north along the English coast, headed for Yorkshire. He will be here any day but now I must deal with the failure of Manchester and the loss of Babylon."

De Russe still wasn't over the fact that Warwick intimated he was a coward. "The loss of both Manchester and Babylon was not expected, I assure you," he said. "It is my opinion that it was not a coincidence."

Warwick's head snapped to him. "Of course it cannot be a coincidence," he spat. "If it was the garrison at Conisbrough, someone must have notified them that le Bec was at Manchester and that Babylon was without protection. Someone must have told them where to go."

Wellesbourne and de Russe glanced at each other; they had already come to that conclusion, discussing it ever since they had fled Babylon for Wakefield. They had ridden hard with almost four hundred men, a far cry from the nearly one thousand that Kenton had taken with him into Manchester. The fact that they had so few men with them spoke to the viciousness of the second battle with the fresh troops and it spoke to the fact that, because Kenton's men were weary, they were more easily fragmented. God only knew how many men were really left and how many had simply fled.

"It had to be a traitor inside of Babylon who knew of our plans," Wellesbourne finally said. "It had to be someone close, someone in the inner circle. We did not even tell the men until we were clear of Babylon where we were going. We kept those plans secret as long as we could."

Warwick scratched at his graying head. "Who knew of your plans, Matthew?" he demanded, standing up wearily from his table. "Le Bec? You? De Russe? Le Mon? Forbes? De Birmingham? Who else?"

De Russe had run through that list, too, and spoke before Wellesbourne could. "It would not be de Birmingham," he said. "He was left in charge of Babylon with our departure. Why sabotage his own command? It was not me or Matt, and it certainly wasn't le Bec or Forbes or le Mon. They are seasoned men, loyal to Henry to the core. That information did not come from any of us in command."

Warwick looked at the big knight. "Then *who*?" he asked, throwing up his hands for emphasis, "for someone sent word to Conisbrough if they were, in fact, the ones who moved on Manchester and Babylon. I cannot imagine who else it would be and Conisbrough is the closest. The entire two-pronged operation was too well planned of an attack for it to be coincidence. Surely you see that!"

He was growing agitated and de Russe simply turned away from him, weary and brittle, while Wellesbourne replied. "Of course we do, my lord," he assured Warwick. "We were in the thick of things. The attack on Manchester, and also Babylon, was well planned. When last we saw Babylon, there did not seem to be an overabundance of men but it seemed to me that she was breached at that point. We did not see any real battle lines, there were simply men crawling all over the place and it's my sense that the gatehouse was compromised."

Warwick rolled his eyes. "Perfect," he snarled wryly. "Babylon is back in Edward's control. I have lost Manchester and I have lost le Bec. What more is there for me?"

De Russe and Wellesbourne looked at each other, with much on their mind, before looking to Warwick.

"We thought you would want to regain Babylon," Wellesbourne suggested. "Gaston and I have discussed it. We will return with your army to retake it. As for le Bec, if he was not killed when he was unseated, then I would presume he is a prisoner of the army who retook Manchester. The only way to know is to send word to Conisbrough and ask. Men were saying it was Conisbrough's garrison that fought against us so that seems to be the logical place to start."

"Did you see other standards flying?" Warwick asked.

Wellesbourne nodded. "The red and yellow bird of Saxilby and I thought I saw Fitzalan."

Warwick eyed the two knights. It was clear that his mind was processing the situation and what to do about it, mostly because warfare and power was all Warwick ever thought of. It was the way his mind worked. He was never at rest and this most recent setback was just that – a setback. Wellesbourne and de Russe were quite certain, given Warwick's objectives, that the loss of Babylon was only temporary.

Le Bec, however, was another matter. They didn't know where he was, or whether or not he was dead or alive, and Warwick was greatly troubled by that. They also knew that Warwick would not walk away from Kenton or leave him to rot, not when Kenton's might meant so much to him. Warwick depended on him too much so the loss of le Bec at this point was even greater than the loss of Babylon.

After several long moments of deliberation, Warwick returned to his seat before his leaning desk, one that had a broken leg that had never been fixed correctly. He had Wellesbourne call forth his advisors, men who were lingering outside where they had come to rest when Warwick had chased them out in preparation for Wellesbourne and de Russe's report of the fall of Manchester.

Warwick had been unwilling to let his advisors hear of a failure, at least not until he had all of the information. Now, he thought he had what he needed, enough to bring it up to the men who surrounded him like courtiers. Men who had fought and lived with Warwick for many years. When the group of them, five in all, re-entered the tent, Warwick fixed on one man in particular, older, with thin gray hair. Even from a distance, the old man smelled like compost.

"Lord Pollard," he said to the smelly man. "It would seem that Manchester and Babylon have been recaptured by those loyal to Edward. Rumor has it that the army came from Conisbrough Castle. What do you know of the garrison and its commanders?"

In spite of his smelly nature, Lord Hugo Pollard was from a very old family and was a man who knew anything worth knowing. He had an infallible memory and although he wasn't much of a military advisor, Warwick kept him around because the man, literally, knew everything about England and its nobility. It was difficult to do without such a man. When Warwick asked the question, Lord Pollard cocked his head thoughtfully.

"Conisbrough is Edward's property," he said. "The last I heard, a man named St. John was the garrison commander."

"Where is he from?"

"North in Cumbria, I believe. You have heard of Eden Castle?"

"I have."

"That is his family, I believe."

Warwick contemplated the information. "Is he married?"

Lord Pollard shook his head. "I do not know," he replied. "But I believe he has a sister who, if memory serves, is a companion to Lady Anne Holland."

Warwick's eyebrows lifted in surprise. "The Duke of Exeter's wife?"

"The same."

Warwick's eyes narrowed with both doubt and possibilities. "Are you certain of this?"

Lord Pollard shrugged. "There is but one way to find out," he said.

"Send to Bradley Manor where Lady Holland resides and ask her."

"Bradley Manor is in Lincolnshire."

"Two days ride at most, my lord."

Warwick's gaze lingered on Pollard for a moment before rising from his chair again, this time with a purpose. He had plan in mind, or at least the beginnings of one. He seemed fueled by something, perhaps an undigested sense of vengeance that was always lingering in his belly when it came to the battle for England's throne. Sometimes he hungered for enemies of Edward and sometimes for enemies of Henry, but at this moment, he was hungering for something against the commander of Conisbrough Castle if, in fact, it was the man and his troops who not only reclaimed Babylon but captured Kenton le Bec. The agitation was in the not-knowing.

He had to find out.

"Send twenty men to Bradley Manor," he instructed his advisors. "If the St. John girl is there, I want her. Tell Lady Holland that the girl's brother has taken ill and has asked for her; anything to take the girl peacefully. I do not want her damaged… yet."

Lord Pollard lifted an eyebrow. "But the information, coming from you, might seem strange," he pointed out. "You do not fight for the same cause that St. John fights for."

Warwick waved him off. "I have been on St. John's side before," he said. "Who is to say I am not again? Do as I say, now. Go get the girl."

The advisors were already on the move, without question, but Wellesbourne and de Russe seemed uneasy about what was happening. Wellesbourne caught Warwick's attention.

"For what purpose would you take this woman?" Wellesbourne asked, unsure if he really wanted to know.

But Warwick fixed on him factually. "Simple enough," he told the young knight. "If le Bec is at Conisbrough, mayhap we can exchange the life of St. John's sister for that of Kenton le Bec. Surely the man would not let his sister die."

It was a ruthless act in a war that had been full of ruthless acts, although no one was particularly thrilled with introducing a woman into that mix. Wellesbourne turned to look at de Russe, to see what the man's reaction was to all of this, but de Russe was characteristically emotionless. He seemed to be focused intently on Warwick, however.

"So you take St. John's sister hostage if, in fact, she is even at Bradley," de Russe said to Warwick. "You exchange her for le Bec. But what do we do about Babylon and Manchester?"

Warwick fixed on the big, young knight quite seriously. "We take them back," he said flatly. "Did you truly believe I will leave both of those valuable assets in Edward's hands? Of course not. We go and take them both back, starting with Babylon."

It was the order Wellesbourne and de Russe had expected, one they had hoped for. But there was one thing in both of their minds, and probably Warwick's, too, that had not yet been resolved.

"What about the traitor?" Wellesbourne wanted to know. "If he happens to be one of the men who survived and is still in our ranks, he could send word on to those who hold Babylon. We cannot let them be forewarned if we are to succeed in regaining the castle."

Warwick was well aware of that. "You say that only le Bec's inner circle knew of his plans?"

"To my knowledge, the knights were the only ones who knew."

Warwick's eyes glittered in the dim light of the tent, a serious and deadly cast. "With Forbes dead, le Bec presumably captured, and de Birmingham presumed dead at Babylon, that leaves you and de Russe and le Mon," he said. "I suppose we have narrowed the field down to find out if there is a traitor among the knight corps."

He meant either one of them and they weren't too terribly insulted by it. Warwick didn't trust anyone implicitly, and they knew they had nothing to hide, so they weren't worried. Still, the thought of a traitor among them was unpleasant at the very least. If it wasn't either one of them, that left le Mon, and they couldn't imagine the man to be a traitor. But stranger things had happened.

As they left Warwick's tent to prepare their mounts to depart once again for battle, Matthew muttered to Gaston.

"Do not say anything to le Mon about this," he said quietly. "Let us keep Warwick's plans between ourselves and only tell le Mon when we have to. If it is he who is sending word to Edwards's camp, then we must discover it before he does any more damage."

Gaston was silent as they walked across the frozen earth, heading for the corral where their horses had been tethered. The sky above was pewter as a storm rolled in and bad weather once again threatened.

"I do not believe it is any of the knights," de Russe finally said. "For all we know, only the knights had been told of Kenton's plans. But we cannot control who *else* Kenton told."

Matthew looked at him. "What do you mean?"

Gaston cast him a long glance. "Who was Kenton close to who had ties to Edward?"

Matthew scratched his head. He replied without hesitation. "Lady Thorne."

"What if he told her his plans and she is the one who sent word to Conisbrough?"

Matthew simply shook his head. He didn't have an answer for that, mostly because it made perfect sense. "But why?" he wanted to know. "She seemed as fond of him as he was of her. Why betray him?"

De Russe's gaze lingered on the horses up ahead, his manner weary and serious. "It is possible she only pretended to be fond of him," he muttered. "It is possible she was using him for information just as le Bec claimed he was using her."

"Do you really believe that?"

"I do not know what to believe."

The men continued on in silence, thoughts lingering on the lovely Lady Thorne. Was it possible that she had only used Kenton for her own means? Was it possible they were both simply using each other? Of course, it was. But what seemed odd to both Matthew and Gaston was the fact that Kenton seemed to let her use him quite freely. Never did the man have his guard up around her from what they had seen. That being the case, he wouldn't be the only man to fall victim to a pretty but vicious face.

It would seem that even great men like Kenton le Bec had a weakness when it came to a beautiful woman.

A viper in disguise.

HE'D BEEN ASLEEP again.

Startled awake, the first thing Kenton realized was the very strong smell of cloves in the air. The air itself was warm and stale, smelling of that rotted smell of fabric that had become wet and not dried out properly. It was a heavy scent, mixed with the cloves, making the entire atmosphere wholly unpleasant.

Kenton lay there a moment, staring up at the canvas ceiling. The cloth was oiled, and draped, and he began to remember where he was: Saxilby's tent. He remembered being brought here, put onto a pallet, but that was the last he recalled. A hand moved to his forehead where he had fallen and he gingerly fingered the lump there, although it wasn't as sore as it had been. His vision was clear, too. As he lay there and fingered the bump, he heard a quiet voice.

"So you are awake?" a man said. "I was wondering if you ever would awaken. That was a nasty bump on your head."

Kenton turned in the direction of the voice, seeing an older man seated upon a rather sumptuous bed. Kenton noticed that his neck didn't hurt like it had earlier, either, and he was able to move better than he had in days. He shifted slightly to gain a better look at the man who was addressing him.

"Forgive me, my lord," he said formally. "It is not usual for me to greet someone lying on my back. The bump on my head feels better but I am not entirely sure I can sit up."

The man smiled faintly. "You look strong and healthy enough to me, Sir Kenton," he said, his gaze moving over Kenton's supine form. "You are, in fact, Kenton le Bec?"

With great effort, Kenton managed to roll onto his right side and realized that all of his pain hadn't gone away, after all. He was still very sore.

"I am," he grunted, breathing heavily. "Would you be so kind as to introduce yourself so I know who I am speaking with?"

The man on the bed stood up, stiffly. "John Saxilby," he replied. "Finally, we meet in person. I have faced many a battle against you, le Bec, and I even saw you once, but I will admit that when you were brought to my tent, I did not recognize you. You appear quite different with your armor on."

Kenton smiled, though it was without humor. "I can only imagine that I do not look like my usual handsome self," he said. "It also seems that my armor and weapons were taken from me, however, things that would make me recognizable."

Saxilby nodded. "I will make sure your things are returned to you," he said. "But you should know that you are now my prisoner."

"I assumed as much."

"My physic has tended to your head for the past two days. He says you will recover."

Very slowly, Kenton managed to push himself up into a sitting position. He was unsteady, and the world rocked a bit, but all things considered, he didn't feel all that bad. More than anything, he was simply exhausted and hungry, with perhaps a bit of apprehension for the immediate future.

"You have my gratitude," he said. "May I inquire to the status of my men? I saw that many were prisoners. What do you intend to do with them?"

Saxilby was moving stiffly because of the gash to his buttocks and hips. Sixty-nine black catgut stitches were holding the skin together. He shuffled towards a collapsible table, scratching gingerly at his arse. "Damn stitches," he grunted. "They itch like the devil. I will have such a scar across my backside that not even my wife will find me attractive any longer. More is the pity."

Kenton watched the man pour a measure of wine into two cups. He then collected the cups and headed to Kenton, extending one to the man. Kenton took it gratefully.

"Women are strange creatures, I am told," he said as he gulped down the very tart wine. "Mayhap she will surprise you."

Saxilby drank with Kenton, eyeing the big man on the floor. "Are you married, le Bec?"

Kenton shook his head. "I am not."

"A betrothed, mayhap?"

"Nay."

Saxilby drained his cup and turned back for more. "Then you are fortunate," he said. "Women are more trouble than they are worth at times. Daughters, especially. I have five that you could have your pick from should you ever decide to lift your sword for Edward."

Kenton's grin turned genuine; it was a far more pleasant conversation than he had expected as a captor to a prisoner. In fact, he was quite astonished at Saxilby's amiability. Even so, Kenton was on his guard. That was natural in his world.

"I am afraid I am not the marrying kind, my lord," he said. "I would make a terrible husband."

Saxilby glanced at him in puzzlement as he poured his wine. "The great Kenton le Bec would make a fine husband for any woman," he said. "Are you sure you would not consider lifting a sword for Edward? My daughters all have vast dowries. It would make you very rich."

Kenton shook his head, trying not to laugh. "Would you really marry one of them off to a man you just captured?"

"Possibly. I have five daughters, le Bec. Capturing their husbands may be the only way I am able obtain husbands for them all."

Kenton couldn't help the laughter now. "That is unfortunate, my lord," he said, "but as I said, I would not make a good husband. Even though I am not married nor betrothed, I am afraid my heart does belong to someone. I suppose that sounds strange coming from a man such as myself, but it is the truth. You will have to look elsewhere for a husband for your daughters."

Saxilby's gaze lingered on him, a sort of appraising sense of amusement in his expression. "Then you are a romantic, le Bec?" he asked. "I find that astonishing. Does this poor woman have a name?"

"If she does, you will never hear it from my lips."

Now it was Saxilby's turn to laugh. He downed his second cup of wine and poured himself another. "That is wise," he said. "But you were correct when you said women are strange creatures. They are, indeed."

Kenton sensed something more to that statement as Saxilby came to him and refilled his cup. He eyed the older man, waiting for him to elaborate, but Saxilby remained silent. Kenton drank deeply of his wine.

"Now that I am your captive," Kenton said, shifting the subject, "mayhap you can tell me what will become of me now."

Saxilby nodded. "It is your right, I suppose," he said, his gaze lingering on Kenton. "Tell me, Sir Kenton, if you were in my position, what would *you* do with a prisoner like yourself? A warrior of such high regard?"

Kenton lifted his dark eyebrows in thought. "I would lock me up in the safest place possible, I suppose," he said. He cast a long glance at Saxilby. "I could possibly ransom me. Or I could send me to Edward as a prize."

Saxilby snorted. "You would not execute you?"

Kenton shook his head. "I would be more valuable alive than dead."

Saxilby could not disagree. "That is exactly what I was thinking," he said, stroking his chin. "It would be a travesty to execute a knight of your caliber. Moreover, I am sure Edward wishes to speak with you. He is a great admirer of yours."

"That is flattering."

Saxilby simply lifted a cup to him, as if saluting him, and turned around to rummage for some food to eat. There was a tray nearby with remnants of an earlier meal and the man went to pick through it. Kenton watched him, thinking that the entire conversation had been far too casual. Jovial, even. He couldn't help wonder if there was an ulterior motive to Saxilby's hospitality although he really couldn't think of what, possibly, that might be. Would they try to probe him for information on Henry and Warwick's movements? That was very likely and Kenton braced himself for that possibility. But before they moved to interrogate him, Kenton had a few things he wanted to know.

"May I ask a question, my lord?" Kenton finally asked.

Saxilby was picking through some stale cheese. "You may. But I reserve the right not to answer."

"Fair enough."

"Then ask."

"You laid siege to Babylon Castle two weeks ago," Kenton said carefully, watching the man for his reaction. "You fled, defeated, but then now you came to Manchester where I happened to be. You came as an army prepared to engage, as if you knew where I was. What made you come to Manchester? And how did you return so strong after so recent a defeat?"

Saxilby managed to find a few edible bits and brought them over to share with Kenton. "You handed us our defeat at Babylon, did you not?"

"I did."

"You and the weather."

"Thank God for all of that snow."

Saxilby snorted ironically. "God had nothing to do with it," he said, handing Kenton one of the less-stale pieces of cheese. "Tell me where Warwick is and I will tell you about Babylon and Manchester. Warwick is in Yorkshire, is he not?"

It was a fair question and, Kenton supposed, no great secret. Warwick never made his movements secret. But more than that, Kenton wanted very much to know how Saxilby knew where he was, or how he had happened upon him. He was very curious and increasingly concerned about Babylon now that Edward's forces knew Kenton was no longer there to protect it. Therefore, he was inclined to give a little information in order to receive some.

"He is in Yorkshire," he said, although he didn't say exactly where the man was. "The last I saw the man and his army, he was heading west."

"*Where* in Yorkshire?"

Kenton shrugged. "Your spies could probably tell you better than I could," he replied evenly. "He said something about Wakefield but that could have easily changed. He could have headed to Leeds or Beeston. He has supporters there, but you probably already know that."

Saxilby nodded, picking at the stale bread. "We had heard Wakefield as well," he said. "My scouts have not returned from Yorkshire so I do not know if, in fact, Warwick has gone there."

"Nor do I," Kenton said truthfully. "My focus has been on Babylon. Now, will you tell me how you came across me in Manchester? I would like to know. We thought you and your men were well gone, at least for a while, but you returned with strength."

Saxilby eyed him a moment before answering. "We returned with Conisbrough."

Conisbrough. Somehow, Kenton wasn't surprised. Warwick had even warned him about the garrison.

"I see," he said. "That is where you went after you left Babylon?"

Saxilby nodded in confirmation. "That is where we went, chased by Warwick until he veered away so as not to confront the garrison," he replied. "Warwick did not send you word of any of this?"

Kenton shook his head. "He did not," he said, "although I knew there was a big contingent at Conisbrough. So you brought the garrison with you, did you? That explains the fresh troops but it still does not explain how you found me. Did your scouts tell you?"

Saxilby, on his fourth cup of wine, was feeling his drink. It usually made him loud and humorous and chatty, and this was no exception. Had he not had so much wine in him, he probably wouldn't have told Kenton anything but given the fact that he was slightly drunk, his usual control was weak. Plus, the conversation had been so casual, as he had intended, that it was almost as if old friends were speaking. He'd hoped to lure Kenton into a false sense of security and pump him for information, but it seemed that his plan was working in reverse. He was the one doing the talking.

"Nay, the scouts told us nothing," he said, reaching for the pitcher of wine again. "Think, le Bec. You conquered Babylon and her occupants who are, in fact, loyal to Edward. Do you think they wanted you there? Do you think they would sit back and do nothing while you took over their fortress? Of course not. It was Babylon who sent a missive to Conisbrough telling us where you were. Even as we speak, Babylon should be back in our hands because hundreds of men went to reclaim her, knowing you had vacated and were heading to Manchester."

Kenton stared at Saxilby, feeling as if he'd just been hit in the gut. He suddenly couldn't breathe and his balance, tenuous at best, was in danger of weakening further. He struggled to regain his breath, and his balance, shocked to the core at what he was hearing.

"*Babylon* sent word to the garrison?" he repeated, stunned. "Who? A servant came to tell you? Or a soldier even?"

Saxilby took a deep drink of wine, wiping his mouth with the back of his hand. "Nay," he said. "It was a missive from Lady Thorne. She told us everything. How she knew of your movements, I do not know, but she was right about you. If not for her, Manchester would be in Henry's hands and Babylon would still be under his control. But I'm curious how she was able to send the missive, le Bec. Did you not lock the woman up?"

Lady Thorne. The room began to spin and Kenton fell back on the pallet, staring up at the ceiling that was moving around, as if he were looking at it underwater. Everything was moving and he felt sick, sicker than he'd ever felt in his life. *It's not possible!* His mind screamed. *Nicola would never do anything like that! She would not do that to me!*

But then he stopped... and he remembered...

... the last time he saw her had been a terrible and tense conversation. God, what had she said to him? That she knew he had only intended to use her? Kenton remembered thinking that someone had poisoned her mind against him and... *oh, God...* poisoned it enough so that she would hate him so terribly that she would send to Conisbrough and tell them of his battle plans?

Hate him so terribly that she would betray him?

Kenton put his hands to his face, closing his eyes, feeling like the biggest fool in the entire world. Nay, not a fool... he felt like a betrayed and defeated man. Nicola knew of his plans because he had told her. She had asked him. *Asked him!* Even then, was that what she had been planning? God in heaven, what on earth could have happened to poison the woman so much against him? What did he do to make her hate him so? He couldn't even fathom what he might have done. Worse yet, she wouldn't tell him. Now, he would never know, for it was clear she hated him enough to betray him to Edward's forces. She had sealed his fate and he was now a prisoner.

It was what she wanted.

"Le Bec?" Saxilby broke into his whirling thoughts. "Are you well, man?"

Kenton still had his hands over his face. "I... I suppose the wine was too much," he muttered, lying, when what he really wanted to do was cry. Aye, he truly did. "I... I will lie down for a time, if you do not mind. I find I have little strength."

Saxilby gathered the food that Kenton wasn't eating and stood up, heading for his own comfortable bed. "And I will join you," he said, shoving bread in his mouth. "This wound is taxing me greatly."

Kenton didn't say anything more. He could hear Saxilby lay upon his bed and he could hear the man as he grunted, moving around and trying to get comfortable with such a nasty wound. But that was the extent of Kenton's interest in Lord Saxilby. His thoughts, mind, heart, and soul were so battered and burdened that he could hardly hold a coherent idea. The one thought that was prevalent, however, rolling over and over in his mind, was something quite simple and factual...

Nicola betrayed me...

... Nicola betrayed me!

Even as the words filled his head, he could hardly believe them. He never knew it was possible to hurt so badly, for Nicola Aubrey-Thorne succeeded in doing what hundreds of thousands of men over the past twenty-two years couldn't do.

She had defeated him.

CHAPTER SEVENTEEN

Babylon Castle

P RIOR TO HER short stay when Kenton had her thrown in, Nicola couldn't remember the last time she was in Babylon's vault. It had been years ago and even so, she couldn't remember why she had come. She thought it might have been because Gaylord had a pair of thieves in his custody, awaiting justice, but she honestly couldn't recall. Looking around at the slick, stone walls, cold and some with a growth of mold, she couldn't see why anyone would come down here voluntarily. It was purely hellish.

The steps leading down to the only level of the vault, which was just below the gatehouse, were narrow and slippery. Nicola found herself gripping the walls as she followed St. John down the steps, illuminated by the torch he held. Dipped in animal fat, it gave off thick black smoke that caught her in the face more than once. Eyes watering, she was fairly amazed that she hadn't slipped on her way down the steps because she could hardly see a thing.

The floor of the vault, dug out those years ago, sloped to one side so it gave one a sense of vertigo when walking on it. When Nicola hit bottom, she listed heavily to the right and almost crashed into the wall because of the floor's angle. Putting her hand out to steady herself against the stone, she struggled to adjust her eyes to the dim light as St. John went to the only cell in the vault and unhinged the big, iron lock.

Blinking her eyes, trying to clear them, Nicola could see a figure lying on the floor of the cell and she made her way over to the cell door just as St. John entered, bending over the supine figure.

"You, there," St. John said, sticking out a foot to roust the body. "Wake up. Someone wishes to see you."

A head swiftly lifted and Nicola immediately recognized Conor, even though she shouldn't have – his face was swollen and beaten, and one eye was so swollen that it was shut. He didn't look anything like the man she remembered. His mouth was bloodied and as he struggled to sit up, she could see that his arms and hands were badly damaged. Two of his fingers were clearly broken. Conor couldn't quite manage to sit up completely so he leaned back against the wall behind him, struggling to look up at St. John. It was fairly obvious how badly the man was injured and Nicola was horrified at the sight.

I did this, she thought, sickened. *Dear God... I did this!*

The more she looked at the knight, the more ill she became. After her brief conversation with St. John up in the gatehouse, Nicola's mind had been whirling with the information she'd been given – Kenton was presumed defeated at Manchester and all of his men left behind at Babylon were now prisoners of Edwardian supporters who had been less than kind in dealing with the conquered.

Nicola had seen the prisoners corralled and beaten, men who had watched her walk by them, men who might be hoping she might help them. Even though her husband had been loyal to Edward, all of Kenton's men knew that Lady Thorne and Kenton le Bec had been friendly towards one another. Of course, they couldn't be certain that her friendliness hadn't been out of a necessity to stay alive, but at this point, they had no hope left.

Because of her treachery, Nicola had taken it away from them.

Now she was looking at Conor as the man lay there, beaten and bloodied. Quickly, she wracked her mind with a way to help him and she could only come up with one thing. It was a lie, and a bold one, but if she didn't do it now, immediately, there would never be another chance. What she had in mind had to look like a gut reaction, an instantaneous response to the man in the cell. At the moment, she was willing to do anything to right her betrayal, to make restitution for sending that missive to Conisbrough. She was willing to lie until she could lie no more.

She had to do something.

"God's Bones!" she exclaimed loudly. "Is *this* the man you thought to be a le Bec knight?"

St. John looked at her, puzzled by her statement. "Indeed, my lady," he said hesitantly, unsure of her reaction. "He was upon the walls and he fought against us. I would assume he was the enemy."

Nicola rushed to Conor's side, falling to her knees beside him. He was looking at her with some dismay and confusion as she reached out, gingerly touching his swollen eye. "This is not the le Bec knight I asked of," she told him, thinking that Conor's eye socket must be broken from the amount of swelling on his face. "I was asking over a big, hairy man with dark hair. I did not mean this man. He is one of my husband's men."

Much to Conor's credit, he didn't react with the surprise he felt. He hadn't expected those words to come out of Lady Thorne's mouth and he was, frankly, astonished. She continued to poke and prod around his face as, behind her, St. John put his hands on his hips and cocked his head in puzzlement.

"A Thorne knight, my lady?" St. John asked. "Who is it? I do not know him."

Nicola sighed heavily. "Do you know every knight in my husband's service?" she asked, rather testily. "Do you know every knight in Henry's service? Of course you do not. This man is my husband's cousin from Scotland."

St. John scowled. Now, great doubt was joining his confusion. "But this man tried to do battle against us," he pointed out. "He was armed on the battlements and came down to the gatehouse with a sword in hand."

Nicola turned to him, frowning. "There is fighting all around him and he is not supposed to arm himself?" she asked, incredulous. "Did you stop to think that mayhap he was coming to fight *with* you?"

The doubt and confusion cooled. Now, St. John was simply stumped. "My lady," he said, trying to make sense out of what she was telling him. "When you opened the postern gate for us, you made no mention of any knights belonging to your husband. Why did you not tell me so I knew what to expect?"

Nicola hadn't expected St. John to blurt the details of her betrayal. Now her secret was out and she turned to look at Conor, who was gazing back at her with the same unwavering expression. But deep in those blue eyes, she could see the rage, the disgust. *Now he knows,* Nicola thought with a sinking heart. *He knows of my sin. Then he must also know I am trying to right it.*

"That is because you ran past me so quickly I did not have time," she hissed at St. John, rising to her feet. She pointed at Conor. "Bring that man up to the keep. You have beaten him so soundly I am not entirely sure he will ever be the same, but I will try to help him nonetheless. Bring him up to me, I say. And then next time, ask a man his loyalties before you nearly beat him to death!"

St. John was feeling quite berated and, truth be told, quite foolish. He looked at Conor, who was gazing at Lady Thorne with his one good eye. There was no discernable reaction in the man's face. Brome thought it all rather odd that the red-headed knight wasn't speaking to the lady or at least showing some measure of relief at her appearance. He focused on the man.

"Why did you not tell me any of this?" he asked Conor. "You have not said a word since we captured you. Why not?"

Nicola interrupted before Conor could speak. "Get out," she told St. John. "Get out immediately. I would speak with him alone."

St. John thought there was something very strange going on but out of respect to Lady Thorne, who had truly been through a great ordeal with Kenton le Bec as her captor, he simply turned and obeyed her wishes. His footsteps were slow and heavy up the slippery stairs, as if he was conveying his displeasure and suspicion at having been sent away.

Nicola remained silent until he was gone and even then, even when his footfalls were gone, she remained quiet for a moment. Knowing that Conor knew it was she who betrayed Kenton's men, Nicola knew her only hope to salvage the situation was to be the aggressor in the conversation and come out swinging. Conor had to understand her reasons and then she would ask him a few questions of her own.

Now, truths would be told. She wanted answers.

"It was I who sent a message to Conisbrough and told them that Kenton had left for Manchester," she said, whirling on Conor. "Do you know why I did it? Because I heard Kenton tell his men that he was only using me for information. He was trying to use a sweet and honeyed tactic against me and I tell you now that I will not be made a fool of. So I sent word to Conisbrough and told them Kenton had left Babylon for Manchester. But you will tell me now, Sir Conor, and tell me truthfully – did Kenton ever tell you that he was using me for information? Did he tell you that he had tried to force me into submission once and it did not work? Did he tell you that his tactic was now charm and affection?"

Conor stared up at her with his one good eye. His features were starting to register some kind of emotion, but mostly, they seemed to be registering confusion.

"My lady," he said, his voice hoarse from having been kicked in the neck. "Kenton has never said anything about you to me, in any fashion. If he was attempting to use you, then I am unaware."

Nicola crossed her arms, her brow furrowed, feeling hurt and furious. Somehow, speaking of Kenton and his actions was bringing about all manner of confusion and sorrow all over again.

"You will not cover for him," she told him, lowering her voice. "He was in my husband's solar a few days before leaving for battle at Manchester, speaking to his men on how he was using me for information. Do you deny you were in that room and heard that conversation?"

Conor was trying to think very hard on the day and location she was referring to and it began to occur to him that it might be the same day that he and de Russe began their animosity towards one another. That was the only time since Warwick left Babylon that Kenton had gathered all of the knights, so it had to be the moment she was speaking of.

"A few days before leaving for battle at Manchester?" he repeated, struggling to work through the cobwebs of both injury and faded memory. "Do you mean when he was speaking to Wellesbourne and de Russe?"

"I thought I heard their voices."

"In the solar?"

"Aye."

Conor chewed his lip with thought, remembering the conversation in that room before he'd been sent away. He sighed heavily, remembering the conference with some clarity, mostly because of the feelings involved between him and de Russe.

"What you heard was de Russe and Wellesbourne confronting Kenton for not following through on Warwick's orders," he said. "I was there when they accused him of spending too much time with you and ignoring his orders."

Nicola's fury took a bit of a dousing. "They said that to him?"

"Aye."

"What did he say?"

Conor tried to shrug but he couldn't quite manage it with his bruised and beaten body. "I am not sure," he admitted, "for I challenged de Russe for slandering Kenton's reputation. Kenton sent me out of the room so that de Russe and I would not come to blows. What, exactly, did you hear Kenton say, my lady?"

Nicola was starting to feel increasingly confused and anxious about the situation. "He said that by virtue of my marriage to Gaylord, I was an enemy of Henry," she said, recalling what she'd heard nearly verbatim. With such hurtful words, she remembered them down to the last syllable. "He said that I would know my husband's allies and that I might have even known what my husband and his allies have discussed. He said that he could not beat the information out of me so it was in his best interest to be gentle with me in order to discover what I know. Surely he said the same thing to you at some point."

Conor was genuinely stumped by her statement. Slowly, he shook his head. "Never, my lady, I swear it," he replied. "I have known Kenton le Bec for many years and I have never known him to be anything other than straightforward and forthright. He would not have tried to ply you with honeyed words in order to find out what you know, for Kenton le Bec does not use subversion tactics. If he was kind to you, or gentle, it was because he wanted to be."

Nicola gazed at the man, her face expressionless for a moment. Then, very slowly, her cheeks began to flush and her eyes grew moist. She blinked, rapidly, and turned away from Conor, wandering away until she came to a stone bench on the side of the cell. She sat heavily, grinding her bum into the moist, mossy stone.

"But I heard him say it," she whispered, fighting back tears. "How was I supposed to know he did not mean it? I heard him say he would use me. He spoke of me as if I were the enemy, which I am. Conor, I *am* your enemy."

Conor was watching her very closely. "You are," he agreed quietly. "But, my lady, I swear to you that I have never in my life seen Kenton behave the way he behaved with you. We all knew he was smitten with you and we assumed you were smitten with him as well. That is why Wellesbourne and de Russe confronted him. It was clear his attention was not where it should be."

Nicola blinked and a tear escaped. She quickly wiped it away. "Where should it be?"

"On Warwick's conquest. He was ignoring all of it because of you."

Nicola hung her head, fighting off sobs. She'd never felt so much remorse or guilt or horror in her entire life. She couldn't stave off the tears entirely so she sat there, quickly wiping at her face.

"I did not know," she whispered. "I thought I heard his true motives. I thought I heard him in an unguarded moment. I was angry… angry because he led me to believe that… it does not matter now. I have done terrible, terrible things. I have destroyed everything he has worked to accomplish."

Conor watched her lowered head, coming to understand that everything he had guessed was occurring between Lady Thorne and Kenton had, in fact, been true. The lady had made that abundantly clear. But she also made it clear that she was the one who had betrayed Kenton and his men, purely out of revenge for a misunderstanding, and he was caught up in a mistake of her doing. Aye, a good deal was becoming quite clear and Conor wasn't sure he was in a forgiving mood.

"If you are looking for absolution, I have none to give you," he said quietly. "There is no forgiveness in war."

Nicola sighed heavily, wiping her face of the tears that would not seem to stop falling. "I am not asking for your absolution," she said, daring to look up at him, "but I thank you for explaining the situation to me from your perspective. I am sorry that the men from Conisbrough beat you and I believe I can convince them that you are my husband's knight. Will you at least let me do that for you so you do not rot away in this vault?"

Conor's swollen lips twitched in an ironic smile. "I will not surrender my honor to save myself, my lady," he said. "Your offer is generous, but I will decline."

Nicola forced herself to stop weeping, focusing on Conor and what needed to be done. She was quite serious when she spoke. "I am not asking you to surrender your honor," she said. "I may need your help, Sir Conor, and I have no one else I can turn to. You understand what is happening here and I will need your counsel. If you hate me for all of this, I do not blame you, but I must try to right the wrongs that I have committed. I am told that Manchester fell to Edward, which means Kenton is either dead or captured. I must do all that I can to discover what has happened to the man and when I do, I may need your assistance. Or I may release you and let you go to him. Either way, it is a better ending for you than moldering away in Babylon's vault."

Conor considered her words. Dying in this moldy hole certainly did not appeal to him and if Lady Thorne was sincere about discovering what had become of Kenton, then he was not opposed to helping her. Perhaps she really did want to right her wrong; perhaps she was only fearful of her immortal soul for the moment and said such words to convince him to join or forgive her. He would not do either of those things. But if there was a chance to get free and go to Kenton, he would be a fool not to take it.

"Very well," he agreed. "I will go along with your charade if you sincerely mean to locate Kenton. But know that you do not have my trust."

Nicola wasn't surprised or offended by his statement. "I do not need your trust," she said. "All I need is your cooperation. I must have it or you will remain here in the vault. I cannot help you beyond that."

Conor nodded shortly. "I give you my word that I will cooperate with whatever plan you may have in mind purely because I will be unable to help Kenton, at this point, any other way," he said. "What did you have in mind?"

Nicola stood up from the cold, stone bench, brushing at her wet and dirty bum. "I will find out from St. John where they have taken Kenton if, in fact, he is still alive," she said. "St. John suggested he would be taken to Conisbrough, as the nearest stronghold for Edward. I will insist that St. John send word to the men in Manchester to see what has become of Kenton and then we shall know how to proceed."

Conor watched her as she moved towards him. "And Forbes, le Mon, de Russe, and Wellesbourne," he added. "You should find out what has become of them, too. All of those excellent knights... it is hard to comprehend if they are all lost."

Nicola stood over him, feeling extreme guilt with his words even though she didn't sense he had said them to offend her. He was simply stating his thoughts.

"I will find out what I can, I swear it," she said. "I did this. I will do what I must to right it, no matter what the cost."

Conor's eyes flickered. "You speak of enemy knights, my lady."

"I speak of men who were kinder to me than my husband, or his men, ever were."

Conor could hear the emotion in her voice when she spoke. "Then what now?" he asked. "What would you have me do if I am to be an accomplice in your plan?"

Nicola pondered that a moment. "I will claim you as one of Gaylord's men and none who are loyal to me will dispute that," she said. "Hopefully we can carry on the charade until we find out what has happened to Kenton. When we do, we will decide what course to take."

There wasn't much Conor could say to that although he didn't think her plan for him was going to work. Sooner or later, someone would talk. They would mention the big knight who had come with le Bec, a knight who was now being claimed by Lady Thorne as one of Gaylord's men, and St. John would realize he had been lied to, which made Conor realize that he could not remain at Babylon for any length of time. He had to escape and allowing Lady Thorne to think that he was going along with her scheme was essential to his own scheme.

He had to flee Babylon and find Warwick.

With his own plan in mind, Conor watched Nicola as she left the cell and went to the stairs, calling up to the guards and to St. John on the level above. She was demanding help in removing him from his cell and shortly, men appeared to carry him out. He could walk, but barely, and it was slow-going until he reached the light of the inner ward above. After that, he ended up in the third floor of the keep in the room where Lady Thorne's boys used to sleep. There was a single bed there now, restful and padded, and he was grateful for the peace and comfort.

Now, he had his own plans to make.

CHAPTER EIGHTEEN

March (Spring)

T HEY HAD RETURNED everything to Kenton but his weapons. They'd
even returned his horse. Several days after his defeat at Manchester, Kenton and Saxilby and about five hundred men had made the trek
back to Conisbrough Castle, including a couple of hundred of Kenton's
men who were prisoners.

They departed Manchester on a bright day, nearly the first of
spring, but it was still terribly cold. The roads, because of the late snows
and wet weather, were terrible and nearly impassible at points, but the
Saxilby army managed to move through or around anything that
seemed like a blockade. Travel was slow-going, however, due to both
the road conditions and the number of wounded they were carrying,
and a trip that should have taken two days in decent conditions ended
up taking four.

Kenton had seen Conisbrough Castle many times from a distance
but he had never been inside the structure, which was quite vast. Much
like Babylon, it had an enormous keep with mural stairs that led to
different levels, and a great hall in the bailey. While his men had been
shuttled to a protected area next to the hall, Kenton had been taken
inside the keep.

Surprisingly, Saxilby didn't put him in the vault, which is what he
had mostly expected. He was a prisoner, after all, and a valuable one, so

Saxilby treated him with a goodly amount of courtesy by placing him in a small, guarded chamber on the fourth floor of Conisbrough's keep. His armor was taken from him, however, and he was left with nothing but his clothing. He was not allowed to attend meals in the hall or outside of his room, but the meals were generous and he did not want for food. He was given no utensils at all, nothing that could be used as a weapon, but it didn't particularly bother him. In fact, nothing seemed to bother him any longer.

Nothing seemed to matter to him any longer.

Kenton was a career knight from a long line of career knights. His grandfather had been the great Richmond le Bec and his grandmother a bastard daughter of Henry IV, so he was distantly related to the current king. From the time he was old enough to understand, he knew what had been expected of him – serving men sworn to the king and making a difference in his world. He had earned a great reputation alongside The Lion of the North, Atticus de Wolfe, but he'd amicably parted ways with Atticus years ago to pursue his career with Warwick. Atticus was more concerned with holding down the north and the Scots borders while Kenton headed into heavy battles flying Henry's banners. It was a life he had been trained to do and something he did very well. But the most recent events in his life, particularly with a widowed lady whose husband had once served Edward, seemed to have sucked everything out of him.

Everything he thought he ever knew was unimportant any longer.

Nowadays, instead of plotting his escape, he seemed content to be a prisoner. As long as they were treating him well, there was no real reason to try to break from Conisbrough, which he couldn't do anyway. The place was virtually impenetrable and, not knowing the layout, he would be foolish to try and escape. Until he knew the place a little better, or perhaps until he had more of an opportunity to escape, he wasn't going to make the attempt. He'd find himself worse off than he already was and he knew it. He had their trust for the moment and wanted to keep it.

But it was more than that. He simply didn't feel the urge to escape. What was there to escape *to*? The woman he loved had betrayed him and he still couldn't believe what she had done. He'd tried not to think back to the stolen kisses they had shared, or the joyful times in Manchester shopping or even the gaiety after they had returned home. Everything had been more delightful and satisfying than he'd ever known. Spending evenings supping with Nicola and her children, or helping the boys learn to fish… it was a life he'd never known to exist, a life that revolved around a beautiful woman and her intelligent boys whom he was quite fond of. He was quite fond of them *all* so to know that what he had enjoyed so much, that fleeting taste of heaven he'd experienced, was all a lie was something he could not accept.

So he stood next to the tiny lancet window of his tiny chamber, peering out into the sky and thinking of things he probably shouldn't think of. He could hear the bailey down below, the hustle and bustle of it, and at night he could hear the sentries on patrol, but he didn't pay much attention. His mind wandered back to Babylon every night, remembering how difficult it had been for Nicola to put the boys to bed because they wanted to remain in the hall and watch the knights play their games of chance. He remembered sitting with Tab when the crazed old woman burst out of her closet and explaining to the terrified young lad that the frightful creature in white tatters was not, in fact, a ghost. He helped the child to grow, to realize that there was nothing to be afraid of.

He'd liked that feeling of accomplishment.

He couldn't even become upset at himself for letting him grow close to Nicola's boys because there had been no way to prevent it. For some reason, he had been drawn to the boys and they to him, and he had enjoyed every moment of Tab's boldness, of Teague's sweet lisp, and Tiernan's expressive silence. It made him want sons just like them, sons from Nicola, but that had been a fool's dream. He had been foolish to even think such things.

Nay, he couldn't muster the strength to become angry with himself in any fashion for what had happened. He kept going back to his conversation with Nicola in the storage vaults of Babylon when she had screamed at him. It was at that moment that he realized things between them had changed and he was convinced someone, perhaps one of his own men, had convinced Nicola that his intentions were dishonorable. That *he* was dishonorable. He didn't blame her because she didn't know any better. She was a woman, after all, and a very smart one, but their relationship had been so new and so tenuous. It hadn't even been a relationship at all, to be truthful.

It had simply been his dream.

Therefore, he stood against the wall, gazing from the window and reflecting on what could have been. He hadn't the strength or need or urgency to do anything else and on this dusky evening as the sun set against the western sky, his thoughts and intentions were no different. He didn't even know how many days had passed since he'd been brought here; he hadn't been keeping track. But he knew, by the color of the sky, that soon his meal would be brought to him, another meal in an endless line of meals that he wouldn't particularly eat. Food made him think of Nicola. In fact, *everything* made him think of Nicola. As he lingered by the window, the bolt on the outside of his door was thrown.

Kenton turned just about the time Saxilby entered the chamber. The man was combed and shaved, which was far more than Kenton could say about himself. In fact, he had a bit of beard growth that he kept scratching on his chin and he hadn't bathed in weeks. He stood by the window in his filthy clothes as Saxilby closed the chamber door and pulled up the only chair in the chamber. He settled himself, getting comfortable.

"Greetings, le Bec," he said. "Have you been content in this chamber so far?"

Kenton nodded. "For a prisoner, I am astonishingly comfortable," he said. "And the food has been plentiful. You have my thanks for your kind treatment."

Saxilby waved him off. "It is no trouble," he said. "Moreover, I would not send you to Edward half-starved and exhausted. That would not do for a man of your status. Speaking of half-starved, however, it has come to my attention that you have not been eating well. Is something the matter? Are you ill?"

Kenton exhaled slowly. "Nay," he said, his tone rather dull. "I am simply not hungry these days."

Saxilby grunted. "I suppose that I can understand that," he said. "Captivity is not normally an appetite inducer, which is why I have come to escort you on a walk about the grounds. I thought you might like to see some of Conisbrough while we discuss a few things. It might help your appetite."

Kenton came away from the window, arms folded across his big chest. "What things did you wish to discuss?"

Saxilby was treating it all very casually. "The changes that are coming in the near future," he said. "In fact, you are to have a visitor, although I am not entirely sure this will be good news to you."

"Visitor?" Kenton repeated. "Who?"

Saxilby wriggled his eyebrows as if about to relay particularly interesting information. "I received a missive from Brome St. John on the day we arrived from Manchester," he said. "If you do not know the name, you should. He is the garrison commander of Conisbrough and also the man who led the successful recapture of Babylon. He wanted to know what happened at Manchester and if we had managed to capture you. I sent a missive informing him that we had."

Kenton mulled over the information, finally turning away and going to his bed, where he sat heavily on the end of it. "I have heard the name of St. John," he said. "I do not know him personally. But what does this have to do with me having a visitor?"

Saxilby continued. "Upon learning that we hold you at Conisbrough, St. John sent another missive to inform me that he is returning to Conisbrough now that Babylon is secured and that he is bringing the Lady of Babylon with him." Saxilby's gaze lingered on Kenton. "I would assume you know Lady Thorne, le Bec."

Kenton's calm demeanor took a hit. "Of course I do," he gushed before he could stop himself. He was suddenly wildly curious as to why Nicola should be coming to Conisbrough, electrified by the news. But not wanting to look like a fool, he struggled to calm himself. "Why would Lady Thorne come to Conisbrough?"

Saxilby shrugged. "Why do women do anything?" he asked, a somewhat snide rhetorical question. "Women get it into their minds to do something and they do it. You are not married, le Bec, and would not understand this, but women are unpredictable and even mad at times. According to St. John, Lady Thorne wishes to see the man who held her and her family captive. I would assume she wants to berate you or take a stick to you. But have no fear; if she wants to beat you, I will not let her."

Kenton's mind was racing with the possibilities, the reasons, behind Nicola's arrival. But the more he thought on it, the more something became quite clear to him. Whatever happened, whatever reason she had, her appearance would end the feelings he had for her. He was in love with the woman, that was true, but after what she had done, after the words she had said, he was convinced she held no such feelings for him and it was therefore foolish for him to hold any feelings for her. He was positive she was coming to Conisbrough to tell him what a fool he was and how much she hated him.

Odd how only moments before, he was wallowing in memories of her, but now that he knew she was coming, he felt a sense of closure approach. He felt defensive, as if he wanted to protect himself emotionally. He wasn't entirely sure he liked that feeling, but there was nothing he could do about it. Nicola must be coming to tell him what she really thought of him and he would have to accept it. Whatever she said, he would have to accept it.

And he would have to move on with his life.

"She is not a very big woman," he said after a moment, trying to pretend her visit meant nothing to him. "I am sure I could defend myself."

Saxilby watched the man, noticing he would not look at him. He thought it rather odd behavior from the usually mannerly le Bec. "Mayhap," he said. "I knew her husband, Gaylord. Did you know him?"

Kenton shook his head. "I knew of him but I did not know him personally," he said. "He is dead, you know. He is buried in Babylon's chapel."

"Did Lady Thorne tell you this?"

"I saw his body myself."

Saxilby nodded but there was something ominous on his mind. "You did not desecrate the body, did you?" he asked fearfully. "Is that why she is coming to Conisbrough? Because you destroyed the body?"

Kenton shook his head. "We destroyed his crypt to identify the body but the body itself was left intact," he replied. "We did not damage it."

Saxilby grunted. "I see," he said. "Well, then mayhap Lady Thorne wants to curse you for smashing her husband's tomb, although I cannot believe that to be the case. He was a very unpleasant man, you know. I am not entirely sure how much his wife knows about his activities, but it is said that there are a few Thorne bastards running about in Yorkshire. The man had more than one mistress."

Kenton looked at him, then, not particularly surprise at what he was hearing but he naturally felt disgusted on Nicola's behalf. She had never mentioned anything about Gaylord's life or practices, and especially not rumors of bastards. It would have been a shameful thing for a wife to admit but it was more than possible that she didn't even know. Still, what a terrible thing for such a proud woman. She didn't deserve that. She deserved a husband who would ply her, and only her, with his attention.

"I would not know of this," Kenton finally said. "All I can tell you is that Gaylord Thorne is, indeed, dead."

Saxilby nodded, standing up wearily. "I have heard that as well," he said. "Months ago, I was told. Any idea how it happened?"

"A fever, I believe."

Saxilby accepted Kenton's reasons. He had no reason not to and no reason to believe that the truth was much more horrific than Kenton made it out to be. *His own son killed him*, Kenton thought, *because the man was beating his mother.* Kenton would keep Nicola's secrets even if she had betrayed him. Just because she created a wrong didn't mean he had to match her. He had more sense, and decency, than that.

He had more respect for the woman than she had ever shown him.

"Come along, le Bec," Saxilby broke into his thoughts. He knocked on the door and pulled it open when the guards on the other side threw the bolt. "Let us walk this vast complex and speak on things that do not involve warfare. I have a farm outside of Norwich, by the way. I breed war horses. Do you know much of horses?"

Kenton nodded. "I know enough."

"Then we will talk about horses for the time being," he said, leading Kenton from the room. "Soon enough St. John will be here and his conversation will not be so pleasant. He will want to know things. You had better prepare yourself."

Kenton didn't care about Brome St. John's arrival. He was only concerned with Nicola's arrival and why she was coming, what she had to say to him. He was eager to see her but on the other hand, he was wary to see her. God, he should hate her. He should utterly hate her for what she did. But he couldn't seem to bring himself to do it. Was he too forgiving or was he just foolish? Truthfully, Kenton had no idea. Perhaps he was neither.

Perhaps he was simply in love.

Stupid, but in love.

Babylon

NICOLA WAS IN the three small rooms she shared with her family. Her sons, as well as the serving women, were watching her shuttle things from the wardrobe to her bed where she had an open satchel. Conor was watching her, too. Several days after his near-death beating at the hands of Conisbrough soldiers, he was up and moving quite ably. And he never left Nicola's side, not for a moment. St. John had permitted it even though he didn't believe that Conor had been Gaylord's knight. There was just something about the relationship dynamics between the lady and the knight that were off somehow, leading him to believe that all was not as she was telling him.

Nicola knew this. She could see the doubt in St. John's eyes when it came to Conor, but to his credit, he never said anything. He permitted Conor to escort Lady Thorne about in a fortress that was full of unfamiliar soldiers. Nicola was grateful for St. John's generosity and she was further grateful that the man was polite enough to keep her informed about what was happening where it pertained to le Bec and Warwick. He'd sent a missive to Conisbrough several days ago asking for the status of Kenton, and had received word back that Kenton was, in fact, alive and at Conisbrough.

The news had brought tears to Nicola's eyes although she refused to let anyone see that reports on Kenton le Bec made her emotional, so the tears of relief she had shed for him had been done later in the privacy of her rooms. The realization that Kenton was alive had been overwhelming for her, overwhelming in the sense that she was vastly relieved and deeply happy. But the realization he was also a prisoner frightened her. She was gravely concerned for him. More than anything, she was desperate to see him.

After St. John received the missive informing him that Kenton was, indeed, at Conisbrough, Brome made immediately plans to depart Babylon and return to his garrison. He'd been away from it for weeks now and was anxious to return, which worked in Nicola's favor since she was eager to go with him. With a schedule that had them departing at dawn the next day for Conisbrough Castle, Nicola spent the evening in her chambers, packing her satchel, while Conor stood at his post by the door and the boys, with too much pent-up energy, were running through the rooms chasing each other.

"But... I do not understand, my lady," Janet said as she helped Nicola pack. "Why must you go to Conisbrough, too? You are not a prisoner and it is not your home. Why is Sir Brome taking you with him?"

The servants, as well as her sons, were in the dark regarding the reason for her traveling to Conisbrough. Nicola had purposely kept any information of Kenton from them, mostly because she was feeling guilty enough for what she'd done and she also wasn't one to share her private life with those who served her, so she'd simply kept quiet about it. Her serving women knew enough about her feelings for Kenton, whether or not she wanted them to, and she'd reached the point where she simply didn't want to speak of him or share anything about him. At least, that had been her mantra for the past several days, ever since they had spoken of the confrontation between Wellesbourne, de Russe, and Kenton regarding Kenton's failure to comply with Warwick's orders. Therefore, in the past few fragile days, nothing about Kenton le Bec had been mentioned to either the servants or to the boys. Nicola simply didn't speak of him at all.

But the same rules didn't apply to Conor. De Birmingham knew why she was going to Conisbrough because she had kept him apprised of the information St. John was giving her. He was accompanying her to Conisbrough, as she had requested it of St. John, and the man had naturally granted her request. He always granted her request, whether or not he wanted to, and Nicola was fairly certain he didn't want the big red-haired knight along with them, but he was submissive to the lady's wishes and Nicola didn't feel the least bit guilty about it.

Janet's question hung in the air as Nicola continued packing her satchel, mulling over what to say and how, precisely, to answer. She'd never admitted to anything between her and Kenton, not ever, and she wasn't going to start now, which would make explaining away her visit to Conisbrough to see Kenton rather difficult. Still, she had an idea and when the curious silence for her answer became excessive, she spoke.

"I am going to Conisbrough Castle because I have asked to go," she said. "It would seem that Sir Kenton is a prisoner there and I have a few things I wish to say to him."

The mention of Kenton being a prisoner brought horror and excitement to the women. "And Sir Matthew, my lady?" Raven gasped eagerly. "Is he a prisoner, too?"

Nicola glanced up at the dark-haired lass. "I do not know," she said honestly. "I was only told that Sir Kenton was at Conisbrough and it is my intention to speak to him about a few things, not the least of which is the tomb his men smashed in the chapel."

The servants knew about that but the younger boys did not. Instinctively, Nicola and her serving women looked to Teague and Tiernan to see if either one of them found interest in their mother's words. But there was no interest. Tiernan was under one of the beds, making a tent with a blanket, and Teague was over next to Conor, putting his wooden soldiers into Conor's open palm. Seeing that the twins were oblivious, Nicola continued in a softer tone.

"In any case," she said, shoving the last of her items into the satchel, "I will be at Conisbrough for a few days, mayhap even a few weeks. It will be your task to tend to the children during that time. I will leave them in your care."

Tab, who was watching his mother seriously, spoke. "I want to go with you, Mam."

Nicola shook her head. "That is not necessary," she said. "Sir Conor is going with me. I need you to stay here and protect your brothers. You are the head of the house and hold now, Tab. Teague and Tiernan are your responsibility until I return."

Tab frowned, looking over at Conor, who was dutifully holding his hand open while Teague put tiny toy soldiers and little spears into it. "I must go and protect you," he insisted. "I will go!"

Nicola shook her head patiently, stepping away from the satchel as Janet and Liesl tied it up. "Your brothers need you here," she said. "I need you here, Tab. If you go with me, I will be terribly worried about your brothers. But if I know you are here watching over them, then they will be safe. That is all I can ask for."

Tab was very unhappy that his mother was denying his request to go with her. It was more of a demand, anyway, but regardless, she was refusing him. Frustrated, Tab wandered in her direction, brow furrowed, feet shuffling. He kicked at the wooden floor.

"I want to see Sir Kenton, too," he finally muttered.

Nicola could see that he was disappointed more than anything. She put her hand on his slender shoulder. "I will tell him that you wanted to see him," she said quietly. "I am sure that will make him happy."

Tab looked up at her. "Will you ask him when he is coming back?"

Nicola sighed heavily. "He is a prisoner, Tab," she said. "Do you know what that means?"

He nodded without hesitation. "It means that he will fish and feast and go into town," he said. "We were prisoners and we did all those things."

Nicola cleared her throat softly, seeing that her son had a skewed view of what, exactly, being a prisoner entailed. She sat on the end of her bed, focusing on her serious son.

"Nay," she said. "That is not what it means. Being a prisoner means that Kenton will be kept in the vault. He will be unable to go anywhere he pleases. It means that those holding him can do what they wish with him."

Tab was puzzled. "But we were prisoners and we were not held in the vault."

Nicola lifted a finger, indicating the chamber surrounding them. "But Sir Kenton moved us out of our chambers and put us up here, did he not?" she asked. "He kept us here and would not let us go at first. Do you recall?"

Tab nodded. "But he let us out and he took me to fish," he said. "Mam, why do we not move back into our old chambers? Are we still prisoners?"

I am a prisoner of guilt, Nicola thought to herself. She forced a smile at her son. "We are not," she said. "I... I do not know why we do not move back into our former chambers. I have not thought about it, to be truthful. Would you like to direct the moving when I am away?"

That was perhaps a bit attractive to Tab, ordering people about and moving chambers, so he nodded even though he still wasn't entirely happy about not going to Conisbrough with his mother. Nicola, seeing his indecision, capitalized on it.

"There's a good lad," she said, kissing his head. "You will stay here and protect your brothers while I am away. I will return as soon as I can."

She stood up, hoping to move away from Tab before he started bombarding her with more questions, but she didn't move fast enough. He latched on to her hand.

"But Sir Kenton?" he wanted to know. "What will become of him?"

Nicola wasn't entirely sure how to answer him. "I... I do not know, Tab."

"Will they kill him?"

Her heart lurched, sickened at the mere thought. "I do not know."

Tab yanked on her. "You must make sure they do not," he insisted. "Sir Kenton is my friend! I do not want him to be killed!"

Nicola squeezed his hand, trying to soothe him. "I will do what I can to ensure they do not, I promise," she assured him. "Do not worry overly. I am sure Sir Kenton is well and I will tell him that you have asked for him."

Tab was frowning, still dwelling on the thought of Kenton being executed, as his mother pulled away and went back to her task of finalizing her packing. Nicola, however, didn't look at her son; she was too busy trying not to look at him, trying not to think on thoughts of Kenton's execution. Honestly, the thought had never crossed her mind until now and, at this moment, she was fighting off the panic the mere idea suggested. What was it Kenton had told her once, back when Saxilby and the others had lain siege to Babylon? *If I am captured by Edward, I will probably stand trial for treason and be executed.* Dear God, why had that not occurred to her before now? He'd spoken those words back in the days when they were harassing each other constantly, back in the days when her attraction to the man, so strong, was something that confused and frightened her.

But now, she remembered his words. She was terrified by them. She swore, at that moment, that even if he didn't want her to, she would beg for his life to be spared. Perhaps those who held him would listen, perhaps not. All she knew was that she was not going to let Kenton le Bec face execution without a fight. She would do all in her power to prevent it.

Somehow, the trip to Conisbrough seemed more urgent than ever before.

She had to get to Kenton.

CHAPTER NINETEEN

Bradley Manor, Lincolnshire

"**N**AY!" THE YOUNG woman screamed as the knight dragged her from the reception room of the large manor house known as Bradley Manor. "I will not go with you! Let me *go!*"

Unfortunately for Lady Holland, Duchess of Exeter, Bradley Manor did not have the retinue of soldiers that most of her husband's properties had, mostly because she didn't like for her home to have the feel of a military installation. At this moment, her preference was her undoing, for about twenty soldiers bearing the red and blue of Warwick had burst into her home and taken hold of one of her wards, a young woman named Katryne St. John. Now, a few men were dragging the girl from the house while the rest of the Warwick solders were holding her servants and guards at bay with big swords and well-aimed crossbows.

"Where are you taking her?" Lady Holland, extremely well dressed in heavy silks and with a tight white wimple around her head, scooted after the men who were dragging her young ward away. "How dare you break into my home and take Katryne with you! Where are you taking her?"

The Warwick soldier who seemed to be giving the orders came to a halt as his men pulled the hysterical Katryne behind them. He stopped Lady Holland from following by gently raising his hands to her, being very careful not to touch her, but Lady Holland slapped at his hands furiously.

"You will not raise your hands to me!" she screeched, smacking at him. "Move out of my way! Bring that woman back here!"

The soldier was trying to be very careful with the Duke of Exeter's wife. He didn't want to harm or overly harass the woman because it would bring Holland down on Warwick. Not that the man wasn't going to come down on him, anyway, for bursting into his wife's residence and stealing away one of her wards, but the soldier was trying to be as careful about it as he could. He didn't want to use more force than absolutely necessary but he had his orders – bring St. John's sister to Warwick at all costs. The woman was to be used in exchange for Kenton le Bec's life, as her brother was le Bec's captor, but Lady Holland need not know any of that. Fed a proper lie of Warwick's creation, that was all she ever need know.

"She will be treated well, my lady," the soldier explained, saying the same thing he had said when he had first come to Bradley Manor and politely asked for St. John's sister. "It seems that the lady's brother has been badly wounded and wishes to see his sister, so we are taking her to him. Warwick has sent us on this mission. I explained this all to you before, Lady Holland."

In the distance, Katryne screamed as she was unceremoniously tossed onto the back of a horse. Lady Holland yelped at the sight of her manhandled charge.

"But she does not want to go!" Lady Holland gasped. "Why must you take her now? Can we not bring her later in a carriage and with proper chaperones?"

The Warwick soldier shook his head. "Her brother may not live long enough for that, my lady," he said, moving in the direction of his men as they secured Lady Katryne atop one of the horses. "He is dying, my lady. He wishes to see his sister. You must allow her to go to him."

Lady Holland scurried after the soldier, out of her front door and across the grassy garden that comprised the front of her manor home. It had been a wet spring so far and the bottom of her fine silk gown soaked up the mud as she ran.

"But… but…!" she cried, trying to stop what could not be stopped. "This is completely improper for the young lady to ride unchaperoned with a gang of soldiers! This simply will not do!"

The Warwick soldier suddenly came to a halt. "Whether or not it will do makes no difference to me," he said, his manner suddenly not so polite. "We are taking the girl and you cannot stop us. She will be well treated and I personally guarantee that she will not be molested or harassed. Warwick has ordered me to bring her and that is exactly what I intend to do. Good day, Lady Holland."

With that, he turned away, swiftly, jogging off across the muddy grassy until he reached his horse. He mounted swiftly as Lady Holland ran after him, waving her hands and screaming for them to stop. Katryne's loud and fearful weeping did nothing to ease the old woman's anxiety and she finally came to a halt in her running, watching the group of soldiers as they thundered off the same way they had come, joining up with the road and then disappearing when the road moved into a thick cluster of trees to the north.

She lost sight of them, then, and for a moment, Lady Holland simply stood there, gasping and shrieking, terrified that her young ward was in great danger. But she didn't have the manpower to stop Warwick's men, prevent them, or even to fight them. She didn't even have enough men to follow them.

Fearful that she had just let Lady Katryne St. John go off to her death, Lady Holland stood there and screamed.

~ A TIME OF HOPE ~

CHAPTER TWENTY

Early April

K ENTON HAD NEVER paid an overabundance of attention to the weather unless it had to do with planning battles, but he had little else to do in his chamber prison than stare from the window and sometimes watch the sky, and today was no exception. The weather was surprisingly pleasant, away from the freezing temperatures they'd suffered as of late, and the sun that streamed in through the lancet window was actually warm. He stood in it, warming his body, basking in the heat.

He'd started counting the days since Saxilby told him Nicola was coming to Conisbrough. He'd marked them on the wall near the door, using a chip of wood he'd pulled off the bed frame. *Six days.* It had been six days since he'd been told Nicola was coming. Six long days to plan what he was going to say to her. Six long days that saw him torn between simply accepting her actions and berating her for them.

But berating wasn't in his nature, at least not in this case. He would keep his dignity and not lower himself to bellowing at her, telling her exactly what he thought of her betrayal. Telling her just how much she had hurt him. *Someone poisoned her against me*, he kept reminding himself. She'd said as much. But what Kenton very much wanted to know was who had poisoned her.

Who did it?

Try as he might not to dwell on that question, it was forefront in his mind. As he stood by the small lancet window in his usual place, thinking on Nicola and her betrayal and who could have turned her against him, he thought back to more pleasant days, of days watching Tab fish with three lines or of watching Teague as the child tried to throw a pair of bone die and threw them right into the blazing hearth. He chuckled when he remembered Gerik trying to fish the die out of the embers with his bare hands. He would yell in pain and the boys would scream with laughter. All these memories, so many memories for so short a time, filled his brain. He'd never known distraction such as this, but lovely distraction it was.

Kenton was wrapped up in his thoughts, so much so that he didn't hear or notice when the bustle in the bailey grew. Men began shouting and calling to one another, and the great portcullis of Conisbrough Castle lifted to admit visitors. There were several hundred of them, including a lady, and the big bailey of Conisbrough was soon chaotic with activity.

Kenton was usually attuned to what was going on in the bailey below but this time, he simply wasn't paying attention. Perhaps it was because he was thinking of the time that Tab, trying to compete with the knights, belched so loudly that he ended up vomiting. It still made Kenton laugh to think of it. Or perhaps it was because he was remembering the feel of Nicola's flesh in his hands. He was distracted, to be sure, and unaware that, four stories below him, the object of his obsession had arrived.

Nicola had come to Conisbrough.

"My castle appears intact," St. John said as he politely led Nicola inside the keep of Conisbrough Castle, followed closely by Saxilby, Conor, and several other men. "I am glad to see that you did not burn it down or let it fall into enemy hands while I was away."

Saxilby gave him a humorless purse of the lips. "Careful, St. John," he said. "You are bordering on slander. The lady will have a bad impression of me before we have formally met."

Nicola had been listening to the banter between St. John and a short, gray-haired man but she was more interested in Conisbrough as a whole and where, in fact, Kenton was located in this mammoth maze of walls and rooms. Their trip from Babylon had been uneventful in surprisingly good weather and now that they had arrived, Nicola had one thing on her mind and she didn't want to wait. She wanted to see Kenton immediately.

The entire ride from Babylon had been filled with angst for Kenton, mostly for his safety. She had frightened herself into thinking that he might be slated for execution, creating terrifying fantasies about Kenton being executed without her knowledge or before she could tell him how sorry she was for misunderstanding his words. It *was* a misunderstanding, for based upon her conversation with Conor the day that Babylon fell back into Edward's hands, it could not have been anything else. Fearful, and vulnerable, and feeling emotion she had never felt before, she had heard Kenton's words and believed the worst. At least, that was what she wanted to tell him. She didn't blame the man if he never spoke to her again.

Therefore, as St. John led the group into a rather large solar with a large, sooty fireplace and expensive rugs upon the floor, Nicola came to a halt just inside the doorway and faced both St. John and the gray-haired man. Mostly, she was looking at the gray-haired man who was about her height.

"I am Lady Thorne," she said to him. "We have not been introduced."

Saxilby smiled at the very beautiful young woman. "Lord Saxilby at your service, Lady Thorne," he said. "May I say that you were extremely brave to send the missive to us regarding Kenton le Bec's movements. Without you, we could not have captured the man or eased Manchester and Babylon from his grip. We own you much."

Nicola had no time for the man's gratitude, reminding her of her treachery as it did. "Where is Sir Kenton?" she asked.

If Saxilby thought her tone was rather curt, he didn't let on. He pointed to the ceiling of the chamber. "Up there," he said. "He is locked in a chamber awaiting transport to London."

Nicola's brow furrowed, puzzled. "What does that mean?"

"He will be turned over to Edward."

"And what will Edward do with him?"

Saxilby shrugged. "That is difficult to say, my lady," he replied. "Please, may I offer you wine? You must be exhausted after your travels."

Nicola shook her head, almost violently. She was starting to shake, anticipation of seeing Kenton almost too much to bear. "Nay," she replied. "I would see Sir Kenton immediately."

She was most adamant about it. Saxilby looked at St. John, bewildered by her passion, before returning his attention to her. "I do not understand, my lady," he said. "*Why* must you see him?"

Nicola's jaw began to tick. "It is my right. He held my castle captive. He… he stole from me. I want to see him *now*."

Saxilby realized that he had the unhappy task of trying to keep the irate lady calm. "Most understandable, my lady," he said, trying to soothe her. "It must have been very frightening to have Kenton le Bec confiscate your castle and occupy it, but I assure you that he can no longer harm or harass you. He is locked up safe."

Nicola was only growing more agitated. "You will take me to him now," she demanded again. "He smashed my husband's crypt, for God's sake. I have every right to tell the man what I think of his behavior and I will not wait. I have traveled three days to come here and you will not deny nor delay me. Take me to him *now*. I will not ask you again. I will simply go look for him myself."

Her words were final and Saxilby believed her implicitly. He stopped trying to soothe or delay her, for he saw her point. He could see how upset she was.

"Very well," he said after a moment, his gaze moving down her arms to her glove-covered hands. "You are not bearing any daggers, are you? No weapons of any kind?"

Nicola shook her head. "Of course not."

Saxilby lifted his eyebrows, unapologetic. "I had to ask," he said. "I would not be surprised if you came to kill the man who disrupted your life so."

He did disrupt my life, but in ways you cannot begin to comprehend, Nicola thought to herself. Again, she shook her head. "I am not here to kill him," she said. "I simply wish to speak with him and tell him... tell him what I think of him."

It was the truth, although everyone in the room took it to mean something other than what she had intended. Without another word, Saxilby motioned her with him and she immediately pursued, on the man's heels, as St. John and Conor followed. When St. John realized that the lady's knight was in tow, he waved the man off and, unhappy, Conor remained at the door to the solar, watching Nicola and the two men walk away, disappearing into a darkened stairwell.

But Nicola didn't know that Conor had been left behind nor did she care. Her palms were beginning to sweat because she knew Kenton was close, nearer to her than he'd been in weeks, and it was as if her heart knew it. It was as if it could sense him, beating so strongly she was sure it was about to burst from her chest as she followed Saxilby up three flights of mural stairs built into the thickness of Conisbrough's walls. By the time they reached the top floor, the ceiling was low, the landing was darkened, and there were four heavily-armed soldiers on this level guarding two doors from what Nicola could see.

Suddenly, she felt a bit nervous, intimidated even. The armed men were looking at her with suspicion, curiosity, and some interest and she felt exposed and fearful even though St. John and Saxilby were escorting her. She was so overwhelmed and excited to finally be within feet of Kenton that she was starting to feel faint. She wanted to see him in the worst way but her anxiety had the better of her. As St. John led her to one of the doors and put his hand up to throw the bolt, she stopped him.

"I will see him alone," she said, looking at the disapproving faces of Saxilby and St. John. "I will scream if I need assistance, but what I have to say to le Bec will not be heard by anyone but him. Is that understood?"

She was making demands and the men, though wary, naturally agreed because a lady was always to be accommodated. Moreover, they figured the woman had been through enough with le Bec and deserved to verbally abuse the man after what he'd done to her family and to her fortress. St. John, the most reluctant of the men, sighed heavily.

"This is not advisable, my lady," he said quietly. "Kenton le Bec is a very dangerous man."

Nicola nodded impatiently. "I know he is," she said, "and I will call you if I need you, but for now, you will remain out here. Please."

So she was trying to be polite about it now even though she'd practically bullied and demanded to see Kenton since she had arrived at Conisbrough. St. John simply threw the bolt and pulled the door open. Nicola, with only a slight hesitation to reveal the apprehension she was feeling, entered the chamber.

St. John closed the door behind her, wondering how long it was going to be before he started hearing cries of help, from either one of them.

AT FIRST, KENTON thought he was hallucinating.

He'd been standing by the window, the sun on his shoulders, when the door to his chamber opened. He turned, casually, thinking it was Saxilby, but the figure stepping into the room wasn't Saxilby at all. It was a vision he'd been dreaming of, fantasizing over, and agonizing over for days and weeks. It seemed like years. He couldn't even remember how long the vision had been on his mind because it seemed like forever. Suddenly, Nicola was standing just inside the door and Kenton actually staggered. His shock was so great that he came away from the wall, stumbled and nearly pitched forward. His face, an open mask of astonishment, gazed at Nicola with more vulnerability than he had ever displayed. Before he could say anything, however, Nicola spoke.

"Are you well, Kenton?" she asked softly.

He nodded, once. Then, his head jerked and he nodded several times, rapidly. He could hardly draw a breath as he drank in her pale, lovely face.

"Aye," he said hoarsely. "Are you?"

"Aye."

"Are your boys well?"

"They are."

"Then why have you come?"

Nicola just stared at him. Her jaw worked, as if she were trying to speak, but no words came forth. Kenton stared back at her, feeling the tension and apprehension in the room thicken and tighten around them both. They both had so much to say but neither one of them could seem to speak. Emotions, sometimes, ran stronger than words could express and this was one of those times.

But someone had to speak. Someone had to give. It was Nicola.

"I came here because I had to see you," she finally said, her eyes filling with a lake of tears that spilled over as he watched. "Our last words at Babylon were hateful... so hateful. I hated you that day, Kenton, or at least I thought I did until I realized I did not hate you at all. It was anything but hate and that was why I spoke so terribly to you. Before you left to go to war at Manchester, I heard you speaking in the solar to your knights and telling them that you were simply being kind to me in order to get information from me. I heard you say those words and... and they were daggers to my soul. I thought you and I... I thought... that is, we had a pleasant existence and you kissed me and told me you did not want me to leave Babylon when I asked to go, and you led me to believe... to think that there was some part of you that cared for me. But when I heard you tell your men that you were only using me, I thought that all of the sweet and noble things you said to me were lies. I hated you for it."

Kenton learned a great deal in that rambling diatribe. *I heard you tell your men that you were only being kind to me to gain information.* Aye, he remembered that he'd said that to Wellesbourne and de Russe, but he'd only said that to throw them off his scent. He was attracted to the Lady of Babylon and they had known it, which could have been a dangerous thing for them all. Kenton had therefore lied to them to convince them otherwise, but in that lie, Nicola had heard him. *God, she had heard him!* Now, things were starting to make some sense and his brow furrowed, more from shock than anything.

"You heard me tell de Russe and Wellesbourne that I was being kind to you simply to gain information?" he clarified, watching her nod. "Then why did you not ask me about it? How could you think… Nicola, I told them that because I had to, because they were suspicious of my attention towards you and towards the fact that I had completely ignored Warwick's orders up until that point. I was supposed to launch an attack against Manchester but I had postponed it, mostly because… mostly because I did not want to leave Babylon. I did not want to leave you. So I lied to them so they would not be suspicious."

Nicola slapped a hand over her mouth, stifling a sob. The tears were flowing faster and harder now. "I did not know," she whispered. "I did not know your heart, Kenton. I thought you were using me to gain your wants and… oh, Kenton, I did not know at all and I was too angry and hurt to confront you. I vowed that you would not use me… that I would use you… so I did. To punish you, I told the Conisbrough garrison of your plans to march on Manchester and that is why you find yourself here."

She broke down into sobs, hanging her head miserably. Kenton, however, smiled faintly. He already knew everything she had confessed to. He was simply touched and relieved that she would admit such a thing. *Mayhap there is hope*, after all, he thought. *God, let there be hope….*

"I know," he told her hoarsely. "I know all of that. What I did not know was why you did it and now I know."

Nicola nodded, tears and mucus running off her face and she struggled to wipe at it. "I am so sorry," she cried, lifting her head to look at him. "I am so sorry I did this. I do not expect you to forgive me but I wanted you to know… know what I had done. And I wanted you to know that I am very sorry."

Kenton's smile broadened, so relieved he could hardly stand. His legs felt weak, boneless, and all he wanted to do was draw her into his arms and never let her go. Her tears cut at him, tears of guilt and remorse.

"I forgave you even before I knew what had happened," he said softly. "There is no need to ask my forgiveness, Nicola. I loved you then and I love you now, no matter what has happened. I will always love you and because I love you, you will always have my forgiveness."

Her tears came anew at his declaration, painfully relieved at his generous forgiveness. It was too good to believe.

"You should hate me at the very least," she said, choking on her own tears. "You should tell me to go and turn your back on me. How can you say that you love me after what I have done?"

He shrugged, wishing very much that he could wipe her face. He wanted to touch her in the worst way but wouldn't do it; against his usual behavior, of taking initiative when it came to touching the woman, this time he would not do it. If she wanted his comfort, then she would come to him or she would ask for it. He still wasn't sure how she felt other than her obvious remorse. He had told her he loved her but she had not reciprocated those words. Slowly, he was dying inside.

"Because I do," he murmured. "I love you and those wild children you have raised and if you will have me, when my part in this war is over, I will return to Babylon to marry you."

"But I…!"

"It does not matter," he said, cutting her off. "I understand why you did what you did. You did it to protect Babylon against a man you believed to be using you. You did what anyone would have done had they learned of deception. But you know that I was not deceiving you. I would live for you and I would die for you, Nicola, but I would never deceive you. Do you believe me?"

She nodded, wiping at her nose with the back of her hand. "I... I do," she sniffed. "But you are quick to forgive a woman who tried to kill you. I am not entirely sure I would be so forgiving."

He laughed softly. "Aye, you would," he said. "When love is involved, and understanding, forgiveness is a simple thing. *Do* you love me, Nicola?"

Her movements slowed, wiping at her face, the tears on her chin, and the miserable expression on her features suddenly lifted. In its wake was an expression of warmth that Kenton couldn't begin to describe, as if the sun had just emerged from behind the storm clouds, and suddenly she was nodding her head.

"Aye," she whispered. "I do, Kenton. I love you. I cannot remember when I have not loved you."

Kenton didn't even remember moving across the floor of the chamber, but suddenly, he was standing in front of her, cupping her wet face with his enormous hands. He simply stood there, holding her face, gazing into her watery eyes and thinking that this was the moment he'd waited for his entire life. This moment of brilliance and comfort, erasing the life of solitude and warfare he had always known. He wanted this moment, this space in time, to last forever. Slanting his mouth over hers, he could taste the salt of her tears along with the sweetness of her flesh, and it was as if his entire life was now complete.

It would be a moment he would remember forever.

Nicola clung to him as he suckled her lips, his tongue gently pushing into her mouth, acquainting himself with the essence that was her, and all of her, because it was something he intended to gorge himself on. Moments like this were only meant for angels and sometimes, not even for them, but Kenton and Nicola were experiencing it nonetheless. For a bright and shining moment, heaven came into that little room and the illumination was blinding.

Nicola had no idea how long she remained in Kenton's arms, surrendering to his powerful kiss. All she knew was that she never wanted it to end. It was everything she had ever hoped for but nothing she could have possibly imagined, even in her dreams. When Kenton was finished kissing her, he simply held her close, his face buried in her neck, his big arms wrapped around her slender body. He had her now, never to let her go.

Nicola's arms were around his neck so tightly that she was positive she was strangling the man, but it underscored one thing – she never wanted to let him go, either. She had no intention of releasing him. But the reality was that he was in a very precarious position that needed to be dealt with. Someone had to broach the subject and Nicola, out of fear, was the first to speak.

"What do we do?" she whispered into the side of his dark head. "How do I get you out of this place?"

Nicola felt his hot breath against her neck as he exhaled slowly. "I am not sure there is an easy answer to that," he whispered. "You cannot release me from Conisbrough. There is no way for you to do that. The only way I would be able to break away, or be broken away, is if I was not surrounded by layers of stone walls. They plan to turn me over to Edward at some point so it would be logical to presume that would be the best time to try to escape."

"How?"

He shook his head, pulling it free of the fragrant haven of her neck. He fixed her in the eye, his arms still around her.

"I am not sure," he admitted. "But you must not mention any of this to anyone. What we discuss here must stay between us."

She nodded solemnly. "Of course, Kenton," she said. "I would never say a word to anyone but Conor. He has come with me."

A look of surprise crossed Kenton's features. "Conor is here?"

"Aye."

"But... but I left him in charge of Babylon," he said, confused.

"When Babylon fell, I was certain he would have been killed, or taken prisoner at the very least."

Nicola nodded. "He was a prisoner," she conceded, "but I convinced Brome St. John that he was one of Gaylord's knights. I do not know if St. John truly believes me, but he has not disputed me. He has allowed Conor to be by my side."

Kenton mulled over that particular revelation. He was astonished, but pleased, to know that Conor not only survived the siege on Babylon but that he was here at Conisbrough. "I see," he said thoughtfully. "What of Wellesbourne and de Russe and le Mon? What of them?"

Nicola shook her head. "I do not know," she said. "I have not seen nor heard of them. What of Forbes? You did not mention him."

"That is because I know he is dead."

She sobered. "Oh," she murmured. "Do you think the others are dead, too?"

Kenton cocked a reluctant eyebrow, reluctant to think the worst. "It is possible although I cannot truly believe it," he said. "Wellesbourne and de Russe especially would have stopped at nothing to remain alive."

"Do you think they fled back to Warwick after the defeat?"

Kenton nodded. "That would be my guess," he said. "I truly hope that they have, at the very least to tell the man what has happened. That is what I would have done."

Nicola watched him as he thought on his knights, the men he'd fought so closely with. "Even if they have fled, they do not know what has become of you," she said. "I am the only one who knows. How can I help you escape? What can I do?"

Kenton pondered her question. "I am not entirely sure," he said. "It will take a plan of great cunning to help me escape. They plan to turn me over to Edward at some point and when they move me would more than likely be the best chance for me to escape. While I am within these walls, there is no hope of release, so it makes sense to make the attempt when I am in transit. The only person who can plan that kind of operation is Warwick."

Nicola shook her head. "I do not know if he is aware you have been taken prisoner," she said. "I have not heard from him at all. I know nothing of his movements."

Kenton released her, sitting her down on the bed as he sat beside her. He held her hands tightly. "Then you must get word to him somehow," he told her, his voice low. "Send Conor if you can. Warwick must be told that I am at Conisbrough and that they plan to turn me over to Edward. Once I am given over to Edward it will more than likely be impossible for any manner of an escape attempt, so it is imperative that any attempt be made once I leave Conisbrough."

Nicola was listening with great seriousness. "I do not know of their plans for you, but I can find out," she said. "They believe I am on their side because it was I who sent them the missive about your attack on Manchester. I am sure they believe I am in their confidence."

Kenton's expression was serious as well. "Then it is important we lead them to believe that you have no loyalty towards me," he said. "We will have to pretend we hate one another. I am not entirely sure what else we can do. If they believe we are bitter enemies, then they may tell you their plans for turning me over to Edward."

Nicola nodded, watching him as he kissed her hands. "I am not sure if I can be convincing about hating you," she whispered, her eyes starting to well again. "Kenton, I'm so afraid for you."

He kissed her hands again, her lips to quiet her. "I know," he comforted. "But you are strong and wise. You are the strongest woman I know. I have faith that you will be able to obtain their plans for me and send word to Warwick. We will be together again someday, I swear it, but you must help me keep my promise."

She wiped at her eyes, squaring her shoulders and trying very hard to be brave. "I will do it," she said, sniffling again. "I did this to you. Now I shall get you out of it."

He smiled at her, drinking in her brilliant beauty, more relieved than he could express that things were well between them again. But he had a feeling there would be much more fear and perhaps even heartache before all of this was finished. But as long as they had faith in each other, and loved each other, that bond could move mountains.

"I know you will," he said, kissing her again. "But for now, we must pretend to hate each other. Can you do that?"

She nodded, somewhat wryly. "I made a good show of it before."

He laughed. "You did," he said. "But right now, I want you to slap me as hard as you can."

She looked at him, shocked. "*Slap* you?"

"Aye," he said firmly. "As hard as you can. And then scream at me and tell me what a bastard I am. It will show them that you truly hope I rot for what I did to Babylon. You must be convincing, love."

Nicola sighed. She understood what he was saying and she knew that it was a necessary ruse, especially if she was going to try and gain information about their future plans for Kenton. It was important that St. John and the rest of them believe there was no love lost between her and Kenton le Bec.

"Very well," she said, standing up. But first, she bent down to kiss his cheek, the one she was about to slap. "Hopefully this will take the sting out of what I will do."

He grinned, touching his face where she had kissed him. "It will undoubtedly," he said softly. "Now hit me, *hard*."

Nicola hesitated a moment before hauling off and slapping him across the face so hard that his head snapped. She looked at him in horror for a split second but all he did was grin, putting his hand to the cheek that was already turning an angry shade of red. She began screaming at him.

"You contemptable bastard!" she yelled. "How dare you... you smashed his tomb! You smashed it! I told you not to do it, I *begged* you, but you still did it! How could you have destroyed Gaylord's tomb like that?"

Her screams brought the cavalry. The door swung open and St. John and Saxilby appeared. Nicola saw the door fly open from the corner of her eye and she launched herself at Kenton, slapping him in the head and trying to kick him. St. John moved swiftly to pull the angry lady away, but Nicola struggled against him, swinging her fists in Kenton's direction.

"I... want... my... *vengeance!*" she grunted, trying to hit Kenton. "You will not deny me my right!"

Saxilby was beside himself, putting himself between the swinging lady and the seated prisoner. "My lady, *please*," he begged. "Please calm yourself!"

Pretending to be furious was fairly easy for Nicola. She lashed out a booted foot and caught Saxilby in the knee. "But you do not know what he has done!" she screeched. "He smashed my husband's tomb and... and he tried to steal my children!"

St. John had her around the waist, easily lifting her and carrying her to the door. "Come along, my lady," he said calmly. "You are simply overwrought from the events of the past few weeks. You must rest and I am sure you will return to reason."

Nicola was struggling and twisting, now trying to hit St. John. "Nay!" she yelled, grabbing on to the door frame as he tried to pull her through. "I will not leave! I must stay and punish him!"

St. John and one of the armed guards outside the door had to peel her hands off the door frame in order to pull her completely from the room; it was clear that she was not going easily. She was fighting and yelling the entire way. Kenton could hear her as St. John took her down the steps, his calm voice against her frenzied one. When their voices faded away, Saxilby, who was still in the room, turned to Kenton.

"God's Bones," he hissed in relief now that Lady Thorne had been taken away. "What on earth did you say to the woman?"

Kenton shrugged carelessly, standing up from his bed. "I do not know what set her off," he said. "She is volatile as it is, so it could have been anything. We were discussing my incarceration, the condition of Babylon after the siege. I told her I should have sold her children off into slavery because they were wild ruffians and suddenly the woman becomes enraged."

Saxilby frowned at the man. "You said that you should have sold her *children*?"

"Aye. They serve no purpose in a military installation, which was what Babylon was after I confiscated it."

Saxilby shook his head in disbelief. "I was worried about her attacking you," he muttered. "I should have been more worried about *you* provoking *her*."

Kenton merely shrugged and turned to the window, his usual position. He was trying to convey disinterest in Lady Thorne, hoping he was able to do it adequately. "She said what she wanted to say," he said. "Mayhap she will leave me alone from now on."

Saxilby wriggled his eyebrows, turning for the door. "I have a feeling she might sneak up here to try and stick a dagger in your ribs," he said. "Make sure you watch that door, le Bec. If Lady Thorne manages to bribe the guards to let her in, you may have to fight for your life."

Kenton shrugged again, as if he didn't care in the least, and Saxilby left the room without another word. When the door shut and he heard the bolt thrown, that was when Kenton's guard came down.

Bravo, love, he thought.

The man had a smile on his face for the rest of the day, for the hope he had prayed for, had wished for, was indeed alive and well. Hope, and love, had worked miracles.

Now they would see if it could work another.

CHAPTER TWENTY-ONE

Outside of Wakefield, Yorkshire
Warwick's encampment

T REMBLING AND TERRIFIED, Brome St. John's sister stood by the brazier in Warwick's big, lush tent, wrapped up in a heavy blanket that one of Warwick's advisors had given her. Standing next to her was Lord Pollard, trying to speak with her, but Lady Katryne refused to speak at all. She was traumatized and furious and frightened, a volatile combination.

Warwick had been away from camp when Katryne had been brought in early in the morning and was only now returning as the day neared noon. The woman had spent several hours in Warwick's tent, ignoring Pollard and weeping on occasion when Warwick, weary from his ride and not in the best of moods, finally made an appearance. De Russe and Wellesbourne were with him and when the three men entered the tent, especially the two enormous knights, Lady Katryne stiffened with terror.

"My lord," Pollard said, eyeing the terrified woman. "You have a guest. Allow me to introduce...."

Pollard was cut off by Warwick as he moved to his broken-legged desk. "It can wait," he snapped at the man. Then, he gestured wildly to Wellesbourne and de Russe. "And that is something else, good knights, our winter stores are very low and require replenishment. It is my suggestion we purchase goods immediately because we are returning to Warwick Castle very soon. From what we heard this morning whilst we were in Wakefield, it appears that Edward has gathered sufficient force and is moving south towards London. We need to move as well, quickly, and will need the supplies to sustain the men on the march."

De Russe was removing his gloves as he spoke. "What about regaining Babylon and Manchester?"

"Our focus is elsewhere now, de Russe. Edward is on the move."

The knights understood. They'd been told that morning by their scouts whom they met at a tavern in Wakefield that Edward, who had landed in Yorkshire the previous month, had gathered a significant army and was moving south, towards London. They had known of Edward's landing in Yorkshire right after it happened but they hadn't heard about the army he'd collected until recently. Now, things were changing all around them and the reclamation of Babylon wasn't a priority any longer. Stopping, or engaging, Edward was now the focus. The situation was fluid and rapidly changing.

"How soon do we leave, my lord?" Wellesbourne asked.

Warwick took a deep breath, evidently laboring to calm himself. His entire focus was now on Edward's movements and he was brittle and preoccupied.

"Within a few days," he said, eyeing Lady Katryne in the dim tent as if just remembering someone else was there. Realizing it was a young woman, thoughts shifted from Edward as he found interested in her. "We will speak more of it later, but for now, do as you are instructed. We must rally supplies."

De Russe and Wellesbourne nodded, quitting the tent with orders to fulfill. It was at that point that Warwick turned to Pollard and to Lady Katryne, who was holding the blanket tightly around her small body. Warwick fixed on her.

"Ah," he said appraisingly. "Who can this be?"

Pollard spoke. "This is Lady Katryne St. John," he said. "She has been brought from Lincolnshire, at your request."

Warwick's face lit up and his expression relaxed. "St. John," he repeated with great satisfaction in his tone. "Can this be the sister?"

"It is, my lord."

Warwick stepped out from behind his desk, his attention riveted to Katryne. "So she was with Lady Holland?" he said, more to Pollard, who nodded his head. "How splendid. Welcome to my humble encampment, my lady."

Katryne, a small and very pretty girl, obviously backed away from him as he moved towards her. "I was told my brother was ill," she said, her voice trembling. "Where is he?"

Warwick smiled thinly. "Were you well-treated on your trip north?" he asked, avoiding her question. "Were you well-fed? Were my men polite?"

Katryne backed away as he came close. "I was well-fed," she said. "But where is my brother? I was told he asked for me."

Warwick stopped stalking her because she was moving away from him with every step he took towards her. He scratched his chin thoughtfully.

"Your brother is not here," he said. "Your brother is Brome St. John, is he not?"

Confused, frightened, Katryne nodded. "If he is not here, then where is he?"

Warwick jerked his head in a westerly direction, off in the general direction of Conisbrough. "He is the garrison commander at Conisbrough Castle, so I am told," he said. "Can you confirm this?"

Katryne was puzzled at the moment more than she was frightened. "Aye," she said. "The last I heard from him, he was. Why do you ask? And why am I here?"

Warwick moved away from her, back to his leaning desk where a covered pitcher of wine sat surrounded by dirty cups. He uncovered the pitcher, picked up a cup and shook it out, and filled it with some of the contents from the pitcher.

"Because I have need of you, my lady," Warwick said, extending the cup to Pollard but indicating it was meant for the lady. "Will you please sit? I should like to discuss something with you."

Katryne was standing far back from Warwick, in the shadows, but she timidly accepted the cup of wine when Pollard came near, mostly because she was very thirsty. Pollard indicated a chair for her to sit in, one he'd been trying to coerce her into for the past two hours. This time, she moved near the chair but she didn't sit. She stood near it, very much on her guard. She didn't want to be trapped by the man in armor, the man who had yet to tell her his name, so she remained on her feet, ready to run at a moment's notice. Not that she could go anywhere, but she was ready to run nonetheless.

"I want to know why I am here," Katryne said, firmly, although her voice was tremulous. "Why have you brought me here? *Who* are you?"

Warwick was seated at his desk, near the brazier. "I am Richard Neville," he said. "Have you heard of me?"

Katryne frowned, thinking. "I… I believe so."

"I am the Earl of Warwick."

Her eyes widened as her fear returned, full-bore. "Warwick!" she gasped. Then, she started to move away from the chair again, preparing to run even though she knew she had nowhere to go. "What do you want of me?"

She was frightened. Warwick could hear it in her voice as well as see it in her actions. He didn't move, watching her as she tried to angle towards the tent opening, possibly to make an escape. "You are quite important to me right now, Lady Katryne," he said. "I wish you would sit so that we may discuss this rationally."

Katryne shook her head. "Tell me what you want!"

Warwick was unmoved by her terror. He sipped at his wine. "Do you want to see your brother?"

"Of course I do!"

Warwick glanced at her. "Good," he said. "He will want to see you, too. You see, he has one of my men and I very much want him back. In fact, I need him back now more than ever so it is my intention to offer you in exchange for my man. A rather fair trade, I would say. Your brother gets you and I get my man back. It is really very simple, truly."

Oddly enough, Katryne seemed to calm significantly now that she knew why, exactly, she was here. Her trip to Warwick's encampment had been based on lies and she really wasn't all that surprised to realize that. In hindsight, she'd known all along. But the unknown of why, exactly, she had come fed her fear for the most part so now that she knew the reasons behind the abduction from Bradley Manor, she seemed to relax. Still, she stood near the door. She would not sit down, not yet.

"Then... then the tale the soldiers told Lady Holland about my brother asking for me was a lie?" she asked.

Warwick nodded. "It was," he said regretfully. "It was necessary to bring you here, although I cannot imagine it was an easy task. You look as if you did not make it easy in the least."

Katryne wasn't sure what he meant. She looked down at herself, all wrapped up in the heavy blanket, and was puzzled. "Why would you say such things?" she asked.

Warwick drained his wine cup. "Because you are fearful and combative," he said. "Am I wrong?"

"Nay, my lord."

"Then, for Christ's Sake, come over and sit down before you fall down," he commanded softly. "Take some wine with me and let us discuss what will happen from this point on. Will you do this? No one is going to hurt you, my lady, I swear it. Do you believe me?"

She eyed him dubious. "Well...."

"Has anyone hurt you yet?"

No one had. Katryne began to see his point. Moreover, she had no real choice. Reluctantly, she finally went to sit in a chair opposite Warwick, near the brazier that was giving off a good deal of heat in the damp and cold tent. Pollard pulled up another chair and sat near Warwick, eyeing the fair young maiden who appeared vastly uncomfortable and vastly nervous.

"Now," Warwick said as Katryne perched in the chair with her cup of wine still in hand, still untouched. "I will send a missive to your brother and relay my terms to him. We should have an answer shortly, as we are a two-day ride from Conisbrough. I am sure your brother will be more than happy to exchange his sister for the man he holds prisoner."

Katryne watched him as he poured himself more wine. "And if he does not?"

Warwick lifted his eyebrows thoughtfully. "Then you and I shall discuss your future," he said. "I could marry you off to the highest bidder or I could send you to the nearest convent. Those are things we will discuss."

Katryne eyed the man, a hardened man she thought. "You... you do not intend to kill me to punish my brother for refusing your terms?"

Warwick's gaze lingered on her. "Does this frighten you?"

She thought on the question a moment. "Not as much as being ravaged does."

Warwick smiled faintly. "You fear a man's touch more than death?"

She shrugged. "I was educated by nuns, my lord," she said. "I fear many things more than death."

Warwick liked that answer. In fact, he was coming to respect the girl just a little. She was flighty and silly, but at least she was honest. He turned back to his wine. "In answer to your previous question, a dead young woman is no good to anyone," he said. Then, he grinned. "Mayhap I will marry you off to your brother's worst enemy. Is there anyone he hates in particular?"

Katryne could see humor in his face although she was unsure what, exactly, was so funny. "I do not know, my lord," she said honestly. "It has been two years since I last saw my brother and would not know his mind these days."

Warwick shrugged. "Well, it is something to think on," he said, drinking his wine. "Meanwhile, I will send him a missive and we will wait eagerly for his answer. While we wait, you will be my guest. I am an excellent host, by the way."

Katryne watched the man as he drank more wine and unlaced his boots, evidently weary after a busy morning. She had no way of knowing just how fatigued or how worried he was about Edward's movements. And she couldn't know how very badly he wanted Kenton back with Edward on the march. She simply kept the blanket wrapped around her tightly, like a shield, especially when the same two big knights entered the tent and Warwick engaged them in a discussion she could not hear.

She should have been rightly terrified at being a captive of the Earl of Warwick and, truth be told, she *was* frightened. But she was also oddly intrigued by it all. She was fairly certain her brother would negotiate for her release so she wasn't worried in that regard. She was the only sister he had and she knew he would not let her languish, so her fears were somewhat eased by that thought. Therefore, she would be a prisoner of the Earl of Warwick for a few days until her brother delivered his prisoner in exchange for her, and she would have quite a tale to tell her friends. It wasn't every young maiden from the dales of Cumbria who became a prisoner of the Earl of Warwick. She would be quite special in that regard.

Before the day was through, a messenger was riding hard for Conisbrough with a missive proposing the terms of a prisoner exchange – St. John's sister for Kenton le Bec. If the terms were not agreed to, Warwick warned, St. John would get his sister back in pieces.

Katryne never knew that part of it and it was probably best that she didn't.

CHAPTER TWENTY-TWO

Conisbrough Castle

"I WILL NEVER see my sister again," St. John said, his face drawn and pale. "Dear God, what am I going to tell my mother?"

In the large solar at Conisbrough on a bright spring morning, St. John was leaning against the hearth, an opened parchment in his hand bearing terrible words from Warwick. Saxilby, who had just wandered into the solar to find St. John distraught over the missive, went to the man.

"What are you talking about?" Saxilby demanded. "What has happened to your sister?"

St. John held up the parchment. "Warwick has her," he spat, distressed. "Somehow, someway, he found out that I am holding le Bec and he is trying to use my sister in an exchange. My sister for le Bec."

Saxilby was horrified. "Your sister?" he repeated, aghast. "But how...? I do not understand! How did he find her?"

St. John sat heavily in the nearest chair, raking the fingers of one hand through his blond hair. "I do not know," he moaned. "She is a ward of Lady Holland. Warwick has ways of discovering things that would lead people to believe he has a mystical gift for divining knowledge. He calls forth the demons of darkness and they tell him what he wants to know. They must have told him where my sister was and somehow the man took her. He *took* her!"

Saxilby patted St. John on the shoulder for the man was truly distraught. He endeavored to remain calm as St. John grunted and moaned. "So he knows we have le Bec," he said, trying to think rationally and logically. "I suppose that would be no great feat, Brome. Men escaped from Manchester, men who knew the Conisbrough garrison had clashed against le Bec's army there. Mayhap they even saw us take le Bec prisoner. Word has reached Warwick. There is no great mystery in what he knows."

St. John was hanging his head, looking at the missive as if it were poison. "But he knew enough to know that I am garrison commander at Conisbrough," he said. "Someone told him who I was."

"Again, no great mystery," Saxilby said. "There are men supporting Henry who know more of Edward's allies than Edward does, and Warwick most of all. He knows le Bec is at Conisbrough and he knows you are the garrison commander. But I would truly like to know how he found your sister. That was quite cunning of him."

St. John wanted to know, too. He grunted unhappily. "What manner of man would use a woman in such a way?" he asked rhetorically. "Katryne is young and innocent. Warwick must have killed Lady Holland to get to her for I know that woman would not have let my sister go without a fight. If he killed Lady Holland, then surely her husband is out for blood."

"Her husband is on our side," Saxilby said quietly. "Where *is* Henry Holland?"

St. John shook his head. "I would not know," he said. "The last I heard, he was south, near Cambridge. His son-in-law was involved in a minor skirmish there, or so I was told. But that was months ago."

Saxilby kept his hand on St. John's broad shoulder. "I wonder if the Duke of Exeter knows that Warwick has gone after his wife," he muttered thoughtfully. "It seems that Warwick will stop at nothing to gain what he wants. We should have anticipated that he would want le Bec returned to him."

St. John was still staring at the missive, at the wicked, black letters that spelled out his sister's fate. Slowly, he began to shake his head.

"I cannot give him le Bec," he said painfully. "We have already sent word to Edward. He knows that le Bec is our prisoner."

Saxilby sighed heavily, reaching down to take the parchment from St. John. He read it, twice, before re-rolling it and handing it back to St. John.

"He says he will send your sister back to you in pieces if you refuse," he said. "I cannot believe Warwick would do such a thing. It is too barbaric to imagine."

St. John was calmer than he had been only moments earlier, having gained some control over his emotions, but he was still deeply upset. He took a deep, cleansing breath.

"I have never heard of him doing such a thing," he said, trying to be logical, "but Kenton le Bec means a great deal to him. The mere fact that he has my sister and is trying to bargain with her speaks volumes of his determination."

"Whose determination?"

An inquisitive female voice came from the solar door. St. John stood up as he and Saxilby faced Nicola as she entered the room. She was smiling pleasantly at the pair, who displayed forced smiles in return at her unexpected appearance. Especially St. John; he was fairly grimacing at her.

"Good morn to you, Lady Thorne," Brome said. "I trust you slept well after your difficult day yesterday?"

Nicola nodded. "I slept better than I have in quite some time," she said. "There is something about clearing my conscience and my soul that brings about restful slumber. Thank you again for allowing me to see le Bec yesterday. It did me a world of good."

"That is good to know."

Nicola could sense that she'd walked into the middle of a serious conversation but she had no intention of leaving. She had just come down from her chamber when she heard their voices, the tension in them, and thought they might be speaking of something that had to do with Kenton. Who else but Kenton could bring about such tension to the commander of Conisbrough, she thought, and if Kenton was the subject, she wanted to know what was being said.

"Please forgive me if I interrupted something important," she said, looking between the two because they'd essentially stopped their conversation. "You were speaking of someone's determination. Could it possibly be mine?"

She was being quite charming with her question as she probed them, her eyes twinkling and a grin on her lips, and St. John smiled weakly. "Nay, not you, dear lady," he said. "There are many determined people in this world, although I will admit you are one of the more determined ladies I have seen."

Nicola laughed, meant to be a lovely and flirtatious sound. She didn't want to leave until they told her what they had been speaking of because something told her that it, indeed, had to do with Kenton. She moved to the nearest chair and primly seated herself.

"My husband often said that to me," she said. "I have three young sons who are just as determined, which I think one needs to be in this world. You cannot let people take advantage of you and, at times, you must fight for what you believe in. Don't you agree?"

St. John wasn't in the mood for a polite conversation. He was still lingering on the missive from Warwick and his sister's predicament, but he remained courteous to Nicola as she all but barged into their conversation.

"Indeed I do, my lady," he said. "There are unscrupulous people in this world that one must fight against."

Nicola nodded, pleased he was agreeing with her, but she couldn't help notice the parchment in his hand. He seemed to be gripping it rather tightly. She pointed to it.

"A missive has come?" she asked. "Could it be about Sir Kenton?"

St. John's head snapped to her, startled by the question. "Why would you ask that?"

She shrugged. "Because you mentioned to me that, eventually, you would be turning le Bec over to Edward," she said. "Has any progress been made on that subject?"

St. John looked at the parchment in his hand. He was still reeling from it, still feeling quite shaken by the entire thing. Without his usual control, now weakened by his emotions, he shook his head before he could stop himself.

"No progress as of yet," he muttered. "We may have an obstacle to overcome first."

Nicola was genuinely curious. "What obstacle would that be?"

St. John glanced at Saxilby, who vaguely shook his head, indicating he should not speak on the contents of the missive to the lady. It didn't involve her, anyway, and would more than likely only upset her. But St. John was feeling emotional, and angry, and was unable to hold back his disgust.

"It would seem that Warwick has discovered that le Bec is my prisoner," he said bitterly. "Somehow, he knows and he has done something unspeakable because of it."

Nicola was deeply concerned. "What did he do?" she asked, gasping.

St. John turned away from her, looking at the missive in his hand before tossing it onto the nearest table. "He abducted my sister and has now proposed a trade," he said. "My sister for le Bec. He says that if I do not agree to the trade, he will send my sister back to me in pieces. In fact, I should send le Bec back to him in pieces for what he has done. No man will give me an ultimatum such as that."

Nicola was genuinely shocked at what she was hearing. "Warwick has your sister?" she repeated, aghast. "That is the most terrible thing I have ever heard. How in the world did he find her? How did he even know you had a sister?"

St. John was quickly becoming distraught again. "I do not know," he said. "That is what Lord Saxilby and I were discussing when you entered the room."

Nicola looked to Saxilby, who seemed rather perturbed that St. John had told her of his troubles. He wouldn't look at Nicola at all. He simply turned his back on them both and went to sit on a chair near the hearth. Nicola watched the man as he seated himself, seemingly ignoring the others in the room. She returned her attention to St. John.

"What are you going to do?" she asked Brome. "Surely you cannot let Warwick harm your sister."

St. John shrugged, clearly despondent. "I cannot give him le Bec," he said. "Edward already knows we have him. He is expecting le Bec to be delivered to him."

It didn't take Nicola much more prompting to realize two things – that St. John was in a talking mood and that they had drifted onto the subject of Kenton being given over to Edward. She capitalized on it as quickly as she could because this was the information she had wanted all along, the information Kenton wanted to know. It was information Warwick would want to know. Going over to St. John, she put a comforting hand on the man's shoulder.

"I am so terribly sorry," she said sincerely. "But when do you plan on moving le Bec? Is there some way that you could put Warwick off?"

St. John shook his head but he was, not strangely, comforted by Lady Thorne's concerned touch. "I am not sure how it could be done," he said. "It was my intention to send le Bec to him in a few days, as Edward is moving south through Yorkshire as we speak."

Nicola looked surprised. "Edward is in Yorkshire?"

St. John nodded. "Aye," he replied. "He has been for some time. He is gathering men to march on London and we have been told he is moving south and will be at Doncaster by early next week. That is where I plan to meet up with him and deliver le Bec."

Nicola hadn't heard any of this. It was true that Babylon was her world and she only functioned within that world without being particularly knowledgeable on the current plans of movements of Edward, but with Edward in the north, he was much closer to Kenton than she could have imagined. The news that he was to be turned over to Edward in a few days in Doncaster was horrifying. Nicola wasn't entirely sure she could send word to Warwick in time and once Kenton was with Edward, the chances of his escape would be greatly diminished. He would be at the mercy of Edward entirely. Terrified, her heart began to race.

"And... and Edward knows you have le Bec?" she asked. "You have already sent him word?"

St. John nodded. "I sent Edward a missive when I was first told le Bec had been captured at Manchester," he said. "We knew Edward was in Yorkshire, and the general area, so the messenger went to find him. The same messenger returned a short time ago and was able to deliver the message to Edward personally. That is how we know Edward will be in Doncaster by next week."

So now it was all explained. Missives had been flying back and forth, missives of Kenton and Manchester and probably Babylon. Missives were flying everywhere, discussing Edward, and Kenton, and Nicola had known nothing about them. Not that she made it her business to know everyone else's business, but still, much had happened that she had not been aware of. Edward probably knew everything about what had happened with Babylon and with Manchester.

Secrets, and battles, had been revealed.

Oh, God, Nicola thought as she lifted her hand from St. John's shoulder and began to pace away. *What now? What do I do?* Quickly, oh so quickly, she began to think of a way to salvage the situation, to send word to Warwick quickly enough. She didn't have time to go back to Kenton and ask his advice on the matter so she had to think on this one all on her own. She knew she had to get word to Warwick and get it to him quickly; that much was imperative. Edward knew about Kenton and, already, his delivery to Edward had been planned.

"So we must save your sister before next week," she said, pretending to be very concerned for St. John's sister when, in fact, it was only Kenton she was concerned for. "I... I have an idea that you may not like but it may be the only thing we can do to save your sister. It would seem to me that if you cannot, or will not, exchange Kenton for your sister, then mayhap we must give Warwick something that is equally attractive."

St. John was looking at her with great interest and curiosity, as was Saxilby. "What could be equally attractive to the man?" St. John wanted to know. "He wants le Bec. What else could we possibly give him?"

Nicola fixed him in the eye. "Something that belongs to me, something he very much wants," she said. "Offer him Babylon in exchange for your sister's life. Surely the man must consider it. He wanted Babylon badly enough to send le Bec after it those weeks ago. I will send my husband's knight with a missive to Warwick to tell him that, although you cannot give him le Bec in exchange for your sister, you will offer Babylon instead. How could he possibly refuse? He will regain the fortress that he very badly wanted."

It was, in fact, a brilliant and shocking suggestion and for the first time since reading the missive from Warwick, St. John felt some hope. He truly felt hope. He looked to Saxilby anxiously.

"What do you think?" he asked the man. "Do you think it will work?"

Saxilby was a bit more skeptical. "That is difficult to say," he replied, eyeing Lady Thorne who was so willing to turn her fortress back over to the enemy. "Certainly, Babylon is not Kenton le Bec but it is nonetheless a prize. Lady Thorne, why would you so willingly give over your home to the man? St. John's sister means nothing to you. Why would you suggest such a thing?"

There was suspicion in his tone. Nicola could hear it. It wasn't difficult to think of a believable answer.

"Because Babylon holds nothing but terrible memories for me," she said, which was the truth. "My husband was not a kind man, Lord Saxilby. If you knew him, then you know that is the truth. He was brutal and unscrupulous. When I see Babylon, I think of him, so it is no great sacrifice for me to offer the fortress in exchange for a young woman's life. The fortress means little to me. Warwick can have it and welcome to it."

It was a reasonable answer and one that Saxilby could understand; he did indeed know of Gaylord Thorne's character. "So you would give it away?" he asked softly. "But you have children. Where will you go?"

"She can stay here," St. John said quickly, perhaps *too* quickly. There was something suddenly warm in his expression as he looked at Nicola. "She and her children can come and live here, with me. It is the least I can do for the lady if she is willing to sacrifice her home for my sister."

Nicola realized, almost too late, that there was something of a romantic interest abruptly in St. John's manner. It wasn't so much what he said but the way he said it and she resisted the urge to back away from the man. He was looking at her with great admiration and gratitude and something more... something she didn't want to see in his expression. He was a handsome man, and seemingly kind, but she wanted no part of him. At least, not in the manner his tone was suggesting.

"Your offer is very kind," she said, trying not to sound put-off by it. "But that is not necessary. I have a widowed aunt near London who will take us in. Now, let us get on with this missive to Warwick offering Babylon in exchange for your sister. If you will write the missive, I will go and tell my knight of his coming mission."

She was swiftly changing the subject away from her possibly seeking refuge at Conisbrough, away from anything that had to do with St. John, and Saxilby took the bait, thankfully.

"We can just as easily send a messenger, my lady," he said. "There is no need for you to send your knight."

Nicola smiled wryly. "You will forgive me, Lord Saxilby, but sending a missive to Warwick will take a man of some determination, strength, and fearlessness," she said. "No offense to your messengers, but I would feel more comfortable sending Conor. He is resourceful and seasoned, and will deliver the message without fail. I do not want to trust something of this importance to anyone other than a man I have implicit faith in. We are speaking of my fortress, after all, so you will indulge me."

Saxilby didn't argue after that. Lady Thorne seemed to have taken over the negotiations with Warwick and St. John was content to let her, so Saxilby sat back, watching as St. John rushed to his desk and rifled through the clutter to find a piece of parchment to write his missive on.

Eagerly, St. John began scribing his reply to Warwick. Most knights had others write their missives for them, and some knights couldn't write at all, but St. John was an educated man who wrote quite well. As he carefully stenciled out the letters, Nicola excused herself and went in search of Conor to tell the man of his coming mission. She tried not to run, but she could hardly wait to tell him.

It was cold and bright outside, typical of spring weather. Nicola wandered the keep a bit before braving out into the ward, finding Conor in the great hall breaking his fast amidst servants sweeping the floor and cleaning out the hearth, which had a blockage in the chimney. Nicola sat down next to Conor as he enjoyed warmed-over beef and bread from the previous night, hardly able to contain her excitement.

"Much has happened this morning," she said to the knight, her voice low. "It would seem that you are riding out to Warwick today."

Conor looked up from his meal. "Why?" he asked, surprised. "What has happened?"

Nicola looked around to make sure there were no servants to hear what she had to say. "St. John received a missive early this morning from Warwick," she said quietly. "Evidently, Warwick knows that Kenton is being held prisoner at Conisbrough and he knows that St. John is the garrison commander. Somehow, he was able to abduct St. John's sister and he is offering her in exchange for Kenton."

Conor's eyes widened. "Is this true?"

"It is," Nicola said, speaking quickly. "But that is not all. Brome has already informed Edward that he has Kenton as a prisoner. Did you know that Edward is in Yorkshire? I did not, either. He is evidently moving south to London and will be in Doncaster in the next few days. That is when Brome plans to deliver Kenton to him. We cannot allow this to happen, Conor. Warwick must be in Doncaster, too, and take Kenton before he can be delivered to Edward."

Conor stopped eating; he found he had no appetite left at the revelations Lady Thorne was delivering. It was all quite staggering, as if a great deal had happened overnight.

"But what of St. John's sister?" he asked. "What does she have to do with any of this?"

Nicola held up a hand, indicating for him to keep his voice quiet. In an empty hall, voices tended to echo. "Brome was distraught that he could not exchange Kenton for his sister," she whispered. "Edward is already expecting Kenton, evidently, so I suggested that Brome write to Warwick and offer to give him back Babylon in exchange for his sister. Brome is writing that very missive right now, a missive you will take to Warwick."

Conor cocked his head curiously. "I will?"

Nicola nodded firmly. "Aye, but the missive means nothing," she said. "Throw it away after you leave Conisbrough for all I care. You are really going to Warwick to tell him about Kenton and Doncaster."

"But does Warwick truly have St. John's sister?"

"That is what he said."

Conor lifted his auburn eyebrows. "So St. John believes I am only going to deliver the missive offering Babylon in exchange for his sister."

"Aye."

"You have offered him the fortress to exchange for the woman's life?"

"I have."

"But why?"

She shrugged. "I will tell you what I told St. John," she said. "Babylon holds only bitter memories for me. It was Gaylord's fortress, never mine. It does not pain me to be rid of it."

"But it is your sons' legacy, is it not?"

She drew in a deep, pensive breath. There as something in her manner that suggested some regret at that point. "Aye," she said. "But I do not want them there. Mayhap I will find a better legacy for them elsewhere, away from a place of such terrible memories."

Now, Conor wriggled his eyebrows, a bit stumped at all of the happenings going on, happenings he found himself involved in. "God's Bones," he muttered. "A good deal has happened this morning already, hasn't it?"

"Aye."

"When are they moving Kenton?"

Nicola's expression washed with uncertainty. "They could only tell me within the next few days," she said. "They could move him tomorrow or move him next week. Regardless, you must go to Warwick immediately and tell him to ride for Doncaster. He must be there when St. John tries to deliver Kenton to Edward."

Conor knew that. He drained the watered wine left in his cup and wiped his mouth with the back of his hand, flicking bits of bread off his auburn beard.

"It will be done, Lady Thorne," he said. "I will go and prepare my things."

Nicola nodded shortly. "Do," she said. "And hurry. As soon as St. John is finished with this missive, you must leave."

Conor stood up, politely helping her to stand as well. Odd how they were allies now when, only days before, he had learned of her betrayal and had been most mistrustful of her motives. Conor had come to see that Lady Thorne was an intelligent, determined woman who, so far, had kept her word. She wanted to free Kenton from Edward's grasp and it would seem that she was making plans to do exactly that. At this point, Conor had no reason not to trust her. It was clear she had been trying to earn his trust back, just a bit, and so far she was succeeding.

"So I will ride to Warwick," he said quietly as they headed for the exit to the great hall. "The last we knew, he was outside of Wakefield, or at least that was where he told Kenton he was going. I will look for him there."

Nicola nodded, looking around to make sure, once again, that no one was listening. "Very well," she said. "But you must hurry, Conor. We do not know when they are moving Kenton and if Edward gets to him before Warwick has a chance to free him, I am afraid we may never see him again."

Conor paused in the hall entry, his gaze lingering on her. "And that would upset you."

"It would destroy me."

There was great finality and emotion in her words. He could see that she meant what she said. "You never told me what was said when you saw him yesterday upon our arrival," he said. "We have not had a chance to discuss it."

She smirked. "And you shall never know what was said," she said. "That is between me and Kenton. Go, now. Prepare to depart."

With a grin, Conor started to move but soon came to a halt. "That reminds me," he said. "Where will you be? Surely you do not plan to remain here at Conisbrough."

Nicola shook her head. "Nay," she said, thinking of St. John and how he would like nothing better than for her to remain. "I will return to Babylon. When you free Kenton, bring him back to Babylon. I will wait for him there."

Conor cocked an eyebrow dubiously. "Edward's men are still at Babylon," he pointed out. "They will find it odd when Kenton and I return, don't you think?"

Nicola shook her head. "It will not matter," she said. "We will leave shortly thereafter and leave Babylon to Edward. You are simply returning Kenton to Babylon so he can collect me and my children. Where we go after that, I do not care."

"So you intend to leave Babylon?"

"Forever."

"Does Kenton know any of this?"

She shook her head. "He knows nothing and I am not sure when I will have the chance to tell him, so hurry and go about your business. St. John will be finished with the missive soon and you will have to leave."

Conor didn't say any more. He had his orders and he was determined to fulfil them. Lady Thorne had made it possible to free Kenton and Conor was determined to find Warwick and enlist the man's help.

This was the moment they had been waiting for, the opportunity of the moment, and it would not be wasted. Perhaps the woman had betrayed Kenton once before but it was clear she was trying very hard to make up for it. Actions often spoke louder than words and if Conor had to guess, he would say that Lady Thorne's actions bespoke of deep remorse for what she'd done and an even deeper affection for Kenton le Bec. She was risking everything, including her fortress, for the opportunity to free him, and Conor would not disappoint her.

When he left Conisbrough later that morning with a missive meant for Warwick, he headed straight northward, towards Warwick, and prayed he could find the man before St. John decided to move Kenton to Doncaster.

The following day, his prayers were answered.

CHAPTER TWENTY-THREE

Outside of Wakefield, Yorkshire
Warwick's encampment

I T WAS VERY early in the morning when Conor barreled into Warwick's camp, lured by the familiar crimson color of a cluster of tents surrounded by an army encampment. He had ridden straight from Conisbrough, north through fairly open country, for most of the night, only stopping to rest the horse. Well before daybreak he was on the road again, entering the southern outskirts of Wakefield as the sun started to illuminate the eastern horizon.

The sky was clear which mean the night had been very cold, and the colors of the east were glorious pinks and blues as Conor continued to head north. His plan was to enter Wakefield and stop at taverns, one after another, until someone could tell him that they'd seen Warwick's army – perhaps on the outskirts of town or perhaps even moving past it. If he had a direction, and a witness, he was certain he could locate Warwick.

Thankfully, he didn't need any of those things because Warwick had camped on the south side of Wakefield and Conor recognized the tents from a distance. Warwick had very recognizable crimson tents and most of the time he flew his standards over his encampment, but he wasn't flying the standards on this day. The camp was already awake at this early hour and the smells of cooking fires were heavy in the air.

Vastly relieved and saying a swift prayer that Warwick had been placed right in his path, Conor charged towards the camp and straight to the sentries.

The men on guard duty didn't recognize him, however, and Conor had been forced to raise his voice, demanding entry and arguing with the four sentries who were holding him stationery, until one of Warwick's advisors heard the commotion and came forth to berate the sentries for not recognizing one of Kenton le Bec's knights.

The sentries let him pass, Conor dismounted, and turned his exhausted horse over to a nearby soldier before following Lord Pollard across the encampment towards Warwick's big tent. Warwick, having heard Conor's shouting even from where he was, met the knight at the door.

"De Birmingham!" he gasped, reaching out to grab the weary knight. "God be praised! We heard you were at Babylon when it fell to Edward's forces."

Conor nodded as Warwick practically dragged him into the warm, slightly rotten-smelling tent. "Indeed, my lord," he said, breathing heavily with exertion. "I was in command when we were overrun by Conisbrough troops."

Warwick pulled him over to the nearest chair. "Sit, man, *sit*," he commanded, hovering over him as Conor all but collapsed into the chair, which groaned dangerously under his weight. "What has happened? Why have you come?"

Conor accepted a cup of watered wine, cold from sitting out all night, from Pollard, but he hardly cared. He drank it down and smacked his lips.

"There is much to tell, my lord, and little time," he said, handing the cup back to Pollard. More of Warwick's advisors were filtering into the tent now, having heard the shouting and bustle in camp, but Conor ignored the advisors and remained fixed on Warwick. "I have come with a message from Lady Thorne. She has sent me to tell you that Kenton is being moved from Conisbrough to Doncaster where he is due to be delivered to Edward. Edward, it seems, is moving south through Yorkshire. Were you aware, my lord?"

Warwick was listening carefully. "I was aware, aye," he said, but he was far more focused on the mention of Lady Thorne. "You say that the Lady of Babylon has sent this message? Why on earth would she send such a message about le Bec?"

Conor wasn't quite sure how to explain the dynamics between Lady Thorne and Kenton. He wasn't even sure of the dynamics himself and he didn't want to divulge any information that was not his privilege to give. Uncomfortable, he shifted in his chair.

"Much has happened at Babylon since Kenton took control, my lord," he said, trying to be truthful yet sparing with the information. "Suffice it to say that Lady Thorne is now an ally. She has risked herself to discover the information regarding Kenton."

Warwick was greatly puzzled. "She is an ally?" he repeated in disbelief. "But Gaylord Thorne was a fanatical supporter of Edward. It makes little sense that his wife would not be the same."

Conor had no idea how to further explain the loyalties of Lady Thorne. "It is my understanding that her husband was a cruel and brutal man," he said. "Mayhap she wants to defy him. In any case, you must believe me when I say that it was Lady Thorne who discovered Kenton's whereabouts and discovered the intention to send him to Edward."

Warwick found it all quite puzzling but he knew Conor was not a fool. If he said Lady Thorne was an ally, then Warwick would do the man the courtesy of believing him. He surely had good reason to say such a thing. Still, it all seemed very puzzling and shocking.

"You are certain of this?" he asked Conor, just to be sure. "You believe her?"

Conor nodded firmly. "I do, my lord. She has risked much to help Kenton."

Warwick glanced at Pollard, who appeared equally puzzled. Still, the man shrugged as if to give Conor the benefit of the doubt as well. So they had an ally in Lady Thorne. Warwick wanted to know more about that alliance when time permitted, but at the moment, he was fixated on the information Conor was delivering about turning Kenton over to Edward. He resumed his focus.

"If you say she is an ally, I will accept that for now," he said after a moment. "But let us return to the subject of Edward and his movement south. I am aware of such a thing, as my scouts have been watching Edward's movements. I, too, will be moving south, back to Warwick Castle. We were planning on preparing for our departure today and leaving tomorrow. But you say that Kenton is being moved to Doncaster?"

Conor accepted a second cup of wine from Pollard. Now, there were a half-dozen men standing around him, in various stages of dress, listening to his message. Conor recognized all of them but he continued to stay focused on Warwick.

"He is, my lord," he said, gulping at his second cup of wine. "Allow me to explain the circumstances if you have not already been told. Kenton was taken prisoner at Manchester when Conisbrough troops overran the city. They took him to Conisbrough Castle where he has been a prisoner ever since. Brome St. John, the garrison commander at Conisbrough who is loyal to Edward, sent Edward word that Kenton was his prisoner. Of course, Edward wants Kenton, so it has been arranged to meet Edward in Doncaster where Kenton will be delivered to him."

Warwick understood everything now and his features were grim. "I did not know all of the circumstances behind the fall of Babylon and Manchester," he said. "I only knew of certain things, but not all. When is Kenton being moved?"

Conor swallowed the wine in his mouth. "Soon," he said. "Lady Thorne, who has been acting as a spy on Kenton's behalf, told me that they plan to move him very soon. Within days. She says that it is imperative you intercept Kenton in Doncaster so that Edward cannot take him."

Warwick processed what he was being told. Lady Thorne seemed to have a big part in all of this, which was increasingly puzzling to him. A foe's wife was assisting them, the very woman who once nearly beat him senseless when he made a grab for her back at Babylon. Warwick still laughed at the memory. But all laughter aside, it was quite early in the morning for such madness yet there was little choice but to digest it. De Birmingham had obviously ridden all night to deliver the message and it was clear that there was no time to waste. With a grunt, Warwick turned away, found the nearest chair, and lowered himself into it. His manner was pensive.

"Doncaster is not far to the south," he muttered. "If Edward is passing through Doncaster, then he must be passing fairly close to my camp."

Lord Pollard, standing next to Conor, spoke. "That is very possible, my lord," he said. "There are two roads to the east of us that pass fairly close. It is entirely possible he will see the smoke from our fires."

Warwick stroked his chin in a worried gesture. "Is it possible he will engage me if he sees me?"

Lord Pollard shrugged. "It is more possible that he will not," he said. "You have a few thousand men and I cannot imagine Edward has more than we do at this time. Moreover, he is moving south towards London. Oxford and his very big army are between Edward and London. It is my guess he will continue to gather men on his journey south and will forego engaging you at this time."

Warwick trusted Pollard for the man was correct much more than he was incorrect. But Edward's army passing so close to him gave him an idea.

"Wait," he said, holding up a finger as he began to formulate a plan. "If Edward sees my army here, camped, he will not be expecting any manner of confrontation when he reaches Doncaster, at least not from me. He will only be expecting the delivery of Kenton le Bec. But if we move a small force down to Doncaster, mayhap to the west of the town on the road leading from Conisbrough, we can snatch Kenton away from his Conisbrough escort before he even reaches Doncaster. Edward will be left wondering where Kenton is and what has happened."

Pollard lifted his eyebrows. "He will know it is you," he said. "If he see the camp and knows you are near Doncaster, then of course he will know it was you who took Kenton."

Warwick looked at him. "But you said he will not engage me," he reminded him. "Even if he suspects it is I who has Kenton, he will not waste the effort of trying to gain Kenton back. Kenton will be protected by my entire army."

Conor had been listening to both Warwick and Pollard, who seemed more concerned with Edward than anything. "Whatever you do, my lord, it must be done immediately," he interjected, stressing that Kenton was the issue here. "You must get to Kenton before Edward does and, that being the case, you must move now."

Warwick couldn't disagree. An old male servant entered the tent at that moment with Warwick's morning meal, but Warwick only took the steaming wine from the tray and had the man give the rest to Conor, who wolfed down the meal of bread and cheese. All the while, as Conor gorged himself, Warwick was thinking of the easiest way to free Kenton le Bec from his captors.

"Do you have any idea how many men are moving Kenton?" he asked Conor.

Mouth full, Conor shook his head. "I do not, my lord," he said. "I am sure if Lady Thorne knew, she would have told me."

Before Warwick could reply, the tent flap flew back and two very big knights entered the tent. Conor nearly choked on his food when he saw de Russe and Wellesbourne enter the tent. He shot to his feet.

"De Russe!" he gasped. "Wellesbourne! You are alive!"

Odd how men who had been adversarial only weeks before were now acting like long-lost friends. The bonds of the knighthood could be odd that way. Wellesbourne was the first to reach out and grasp Conor's hand, a smile on his fair face.

"So you survived," he said, satisfaction in his voice. "When last we saw Babylon, she was greatly overrun."

Conor squeezed the man's big hand. "So you saw Babylon as it was attacked?" he clarified. "I thought you were in Manchester?"

Wellesbourne nodded. "When Manchester was overrun by Conisbrough, we retreated back to Babylon but came upon it as it was under siege," he explained. "When we realized we could not find refuge at Babylon, we came on to Warwick to tell him what was happening."

Now, a good deal was making sense to Conor on how Warwick had known what had happened with Manchester, Babylon, and even Kenton. "I understand," he said. "Thanks to God that you both survived."

"Le Mon is with us, too."

The statement came from de Russe, who now had a hand extended to Conor. With a smirk, Conor took his former enemy's outstretched hand and shook it firmly. "So le Mon survived," Conor said, looking between the pair. "That is good to know. What of Forbes?"

The smiles faded from their faces. "He did not survive Manchester," Wellesbourne said. "What of Kenton? Have you heard anything about him?"

Warwick interjected. "De Birmingham has come to tell us that Kenton was captured," he told them. "The garrison at Conisbrough is moving him to Doncaster to deliver him to Edward. Good knights, we must make sure Kenton never makes it to Edward."

De Russe and Wellesbourne were startled by the news but, nonetheless, they were already prepared to move. Knights often had to make instantaneous decisions and they were therefore ready and eager to ride to Kenton's aid.

"Now, my lord?" Wellesbourne asked.

Warwick held up a hand to cool the enthusiastic warrior, at least for the moment. "We will waste no time," he said. "The word is that Kenton will be moved very soon, mayhap even today, so we must make sure we are in position to stop the escort from delivering Kenton to Edward. I will need two men to ride forward and select an excellent spot for an ambush on the road between Conisbrough and Doncaster. Will you two volunteer?"

Warwick knew he didn't even have to ask, for both knights were virtually out of the door already. "Of course, my lord," de Russe said. "I know the land around Doncaster fairly well. We will find a suitable position."

Warwick nodded. "Excellent," he said. "I want a contingent of fifty men for this task, fifty of our best. We must get Kenton at all costs. Make sure the men are well-armed because you know the contingent guarding Kenton will be."

"Aye, my lord," de Russe replied.

"Prepare a mount for de Birmingham as well," he said. "I suspect he will want to go with us."

"Aye, my lord."

"Get about your business."

The knights quit the tent immediately, leaving Conor standing with Warwick. Exhausted, but determined not to be left behind, he struggled not to look completely spent.

"My lord, if you have no further need of me for the next hour, I should like to rest," he said.

Warwick shook his head. "Rest while you can," he said. "It is my intention to leave as soon as de Russe and Wellesbourne have the men prepared."

Conor nodded. "Very well, my lord," he said. "Is there a place to lay my head?"

Warwick shook his head. "There was, but I have a guest occupying that space," he said. Then, he looked at Conor with a strange gleam to his eye. "Do you know anything about St. John receiving a missive from me?"

Conor gave him a half-grin. "I do," he said. "With the news about Kenton I'd almost forgotten to tell you. I have a missive that St. John himself personally wrote to you in response to the exchange you offered – his sister for Kenton."

Warwick's eyebrows lifted in surprise. "Ah," he said. "So he did receive it? But he chose to send Kenton to Edward in spite of the fact he knew that I had his sister?"

Conor shrugged. "Apparently he fears Edward more than he fears you," he said. "Moreover, the missive contains a counterproposal – with Lady Thorne's blessing, St. John is offering you the return of Babylon in exchange for his sister."

Warwick was not expecting that counteroffer, struggling not to appear off-guard. "Is that so?" he asked with great interest. "That is surprising considering I threatened to send his sister back to him in pieces if he did not comply with my terms."

"Are you planning on doing that, my lord?"

Warwick shook his head. "Nay," he said. "A dead young woman is of no use to anyone. At least, that is what I told her. But I also told her I would marry her off to the highest bidder if her brother refused me. Are you looking for a wife, de Birmingham?"

Conor shook his head vigorously. "Nay, my lord."

"Are you certain? She is quite pretty."

Conor moved to shake his head again but the mention of beauty had him naturally intrigued. "Is she?"

"She is," Warwick said, sensing the man's curiosity. "She is in the tent right next to me if you care to see her."

Conor lingered on that suggestion for a moment. "Mayhap I will, my lord," he said. "But I will determine the price, not you."

Warwick grinned. "She is worth a great deal."

"Then am I to understand you will refuse St. John's offer of Babylon for his sister returned?"

Warwick laughed softly. "I am not entirely certain yet," he said. "I would like Babylon returned, that is true, but you deserve a reward for risking yourself to deliver the message regarding Kenton. If you do not want the girl then mayhap I will take the castle in exchange for her."

Conor simply grinned as Warwick moved away to discuss the latest events with his advisors, who had overheard most of the conversation.

As Warwick went into conference with the group of rather vocal men, Conor found himself wandering from Warwick's tent. He didn't know why he had any interest in seeing St. John's sister, but for some odd reason, he did. Perhaps because he wanted to see the woman whose life was worth an entire castle. For whatever reason, he was curious. And curiosity drove him to her tent.

Lady Katryne was sitting on the floor of the tent, on a woolen hide perched before a small but red-hot brazier, when a very big knight with red hair stuck his head into the tent. He seemed to be searching for something and when his eyes fell upon her, Katryne felt something like a jolt, as if she'd been slapped. But it wasn't a fearful sensation. It was, in truth, an exciting one. She'd never known anything like it and when the knight smiled at her, she felt another shock run through her. Most unusual.

Conor, in fact, felt the same sensations when he first beheld the vision of St. John's beautiful sister. He, too, had never experienced anything like it.

He soon came to think that Warwick might never get Babylon back, after all.

CHAPTER TWENTY-FOUR

Five days later
Two miles southwest of Doncaster, Hagg Forest

THE MOISTURE HAD been very heavy in the air overnight, which meant by morning, a thick fog was blanketing the land. Having departed Conisbrough Castle before dawn, Kenton rode in the center of about fifty men, all of them heavily armed, all of them with one focus – Kenton le Bec. This was a transport troop, designed to move an important prisoner, and it was of such importance that St. John had taken command of the troop and was riding point. The man wasn't going to let anything go wrong, at any time, and was determined to take control of every aspect of the movement.

Kenton, however, wasn't thinking on St. John or the fact that he was being moved. St. John had said very little to him about the action, only enough to tell him that they were meeting with Edward in Doncaster, which was very close to Conisbrough, a mere five miles away. All Kenton could think of was the fact that he hadn't seen Nicola since the day she arrived at Conisbrough, but he supposed that was to be expected. She didn't have any reason to see the prisoner beyond her initial visit but he still yearned for her, wishing he could have seen her at least once more before he departed Conisbrough. He still had the taste of her upon his lips, something he kept tucked close to his heart. He hoped it wouldn't be his last taste.

More than that, he had no idea what had transpired in the five days since he'd last spoken with her. They had separated with a plan in mind, of getting word to Warwick, but he had no idea if she'd been able to accomplish that. Therefore, he was operating in the dark, edgy and concerned about what was to happen, and especially concerned that he would be seeing Edward this day. If Nicola hadn't been able to send word to Warwick about him being moved from Conisbrough, then it was a certainty that he would be dining with Edward that night.

Already, he had no appetite.

Kenton's anxiety made travel uneasy. He had been given back his armor, and his horse, everything but his weapons, so he looked just like any other knight as he was escorted on the road towards Doncaster. The truth was that, for a prisoner, he had been extremely well treated and afforded a good deal of respect from both Saxilby and St. John, so he really had no complaints about his treatment. But he simply didn't want to be there, having grown bored and unnerved in his captivity. He wanted to see Nicola and he wanted to go back to his last memories of Babylon, fishing with little boys or gently flirting with Nicola, although he wanted to do far more than flirt with her this time. He had a taste for her flesh that he would never be free of.

So his mind wandered as they plodded along the muddy road, through the heavy fog, and towards a fairly dense stretch of forest that lined both sides of the road. He could smell water and could see the hints of a lake off to the south, through the mist. Creatures were foraging in the early morning and he saw more than his share of rabbits and foxes as they darted about, startling the horses as they went. He was peering off to the south, thinking he saw the dark shadows of people in the distance, when St. John pulled his horse up alongside him.

The men acknowledged each other silently. The truth was that Kenton didn't have much to say to the man so he simply kept his mouth shut. He wasn't one for meaningless conversation, anyway.

"We should be in Doncaster within the next hour," St. John said. "I have no way of knowing when Edward will be passing through so we may be forced to pitch camp there. If you tell me you will not make an attempt to escape, I will not shackle you."

Kenton looked at him. "That is your choice."

St. John eyed him for a moment, sensing that he had insulted the man with the shackle comment. "Sorry, le Bec, but you are a valuable commodity," he said. "Were you to escape, Edward would probably throw me in my own vault and lose the key."

Kenton really didn't care about that. He returned his attention to the misty field to the south, which was now becoming increasingly dotted with trees as they drew near the dense forest to the east.

"Where is Saxilby?" Kenton asked.

St. John, sensing that Kenton had no real desire to carry on any manner of conversation, turned his attention forward, towards the forest that they were approaching. "He has gone with Lady Thorne back to Babylon," he replied. "She wanted to return home so he escorted her."

Kenton didn't react outwardly, but inwardly he was thrilled to know where Nicola was. He'd been desperate to know. "Good," he said, but realizing that sounded as if she meant something to him, he added: "Send the woman back where she belongs and far away from me."

St. John sensed a great deal of bitterness in his words and he grinned. "I can only imagine how difficult she must have been," he said. "Why you did not confine her to the vault, I will never know. If you trusted her, it was your undoing, for the woman certainly did not trust you. It was by her hand that we were able to capture you."

Kenton felt as if he were being chastised. "She had a working knowledge of the fortress," he said as if explaining the obvious. "She served a purpose as chatelaine. As long as she served a purpose, there was no reason to confine her to the vault."

St. John scratched his cheek beneath his open visor. "As you say," he said, although it was clear he didn't particularly agree. "Had it been me, I would have locked her up. She is an aggressive, pushy woman, but she is also quite beautiful and I suppose you are only a man, after all.

Greater men than us have fallen to a beautiful woman."

Kenton turned to look at him. "Who says I fell to her?"

St. John gave him a half-grin. "You *did* fall to her," he said. "The woman betrayed you. I would call that falling to her. But she is so lovely that mayhap I would not mind, either. In fact, when this is over, I may return to Babylon and marry her."

Jealousy reared its ugly head. Kenton's eyes narrowed at the man as the ancient primal sense of defending a mate filled his chest. Nicola belonged to him and he would not tolerate any competition for her but he certainly could not say so. If he did, it would jeopardize Nicola and everything she had worked for. For all St. John knew, Nicola and Kenton were bitter enemies and no matter how much Kenton wanted to tell St. John otherwise, he would not do it. He couldn't. So he had to bite his tongue and turn away.

Stay away from her, you bastard!

"Then I wish you luck," he said, not meaning a word of it. "Be careful that she does not end up ruling the house and hold, and you along with it. I get the sense that she would be quite adept at doing all of it."

St. John chuckled. "I would not mind," he said. "She is a lovely bit of flesh."

Kenton's jaw began to tick, struggling so hard not to say anything in return. St. John was speaking of the woman he loved, the woman he intended to give up everything for, so it was a fierce struggle not to rush the man and wrap his hands around St. John's neck. He was thinking of St. John's face turning purple as he squeezed, taking fiendish delight in it, when they entered the dark confines of the forest that surrounded the road.

It was moist and sticky as they began to pass through the heavy canopy of trees. The white mist seemed to stop at the treetops, as if the canopy were holding it aloft, so the passage through the forest was fairly clear. Birds were chirping and forest creatures were making noise, rustling through the ground cover, but Kenton thought it all felt rather eerie. St. John must have, too, because he ordered his men to fan out and carry weapons at the ready. Kenton was fairly open in the middle of the pack, watching the men around him tense up. He was vigilant, looking around him as he would have normally done on any given patrol, sensing there were things in the trees that he could not see. Perhaps it was the warrior in him imagining things or perhaps it was experience telling him that something was really there. He had just turned his eyes forward, down the road, when something whizzed by his head.

Suddenly, chaos broke loose. Arrows were flying and men on horseback were charging from the trees, aiming for St. John and his men. Startled, Kenton struggled to keep his horse from bolting, knowing he was weaponless and had no real way to fight back. He was quite concerned momentarily, enough so that he considered running from the charge. But then a strange thing occurred.

Knights were emerging from the forest atop horses that Kenton had seen before. In fact, he recognized at least three of the animals, maybe more, as a very big knight came forth and began swinging a massive broadsword at St. John's men-at-arms. Two men near the front of the company fell almost immediately, beheaded by a massive knight with a serrated-edged broadsword. The knight continued to charge back through the ranks, swinging that sword, as another enormous knight fell in behind him, killing men the first knight missed. It was a precisely planned destruction that took a great deal of skill, and those two knights obviously had it.

As Kenton watched with some fascination, it was a blood bath. He didn't even know where St. John was; he didn't even look for the man. He was fixated on the two massive knights who were charging in his direction and would soon be upon him. Being weaponless, his only choice was to try to outrun them. But the fact that he recognized the animals was the only thing that kept him from doing so. He held his ground as St. John and his army rapidly fell beneath the swords of a well-planned ambush.

"Kenton!"

Someone shouted his name and he turned to see Conor charging towards him. The man was holding a broadsword out to him, hilt-first, and Kenton was seized with the fact that this ambush wasn't random; suddenly, it began to make sense. This attack, this flood of armed mean, was meant for *him*.

Help had arrived!

Kenton could hardly believe what he was seeing, astonished to the bone. But in the same breath, he knew that this was Nicola's doing. She must have discovered St. John's plans to deliver him to Edward and, somehow, she'd gotten word to Warwick about it. Now, days of wondering and darkness were coming to light as Kenton realized the plans they had made, and all that they had hoped for, were coming to fruition.

She did it!

The relief he felt was indescribable. Kenton found himself reliving the conversation they'd had at Conisbrough where he had told her the only real chance to free him was when he would be out in the open, away from the walls of Conisbrough, as he was being transported to Edward. Although they'd spoken of the plans very seriously and she swore to find out what she could from St. John, perhaps deep down, Kenton really didn't believe that his extraction could be arranged. So much was involved, from discovering the plans to notifying Warwick to actually being in the right place at the right time to free him, but somehow, someway, the stars had aligned and there were men fighting for Kenton's freedom. They were saving him from Edward.

He had to save himself as well.

Kenton took the sword from Conor with a warm, grateful expression. "I was wondering when you were going to show up," he said. "What took you so long? I have been on the road for hours."

Conor grinned, displaying his big, white teeth. "We have been here for days," he told him. "What took *you* so long?"

Kenton returned the smile but, suddenly, the two enormous knights who had been destroying the front half of the escort were in their midst, bloodied swords in hand. Visors went up and Kenton recognized de Russe and Wellesbourne.

"Are you well, le Bec?" Wellesbourne demanded. "The last we saw you, you were falling off your horse at Manchester."

Kenton nodded, so incredibly grateful to see his friends and colleagues, men risking their lives to save him. He'd never felt more blessed in his life than he did at that very moment.

"I am well," he said. "But we need to get out of here. You have done enough damage. Let us retreat to safety."

It was the logical path now that St. John's escort was nearly destroyed. There were still pockets of fighting going on towards the rear of the column and the four men turned to see St. John in a serious struggle with three other Warwick men. Emerging from the edge of the tree line nearby came another mounted knight, and a few more mounted soldiers, and Kenton recognized Warwick's armor immediately. Before he spurred his horse to the man, he turned to his three friends.

"That is Brome St. John, garrison commander of Conisbrough," he said, pointing out St. John. "Do not kill him. He is to be spared."

De Russe, Wellesbourne, and Conor strained to see who he was speaking of. "That knight back there?" Conor asked, pointing to the rear of the column.

"Aye," Kenton said. "Spare him. I will go see Warwick now."

The four of them separated. Kenton rode straight for Warwick whilst de Russe, Wellesbourne, and Conor headed back to prevent St. John from being killed in his fight against three heavily-armed men.

As Kenton reached the elevation above the road where Warwick was, he turned to see that most, if not all, of St. John's escort had been killed or wounded. Bloodied men were lying everywhere on the muddy road. His gaze lingered on the carnage a moment, feeling incredibly grateful to be alive, when he heard a voice beside him.

"'Tis good to see you again, Kenton," Warwick said. "How foolish of you to permit yourself to be captured. Do you see what lengths we had to go to in order to get you back?"

Kenton smiled weakly. "I was not captured by choice, I assure you," he said. "Being hit on the head and falling on my face ensured that I was unable to fight back. Had I had any opportunity to resist, I am sure you know that I would have."

Warwick was visually inspecting Kenton, peering closely at his face and still slightly-bruised forehead. "You look well enough to me," he said. "How do you feel?"

Kenton noticed that Wellesbourne and de Russe now had St. John between them, trying to force the man to drop his sword, which St. John seemed reluctant to do. "I am well enough," he said. "I was treated very well, considering. And that man that de Russe and Wellesbourne are attempting to subdue is Brome St. John, the garrison commander of Conisbrough. He should be given all due respect, my lord. He was humane and fair in his treatment of me."

Warwick turned to see what Kenton was looking at; four knights in a standoff. De Russe and Wellesbourne were trying to convince St. John to drop his sword as Conor got up behind St. John, making sure the man didn't make any swift or foolish moves.

"That shall be up to him," Warwick said. "If he does not drop his sword, we cannot treat him fairly."

Kenton knew that. He spurred his horse towards St. John as the man held off the three heavily-armed Warwick knights. Warwick followed close behind and, as the men came close to the standoff, Kenton spoke out.

"St. John," he said loudly "Drop the sword. Your escort is finished and so are you. Please do not make this difficult."

St. John looked at Kenton with resistance, hesitation, and some frustration in his expression. "You know that I cannot surrender, le Bec," he said. "If I go down, it will be with a sword in my hand."

"Do you want your sister returned?" Warwick suddenly called to the man. "If you want your sister returned and not sent back to you in pieces, then you will drop your sword."

St. John looked to the older man behind Kenton, suspecting who he might be simply because of the very fine but well-used armor he wore, and the horse he rode upon was an utterly magnificent beast. He wore the crimson Warwick tunic that St. John had seen, many times and, after a moment, Brome sighed heavily. He knew he was already defeated but he simply wasn't ready to give in yet. He couldn't believe how sour his luck had turned.

"What do you know of my sister?" he asked.

Warwick shrugged. "I know she is my guest," he said. "I know that I sent you a missive telling you that I would exchange your sister's life for the life of Kenton le Bec. Now I have Kenton but you do not have your sister. Swallow your pride and lower your sword, St. John. I will not tell you again."

The conversation suddenly took an ominous turn in that threat. Warwick meant what he said. Kenton, who truly didn't want to see St. John killed, put up a big hand and motioned for him to lower his sword. It was a plea. St. John looked at Kenton with an expression that suggested he was the one who felt betrayed, as if this entire ambush had been Kenton's doing as a personal attack against him. But St. John's expression also suggested that he wanted to live so, with a heavy sigh, he handed the sword, hilt-first, to de Russe, who took it.

The ambush, officially, was ended.

"Now," St. John said to Warwick. "Tell me your name and tell me of my sister's health."

Warwick eyed the young, strong knight whom Edward had placed a good deal of faith in. He could see the faint resemblance between the man and his sister.

"I am Warwick," he told St. John. "Your sister's health is fine. She is doing quite well. I read the missive you sent to me with a counterproposal to my original offer; in exchange for your sister's life, you are offering to withdraw from Babylon Castle and return it to me."

St. John nodded, looking and sounded defeated now that Warwick's identity had been confirmed to him. "Aye, my lord," he said glumly.

"That was my offer."

Around them, the fighting had stopped now that St. John had surrendered his sword. Warwick's men began gathering their own wounded, which there were only two, and the able-bodied began assessing St. John's wounded. Men were being picked off the road and brought onto the cold, damp grass, but none of the knights or Warwick seemed to notice. They were entirely focused on what was appearing to be negotiations for the release of St. John's sister.

"You know," Warwick said, leaning on his saddle horn and shaking a finger at St. John, "I could become quite upset at you for ignoring my demand for Kenton. You were taking him to Edward in spite of my threat against your sister. Is it true that you fear Edward more than you value your sister's life?"

St. John shook his head. "In a sense, my lord," he said honestly. "Edward knows I have Kenton and he wants him very badly. Should I fail to deliver him, the repercussions would go beyond simply me. My family would be involved and our honor would be at stake. I was planning on the fact that you would not kill a defenseless woman in spite of your threat and that we might be able to negotiate for something just as valuable. You wanted Babylon badly once, badly enough to lay siege to it. I assumed you would want it back so I offered it."

Warwick had to admit that the knight's logic was sound. He looked at Kenton, who seemed to think the same thing because Kenton nodded faintly at Warwick as if to concur with St. John. It was a silent confirmation of an agreeable point. Warwick returned his attention to the captured knight.

"I do want it back," he said. "You were actually quite wise with your negotiation tactics in suggesting it. But now that I have Kenton back, I still want Babylon returned to me. Clear out your men immediately and I will give you back your sister."

St. John looked at the knights around him, obviously holding him prisoner. "In order to do that, I would have to be permitted to return to Babylon," he said, pointing to de Russe. "This very big knight might not let me leave so easily."

Warwick cocked an eyebrow. "That very big knight, as well as a few others, will escort you back to Babylon where you will order your men to leave," he said frankly. "Once your men have vacated, those same knights will send word to me that your part of the bargain has been accomplished. Once I receive that missive, I will return your sister to you unharmed. Is that clear?"

Begrudgingly, St. John nodded. "It is, my lord."

Warwick smiled without humor. "Excellent," he said. "Now, collect your wounded and my men will bury your dead. You will return to Babylon this day."

St. John looked around him, at the fact that nearly all of his escort party had been killed. He felt rather sick about it. "What of Edward, my lord?" he said. "He is expecting me in Doncaster."

Warwick shook his head. "If you show up in Doncaster without Kenton, how do you think he will react?" he said, pointing out the obvious. "To say the man will be displeased is putting it mildly. Nay, St. John, you will return to Babylon this day without further word to Edward. He will wonder what has happened to you and to Kenton, of course, but it is my suspicion that he will not waste an overabundance of time on it. He has much larger things to deal with right now. Return to Babylon and deal with Edward at a later time."

St. John had no choice. He could see that. Around him, men were gathering up his wounded and putting aside his dead. He couldn't do anything about Kenton any longer. Now, he had to focus on his sister and the bargain he made for her release. Edward wouldn't even know about that part because he more than likely didn't even know Babylon was currently being held for him by the Conisbrough garrison. Warwick was right; Edward had more important things to worry about than whether or not he held Babylon Castle. With that in mind, he simply nodded his head.

"Very well," he said. "Let us move for Babylon so that I can ensure the release of my sister."

Babylon is where Nicola has gone, Kenton thought. Remembering how fondly St. John had spoken of Nicola suddenly spurred him into action.

"I will return with them, my lord," he said, already moving his horse off of the embankment and down to the road. "Babylon was mine and shall be again. I have become rather fond of it."

Warwick stopped him. "Nay, Kenton," he said. "I have need of you with me. Let de Russe, Wellesbourne, and de Birmingham take St. John back to Babylon. They are quite capable."

Kenton stopped but he didn't return to Warwick. Instead, he simply looked at the man, struggling not to argue with him. He hadn't expected Warwick to deny him and now he felt slightly panicky about it. *What if I cannot return to Nicola?* It was all he had thought about, the only thing that kept him sane. He had to be reunited with her, to hold her in his arms again. He didn't want to go with Warwick in the least and he certainly didn't want St. John to return to Babylon with Nicola there and Kenton unable to protect her or stake his claim. Nay, he didn't like that thought at all.

I must return to her!

"My lord, when I left Babylon for Manchester, I was expecting to return," he explained with more patience than he felt. "I left most of my possessions there, things that belong to me and things that I want returned. Allow me to return to Babylon to collect what belongs to me and then I shall join you wherever you may be."

Warwick didn't want to deny the man but he had his reasons for his request. He crooked a finger at Kenton. "Come with me a moment," he said. "We must speak."

Obediently, Kenton went to him and the two of them moved away from the road, away from ears that could overhear their conversation. Kenton had to admit that he felt incredibly resistant at the moment, resistant in that Warwick wanted to prevent him from doing what he wanted to do. He struggled with his manner, trying not to convey how displeased he was, as Warwick came to a halt just inside the tree line and faced him.

"Let me explain what has happened since you have been at Babylon and in captivity," Warwick said quietly. "Edward landed upon the shores of Yorkshire, moved through Percy lands, and gathered a fairly substantial army. It is that same army he is moving south at this moment, the one that is soon to pass through Doncaster. We have heard rumor that he is heading to London but more than that, I have heard specifically that he intends to attack Warwick. That is my home and my seat, Kenton. I cannot allow that. My army is therefore moving south as we speak, heading to Warwick Castle and trying to avoid Edward in the process. I have been told that Oxford is already waiting for Edward further south, preparing to engage him. There are massive dealings afoot, Kenton, and I need you. Edward must not bring his army into London, for if he does, we will lose this fight for Henry. Is this in any way unclear?"

Kenton absorbed what he was being told, the movements of the man who wanted to be king again, and he was not surprised. Nothing Edward did surprised him any longer.

"We have been hearing rumors for months that Edward planned to gather strength in Yorkshire," he said. "Surely this is of no great shock, my lord."

Warwick shook his head. "It is not," he said. "But I am concerned with the size of the force he has gathered. Allies are waiting for us to join with them, further south, but I am retreating to Warwick Castle and I want you to come with me. Will you do this?"

Kenton thought on the greater implications of that question. It wasn't as if he could refuse even though he very much wanted to. He wanted to stay at Babylon with Nicola and the boys and pretend that all of this warfare, battles and kings that had been part of his life for so very long, no longer existed. He didn't want to fight anymore. The promise of a new life was waiting for him, something he very much wanted, but he knew he had no choice when it came to Warwick. He could not leave his old life, not just yet.

The thought greatly saddened him.

"Of course I will, my lord," he said, wondering if his unhappiness showed. "But you must allow me to return to Babylon and retrieve my possessions. It is a three day ride at the very most. I will collect my things and catch up to you as you travel south. Also, I had a great many men with me when I went to Manchester and many were captured in the battle. I do not know what has become of the rest of them but I would like to find out. You will need the manpower."

Warwick waved him off. "The men who were not captured by Saxilby returned to me with de Russe and Wellesbourne when they came to tell me of the disaster at Manchester," he said. "They managed to escape the battle that saw you become a prisoner. I have four hundred of your men under my command, men that will gladly return to you."

Kenton was relieved for the most part. "Thank you, my lord," he said. "But I still worry about those men who were captured."

"Where are they?"

"At Conisbrough."

Warwick pondered that for a moment. "Unfortunately, we cannot do anything about those men at this time," he said. "We are moving south and I cannot deviate to go to Conisbrough and demand their release."

Kenton nodded but even as he did so, a thought occurred to him. He turned to look at St. John, who seemed to be in conversation with Wellesbourne. Kenton scratched his chin.

"Do you think we can include the release of those men along with the surrender of Babylon?" he asked. "We have the commander of Conisbrough at our service, after all."

Warwick realized what he was suggesting. "Brilliant," he said. "Tell St. John we require the release of your men from Conisbrough in addition to the surrender of Babylon or he will never see his sister again."

Kenton cast him a rather dubious expression. "I will not threaten a woman with death," he said. "Suffice it to say that I think I can convince St. John to give me back my men without promising to kill his sister if he does not comply."

Warwick shrugged. "Such threats have worked well enough for me in the past."

"But you are Warwick. I am not."

Warwick snorted. "True enough," he said. Then, he sobered. "Very well. See what you can do about obtaining the release of your men and return to Babylon for your possessions, but do not be gone overlong. I have a feeling the coming conflict with Edward might be something of a decisive one."

Kenton looked at the man seriously. "Why would you say that?"

Warwick shrugged, seemingly lost in thought. "Because I am weary," he said softly. "I am weary of the constant warring, Kenton. Do you not feel like that at times?"

Kenton nodded slowly, with great understanding. "Quite a lot, actually," he admitted. "I wonder what it will be like to live in peace, with no threat of war. I want to marry and be happy, and watch my children grow, so in answer to your question, I feel weary quite often and mayhap never more weary than I do at this moment."

Warwick looked at him, suddenly seeing something different in the man. Perhaps captivity had changed him somehow, or perhaps it was recent events in general. Warwick made a mental note to ask him of the comment at some point, but not now. There wasn't the time to explore it. He gathered his reins.

"Back when you managed to conquer Babylon, I remember saying something that still has meaning to me," he said. "I said that we must end these wars or they will surely end me. I wonder if I will live to see the end of this conflict between Henry and Edward. Something tells me that I will not."

Kenton lingered on that thought for a moment. "If anyone deserves to see the outcome, it is you," he said quietly. "You have done more than anyone to see that the right man sits upon the throne, even if, at times, you sided with Edward."

Warwick smiled faintly. "Yet that did not stop you from serving me."

Kenton shook his head. "Not at all," he said. "You may have switched fealty, but you were never dishonest about it. You were always open and honest with your reasons. As long as we were fighting for the same cause, I had no problem fighting with you."

Warwick chuckled softly, glancing over at St. John and the other knights, knowing it was time to get about their business.

"Go and gather your possessions from Babylon," he said. "Meanwhile, send Wellesbourne and de Russe to me. You may take Conor with you to help you settle things, but I do believe I will take de Russe and Wellesbourne with me. I may need them. As soon as Babylon is ours again, I will expect confirmation from you personally."

"Aye, my lord."

"And you may want to throw Lady Thorne in the vault this time. It seems to me that the woman has been more trouble than she is worth, even if she is on our side for the moment."

Kenton merely smiled and turned his horse in the direction of the road again. When he saw Nicola again, the last thing he intended to do was throw her in the vault.

But Warwick didn't have to know that.

CHAPTER TWENTY-FIVE

Babylon Castle

"TIERNAN, STOP CHASING the chickens," Nicola scolded softly. "They will not lay eggs if you frighten them."

The beginning of the fifth day since having returned home from Conisbrough saw the morning dawn misty and cold. Nicola was out in the kitchen yard gathering eggs for Hermenia, who was moving more slowly these days due to her age and poor health. Because of that, Janet had taken on the bulk of the kitchen duties while Raven and Liesl were mostly in charge of the keep, making sure it was swept and kept clean. The younger girls were starting to show more responsibility these days and Nicola was glad to place it upon them. Things were changing at Babylon and all of them were adapting admirably.

Nicola and the boys were helping, too. Tab was following the stable master around, helping him with the horses, while Teague and Tiernan were gathering eggs with their mother. Or, at least they pretended to gather eggs when they weren't chasing the chickens around. When they grew bored of the chickens, Nicola had to warn them away from playing with the lambs, which were now growing larger but still quite frisky. They liked to head-butt nearly anything, including playful little boys.

Babylon had a feeling of normalcy these days, ever since Nicola had returned from Conisbrough. There were Conisbrough soldiers still there, guarding the walls, but Saxilby had taken some of the men with him when he departed the fortress after escorting Nicola home. Saxilby had left for parts unknown, Kenton's fate was unknown, and most of Nicola's future was unknown, which made her somewhat sad and anxious these days. Gathering eggs with her boys, and maintaining the sense of normalcy, were nearly the only things that kept her sanity. Otherwise, anxiety would have surely overwhelmed her.

Kenton was on her mind every second of every day. She prayed hourly for his safety and for the safety of those who had gone to help him. She prayed that Conor had been able to find Warwick and that, together, they had been able to go to Kenton's aid. But she had no way of knowing if any of that had been successful. For all she knew, Kenton was a prisoner of Edward at this very moment and she would never see him again, although she tried not to think on that. She tried not to imagine the worst. To do so brought tears to her eyes and a lump to her throat; if that was the case and Kenton was indeed a prisoner of Edward, then she considered her life over before it ever really began. Without Kenton, there was no point in going on.

God, she loved him....

Nicola had spent so much time away from Kenton as of late that she was beginning to forget what he looked like, the deep blue of his eyes and the dark color of his hair. More than anything, she could clearly recall the sound of his voice, that deep and smooth tone that brought liquid warmth to her limbs. She hadn't always felt like that, she giggled to herself, but she really couldn't remember those times. She had nearly forgotten about the time he threw her in the vault and all of those arguments they had shared. All she remembered were the moments of warmth between them and the power of his touch, like nothing she had ever known or ever would know again. He was the only man she had loved, or ever would love.

He was her everything.

Depressed, and wrought with the anxiety of Kenton's unknown whereabouts on this fifth day since her return home, she finished collecting the eggs as Teague and Tiernan played over in the corner of the yard with a group of baby chicks. Nicola admonished them to be very careful with the babies and, surprisingly, the boys were quite gentle.

With eggs in her apron, Nicola made her way over to the boys as they sat on the ground and petted the chicks. It made her smile to watch their happy faces, momentarily forgetting her troubles. As she bent over Tiernan, who had a little chick cupped in his hands, she had no idea that, behind her, a very big knight had come into the yard and was now lurking a few feet away.

The mist, so heavy most of the morning, seemed to lift as he stood there, or at least it seemed to lift around him, creating a halo of sorts, as the sunlight reflected through the fog. All that was good and pure in nature seemed to swirl around him, for just a moment, long enough to create a vortex of light that went from his feet, around his legs, swirling around his hair, before disappearing up into the mist above.

For just those few brief moments, there had been magic in the air, the magic of an attachment so powerful that nothing in the world could destroy it. Love had saved him and love had brought him back to Babylon, back to Nicola.

It was the magic of love that had come home again.

"The first time I saw you, you were sitting on the floor of the kitchen," he said quietly. "I remember that day as clearly as if it happened yesterday."

Startled, Nicola gasped and whirled around to find Kenton standing behind her. She hardly took another breath before she burst into tears at the sight of him, all of the apprehension and fear and sorrow she had felt over the past several weeks finding an abrupt outlet. Teague and Tiernan, upon seeing Kenton, leapt to their feet and ran at him, throwing themselves against him as each boy tried to make it into the man's arms. Everyone in the kitchen yard, for the moment, seemed to have lost their minds at the unexpected, but wholly welcome, appearance of Kenton le Bec.

But Kenton retained his wits, at least somewhat. He was over-whelmed at the response, with screaming boys and a crying woman. Laughing softly, he picked up Tiernan because the boy was seriously trying to scale his leg, patted Teague on the head, and went to Nicola as she stood near the wall and wept openly. He was upon her in a second, cupping her face with his free hand, gently kissing her salty lips.

"No tears, love," he murmured. "I am here and I am safe. But I would not be either of those things were it not for you."

Nicola still had eggs in her apron and she tried not to smash them as she fell against him, her head against his chest as his free arm went around her tightly.

"You are here," she wept over and over. "You have come back. You are alive!"

Kenton finally put Tiernan down so he could put both arms around Nicola, who was genuinely distraught. He kissed the top of her head tenderly. "Of course I am alive," he confirmed. "I told you that we would be together again someday, did I not? I swore it to you and I never break a promise."

Nicola remained pressed against him, wrapped up in his enormous arms, and it was the most satisfying and joyful experience she had ever known. She was melting into him, blending with him, becoming one with him in a way that was difficult to describe. It was as if their warmth was mingling into something solitary and fine. Sniffling, struggling to gain control of her emotions, she looked up at him.

"Conor must have gotten through to Warwick," she whispered. "And they found you?"

Kenton nodded, wiping away the moisture on her cheeks. "They did," he said. "Warwick intercepted St. John before he could deliver me to Edward."

Even though his presence was proof enough of that, she still sighed with great relief. "Praise God," she whispered. "Are you well?"

"I am."

"But there was surely a battle when Warwick found St. John! You did not suffer in it?"

"Not in the least."

"And Conor... is he well?"

"He is well."

"Where is he?"

Kenton tipped his head back in the direction of Babylon's big inner ward. "He is here," he said. "He returned with me."

Nicola was so joyful that she was nearly lightheaded with it. "Is it all true, then?" she breathed. "You are back and everyone is well? It will be just as it was when...."

He cut her off, gently. "Wait, love," he said softly. "There is more you should know; Warwick accepted St. John's offer to exchange Babylon for his sister's release, so St. John is here as well, gathering his men. It seems that Babylon will once again be in Warwick's hands."

Nicola realized from the way he was speaking that he was trying to ease her angst about her fortress changing hands again and she hastened to assure him that she had no angst about it whatsoever.

"That is as I had intended," she said, watching his confused expression. She grinned. "Much happened while you were in captivity, my love, that you are not aware of. How do you think I was able to send word to Warwick about your being moved to Edward? It all started when Warwick sent a missive to St. John demanding you in exchange for St. John's sister. Somehow, he found the girl and abducted her."

Kenton nodded. "I heard something about that but I did not know the entire story," he said. "Somehow, Warwick obtained St. John's sister and intended to use her for my freedom."

Nicola nodded. "Exactly," she said. "But St. John had already promised you to Edward. He was quite torn up about it, actually. Therefore, I told him to offer Babylon to Warwick in exchange for his sister, which he did. I knew when Warwick received Babylon, he would naturally put you in charge of the fortress again."

Kenton grinned at her confidence. He gently tweaked her nose. "But that would only happen if I did not make it into Edward's custody, my self-assured lady."

She laughed, seeing his humor. "Exactly!" she agreed. "So I sent Conor to find Warwick with a missive from St. John, offering Babylon in exchange for his sister, but Conor was really going to tell Warwick that St. John was turning you over to Edward. Don't you see? St. John never suspected the real reason I sent Conor to seek Warwick. He thought it was to deliver his missive when it was, in fact, to deliver mine. Warwick then regained you and he regained Babylon as well. It was my hope all along."

He could see her logic, quite impressed with her ability to think through complex plans and situations. His admiration, and his gratitude for her, grew by leaps and bounds, coming to understand this intelligent lady just a little more.

"You would make a fine spy, Lady Thorne," he said with great respect in his voice. "Now I see how everything has come together. I am not entirely sure I can ever completely express my gratitude, but know that you have my undying thanks."

Nicola sniffled away the last of her tears now as the realization that he was here, and he was safe, settled. He was here as if he'd never left her and now that the shock of his appearance wore off, she was left with nothing but gratitude. Gratitude for his very life and gratitude that all of her scheming and planning had saved him. Once, she had sworn to make up for her betrayal, to fix the wrongs she had created.

At this moment, she realized that she had.

"I would do it again, a thousand times over," she professed. "But what will happen now? St. John is here to take his men back to Conisbrough, but then what?"

Kenton shrugged, thinking on the bigger implications of that question, implications he wasn't yet ready to discuss with her. "Babylon will once again belong to Warwick," he stated the obvious. "We will start by assessing what assets we have. I have no idea how many of the men I left behind survived the Conisbrough siege so Conor is looking into that very detail as we speak."

Nicola pondered that question. "I do not know how many men you left behind but very few survived the siege," she said. "They have all been kept prisoner near the stables. I have not been permitted to go near them."

Kenton nodded, contemplating the state of Babylon and the men he was left with now that St. John was vacating the fortress. But the truth was that he could have had ten men left and he wouldn't have cared; as long as he had Nicola, nothing seemed to matter. But he wouldn't be with her for very long and at some point, she would have to understand that. She had to understand that his presence, for the moment, was not permanent so that she could prepare herself. In truth, he was dreading telling her but it was necessary.

"That is of no matter any longer," he said, putting an arm around her and directing her towards the keep. "St. John and his men are leaving and Babylon will once again belong to you."

Nicola began to walk towards the keep with the eggs in her apron, gazing up at Kenton as if she could not take her eyes from him. "It belongs to *us*," she whispered. "It belongs to you and to me."

He smiled down at her, removing his arm from her shoulders because somewhere, St. John was lurking and he didn't want the man to see the obvious affection between them. If he did, he was sure that St. John would realize Nicola had fooled both him and Saxilby, fooling them into thinking she was on their side when, in fact, she had been on Kenton's side all along.

"Aye, love," he agreed. "It belongs to us. But until St. John leaves, there is no 'us'. Remember? He must believe that you and I hate one another."

She frowned deeply. "But why?" she demanded. "You are returned and…."

He cut her off, gently, by grasping her arm. "Not yet," he stressed quietly. "If St. John realizes there is something between us, then he will know you only used him to save your captive lover. He will know he has been made a fool of. As much as I do not want to be St. John's ally, the fact remains that Conisbrough is close to Babylon and I would rather have a peaceful existence with them than have his hatred turned against you."

She understood, somewhat. "So the man can never know about us?"

Kenton let go of her arm. "Eventually," he said. "When I marry you, of course he will know, but for now, we will continue to let him believe we hate each other at least until he leaves here. Let some time pass before he knows the truth and realizes he was used. It will lessen the sting."

Nicola regarded him a moment. "You are being quite considerate to the man who tried to turn you over to Edward."

Kenton shrugged. "He was only doing his duty," he said. "During that time, he treated me with respect and fairness. I am trying to treat him the way he treated me. Moreover, Warwick still holds his sister. He will behave himself until he gets her back."

Nicola understood what he was telling her, trying to understand the code of honor between knights who served different lords. There was still honor amongst enemies and that was something she respected in Kenton's attitude. He was a man of solid character. She smiled faintly.

"Even back when we first met and there was so much animosity between us," she said, "you never treated me with disrespect. You are an honorable man, even with your enemies, Sir Kenton. That is a most admirable quality."

He smiled back. "I did not treat you with respect," he said. "I treated you with utter fear, terrified of what you would do if I was not constantly on my guard."

Nicola smiled and he touched her cheek, gently, as Teague and Tiernan ran up to Kenton, showing him the baby chicks they were holding. As much as Kenton wanted to spend time with the boys and their fuzzy friends, he could not. He had much to do and little time in which to do it. He put a big hand on Tiernan's blond head, dwarfing it, as he addressed Nicola.

"I must go now to make sure that St. John gathers his men and clears out just as he is supposed to do," he said. "Are you well enough to go about your duties now? The shock of seeing me has not been too much?"

She grinned. "It has not been too much," she assured him. "I could deal with the Devil himself today and be perfectly happy and content with it. As long as you are safe, that is all that matters to me, Kenton. All is right with the world."

He took his hand from Tiernan's head, gently touching her hand. "Then please go into the keep and remain there whilst I accomplish this," he said. "I will return as soon as I can and we will sup together. I have not eaten well in a couple of days."

Nicola nodded eagerly. "I will make sure Hermenia prepares a feast," she assured him. "Have you see Tab yet? He was in the stables the last I saw of him. He will want to see you very much."

Kenton nodded. "I will see him when I can," he said. "For now, go inside, please. I will see you later."

He bent down and kissed her on the mouth, gently, but quickly he was drawn in by the overwhelming attraction he had for her. A gentle kiss instantly turned into raging lust and he pulled her against him, forgetting about the eggs, and several of them cracked as their bodies came together. He grinned as Nicola started laughing, now with an apron of broken eggs. Kenton kissed her again, swiftly.

"I love you," he whispered against her cheek. "More than anything on this earth, I love you. Now go inside before you drip all over everything."

Nicola grinned up at him, running a finger across his full lower lip. "And I love you madly even though you broke my eggs."

He swatted her playfully on the behind and she continued to laugh as she went inside the kitchens, dripping egg as she went. Kenton watched her go inside, his heart swelling in ways he never knew it could. It was as if every moment brought new emotions with Nicola, stronger and more deeply than anything he knew to exist. He was with her and things were good once more, if only for a short time before he departed again. Until then, he would enjoy the time they had left.

Once Nicola left his sight, Kenton headed out of the kitchen yard, back the way he came, searching for Brome St. John as the man gathered his men in preparation for leaving Babylon.

His body may have been in the inner ward, but his heart, mind, and soul were inside with Nicola.

He was home now, but not for long.

In truth, he was dreading the dawn.

HERMENIA AND JANET were more than happy to create a lovely meal for Kenton's return and Nicola herself picked out the cuts of meat for the master's table. In the close, hot kitchen of Babylon, she selected nearly everything for Kenton's meal personally, happier than she had ever been. She wanted to spend every single second with him now that he was back but she knew that was impossible at the moment; he still had duties to attend to as there was to be a changing of the guard at Babylon. Kenton had to make sure the transition was seamless. Dropping off her eggs in the kitchen, the broken ones as well as the whole ones, she removed her soiled apron and took Teague and Tiernan out into the hall.

Hermenia had given the boys bread with melted cheese on it and they happily shoved the warm bread into their mouths as Nicola led them out into the hall, which was cold and rather dark at this time of day. She caught sight of Liesl near the hearth, sweeping out the soot, and she quietly told the girl that Sir Kenton had returned.

Liesl immediately asked about Sir Matthew, more than likely on behalf of her sister, but Nicola was unable to tell her anything about the knight. She hadn't asked Kenton the whereabouts of de Russe or Wellesbourne, or even le Mon or Forbes. She had only been concerned with Kenton and Conor, to a lesser extent, because the plan to free Kenton had rested entirely on the red-headed knight. She knew that Kenton and Conor were safe and that was all she could tell Liesl.

Wanting to remain in the hall in case Kenton should come in, she sent Teague and Tiernan with Liesl up to their chamber. Nicola took the broom from Liesl and resumed sweeping the hearth although her mind was wandering to Kenton the entire time. She thought about his pledge to marry her and wondered if it would be soon. She even found herself thinking on the children they would have, undoubtedly strong sons since she was very capable of producing boys. Coupling, which had been so distasteful to her with Gaylord, was suddenly quite curious and alluring with Kenton. She wondered what it would be like for him to touch her in intimate places, arousing her passion. Simply to think on it made her knees weak.

Grinning at her reaction to the thought of his caress, she continued to sweep the soot out of the hearth, wondering what it would be like to actually be touched by a man she was in love with, by someone she wanted to touch her. She was so caught up in her thoughts that she didn't hear the entry to the keep open or the footsteps that approached her. She had her back to the hall entry as she swept the soot towards a basket they used to remove the ashes so her first clue that someone was standing behind her was a soft clearing of the throat.

"Lady Thorne?"

Startled out of her preoccupied thoughts, Nicola whirled around to see St. John standing there. Her eyes widened in surprise as he smiled weakly.

"Greetings, my lady," he said. "It is quite agreeable to see you again."

Nicola heard that same soft tone in his voice, the one she'd heard when he'd offered to let her and her children stay at Conisbrough should she turn Babylon over to Warwick. It was that same sickening tone of interest and warmth, as the man was clearly interested in her personally. She tried not to be put off by it.

"Greetings, Sir Brome," she said evenly. "I understand that Warwick accepted your offer of Babylon in exchange for your sister."

His smile faded. "Who told you that?"

She leaned on the broom, keeping it between her and St. John in case she needed to use it as a weapon to chase him off. "Sir Kenton," she said. "He found me in the kitchen yard and told me what happened. It would seem that he never made it to Edward."

St. John's smile was gone completely now. "He did not," he said, sounding frustrated. "Warwick somehow managed to find us before I could deliver Kenton to Edward. I am sorry if that disappoints you, my lady. I know how you were hoping Kenton would be away from you and away from Babylon, but it seems that is not to be. Warwick has ways of discovering information that leads me to believe... well, it does not matter what I think of Warwick. Unfortunately, now Sir Kenton has Babylon returned to him and it is once again under Warwick's control."

Nicola nodded. "I see," she said. "But all is not lost as long as your sister is returned to you."

St. John shrugged, a humbled gesture. "I can never thank you enough for offering up Babylon to exchange for her life," he said. Then, his gaze lingered on her. "My offer still stands, of course. You and your children are welcome to live at Conisbrough for as long as you wish to stay."

There was that unwelcome offer again. Nicola took a step back from him, resuming her sweeping. "Your offer is kind but not necessary," she said. "Babylon is our home and I am not leaving. We have endured Sir Kenton before and we can do it again."

St. John watched her as she swept, thinking she was quite a determined woman to stay in the same fortress with a man she clearly hated. He began to think that it was because she thought his offer to live at Conisbrough to be most improper, coming to stay with a man she barely knew in a strange fortress. Aye, that must have been the reason she rejected him for, certainly, he could think of no other reason.

"My lady, I apologize if I have offended you," he said. "Please understand that I meant my offer only under the most proper of circumstances. You and your children would be my guests, of course, and guests of Edward, and when my sister arrives, you will have a companion. You have been to Conisbrough and have seen what an excellent place it is. You and your children would want for nothing, I assure you."

He was being quite chivalrous which made Nicola feel the least bit guilty about carrying on a lie about her and Kenton. She'd done nothing but lie to St. John from the beginning but she'd had no other choice given the circumstances. Still, she felt badly for him in the slightest.

"You are most kind. Sir Brome, but again I will decline," she said, easing her stiff stance somewhat. "Babylon is my eldest son's legacy and we are not leaving. If we do, we will never get it back."

St. John simply nodded. He was finished being polite and gallant. Now, he was going to come to the point and dare her to deny him again. It was time to make his intentions plain.

"You will," he said firmly. "Because I will get it back for you. My lady, if I may be so bold, you are a widow and I am an unmarried man. I... I would like to offer for your hand if you will have me. I am healthy, have no bad habits that I am aware of, and come from a fine family. I would make an excellent husband and I would help you raise your sons if you will allow me. My lady, what I am clumsily asking is if you will accept my proposal of marriage. I would be honored if you would consider it."

So he had spelled it out. Nicola wasn't particularly surprised but it did make her feel even sorrier for him than she did before. Brome St. John was a kind man, and handsome, and she was quite sure he would make a very good husband, but she had absolutely no interest in him. She tried to be gentle in her rejection.

"I am sure you will understand when I say that I cannot consider it at this time," she said, lowering her gaze. "My husband has only been gone these few months. I have not been a widow for very long and to marry another so soon... I cannot think on such things, at least not now."

St. John didn't give up. "I understand, my lady," he said. "I just wanted you to know… that when you are ready, I would be grateful for your consideration."

Nicola looked up from her broom. "You are very kind to offer," she said. "But for now, I will stay at Babylon with my children. This is where we belong and where we shall stay."

"Is there nothing I can say to convince you otherwise?"

"Nay. I am truly sorry."

Her words were final and there were no more arguments for St. John to present. He wasn't happy to leave her at Babylon much less leave her under Kenton le Bec's watchful eye, but she was making the choice to remain and he would have to respect that.

Unhappy, he turned away from her because she had made it clear that there was no negotiating the issue at this time. But he made a silent vow not to give up; he would give her a few weeks, enough for her to get a belly full of le Bec, and then he would try again. Perhaps then she would be more willing to listen.

"Very well," he said. "But if you need anything, you know where to reach me. Send a missive and I will come right away."

Nicola nodded, watching the man go even though she was pretending to sweep. His shoulders were slumped and he seemed quite depressed, and dejected, but she couldn't help it. She couldn't tell him the truth and she could not accept his proposal, so she would have to leave things the way they were.

Nicola returned to sweeping, thoughts lingering on Brome St. John. She truly hoped the man would find happiness someday but she knew that happiness would not be with her. She already had the greatest happiness she could ever hope for and she was very much looking forward to a lifetime of it.

Happiness with the man who had once been her captor.

CHAPTER TWENTY-SIX

K ENTON BID ST. JOHN farewell right before sunset, finding it odd that the man refused to stay the night and return home on the morrow. In fact, St. John seemed most anxious to leave Babylon but not before letting Kenton know, in the strongest words possible without actually throwing punch, to be considerate of Lady Thorne. Kenton, already knowing that St. John was attracted to Nicola, kept a straight face and promised to treat the woman fairly.

As a final item of business, Kenton reminded St. John to send the Warwick men he held prisoner on to Babylon immediately and in doing so, Kenton vowed to send Warwick word that St. John had complied with all of the terms regarding his sister's release. St. John agreed to liberate Kenton's men as a final stipulation to his sister's freedom, but he didn't seem nearly as concerned for his sister as he did for Nicola. He seemed far more concerned for her welfare at Babylon with the tyrannical Kenton now in charge and he made clear his displeasure with the entire situation. When the man finally left, Kenton fought off a grin when he was positive St. John couldn't see him.

After St. John's departure, the great gates of Babylon, having since been repaired after the Conisbrough siege, were closed and secured for the night. Conor and Kenton set posts upon the walls and at the postern gate with the forty-two men they had left at Babylon, men that had once been sworn to Kenton and had gone through a great deal of upheaval with the changing of hands. Until this morning, they had been prisoners of the Conisbrough garrison. Kenton was uncomfortable with so few men to protect Babylon's large and complex structure, but they would have to make do until they received the balance of the men from Conisbrough.

Kenton and Conor walked the perimeter of Babylon several times after dark, making sure everything was set, becoming reacquainted with the weak points in the fortress. The postern gate was of particular interest considering that was how Babylon was overtaken the last time, and they put eight men on the postern gate alone. Not that they didn't trust Lady Thorne, because they certain did, but they wanted to discourage others inside the fortress, others who might not be entirely loyal, from thinking the postern gate was an easy breach. Kenton was convinced that in the very near future, he would brick the gate up. He didn't want to have to worry about it in the years to come.

As the night deepened, they caught whiffs of cooking smells coming from the kitchen yard, knowing that a meal would soon be underway, but Conor decided to stay upon the walls this night. The last time he'd been on those walls, the fortress had been overtaken and he was a bit superstitious about it, so Kenton let him do what he was comfortable with. However, before Kenton retreated inside to share a meal with Lady Thorne, he instructed Conor to send a rider into Huddersfield in search of a priest. When Conor wanted to know why, Kenton was forced to let him in on an open secret, which wasn't so much a secret any longer. It was the truth and Conor, he felt, deserved to know.

"What on earth do you need a priest for?" Conor wanted to know as they both stood by the newly-repaired front gates. "You do not appear as if you are in danger of dying any time soon."

Kenton smiled weakly. "Fortunately, no," he said, eyeing Conor. "The priest is for Lady Thorne and me so that Lady Thorne will become Lady le Bec. I apologize if that comes as a shock to you, de Birmingham, but it is the truth. I plan to marry Lady Thorne."

Conor started chuckling, shaking his head as if the entire situation were ridiculous. "A shock?" he repeated. "God's Bones, Kenton, we have known you intended to marry Lady Thorne since nearly the moment we came to Babylon. Of course we knew she felt the same way; why do you think de Russe and Wellesbourne confronted you about it those weeks ago? We all knew you two were smitten with each other, something that was confirmed when she risked her life to save you from being turned over to Edward. You had better marry that woman, Kenton, after all she has done for you. I would be ashamed of you if you did not."

It was Kenton's turn to grin. "You idiot," he hissed, feigning anger. "How can you say such things? I was *not* smitten with Lady Thorne from the beginning."

Conor put up his hands and backed away as if fearful Kenton was about to throw a punch. "Very well," he conceded. "Not from the very beginning, but at least since you threw her in the vault. You waited a day or two before completely falling under her spell."

Kenton growled at him. "Bastard," he grunted, turning away and still pretending to be miffed. "You know nothing."

"I know more than you evidently think I did."

Kenton turned to look at him, fighting off a grin. It was hard not to smile when the subject was Nicola. "Then if you know everything, you should know that I will not wait much longer for you to send for a priest," he said. "I promised Warwick we would return to him as soon as possible but I intend to marry Nicola before I go. The sooner the priest, arrives, the better."

Conor whistled between his teeth, loudly, motioning to one of the soldiers guarding the gatehouse when the man turned to look at him. As the man headed towards him, Conor turned back to Kenton. "Have you told Lady Thorne we will be leaving on the morrow?"

Kenton shook his head. "I have not," he replied. "I will not tell her until absolutely necessary for the news will certainly upset her."

"How *much* are you going to tell her?"

Kenton lifted his eyebrows with great regret. "No more than I must," he said. "I will not tell her that we are heading towards what is mayhap the final battle with Edward. I do not know all of the intelligence or logistics associated with what we are about to face, but Warwick seemed to think it was to be quite large. This could be the turning point."

Conor grew serious. "I received that impression as well."

Kenton scratched his dark head. "I have never had to face this type of situation before," he muttered. "Telling the woman I love that I am going to war and may not return. This is an entirely new circumstance for me."

Conor was studying him as he spoke. He'd never seen Kenton so emotional, which was very strange to him. He never knew Kenton was capable of such feelings.

"She is not only the woman you love," he said quietly. "She will be your wife. I will send for the priest, Kenton, but you make sure that you give her your son this night. Even if you do not make it back to Babylon after this battle is over, your legacy will still live on. She will still have something of you to remember."

Kenton gazed up to the keep, dark and cold against the night sky, as if seeing Nicola within those walls. *A son,* he thought. He'd never really thought of his progeny before but with Conor's advice, he found that it was something that was important to him. He hadn't even realized it.

"Mayhap you are right," he said, turning towards the keep. "Send the priest to me as soon as he arrives."

Leaving Conor to arrange for the messenger, Kenton lumbered towards the keep, mounting the steps. *My steps,* he thought. He'd never had a home, not ever, not one place that he felt belonged to him or that he belonged to it, but Babylon somehow was filling that role. Because it was Nicola's, it was his, and he felt more at home here than he'd ever felt anywhere in his life. God, he felt so happy here, so content, that he never wanted to leave it, but that was the sad reality facing him. He didn't want to go… again.

But he had to.

The hall inside the keep was lit by a blazing hearth and several banks of tallow candles, all dripping fat onto the wood floor. As soon as Kenton entered the keep, he could feel the warmth and hear the boys yelling about something or other. He couldn't even make out their words, only shouting. By the time he entered the hall, he saw the source of the shouting – Teague and Tiernan had brought one of the lambs into the hall to play with it and Tab was telling them, quite imperiously, to take it outside. But as he watched, the lamb broke free and began cavorting around the room with the three boys chasing after it. The more they would chase, the more it would run, and Kenton ended up coming to a halt just inside the doorway, watching the antics with a big grin on his face.

"I apologize for the chaos, my lord."

He turned to see Nicola walking up from his left. She had been over near the big feasting table, making sure everything was set for their meal. He held out a hand to her as she approached and she eagerly took it, being pulled against his torso as they watched the boys chase the lamb around.

"No need for apologies," he said. "This is quite entertaining."

Nicola shook her head with resignation at the frolics of her sons. "Teague and Tiernan are determined to make a pet out of this lamb," she said. "I haven't the heart to tell them that, eventually, the animal will end up on our table. I do not think they will like to hear that."

Kenton laughed softly, watching the lamb as it turned on its pursuers and ended up butting Tab so hard that the boy flew back on his arse. That cause Kenton to guffaw with laughter, and he wasn't the guffawing type. But he'd never seen anything so funny or so charming. Beside him, Nicola giggled.

"Mayhap I should go and save Tab from the wicked lamb," she said. "Moreover, it is time to eat. There will be time for play later."

She broke away from Kenton, instructing the boys to remove the lamb, but they tried to plead and bargain with her. Kenton was more firm about it. He went over to the boys, who by now had corralled the frisky animal, and pointed to the door that led to the kitchen and ultimately out to the yard beyond.

"This may come as a shock to you, but lambs do not belong inside the keep," he said. "Remove the beast so that we may eat the lovely meal your mother has worked hard to prepare."

Tab was still on his bottom; he had the lamb around the head so it would not try to butt him again. "He does not want to go outside!" he declared.

Before Kenton could reply, Teague nearly shouted at him. "He can sit nexth to usth!" he said in his terrible lisp. "He will behave, I promith."

Kenton shook his head and began to direct the lamb towards the door in spite of all of the boys holding on to it. "You cannot guarantee the behavior of the beast, Teague," he said, pushing the fuzzy arse along. "Take him outside and back to his mother where he belongs."

The boys argued somewhat but not too much; they knew, deep down, that the lamb belonged outside. Even Tab, who had originally told his brothers to take it outside, was now reluctant to do so. Sometimes the boys tended to push their mother's patience just because they knew they could. Kenton, however, seemed immune to their will, a big authority figure in their midst. Kenton helped them scoot the lamb out of the hall, through the kitchens, and then he stood in the doorway to the yard and watched as the three of them took it back to the corral where the other sheep were clustered. As he stood there watching, he could feel a soft hand slip into his big one.

"You will make a fine father someday," Nicola said, gazing up at him adoringly. "You have always shown great patience and wisdom with my sons, something their father never did."

He squeezed her hand. "It is good practice for our own children," he said. "I expect at least a dozen, by the way."

Nicola rolled her eyes. "God's Bones, le Bec," she said. "A dozen?"

He nodded. "That would be my preference, aye."

She rolled her eyes again, this time laughing as well. "You are a madman," she said, releasing his hand and turning away. "Come and let us eat. Mayhap it is the lack of food that is causing these great fantasies you seem to have."

He grinned broadly as he followed her from the kitchen, hearing the boys coming up behind them. "Is that so?" he said. "We shall see."

"Aye, we shall."

They entered the hall with smiles on their faces and the three boys ran around them, making a mad dash for the table where Janet and Raven were pouring wine into cups. The hall was empty this night, with just the family to feed, because everyone else was out on guard duty. Kenton made sure to relay orders to the servants to take food outside to the men, which they rushed to prepare. As the servants went off to tend to their tasks, Nicola, the three boys, and Kenton sat at the feasting table and delved into the steaming food.

Boiled mutton with garlic and onions was the main bill of fare along with fresh bread, apples with cinnamon, and boiled beans. Kenton sat between Tab and Nicola, eating heartily, helping Tab butter his bread, and grinning at Nicola as she tried to keep the twins off the table. Instead of asking for something to be passed to them, like the butter, they would simply climb upon the table to get it, prompting their mother to grab a little leg and pull them back down. It came to the point where the twins gravitated towards Kenton because he wasn't apt to pull them off the table, so Nicola finished her meal with no one on her right side and everyone to her left as the boys crowded around Kenton.

But it was more than simply the fact that he seemed more lenient with them; it was the mere fact that he had returned and the boys were thrilled to see him. Nicola finished her meal with a smile on her face, watching Kenton and her sons interact, so incredibly appreciative of his presence. He seemed to bring out the best in all of them, the man who had once been their captor but who was now quickly becoming the center of their world. It made all of those lonely, fearful nights for Nicola fade from memory, recent nights where she had been unable to sleep, so very fearful of Kenton's fate. Now, his fate was here, at Babylon, as if he had always belonged here. He was theirs and they were his. She couldn't explain the joy, the contentment, any other way.

As she watched Teague and Tiernan tussle over wanting the same piece of bread, the door of a closet in the entryway slowly creaked open. Nicola caught movement out of the corner of her eye, turning to see the mad, old woman emerge from her cave and begin her nightly dance. Kenton, too, saw the movement as the old woman flitted about in the entry hall, just outside of the reach of the light. He could see her silhouette in the darkness, moving about. The twins, naturally, were frightened and climbed upon Kenton for protection, while Tab stood up from his seat, moving around his mother so he could have an unobstructed view of the dancing woman.

Tab had seen the old woman many times in his life but when he came to realize she was not a ghost, as Kenton and the other knights had explained to him, he began to be more curious about her. Most nights she came forth but, as of late, her appearances were less and less frequent. Even her dancing seemed to be slower and less energetic. But to Tab, she was of increasing interest now that he was more aware of her. As the woman danced in the darkness just beyond the hall, Tab turned to his mother.

"Mam," he said, pointing to the woman. "Who is the ghost?"

Nicola looked at Tab, surprised to hear the question. He'd known of the "ghost" for years but had never shown much interest in her, so his question naturally had his mother surprised. He was almost six years old now and as Nicola thought on his question, she presumed he had a right to know the truth. He was old enough and certainly becoming more curious and aware about things. Her little boy was growing up.

"That is Lady Aspasia Thorne," she said, putting her hand on Tab's shoulder. "She is your father's mother. She is your grandmother."

Tab continued to watch the woman, now with his brow furrowed. "She *is*?" he asked with some awe in his tone. "Then why does she do that? Why does she live in the closet?"

Nicola squeezed his shoulder. "It is sad to say that she is not in her right mind," she said. "She has not been in her right mind since I came to live here many years ago. Your father made her live in the closet because she was not fit to be around other people, so she has lived in that closet so long I do not believe she knows anything else. You know that she will not harm you as long as you leave her alone."

Tab was rather rocked by the information that the woman in the closet was his grandmother. "It was not right for Papa to make her live in the closet," he said. "She should not be there."

"She likes to be there, Tab. As long as she is content, then you must leave her alone."

Tab wasn't so sure. Something in his young, growing mind felt sorry for the woman, feeling empathy his father never had. The woman was evidently his family, after all, and he was coming to understand a good deal about family and taking care of those he loved. He never understood that so much as when Kenton started to take interest in him and his brothers, and now the man had returned to them. He had learned a great deal from Kenton in the short time he'd known him. He was a man that Tab wanted to emulate.

His father had never been kind. He had always known that. He never regretted stabbing the man when he had been taking his fists to his mother on that terrible night, stabbing him with a sword he had stolen off of one of the old, drunk soldiers. His father had been ill after that and then he had died, so Tab had always suspected that perhaps he had killed his father. He'd never told his mother his suspicions, however, because he didn't want to upset her. Maybe she didn't realize that what he did had caused his father's illness and eventually killed him, so he didn't want to tell her. Let her believe that his father simply died and that was the end of it, because to Tab, it *was* the end. Gaylord Thorne, the man who had fathered him, had finally ceased to exist.

And then came Kenton.

Kenton had been the enemy but he had shown them all more attention and affection than Gaylord Thorne could have ever dreamed of.

Nay, Tab wasn't sorry at all for what he'd done. In his view, he'd had to do it. He had to protect his mother from his father. But he did not have to protect her from Kenton. Watching the gray-haired old woman dance around in the dark, Tab was coming to think there was one more woman who had needed protection from his father, only Tab hadn't realized that until now. Maybe he could help her somehow. Picking up a piece of bread from the table, Tab made his way towards the old woman spinning in the dark.

Nicola, puzzled, opened her mouth to stop her son but Kenton put a hand on her shoulder, quieting her when she turned to look at him quizzically. Together, they watched Tab as the boy walked slowly and carefully towards the mad, old woman. He continued through the doorway and into the darkened entry, and when the woman saw him, she came to an abrupt halt and hissed at him. Tab jumped but he didn't walk away. He simply extended the bread to her.

The old woman stopped her hissing, looking at the bread very curiously. Since she ate only what she could steal, scraps from the dogs or rubbish to be burned, the concept of fresh bread was foreign to her. She sniffed the air in the direction of the bread and, realizing it was quite appetizing, timidly reached for it. Tab held it out, steadily, until she finally snatched it and ran off, disappearing back into her closet and slamming the door. Tab went up to the closed door and tried to listen, to hear what was going on inside. All he could hear was rustling and grunting.

"I shall bring you more bread tomorrow, Grandmother," he said loudly. "My... my name is Tab. I will bring you more food tomorrow."

With that, he turned around and headed back into the hall, where Nicola was quickly wiping tears away at the compassionate gesture from her young son. She knew, without a doubt, that Kenton was to thank for it. Through his compassion and honor, her boys were learning the same. They were learning traits they would have never learned from their own father and it was yet one more thing to thank Kenton for.

"That was very kind of you, Tab," she said as her son resumed his seat next to Kenton. "I am sure she appreciates your gesture."

Tab shrugged, picking at his cinnamon apples. "I will bring her more tomorrow."

Nicola smiled. "I am sure she will appreciate that."

Kenton interjected. "That was a very gracious thing to do, Tab," he said. "I am proud to have witnessed it."

Tab looked up at Kenton. "Will you help me?" he asked. "What I mean to say is that she may like more food, too. Will you help me carry it to her?"

Nicola answered before Kenton could. "Kenton has many duties to attend to, Tab," she said. "He will be quite busy tomorrow, I am sure. He has only just returned to Babylon, after all. I will help you carry the food if you wish."

He will be quite busy tomorrow. Kenton heard the words, thinking that now might be the best time to mention that his plans for the morrow were set. As much as he wanted to put it off, he knew that he could not. Nicola needed to know and the longer he waited, the worse it would be. He might end up not telling her at all and not leaving Babylon, and that would not be good for any of them. Sooner or later, Warwick would come after him and he didn't want that. He had an obligation to the man that he had promised to fulfill.

"You have brought up a very good point, love," he turned to Nicola, gazing into her lovely eyes. "In fact, I will be quite busy tomorrow. I have duties to fulfill that will take me from Babylon, so at dawn tomorrow, I will be leaving."

The warm expression vanished from Nicola's face. "Leaving?" she repeated, her brow furrowed. "Where are you going?"

He reached out and put a big arm around her shoulders, pulling her against him. He simply wanted to feel her against his flesh, memories to keep him sane for the days and weeks ahead. For a moment, he simply looked at her, thinking of what to say. He ended up kissing her cheek to soften the blow for what was to come.

"Warwick still has need of me," he said quietly. "I was almost prevented from coming back to Babylon because of it. It would seem that Edward is gathering a force and moving south towards London. Warwick must prevent him from getting into the city and he requires my sword. I could not deny him, you understand. The man had just freed me from Edward's clutches and to refuse would have been to appear ungrateful and insubordinate. I have no choice. He has already taken de Russe, Wellesbourne, and le Mon with him. Conor and I will be departing Babylon tomorrow to join them."

Nicola's expression changed during that speech; at first she was concerned, then resistant, then even angry, to finally saddened. Kenton watched all of those things roll across her features, an inkling of what she was feeling as he explained his immediate future. When she finally spoke, there was resignation in her tone. She was trying very hard to be brave.

"Where are you going?" she asked softly.

He shook his head. "I do not know yet," he said. "All I do know is that I will go to Warwick Castle first but after that, I do not know. It will depend on Edward."

"How long will you be gone?"

Again, he shook his head. "I have no way of knowing, love," he said. "It could be one month or six. That being the case, I hope you will understand when I say that I do not wish to wait to marry you. I will marry you tonight so that when I depart tomorrow morning, I will be bidding farewell to my wife and not simply the woman I love. You are, and always will be, everything to me. As my wife, you will become more than that. You will become all of me."

Nicola was struggling not to weep. To have him back at Babylon, so briefly, and then cruelly taken away again was almost more than she could bear. She lifted a hand to his cheek, a tender and comforting gesture, and Kenton kissed the palm of her hand, waiting for great arguments to come forth. He knew she did not want him to leave; he could see it written all over her face. But to her credit, she was not making a spectacle of herself by begging him to remain for she knew it would do no good. Kenton was a warrior; *Warwick's* warrior, his attack dog, and someone Warwick has also risked much to save from Edward.

He owed the man.

"But you *will* come back, won't you?" Nicola finally murmured, tears filling her eyes. "You will not forget about us?"

He pulled her close, kissing her, hearing her soft sniffles in his ear. The twins were crawling all across the table, chasing one another now, but neither Nicola nor Kenton seemed to notice. They were completely focused on one another and on the painful poignancy of the moment. Another separation was coming and there wasn't anything either one of them could do about it. The finality of it was in the air, heavy, like a weight bearing down on them both. Nicola finally buried her face in his chest if only to feel him, and smell him, something she would cherish always.

"I will come back," Kenton whispered against the top of her head. "There is nothing on this earth save death that will prevent me from returning to you. Do you believe me?"

Face still in his chest, she nodded. "Aye."

"Swear it?"

"Aye."

He put his hands on her cheeks, pulling her away from his torso. Head cupped in his big hands, he gazed into her eyes intensely, as if this one powerful look was enough to seal his promise to return more than words ever could. He wanted her to understand that he meant what he said and that he would not fail her.

"I cannot tell you how much I love you more than I already have," he said huskily. "You already know that you are the very air I breathe. You belong to me and after this night, we will be a part of one another more than any two people have ever been."

She nodded as if she agreed with him, accepted him, but then suddenly she threw her arms around his neck, so forcefully that she hit him in the Adam's apple. As he coughed, the boys, seeing their mother throwing herself on Kenton, thought it was a game and threw them-selves on him as well.

Suddenly, Kenton was being piled upon by three little boys. Tab had him around the neck from behind, Teague had an arm, and Tiernan had climbed onto the table and now tried to drape himself over the man's head. All the while, Kenton was trying to stay focused on Nicola but he simply couldn't do that any longer when Tiernan ended up falling over his face. He started to laugh and Nicola laughed right along with him.

"I will have to become accustomed to this, I suppose," he said as he lifted Tiernan off of his neck and set the boy on his feet. "Either that, or we will have to train them not to interrupt us when we are speaking."

Nicola was gently pushing Teague off of Kenton then pulling Tab's hands from around the man's neck. "Tab, please take your brothers up to your chamber," she said. "Do this now. I will be up shortly."

Tab obediently climbed off the seat and took Teague by his tunic sleeve, pulling him along until he came to Tiernan, whom he also grabbed. As he pulled the whining twins from the hall, Kenton called out to him.

"Tab," he said, watching the boy come to a halt and face him. "I have something I would like to say to you and your brothers. Come back here."

Dutifully, Tab went to Kenton, still holding on to Tiernan and Teague, who were starting to struggle with their older brother. Kenton put out a hand to still the tussle, forcing the three boys to look at him.

"I have something very important for you three to do," he said seriously. "You will listen to me now. I am leaving in the morning and I am trusting the three of you to watch over your mother while I am away. Will you do this?"

The three of them nodded solemnly. They had heard parts of the conversation between Kenton and their mother but they were still a bit too young to understand what was happening; at least, the younger boys were. Tab was coming to comprehend more than his brothers were.

"Where are you going?" he asked.

Kenton gazed into the little face of Nicola's eldest son, the boy who would become his own when he married the mother. *My son*, he thought. It seemed like the most natural of things when it came to Tab. *A son I am already proud of.*

"My liege has need of me," he said as simply as he could. "I must go to help him for a while but I will return. While I am gone, I will trust you to take care of your mother. Protect her and make sure she does not come to harm."

Tab nodded and the twins to a lesser degree. "But I am growing big," Tab insisted. "I can go with you and help you fight."

Kenton smiled, putting a big hand on Tab's head. "You are indeed growing big and I would be honored to have your help," he said. "But your mother needs you more. There will be no one to oversee Babylon when I go so you must assume that role. I am trusting you to ensure all remains well. I know you can do this, Tab. You will make an excellent knight."

Tab's eyes widened. "I will?"

"You will."

Feeling prideful, Tab fought off a grin, looking at his little brothers, who still weren't entirely aware of what the conversation meant.

"Will you teach me when you come back?" Tab asked. "I want to fight with you."

Kenton patted his head. "We will speak of your training when I return," he assured the boy. "Now, do as your mother said. Take your brothers upstairs."

Tab did as he was told because all future knights did as they were told. He pulled the twins from the room, herding them away, leaving Nicola and Kenton alone. As the fire in the hearth crackled softly, Kenton returned his attention to Nicola.

"When we have sons," he said softly, "I expect them to be just as fine as those three. You will not fail me."

Nicola laughed softly. "I will do my best."

"See that you do."

Her smile faded, sensing his attempt at humor was a cover for the seriousness of what they now had to face.

"Now what?" she asked softly.

Kenton reached out, pulling her against him. "Conor has sent for a priest," he said. "I will have the priest marry us as soon as he arrives but I do not know when that will be, so you may want to try and sleep for a time. I do not want you exhausted, waiting up all night for the priest to come."

Nicola shook her head firmly. "I will stay with you," she said. "We have so little time left, Kenton. Would you truly deny me that time together?"

He squeezed her. "Nay, of course not," he said. "But I did not want to sound greedy about it and I do not want you to be exhausted from staying awake all night."

"I do not care," she said. "I want to spend these last hours with you. Let us sit in the solar and speak of the dozen children we will have and of other things that will be in our future. Can I assume that I am allowed to have a daughter or two?"

Kenton grinned as he pulled her up from the seat, holding her hand as they made their way across the hall and towards the entry where the solar was situated. "One or two," he said, feigning seriousness. "I am sure you would like daughters to comfort you and I will not deny you your wishes to that regard."

Holding his hand, Nicola laid her cheek against his big bicep as they walked. "I am sure they will be just like me."

"God help me."

She laughed. "I am well enough to marry," she pointed out. "Why would you not want daughters in my image?"

He cleared his throat softly. "You did not let me finish," he said. "I meant that I will need God's help to keep away the thousands of suitors that will come calling for my daughters when they become of age. If they are in your image, then they will be the most beautiful maidens in all the land."

He was flattering her now, trying to pretend as if he had not just mildly insulted her. She shook her head reproachfully at him. "I am very eager to see you chase off your daughters' suitors," she said. "It will be quite entertaining to watch."

"You are a cruel woman."

"That is true, but you already knew that."

They had reached the solar door and Kenton paused, pulling her into his arms again. He gazed down at her, thinking so many things at that moment. Here was a woman who fought him, antagonized him, showed him no fear, yet he ended up falling in love with her. She was also the bravest and most intelligent woman he had ever known. He adored her.

"Aye, I already knew that," he said softly. "I also know that I am the most fortunate man alive. The day I breached Babylon was the best day of my life, although I did not know it at the time."

Nicola was still smiling at him, feeling the warmth and gratitude and adoration that seemed to be flowing from him and into her. "Did you ever imagine you would have to conquer fortresses in order to find a woman to marry?"

He shook his head, a jesting twinkle to his eye. "I should have avoided Babylon at all costs."

"Are you sorry, then?"

His smile faded, the twinkle in his eye turning into something far more deep and emotional. "Never," he murmured. "It has been the greatest adventure of my life. *You* have been the greatest adventure of my life."

He bent down, kissing Nicola sweetly, but it was a kiss that quickly turned deep and lusty. There was no one to interrupt them and no reason for him to stop. The priest was on his way and they had nothing but time and privacy at the moment. Kenton had no way of knowing if that moment would ever come again.

Picking Nicola up, he carried her into the solar that used to belong to Gaylord, the one that had now become his more than it had ever been Gaylord's.

The door shut softly behind him as the real discovery began.

CHAPTER TWENTY-SEVEN

THERE WAS NO proper bed or any comfort, but Nicola hardly cared as she wrapped herself around Kenton and kissed the man as she'd never kissed anyone in her life. It was as if the moment he touched her, a fire was sparked and it was a blaze that was growing more intense by the moment. She didn't want to let him go; she *couldn't* let him go. As Kenton carried her into Gaylord's former solar, there was one thing on Nicola's mind – to feel Kenton's naked flesh against hers.

It was all she could think about.

Kenton didn't give her any argument. In fact, he seemed just as intent on separating her from her clothing as she was on separating him from his. He wasn't wearing any armor, fortunately, but he was wearing heavy tunics, two of them, breeches, and boots. Nicola was simply wearing layers of fabric, a lamb's wool shift and a heavy brocaded surcoat over that. But somehow, things came off, were tossed aside, and in the dark coldness of the room, Nicola and Kenton's naked flesh came together. She heard him groan, softly, when it did.

Kenton had her in his arms, aloft, and she instinctively parted her legs, wrapping them around his slender waist and holding him fast as they shared heated kisses in the darkness. Kenton could feel her wet heat against his belly, resting above his full erection, and the sensation nearly drove him mad. It was like a target he was seeking, and seeking it with a deep and instinctive need, and he shifted her so that she sank lower against him until her wet heat was nearly on the tip of his shaft.

But not quite; he was too tall for him to comfortably take her that way so he carried her over to what used to be Gaylord's table and swept a big hand over the surface, sending parchment and quill and anything else on the tabletop crashing to the floor. Carefully, he set her down on the table, making sure not to drive splinters into her tender bottom, and laying her back on the table, he mounted her.

His swollen staff thrust into her wet and waiting body, and Nicola cried out softly as he possessed her. He was quite enormous, as proportionate with his height and the size of his body, and she wrapped her legs around him, drawing him deep inside of her as he repeatedly thrust into her. His hands were on her buttocks, between her and the splintering table, protecting her skin as he drove into her, but he bent over her as he thrust, suckling her breasts, nursing against them, tasting the sweetness of her flesh as if he were gorging upon it.

His thrusts were so powerful that Nicola had to put her hands over her head, bracing herself so that he wouldn't push her right off of the table, and she lifted her hips to him, begging for every sensation, every hard thrust he could deliver. He answered her silent demands with all of the long, hard, and deep thrusts he could deliver and when he was finished suckling her nipples, he suckled on her neck, her chin, and her shoulders. He tasted everything his mouth could come into contact with.

But the truth was that her soft, supple body had driven him beyond the point of madness and when he finally climaxed, it was such a powerful moment that his weakened knees pitched him forward and he nearly collapsed onto the table. He imagined his seed finding its mark this night, taking root in her womb. He found himself praying for it, praying that he would leave her something of himself come the morning. He could feel her tremors beginning, her climax throbbing around him, telling him that she found as much satisfaction from their coupling as he had. Then he lifted her up into his arms, her legs still around his hips and his male member still partially buried in her body, and held her close.

"I long for you already," he murmured into the top of her head. "I have not even left this fortress yet and, already, I long for you."

Warm, satisfied, but still very aroused, Nicola gripped his shoulders as she continued to grind herself down onto his manhood, feeling the wetness he had put into her, taking great panting delight when she climaxed again from the sheer stimulation. Kenton, hardly able to stand, sat in the nearest chair as she settled on his lap, legs still parted, his body still joined to hers.

Now, it was her turn to kiss his neck, his chin, and finally his full lips, kissing him even as she continued to move her body on top of his semi-arousal, which was quickly growing hard again with her stimulation. Kenton groaned as she latched her mouth to his again, realizing he was quite ready to resume as least some semblance of making love to her. As she slowly, sensually plunged her body up and down on top of him, now bracing her knees against the chair he was sitting on, Kenton began to move his hips against hers, meeting her thrust for thrust.

The groans of pleasure that filled the solar reverberated softly off the walls. Between Nicola's panting and Kenton's grunts, there was quite a chorus going on. Kenton found particular interest in her breasts, which were quite full and beautiful, and his hands moved to them, fondling her tender flesh, feeling her climax around him once more. He slanted his mouth over hers, muffling her pants of pleasure, as he thrust hard into her and released his seed once more, although far less of it this time. The climax was very long although not quite as strong as before, as his body had not yet recovered from the first time, but he was so aroused that his body was responding the best way it could.

In the old leather-cushioned chair that had been made for Gaylord's very fat father many years ago, Kenton and Nicola finally found total, utter contentment. Seated on his lap, still straddling him with his body still embedded in hers, Nicola collapsed against his chest in complete exhaustion. Kenton, his big arms wrapped around her against the chill of the room, held her tightly against his warm flesh, his cheek against the top of her head, thinking that there were no words in existence yet that were powerful enough to describe what he was feeling.

Still, he wanted to try. He wanted to explain to her just how much she meant to him and why. But the moment he opened his mouth, her soft snores cut him off. She'd fallen asleep against him and he hadn't even realized it until now. With a grin, Kenton let her sleep.

It was the best night he'd ever spent.

NICOLA WAS AWOKEN at some point before dawn by Kenton, who heard the commotion out in the bailey as Conor and the priest arrived. Groggy and naked, she climbed off Kenton's lap and stumbled around for her clothing as he hunted around for his. He kept laughing at her because she was quite uncoordinated in her sleepy state and he ended up dressing much more quickly than she did.

Kenton helped her with her surcoat, fastening the laces in the back, the same laces he had nearly ripped free in his quest to remove her from her clothing, but by the time Conor and the priest entered the keep, Kenton was lighting a fire in the hearth of the solar and Nicola was sitting, quite primly, on the same chair they had made love in. Nicola sneezed at one point, thinking the room must have surely smelled like the sex that had so recently taken place there, but if it did, the men were too tactful to make that comment.

Sleepy, and the slightest bit sore from the vigorous sexual activity that she had partaken of only hours earlier, Nicola stood next to Kenton, with Conor and old Hermenia as witnesses, as a slovenly-looking priest from Huddersfield intoned the wedding mass. Normally, a wedding mass was conducted outside of the church doors before the marital party moved inside the church to complete the nuptials, but since there was no church and Nicola did not want to go near the small chapel where Gaylord was buried, for obvious reasons, the priest conducted the uncommon ceremony in front of the door to the keep at Babylon just as the eastern sky began turning shades of purple and pink, signaling the coming sunrise.

Brides normally wore blue to symbolize purity for their wedding but since Nicola had already been married, purity was not an issue and she simply wore the heavy yellow surcoat she had worn the day before. She carried no stones to symbolize other virtues that were expected in brides and there was no ring exchange, so the priest simply conducted a blessing over their heads and pronounced them man and wife. And with that, Lady Nicola Aubrey-Thorne became Lady Nicola Aubrey-le Bec. It was a tradition in her family for the women to retain their maiden name after marriage and Kenton, who didn't particularly care if she did or didn't, allowed her to make the choice.

Conor, with a grin on his face, had been permitted to congratulate the bride with a kiss to the cheek but Kenton had quickly chased the man off when he thought he had lingered too much in his congratulations. Nicola had simply laughed as Conor shuttled the priest away, into the hall where a simple meal had been laid out to break their morning fast. Janet and Liesl were awake and had witnessed the tail-end of the ceremony, very happy that their lady had finally married the man she was so entirely in love with. Finally, all seemed well at Babylon; usually a place of discomfort and unhappiness, at least in the days of Gaylord Thorne, it had now become something warm and peaceful with the introduction of Kenton le Bec.

As the sun slowly lifted the veil of night towards the east, a brand new day was dawning over the inhabitants of Babylon Castle and Kenton faced his new wife upon the steps of the keep where they had met, a place that had become the heart and soul for them. He could hear people milling about in the hall inside and the sounds of sleepy boys could be heard on the floors above. He could hear Tab yelling at his brothers from where he stood. Nicola heard it, too, and she simply shook her head, resigned, as Kenton grinned.

"It will always be like this for us, you know," he said, pointing a finger upwards to the noisy keep. "The joy of the family I never thought to have. I hope to do you all very proud."

Nicola went to him, putting her arms around his trim torso as he swallowed her up in his embrace. "You needn't worry over that," she said, hugging him tightly, knowing it would be her last feel of him before he departed. Already, she found herself fighting off a flood of tears. "You have already done us quite proud, Kenton. Surely you know that."

Kenton kissed the top of her blond head, sighing heavily as his thoughts mirrored hers. He had to leave very soon but he avoided saying anything. She already knew, so to voice those words, to bring to the forefront that which neither one of them wanted to hear, was something he didn't want to introduce into their conversation at the moment. He wanted to spend just a few moments with his wife, enjoying their new marriage and enjoying each other.

His wife.

He could hardly believe it even as he thought the words. It seemed like a dream to him, still a dream even though they were legally married in the eyes of God. He'd never known such satisfaction in his life.

"I apologize that I do not have a ring to give you," he said. "I will make sure I remedy that upon my return. What kind of stone would you like? Garnet? Amethyst? Beryl?"

Upon my return. He acknowledged the fact that he had to leave, for only a man leaving would be returning. She'd hoped he'd forgotten about it, hoping he would simply remain at Babylon and forget all about Warwick and his promise to the man. But she knew that was a foolish thought. God's Bones, it hurt already. She felt his loss to her very soul but she wasn't entirely sure she should let him know. She didn't want him to think her weak or ridiculous, weeping over something she could not control.

"I have always liked red jasper," she said, forcing a smile when she looked up at him. "My mother had a ring of red jasper. Mayhap you can find one on your travels back home."

He nodded. "A fine stone, but not nearly brilliant enough for you," he said. "Would you like a ruby? That is a beautiful stone and worthy of my wife."

Nicola laughed. "You make the choice, then," she said. "Surprise me. Whatever you bring for me, I shall cherish it always."

He started to reply when the noise from the boys grew louder and suddenly, they were on the massive staircase of Babylon's vaulted entry. Raven was with them, trying to keep them quiet, but they thundered down the steps, declaring how hungry they were. Teague said something about going out into the kitchen yard to see the lambs again. They didn't see Kenton or Nicola standing at the entry, running past them and into the hall where there was food and warmth at this early hour.

Outside, Kenton and Nicola watched the boys as they disappeared into the hall to break their fast. Nicola took a step to go inside and follow them when Kenton reached out to stop her.

"Not yet," he said softly. "I must leave right away and I am not entirely sure we will have any more opportunities for a private farewell, so let us say our farewells here and now. I have never faced a situation like this before, leaving a woman I love, so I fear that I may be somewhat inept at it. I have told you how much I love you and how much you mean to me. I have sworn to return to you and I shall do exactly that. But I have not told you how much I have been dreading this moment, because I have... to lose sight of you, even for a moment, fills me with longing that I cannot even begin to describe. All I know is that I will miss you more with every beat of my heart, a pain that will not be eased until we are together again."

Nicola's expression was warm and loving as she gazed into his eyes. "You have spoken everything that is in my heart, Kenton," she whispered. "I do not want you to leave Babylon. If I thought it would do any good, I would throw myself on the ground and refuse to allow you to pass, but I know that it would not do any good at all. More than likely, you would simply step over me and I would make a fool of myself, and as Lady le Bec, I would die before shaming you or dishonoring you. I have never been more proud of anything in my life, other than my children. You are my pride and my joy, Kenton, and I shall be expecting your return every single day that you are gone."

He touched her cheek softly. "We have not spoken of the possibility that I may not be able to return," he said quietly. "If that is the case, and death keeps me from you, then know that it is my wish for you to be happy and if that means remarriage, then you have my blessing. I only want what is best for you, my love. Be joyful and content in whatever life you choose if it is a life I am not a part of."

Nicola was emotional after his speech, swallowing tears that were close to the surface. She couldn't even entertain the possibility of his death but she knew it was ridiculous not to be aware of the potential. She was, but she clearly wasn't happy about it.

"I should tell you something that will guarantee you will return to me," she said, her throat tight with emotion.

He cocked his head curiously. "What is that?"

She fought off a grin. "St. John proposed marriage to me before he left for Conisbrough yesterday," she said. "If you do not return, I am afraid I shall have to marry him."

Kenton's eyes narrowed. "Never," he hissed. "I will be back, Madam. Rest assured. I will crawl out of my grave and return as a living corpse before I let you marry Brome St. John."

Nicola laughed weepy tears. "You see?" she said. "I told you it would guarantee that you will return to me."

He growled, pulling her into his arms, holding her so closely that he was surely crushing her, but Nicola did not complain. She was happily crushed by him, happily devoured by the only man she had ever loved, the only man she would ever love. All things in her world were well and true so long as she was with him.

When Kenton and Conor rode from the fortress a short time later, Nicola stood on the steps of the keep, waving to her husband, smiling bravely and believing that, no matter what, he would return to her. He had promised, after all, and Kenton le Bec was not in the habit of breaking his promises.

She had little doubt that the walls of Babylon would see him once again.

At least, that was her fervent wish.

CHAPTER TWENTY-EIGHT

May

T HESE WERE NOT days of hope.

It was a gloomy, misty morning, one that reflected the mood of Babylon as of late. Days upon days of gloom, of sadness, and of uncertainty.

As Nicola gathered eggs in the kitchen yard and the twins played with their increasingly large lamb, she didn't even have the energy to tell them to stay away. She simply let them do as they pleased, getting butted by the lamb and falling on their arses until Teague ended up tearing his breeches. But still, she didn't stop them. She let it go on.

St. John had come...

Such a heavy, weighty burden his visit had been this time. The first time he'd come, about two weeks after Kenton had left, it had been to see if she had reconsidered his marriage proposal but when she told him that she had married Kenton, St. John's entire attitude seemed to change. His shock turned to outrage and his outrage to bitterness. He tried to hide it but Nicola had clearly seen it. Embarrassed, rejected, he'd politely excused himself and had returned to Conisbrough where Nicola hoped he would stay.

But he hadn't.

Three days ago, he'd come back with news that had traveled up from the south. It was very big news, indeed. *Warwick was killed at a place called Barnet,* he'd told her. *Warwick's forces were scattered and defeated once and for all. His body and the bodies of his generals are in London, exhibited for all to see.* Nicola had listened with such horror that she'd nearly collapsed with it, accusing St. John of lying and ordering him to leave Babylon by screaming it at the top of her lungs.

Her screaming had brought Tab who, fearful his mother was being assaulted by a knight he'd only seen once before, grabbed the fire poker from the great hall and went after St. John with it. Brome had been chased from Babylon by a little boy with a fire poker, but Nicola knew it would not be the last she saw of him. He'd come to gloat, to tell her of Warwick's death, knowing Kenton and his knights had more than likely been with Warwick when the man was killed.

Kenton had been with Warwick....

Nicola hadn't slept since St. John had come with the news. Usually one to recall great detail in a conversation, Nicola could only seem to remember bits and pieces of what St. John had told her. She remembered that he'd told her of the location, a town just north of London called Barnet, where Warwick's massive force had met with Edward's very large army. Something had happened in it... men were confused and Warwick's forces ended up fighting each other... Warwick had been killed in the melee. Then his forces scattered.

That had been in the middle of April, nearly a month ago, and Kenton had not yet returned. St. John intimated that perhaps he wouldn't, that perhaps it was his body on display in London along with Warwick's. She'd been crying since St. John's visit even though at the moment, she was relatively calm. Still, her face was puffy and swollen, unnaturally pale. She felt dead inside, so very dead. Her sweet, noble Kenton dead and on display for all to see. It was too sickening to even think of.

How could a man like that, a man so loved, end up laid out like a slaughtered animal?

God, she was so very miserable. The tears she'd cried for days had dried up simply because there weren't any left. All that was left now was a great hole in her chest where her heart used to be. Why did God allow her to become so happy only to rip it all away, like ripping a fingernail off and leaving nothing but excruciating pain in its wake? She didn't know and, at the moment, she wasn't on speaking terms with God. She had prayed for Kenton's safety and those prayers had done little good. Perhaps she should have allowed Kenton to be taken by Edward those weeks ago because at least he might still be alive. Instead, she had schemed for Warwick to save him and now Warwick was dead.

They were all dead. Edward had taken the throne of England, now for good. There was no one left to fight him. Henry was finished and England was now in the hands of the Yorkists. Nicola should have been happy but she found that she hardly cared. Putting Edward on the throne had cost her far too much. She simply couldn't think any longer. With an aching head and aching heart, she collected the last of her eggs and sat down to watch the boys play with the lamb. She couldn't even find any joy in it.

"My lady?"

Nicola turned, sluggishly, to see Raven standing a few feet away. The girl was noticeably pregnant these days, with a gently rounded belly beneath her apron, but Nicola couldn't even become upset over it. At least she had something to remember the man she loved. Nicola wasn't even sure she had that, although it was still fairly early to tell. Her menses were due but hadn't come and if she did say a prayer to God, it was for that alone.

If you are going to take Kenton from me, at least give me his son….

"What is it?" Nicola answered without any enthusiasm.

Raven pointed to the inner ward beyond the kitchen yard. "Lewis wishes to speak with you, my lady," she said. "He is waiting outside of the gate. Can I show him in?"

Nicola nodded; Lewis, one of the prisoners who had been returned from Conisbrough, was a sergeant whom Kenton had put in charge of Babylon while he was away. Camden Lewis seemed like a good man and he was very polite to Nicola, so she nodded feebly to Raven's question. The girl scooted over to the kitchen yard gate and opened it, motioning forward the sergeant, who had been waiting there patiently. He approached Nicola with great respect and when she turned her attention to him, unenthusiastic, he bowed politely.

"Lady le Bec," he said. "I thought to tell you... I know that the knight from Conisbrough came to tell you that Warwick was killed, but...."

Nicola turned away. "I do not wish to discuss it," she snapped, but just as quickly realized she sounded terrible and rude. She took a deep breath. "I am sorry, Lewis, 'tis simply that... it is a painful subject these days so if you wish to discuss it, I am not one to do it with. I am sure there are a number of other soldiers who would willingly speak with you about it."

Lewis was shaking his head the entire time she was speaking only she couldn't see him because her head was turned away. "My lady," he said, rather urgently. "I came to tell you that we can see men approaching through the mist, remnants of an army bearing the colors of Warwick. They must be Sir Kenton's men returning to Babylon."

Nicola looked at him, stricken. She was so startled that she stumbled as she tried to stand up, dropping all of the eggs in her apron. Raven, who had been listening, began squealing with excitement as Nicola grabbed hold of Lewis before she collapsed completely. The world was rocking dangerously as she stared at the man in astonishment.

"Where are they?" she demanded.

Lewis was already moving, trying to pull her along so that he could take her to the gatehouse, but her legs wouldn't seem to move. He called over to the boys, playing with the lamb.

"Young masters!" he bellowed. "Come and help me with your mother! She must come with me!"

Teague and Tiernan looked over to the sergeant, who was frantically waving them over. With their mother standing there, looking as if she were about to faint, they ran over and began pushing her from behind at the sergeant's prompting. Lewis pulled while the twins pushed, and Nicola began to gain control of her legs. She started to move, slowly at first, but by the time they hit the kitchen yard gate, she was running.

"Where are they?" she demanded again.

Lewis, running alongside her, was pointing off to the east. "They are coming from that way," he told her. "Huddersfield, more than likely. All of the big roads to the south cut through Huddersfield in this area."

Nicola wasn't listening anymore. She broke away from them, running to the gates of Babylon, which were just starting to open. When the gap between the gates was wide enough for her to slip through, she did, tearing down the road as fast as her shaking legs would take her.

It was cold and misty still, with the sun struggling to break through, as she raced down the rocky, muddy road. There was water everywhere; in puddles in the middle of the road or alongside the road, and she plowed through the puddles without missing a beat. She never bothered to ask how far out the army was, but if the men on the walls had sighted them, in mist no less, then they couldn't be too far out.

Nicola ran and she ran until her chest felt like it was about to explode and then she came to a stop, but only momentarily, coughing and struggling to clear her lungs, before taking off again, but this time much more slowly. Her legs were on fire, her chest was swelling, but she had to keep going. She had to make it to the incoming army, men bearing Warwick's colors.

They would know what happened to Kenton. Oh, God...Kenton! Suddenly, she came to a halt, unable to run any further. Weak, dizzy, she stood in the middle of the road, in the middle of the mist. It was like a nightmare; she couldn't run anymore but she so desperately wanted to. She had to know what happened to Kenton.

Kenton....

"Kenton!" she screamed. *"Kenton!"*

There was no reply other than the birds in the trees. *Oh, God... please let him be coming home! Please let it be him!*

"Kenton!" she screamed again. "Kenton, answer me!"

There was no immediate reply, simply more birds. The tears started to come then but Nicola fought them, taking staggering steps in the direction she had been running. She had to make it to the army, to discover what had become of her husband, and the tears she was trying so hard to stave off began to fall as she haltingly wiped them away.

"Kenton!" she screamed one more time, her voice breaking. "Please, Kenton! Ken –!"

"Nicolaaaaaaaaaaaaaaaaaaa!"

A bellow broke through the mist, carving through it like a great broadsword, louder and sweeter than the cries of angels. Nicola gasped when she heard her name, startled to the bone, but in the same breath, she recognized the voice.

Oh, dear God… it's him. *It's him!*

"Kenton!" she screamed again.

She forced her legs to move although they were as weak as a new-born colt's. She started to run again although it was more like shuffling, shuffling through the mist as Kenton's voice came once more, plowing through the fog, echoing off the trees.

"Nicolaaaaaaaaaaaaaaaaaa!"

Nicola shrieked at the second call. "I am here!" she cried. "I am here!"

Suddenly, there were men in front of her, foot soldiers looking beaten and worn, but men who grinned when they saw her running in their direction. She was panting Kenton's name, steady with the rhythmic falling of her feet, and suddenly more and more men were coming into view. They were all on foot but as she traveled back through the column, she could see a wagon and a couple of horses towards the rear. It was too misty for her to see who was on horseback so she simply called Kenton's name again, looking for direction.

"Kenton!" she cried.

"Nicola!"

Suddenly, a man lurched out of the wagon, jumping out of it and landing heavily on the road. The man's right leg was heavily wrapped and it was clear that he couldn't walk on it for he nearly fell when he jumped out of the wagon. As Nicola ran closer, the vision of her husband's face came into focus and at that moment, it was as if no mist or distance were between them any longer. The sun had come out and Kenton's face was there, stronger and more beautiful than she had ever known it to be.

He was alive!

Kenton wasn't moving but Nicola was. She ran at the man, throwing herself at him so hard that he lost his balance and toppled over onto the road. The rear half of the column came to a halt as men rushed forward to pull Kenton and Nicola out of the mud.

But Nicola wouldn't let go of him, not for anything. She clung to him, weeping, even as men righted the pair, and even as he struggled to regain his balance, she continued to hold him as if fearful if she let go, he would disappear before her eyes. But Kenton didn't mind. He had tears in his eyes as he held her, so tightly he could hear her spine crack.

"'Tis all right, love," he murmured. "I have returned. I told you I would, did I not?"

Nicola was so overwhelmed she couldn't even speak. The smell of him, the feel of him, was nearly too much to bear. After the misery she had gone through, the grief she had experienced, to have him alive in her arms was an astonishing turn of events. It took her several long moments before she could gather her wits.

"You did," she sobbed, finally pulling back to look the man in the face. He was shaggy with beard growth, and needed a haircut, but she didn't care. He was the most beautiful sight in the world. She ran her hands over his face just to make sure she wasn't dreaming. "You swore to me that you would return and you have. But we heard that Warwick was killed! Is it true?"

Kenton simply stood there as the men around him began to move again, heading for that great bastion of Babylon not too far in the distance. But Kenton was solely focused on his wife.

"Aye," he said quietly, kissing her twice, tremulously. "He is. Edward is upon the throne now and he is there to stay. But let us speak of it inside where it is warm and dry. I do not believe I have been warm or dry in over a month."

So the news St. John bore had been correct. Nicola pondered the confirmation of such information as she and Kenton slowly began to walk towards Babylon, following the rest of the army. Men were pouring out of the fortress now, coming to help the others along, and there was great joy now that the remains of the army had returned. Weeks of waiting, of speculation, and of fear, had finally come to an end as the army of Kenton le Bec returned to Babylon.

But not unscathed. Many were wounded, including Kenton. He was moving very slowly on his injured leg and Nicola couldn't help but notice. She inspected him closely from head to toe.

"Although I am grateful you have returned, it is not without injury," she said. "What happened?"

He was quite casual about it. "A broadsword cut me down the length of my thigh. An impressive wound if you have the stomach for it."

He meant is as a jest but Nicola looked at him with some horror. "I suppose I must have the stomach for it if I am to tend to it," she said, watching him grin. Reaching up, she touched that grinning mouth as he kissed her fingers. "What of your knights? Where are Conor and Wellesbourne and de Russe?"

Kenton's attempt at humor faded somewhat. "Conor was badly injured," he said. "Matt and Gaston took him to Wellesbourne Castle to be tended, which was closer to the scene of the battle. Gerik, however, did not survive the battle."

Nicola grunted in sorrow, thinking of the fine knights who had sustained injury and death in the midst of such a cataclysmic turning point in the history of the country. "I am so sorry to hear that," she said. "Will Conor survive?"

Kenton nodded. "I hope so," he said, looking up as the great gatehouse of Babylon finally came into view. He sighed with satisfaction at the sight. "He kept speaking of a Lady Katryne and how he wanted to recover well enough to marry her. He was speaking of St. John's sister, you know. He met her at Warwick's camp when he was there. I am not entirely sure how St. John is going to take his sister marrying one of my knights. It would make us all family, I should think, and I am not entirely sure he wants to be related to the man who married the woman who rejected him."

Nicola couldn't help but giggle. It was so good to have him returned and, already, it was as if he had never left. His humor was back, his manner calm and rational, and she was so happy that tears of joy were in her eyes.

Nicola clung to him, holding him tightly, as they approached the gatehouse, but before they could cross the threshold, Kenton suddenly came to a halt. When Nicola looked up at him, curiously, she saw that he was looking up to the great walls, studying them with satisfaction.

"What is it, my love?" she asked softly.

A smile crossed his lips as he studied the great stone fortress, now becoming increasingly visible as the mist lifted.

"I was thinking," he said, clutching her tightly, "that I have never in my life felt as if I had a home, one place to go to above all others. I fostered at an early age and spent my adult life at several different castles, serving different lords, but I never considered any of those places my home. But now, as I look at Babylon, I feel as if I have truly come home. You are here and it was within these walls that we first met. Home is where my heart is and you are my heart. *You* are here. I finally feel as if I have come home."

Nicola smiled at him, leaning up to kiss him on his stubbled cheeks. "You *are* home," she murmured. "This is where you are loved most, Kenton. This is where you belong."

He agreed completely. Carefully, they resumed their walk, allowing the great gatehouse of Babylon to swallow them up as the massive gates slowly cranked closed behind them. Finally, they were both home, both where they belonged, inside the warm, wonderful, sometimes hectic, but always protective walls of Babylon.

Kenton, indeed, had come home.

EPILOGUE

Present time
Yorkshire, UK, East of Huddersfield
Babylon Castle

WHEN THE WIFE got back to the car, she didn't notice that her husband was sitting there, looking rather odd. He wasn't looking at her, either, so he didn't realize she was looking rather strange, too. They both sat there for a moment until the wife realized the car wasn't on. Her husband was simply sitting there, gazing through the windshield.

"Nice try," he said, unhappy.

She had no idea what he was talking about. "What do you mean?"

He sighed sharply and looked at her. "The ghost voice," he said, mocking it. "The one you yelled from inside the castle. Nice try in your attempt to scare me."

She blinked, startled. "You heard, that too?"

He frowned and rolled his eyes, turning on the car. "Oh, brother," he said. "Come on, let's get out of here. Where are we going next?"

"Wait," the wife said urgently, putting her hand on his arm. "Don't go yet. What do you mean you heard a voice? I heard a voice, too. At first I thought it was you just being a jerk, but then I realized... well, it was a woman's voice. It sounded as if she were calling a name – something like Clinton, I think. Did you really hear it, too?"

He was impatient. "Honey, you're cute, but I'm not that gullible," he said. "Nice attempt at trying to get back at me for being a dick, though. I'll give you that. It was a good voice, nice and scary."

The wife's grip on his arm tightened. "But it wasn't me!" she insisted. "You know practical jokes aren't my thing. Why would I do that to you?"

He shook his head. "I don't believe in that stuff, honey. You know that."

"But you heard it!"

"I heard *you*."

The wife looked at him, realizing that all of the debating in the world wasn't going to convince him that they both heard a voice, and it wasn't a voice from either one of them. It was as if it had come from the very walls of Babylon, for it was everywhere yet nowhere. Like a swift wind, it was there and then it was gone. Still, she was quite rattled by it. It had been such a breathy, sweet tone, the song of a lover calling through the mist. Baffled, and the least bit spooked, she simply shook her head.

"Fine," she said, letting the subject drop. "Hold on, I've got mud on my shoes. Let me shake it off."

She popped open the door and removed her shoes, smacking them on the running boards to remove the mud. She was almost finished with the task when, quite close by, they heard another voice coming through the trees.

"*Nicolaaaaaaaaaaaaaaaaaaaaaaaaaaaaaaa!*"

The wife's head snapped up and even the husband jumped, both of them frozen to the spot as a disembodied voice, quite obviously male this time, blew through the mist, through the trees, as if only spoken by a passing breeze. But that breeze had definitely formed a word.

"Oh, my God," the wife gasped. "Did you hear that?"

The husband's eyes were bulging out of his head. "What in the hell *was* that?"

The wife's mouth popped open, suddenly recalling the legend she had heard. *Two lovers, calling for each other in the mist.* They heard the first voice, the woman, and now the man was answering. Good God, was it even possible? Goosebumps shot up her spine.

"He's calling to her!" the wife breathed in astonishment. "Did you hear him?"

The husband might not have believed in ghosts but he sure as hell didn't want to see one. "Close the damn door!" he hissed. "We're getting the hell out of here!"

The wife threw up a hand to prevent him from moving. "No!" she cried softly. "Wait! The first voice you heard was female, right? The voice you thought was me?"

The husband was already putting the car in reverse. "It *was* you!"

"No, it *wasn't*," she insisted. "It was the lady calling to her knight and now he's answering her!"

"Close the door or I'll shove you out and leave you here!"

The wife shut the door, mostly because she believed him. Already, he was backing out of the car park and onto the road, spraying gravel as he went, but the wife was fixated on the trees where the man's voice had come from.

She was absolutely stunned and elated by what she'd heard. Yes, elated was the right word. Elated that a love so deep, and evidently so strong, had endured all these centuries. As certain as she had ever been about anything in her life, she knew she'd heard the cry of the lady from the very walls of Babylon, and now she was equally sure that the lady's love, her enemy knight, was returning that call. The mist had brought them together. Maybe that was why she had been so drawn to Babylon, with its ancient walls and misty secrets. It was because those walls protected something, something that endured until this very day.

Those walls protected a love that not even time could erase.

But there was more, something more the wife saw before the ruins faded from view. She would swear until the day she died that she caught a glimpse of woman rushing from the gatehouse of Babylon, only to disappear before she hit the road. It was a fleeting glimpse of nebulous legs and long, pale hair, but it had been there. The wife was sure of it.

As the car tore down the road and the ruinous old castle faded away, the wife took that memory and tucked it deep into her heart, knowing without a doubt that she had witnessed something few mortals ever experienced. It was a love beyond time.

The legend of the lady and her knight would continue to live on, tucked deeply and safely within the ancient walls of Babylon.

If these walls could talk....

○ THE END ○

About Kathryn Le Veque

Medieval Just Got Real.

KATHRYN LE VEQUE is a USA TODAY Bestselling author, an Amazon All-Star author, and a #1 bestselling, award-winning, multi-published author in Medieval Historical Romance and Historical Fiction. She has been featured in the NEW YORK TIMES and on USA TODAY's HEA blog. In March 2015, Kathryn was the featured cover story for the March issue of InD'Tale Magazine, the premier Indie author magazine. She was also a quadruple nominee (a record!) for the prestigious RONE awards for 2015.

Kathryn's Medieval Romance novels have been called 'detailed', 'highly romantic', and 'character-rich'. She crafts great adventures of love, battles, passion, and romance in the High Middle Ages. More than that, she writes for both women AND men – an unusual crossover for a romance author – and Kathryn has many male readers who enjoy her stories because of the male perspective, the action, and the adventure.

On October 29, 2015, Amazon launched Kathryn's Kindle Worlds Fan Fiction site WORLD OF DE WOLFE PACK. Please visit Kindle Worlds for Kathryn Le Veque's World of de Wolfe Pack and find many action-packed adventures written by some of the top authors in their genre using Kathryn's characters from the de Wolfe Pack series. As Kindle World's FIRST Historical Romance fan fiction world, Kathryn Le Veque's World of de Wolfe Pack will contain all of the great story-telling you have come to expect.

Kathryn loves to hear from her readers. Please find Kathryn on Facebook at Kathryn Le Veque, Author, or join her on Twitter @kathrynleveque, and don't forget to visit her website at www.kathrynleveque.com.

CPSIA information can be obtained at www.ICGtesting.com
Printed in the USA
BVOW06s1745300416

446267BV00006B/38/P